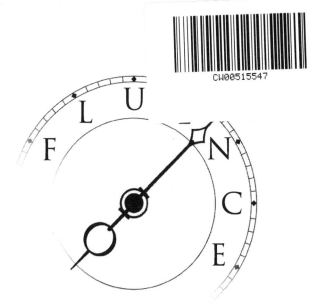

STEPHEN ORAM

SilverWood

Published in 2015 by SilverWood Books

SilverWood Books Ltd
14 Small Street, Bristol, BS1 1DE, United Kingdom
www.silverwoodbooks.co.uk

ISBN 978-1-78132-363-2 (paperback)
ISBN 978-1-78132-364-9 (ebook)

British Library Cataloguing in Publication Data
A CIP catalogue record for this book is available from
the British Library

Set in Adobe Garamond Pro by SilverWood Books
Printed by Imprint Digital on responsibly sourced paper

STEPHEN ORAM lives in Fitzrovia, London. He writes novels and flash fiction that takes a sideways look and asks, *what if.*

As a teenager he was heavily influenced by the ethos of punk. In his early twenties he embraced the squatter scene and was part of a religious cult, briefly. He did some computer stuff in what became London's silicon roundabout and is now a civil servant with a gentle attraction to anarchism.

Visit Stephen's website and blog at stephenoram.net, follow him on Twitter @OramStephen and Facebook Stephen Oram Author.

For my goddaughters: Emily, Kim, Angeline, Stephanie and Ash

THURSDAY

ONE

It was nearly a year since Amber had teetered on the edge of yellow, deciding to drop a level before she was pushed. The annual Pay Day review had come around again and everyone, on every Strata Level, was preparing for the week ahead. The affluence and the influence of the higher strata was within her grasp, she just had to decide what she was prepared to do to get them.

Her four-inch heels click-clacked, tapping out her progress along the polished wooden tiles that reflected the dull light of the corridor. A smell of disinfectant filled the air. She looked down at the source of the click-clacking and smiled; the light-grey brogues always seemed to fit so perfectly with this ageless, but faintly sterile building.

Almost a year ago she'd chosen to drop to the green Strata Level. It was a mistake and she had less than ten thousand minutes to put it right. This was the last week of the Pay Year.

She turned the corner and there was Martin who, according to the algorithms, was one of her peers. A fact that depressed her and made her angry.

'Almost Pay Day then,' he said. 'Or Lay Day, as we used to call it. Everyone trying so hard to get as many points as they could before the deadline.'

'You called it what? How gross,' said Amber. She glanced at him, barely concealing her contempt. She turned on her heels – those brave high heels as he'd once called them – and, with a flick of her long blonde hair, strode away.

She saw his reflection in the glass door. He was staring at her legs. Creep, she thought to herself and gripped the door handle tight. How on earth had she ever fallen for his bullshit? It made her shudder to think she'd ever enjoyed his attention; his fixation on the office gossips bitching that her hair was bleached when he thought it was stunning. And why had she believed his exaggerated stories? Stories of being a hacker, of moving with the in-crowd. Stories of knowing how to crack the algorithms that determined your Strata Level.

During her first few days in the unit she'd been entranced by his piercing blue eyes, which were made all the more captivating by his ruddy complexion. When the bubble of attraction burst, those eyes had become tiny slivers of ice swamped by blotchy skin.

Standing there, she found it hard to believe she'd been attracted to this grey-haired man with ridiculously bushy sideburns. He seemed innocent and childlike, rather than wise and edgy as she'd once thought.

She pulled the door open and walked through into a glass-walled corridor. The left-hand side looked out over tall blocks of fading concrete flats, giving a brief but only partial view of life as an indigo. On the right-hand side were empty glass meeting rooms where later in the day groups of soberly dressed bureaucrats would gather to chew over a pointless detail of their pointless jobs. She couldn't tolerate staying at this Strata Level for another year.

She walked through the communal office, through the depressing row upon row of identical regulation-sized desks. Their neat rows reminded her of a military parade. A line of white carpet tiles flanked on both sides by shoulder-high grey metal drawers mapped the designated path through this physical manifestation of the organisational structures; teams were identified by a sign hanging above their desks. Each desk had a coloured chair to show the occupant's place in the colour-coded Strata. Although the full strata ranged from red down through the rainbow to violet, only yellows, greens and blues worked for the Bureaucracy.

On top of the drawers was the usual array of cakes and biscuits. As she passed a yellow's desk she noticed an apple inside a red cardboard box with the letters RB embossed on the side. It was a rare breed and illegal to buy unless you were from the highest levels. How she ached to have such things. She'd tasted one once when she'd been hanging out with some seriously influential people. The taste was only slightly better than other apples, but the status that came with it was magnificent. People had stopped and stared at her in the street, whispering to each other as she'd held its box in her hand. She'd enjoyed the taste of the envy much more than the taste of the apple.

Sitting in a green chair at a desk underneath the sign for the Disability Assessment Unit was Sam, her boss. Sam was affectionately known as Mother by her small team of eight people because of the way she nurtured and protected them. Amber felt smothered, but had never said anything.

'Hi, Amber,' said Sam.

'Hi. What's on the list today then?'

'A Mrs Joyce. Social Strata Number WP 21 23 71 B. She's been struggling with her job for a few years and she's finally asked to be assessed. Says she can't cope with the stress of performing to standard, day after day, just to keep her Strata Level intact. Especially having to wait until the end of the year to know precisely how she's doing. She thinks she should be assessed for atypical autism.'

'A parasite going for white then?'

'Amber. Do not use words like parasite.'

'I know. I only say it in the office. It helps to dissipate my empathic pain.'

Sam smiled. 'It's hard, I know, but you must try.'

'Sam, any chance of a few days off this week? I need to look after my own FluenceRating. The damn prediction's showing I might only scrape through to the next level. I have to make it back up there.'

'No, you can't. And you know why. It's our most critical week. I explained months ago that it's during this week that people like Mrs Joyce come to our attention, and we have to assess all of them before the end of next Tuesday.'

'Okay. No harm in asking though, eh?'

'No harm at all. I'm glad you feel you can,' said Sam.

Amber wondered how she – a clever, socially bright, career-driven girl – had ended up with this mumsy, slightly plump woman with such bad taste in clothes.

'Dig the boots,' lied Amber.

'Thanks,' replied Sam, visibly pleased with the compliment. 'They're made from vegan leather and they're lovely and warm. Look at this fabulous lining,' she said, pulling back the top of the boot to reveal fake fur.

'Better get on with the day, I suppose,' said Amber. She wasn't in the mood to indulge Sam's enthusiasm.

Sam flinched and turned back to her work.

Amber sat down and Sam casually glanced over. Sam never seemed to pay much attention to the way the others looked, but for some reason, maybe because she wanted Amber's respect, she seemed envious of Amber's style. Blonde hair and hazel eyes were not an easy combination, but she spent time on her nails, her professionally bleached hair and her make-up – they were perfect. She was different to the rest of the team. She'd been a high-flyer since she was eighteen, had dropped a level last year and wanted to climb the Strata Ladder again. She knew that her immaculate appearance was only one of the tell-tale signs of her ambition.

Her day would be spent assessing whether people were disabled and unable to take part in the normal everyday social activity that gave them their place in society. The dismantling of the State and the introduction of CorpCards as the only method of purchase had created a white Strata Level of non-workers and the corporations were obliged to provide for their basic needs. Her job was to keep as many people in work as possible. She assessed people whose friends or employers had declared them physically, mentally or emotionally disabled. In a few cases, they self-declared.

Amber picked up a charta from her desk. The micro-thin sheet of technology would give her access to everything she needed for the day. She placed her thumb on its bottom right-hand corner to identify herself. It recognised her and downloaded all the relevant data and apps for the day's work.

'Ready,' said the charta in Sam's voice. Amber found the use of Sam's voice a bit spooky and was well aware that this was the clumsy way in which the Bureaucracy attempted to keep its employees conscious of their place in the hierarchy.

Amber put the charta on her desk and spoke into it. 'Directions. Current location to the home of Mrs Joyce. SSN WP 21 23 71 B.'

The charta was ready to go. She put it in her bag and walked back along the line of white floor tiles. Martin was leaning on a cabinet next to a yellow chair. She didn't recognise the female occupant, but anyone with half a sense of social awareness could see that she wasn't comfortable. She was only half listening, giving him an occasional nod while continuing to read from her charta. Martin seemed oblivious.

As Amber passed, she overheard him saying, 'Jenny – that's the wife – wants me to throw it all out. Clear out my shed. I'm not sure I want to. A man has to have his shed, doesn't he? This whole spring cleaning lark that the Bureaucracy's advocating has got out of hand. Is there anything you can do to stop it? I'll send you an attachment request. Can you keep me up to date?'

Amber dashed into the ladies' to avoid eye contact. She was embarrassed to be in the same unit as him.

The door closed quietly behind her. The plush room with its expensive hand towels, proper soap and soft-lighted mirrors was designed to make the office workers feel special. And it worked. She checked her appearance and straightened her blue charcoal suit, pleased with the way it complemented her watermelon pink nails, her hair and her eyes. She applied more lip gloss and then left the hushed atmosphere of the female-only room.

A waterfall cascaded down the nine floors from the top of the building in front of her, creating a mini-lake in the centre of the ground-floor entrance hall. It was magnificent. The original wood panels of the hall had been left in place and the old cloakrooms had been transformed into high tech checking-in and checking-out pods.

She joined the small checking-out queue; she was green so she was entitled to travel by communal taxi rather than having to use the hot, sweaty and frequently broken public transport system. Her mind wandered, fantasising about her future after Pay Day. She'd miss the grandeur of the Bureaucracy, but it would be a small price to pay if she could become yellow again.

'Charta please,' said the doorman. He collected a charta from each person in the queue and placed them for a few seconds into a dip in his desk before returning them to their owners.

She stepped outside and into the cold March morning.

TWO

Amber handed her charta to the woman in charge, who then guided her to the fourth taxi in the queue. She climbed in to join three other people. The taxi's navigation system was already loaded with their combined journeys, had calculated the most efficient route, and would charge the cost of Amber's part of the journey to Sam's unit.

She was too busy familiarising herself with Mrs Joyce's application form to pay much attention to the other occupants or to the familiar London streets between the Bureaucracy headquarters in Greenwich and Mrs Joyce in Walthamstow. The form contained data that was directly related to the interview and some additional background data. It was the background data that was of more interest to her because it might help her crack the algorithms that calculated someone's Strata Level.

The form itself covered the twelve basic categories for assessing someone's ability to cope with everyday living – feeding, toileting, washing, dressing, understanding signs and understanding the mechanisms for CorpCard points and Fluence. Mrs Joyce scored zero points, which indicated she had no problems in these areas. It was the additional categories of mobility and engaging with people where she had a problem and where she was disputing her score of six points which was two points away from the threshold for being diagnosed as disabled.

The form included a voice clip of her saying that, 'The thought of going out, of meeting other people and being judged, causes me overwhelming psychological distress.'

It was Amber's job to talk to Mrs Joyce and decide if this was true.

She hated assessing the mentally or emotionally disabled because most of them were just taking advantage, but she wanted their data and wanted to know what was significant to the algorithm about their profile. With this knowledge she'd be able to push herself up the Strata Levels and become rich from selling her algorithm on the black-market. Of course the risks were high – it was illegal to keep any of this data, let alone create a whole database from nine thousand clients as Amber had done.

The charta detected the data-stick in her jacket pocket. She held her breath slightly as she transferred Mrs Joyce's data to it because it was always possible that someone else in the taxi would notice what she was doing or she'd transfer it to the wrong data-stick by mistake. Either way she'd be caught and made violet, with the chance of moving back up removed for twenty years. It hadn't been that long since a woman had been caught stealing NetCorp card data containing the shopping patterns of their customers. She'd been busted down to violet for ten years and a paparazzi campaign had viciously followed her, daily charting her dramatic collapse into isolation. They hounded her so much that she left her family and stopped seeing any friends. She went to and from her cleaning job with her face covered from the spying cameras. She stopped her SMFeed because every time she posted she was subjected to an onslaught of violent threats, including rape and beatings, to make her pay for her betrayal. This scared Amber.

'Home of Mrs Joyce, SSN WP 21 23 71 B,' said the charta in Sam's voice.

Amber got out of the taxi and looked up and down the road. It was a cul-de-sac of two-storey terraced houses that had been rebuilt after the Blitz of the Second World War. A fairly typical blue area. The houses were tiny and tired-looking and a faint whiff of wood smoke hung in the air. The charta directed Amber to an end-of-terrace house with '20' hand painted on a waist-high wooden front gate. Inside the gate was a surprisingly well-manicured front garden.

She didn't know the names of the plants and flowers, but the smells were pungent and reminded her of Katie, her posh school friend from the blue level. In fact, this whole area reminded her of Katie's neighbourhood, sucking memories to the surface; memories of the jealousy she'd felt as a young violet girl. She remembered her mum's mantra, 'Amber, you must better yourself. Don't make the same mistakes as me,' which had been a constant background hum urging her on, urging her to climb the ladder and escape the lower strata of her birth. It finally stopped when a famous musician visited her school and explained that it was possible to be catapulted to the highest levels, rather than carefully climbing one or two above your birth Strata.

She hung her bag on Mrs Joyce's gate and took out a twenty-centimetre dark wooden rod – her ruyi. She had to remain active in the social-media sphere, otherwise she'd start to leak rating points. The ruyi allowed her to remain connected while she was out and about. It was based on the ancient Chinese ceremonial sceptre – a long S-shaped shaft with bulbous ends – and had a validation pad in the middle, a microphone and speaker at one end and a camera and screen at the other. Everyone except whites had one, but they varied in style and quality. Amber's had been a present from her orange ex-lover Francis and was still top of the range. She twisted it so the microphone was near her mouth.

'Update status: Sooo looking forward to all of this week's fabulous parties,' she said.

The front door opened. A woman in her mid-fifties wearing a brown knee-length dressing gown and holding a transparent plastic bag of rubbish stepped out. With a single movement she flipped open the lid of her bin, dropped the bag inside and flipped it shut.

'You must be Ms Walgace. Come in,' she said.

Amber lifted the latch on the weather-worn gate. 'Lovely garden you have,' she said, as she walked up the path.

'Thank you. I try, but it's so hard when you have to keep feeding this social-media thing. I can't cope. You do know that unless you grant me a white rating it'll be the end of this beautiful garden. The end of me most likely.'

Amber interrupted. 'Mrs Joyce. Can we wait until we're inside and I have the necessary documents in front of me?'

'Of course. Sorry. I'm just so stressed. I need you to understand.'

'I do,' said Amber in a soft, professional tone.

Mrs Joyce guided Amber into a long and narrow lounge where the two sofas on either side were so close that her seated guest's knees would almost touch. Amber chose to sit on a dining-room chair at a small table in the front window. Attached to the wall above one of the sofas was a small StrataScreen.

Mrs Joyce pointed at the screen. 'That thing. That's what stresses me out the most. The constant reminder of my place in the world. Having to feed it with irrelevant snippets of garbage just to give the impression that I'm taking part. As if I'm interested in their stupid trivia. I can't cope with it.'

Mrs Joyce's StrataScreen was no different to anyone else's. Around the edge was a blue border, the colour of her Strata Level. At the top was her social-media feed – her latest contribution. Alongside was its influence rating, which was calculated using the number of people who saw it and the number who then passed it on. In the middle of the screen on the left-hand side was a steady stream of the top influence rated posts and on the right-hand side was an empty eHistory that should be full of photos, videos and comments. Each would have had statistics to show how many people had seen them, liked them and interacted with them. Underneath was a minute-by-minute graph of her predicted FluenceRating, showing that she was at the lower limit of her level. On the bottom left-hand side was an empty space for the tally of pending incoming and outgoing attachment or tag requests and the number of minutes they'd been there. This was known as the lag. On the bottom right-hand side was her current CorpCard Points balance for each of the five corporations. This was the amount of Fluence she had at her disposal to spend.

She sat down on the sofa with her back to the screen. 'I worked in a care home, you know. A supervisor. Looking after the old folk. I liked it. And then that damn thing arrived.'

'I'm sorry, Mrs Joyce, I don't see the connection,' said Amber.

'You know what they're like. Always pestering you to make more connections. Get more points. Get ahead.'

'Nothing wrong with that, surely?'

'I liked being a supervisor. Then I moved into the office. Became a secretary. And this thing, nagging me every evening. The scores dropping. Tracking my life, minute by minute. I hate it. I want out.'

'That's why I'm here,' said Amber. She put her ruyi on the table and took out her charta. 'File for SSN WP 21 23 71 B.'

Mrs Joyce pointed at the ruyi. 'And as for those ridiculous sticks you all carry around as if your life depended on them. Lumps of pointless technology.'

'They're great, you just need to get used to them.'

She snorted. 'Typical. The reds have something so everyone else must have one. Pathetic.'

'Mrs Joyce, they're the only choice on the market. Now, please let me read.'

They sat in silence as Amber scrolled through the file. She didn't really need to read it again, but she felt it gave a sense of occasion and more importantly made it clear who was in charge.

'Edith. May I call you Edith? You say that you have problems engaging with people? Before I ask a bit more about that, could you tell me something about your background?'

'Of course. If you think it'll help.'

'It'll be very useful to me. What was your Birth Strata?'

'Indigo. My dad ran the meat counter in one of the large RetailCorp supermarkets. They offered him a franchise for his own local shop, you know. He turned it down, so we stayed indigo.'

'Thanks,' said Amber. 'You don't mind me recording this do you?'

'That's fine.'

'And a photo for our records?'

'If you must.'

Amber took a photo with her charta, making sure she caught a good shot of Mrs Joyce's clothes and hair as well as the room itself.

'Which of the corporations do you spend most of your Fluence with?' asked Amber

'RetailCorp.'

'Why?'

'Loyal to my dad, I guess. I only really buy food and a few bits and bobs. I know they all sell everything, but somehow I can't get used to buying food from an oil company or a pharmaceutical firm.'

'May I take a look at your StrataScreen?'

'That thing? Why do you want to see that?'

'It gives me a fuller sense of who you are. The difficulties you face,' said Amber.

'Go ahead. If you must.'

Amber strolled over to the screen. 'Three thousand and twenty-two minutes since your last SMFeed – "leaving for work". Your eHistory is empty. Your predicted FluenceRating is steady at the bottom of your Strata Level.'

'So?'

'You're not trying,' said Amber.

'I can't. Like I said, the stress is too much.'

'Why should we help you, if you're not trying to help yourself?'

'Please. Do the assessment. I should be white. You must see that?'

Amber returned to the chair in the window. 'Let's see. You say you have trouble engaging with people. And yet you go to work every day.'

'Yes. I'm in the office though. I don't really see anyone.'

'Edith, I have four descriptors here and it's my job to work out which of these fits you best: A – you can engage with people unaided; B – you need prompting; C – you need support; or D – you simply can't engage because it creates overwhelming distress.'

'That one. The last one. That's it.' Edith was clearly agitated, stabbing the air in Amber's direction.

'You say that and yet you have engaged with me perfectly well and unaided. I'll have to take this back to the Bureaucracy to get a second opinion, but my initial assessment is that you are perfectly capable of engaging with people. I believe the driving force behind your request is that you want to drop out. You want us to look after you and you don't want to take any personal responsibility for your life. That's not what we're about, I'm afraid.'

'You can't do this to me!' Edith stood up and paced around the room, shouting at the StrataScreen. 'You fucking monstrosity! How did we ever come to this?' She turned to Amber. 'Please. You must help me.'

'I'm helping you help yourself, Mrs Joyce. Do you realise that if you become white you'll no longer be able to connect to a StrataScreen and you'll have to move house?'

'No, I won't. I own this house. It was my dad's. He bought it outright. You can't make me move.'

'You're right, they can't make you move. However, I have to inform you that you won't be able to shop in any of your local shops with white points; you can only use them in the white areas. You'll end up moving. I've seen it so many times over the past year. Do you still want me to consider you for white?'

'Yes. I don't believe you. You're trying to scare me.'

'I'm not.' Amber patted Edith on the shoulder as she walked past her to the front door. 'I'll see myself out.' She opened the door, smiled at Edith and then walked away without looking back.

She sat down on a bench by the side of the road and asked the charta to call her a taxi. It confirmed that a taxi would take about fifteen minutes to arrive. If she'd been in an indigo or violet area, especially as a lone female, it would have arrived much quicker. She'd often confessed to her husband Terence that she had mixed feelings about the prioritising of lone females. It seemed patronising, but also a relief. He tended to shrug and say, 'Gets you home quicker. What's the problem?'

She was engrossed with her own ruyi version of the StrataScreen when the taxi arrived. Her rating was stable and was unlikely to change during the day because the software was sophisticated enough to ignore contact with clients unless she specifically requested otherwise.

Inside the taxi she took out the data-stick and pushed the rubber nub at the end to scroll through and check the data had transferred. The driver glanced at her in his mirror and she quickly, maybe too quickly, tucked it back into her jacket pocket.

THREE

Amber stepped off the driverless train at Deptford Bridge Station, having completed four more assessments during the day. On the train journey she'd changed from the grey brogues into ankle-high walking boots. They were new and were no ordinary walking boots. She was in love with them. They were comfortable like her brogues, but in a different way. The heels were only half the height and they were made from the same elasticated material as running shoes. Around the white heel was a spiral of grey that opened out to run along the half-inch sole, up the side of the boot and then continued to cover two-thirds of the foot. 'Completely brilliant' was how she'd described them on her eHistory video feed.

She relished the twenty-minute walk home. It gave her time to mull things over, to think about the evening to come, to shed the tough outer skin of Amber Walgace and the day job, and to put on the silky skin of Amber Huddson, wife and homemaker.

She'd spent the final hour of the afternoon completing paperwork, including the report on Mrs Joyce. It wasn't a difficult report to write. In fact none of them were, as far as she was concerned. A simple summary of the situation and visit, a recommendation and then pages and pages of background information copied from the original report. Mrs Joyce would be going nowhere – Amber could see no reason for the corporations to support her. She simply needed to pull herself together and, like the rest of the population, get on with it.

By the time she arrived home she was well and truly Amber Huddson. She paused and looked up at the house that Francis, her rich orange-strata lover, had left her in his will. The four-bedroom Victorian house stood there tall and proud – as proud to exist as

Amber was to own it. It was a dream that the young blue-strata girl wouldn't have even dreamt of before she'd met him at that party and then spent two incredible years with him. Dropping to green when he died had been difficult, but the house and the Fluence he'd left her had helped a lot.

She pressed her finger to the lock and said, 'Amber Huddson wants to come in.' The door clicked open.

'House: I want music,' she shouted, as she threw her coat and bag on the floor.

The house sound system obliged, pumping a loud beat along the hallway. The music followed her, switching on in front of her as she climbed to the first and then the second floor. At the top of the stairs she glanced out of the window and across the spectacular view of London.

She half sang, half screamed along to the words.

She sat on the toilet and carried on singing as she took off her shoes. She loved that first piss on her own toilet after a day at work. She finished with a little squeeze, sighed and then picked up her knickers. She took them into the bedroom and threw them on the floor – an intimate treat for Terence.

Her first burst of energy was expelled, Madonna had sung her stuff and Amber was well and truly home.

'House: DJ for me. And some lights, please.'

The bedroom lights started to flash blue, then red, then green. A strobe on top of the wardrobe pulsed in the corner. She danced and sang to the tunes that filled the room. She imagined that she was deep inside a club packed tightly with beautiful people, completely lost in the music.

A piano started to play and Amber instantly recognised the sad song. She slumped on to the bed and sang along. This had been one of her mum's favourites. She stopped smiling. The song made her think of Terence; if she could make it with anyone it would be with him, but she had to climb the Strata Ladder and he didn't have the same drive or ambition as her. One day she might have to choose between the life she wanted and the person she wanted to spend it with. It unnerved her, making her think about things she didn't want to – she couldn't let her doubts about Terence surface too much, especially this week, because she'd never get enough points if she got distracted.

I must tidy up and check my rating, she thought. 'House: Stop DJ.'

She undressed and carefully hung her suit in the walk-in wardrobe. It covered the entire length of her bedroom's twelve-foot wall and was packed full of one-off made-to-measure items that she'd been given during her days of celebrity tagging with Francis.

One of her cleaner's jobs was to choose a home outfit for Amber each evening and neatly folded on the bed were a pair of black ruched leggings and a rust-coloured singlet with the words *Not Known At This Address* printed diagonally across the front. This gave Amber an exquisite sense of high status.

'Good choice for this week,' she thought. 'All that training's paying off.'

She dressed and checked herself in the full length mirror. 'Okay, but not stunning,' she thought. She ran her hands over the leggings, enjoying the crumpled feel of the ruche, and messed her hair to give it that lived-in look.

She bounced down a flight of stairs to the middle floor where the cleaner had left fresh flowers for her to arrange. She picked up the lemon and white freesias and put them one by one into the vase of fresh water the cleaner had also provided. They smelt sweet and crisp. She scanned the information label with her ruyi. It suggested that the smell should remind her of running through a field of strawberries in a freshly washed blouse.

She sat down, enjoying the luxury of the sofa's deep pile against her feet and the perfectly positioned chocolate-brown cushions against her back. She wriggled her toes; the matching tones of her watermelon-pink nails and the chocolate brown of the sofa were wonderfully satisfying. This was the most precious part of the day – alone in her fantastic house with the gorgeous smell of fresh flowers and only her SMFeed to worry about. Directly opposite the sofa, embedded into the plaster of the wall, was her six-foot by four-foot StrataScreen.

'House: StrataScreen, please,' she said. She became Amber Walgace again for the purposes of her SMFeed.

The screen recognised her voice and came to life with all her details already loaded. Her latest post, which had simply said that she was off to work and would be back as soon as she could, had an influence rating of twenty out of a possible one hundred. It was lower than she'd hoped. It had been seen by all of her contacts, but only her best friend Opo and Terence had reposted.

'Screen: send public message to Terence Huddson: Fancy spending the night in together? The rest of the week's going to be mad busy.'

The screen obliged. The message was immediately displayed in her eHistory with a corresponding tick and a text bubble – 'seen by Hudders'. Her screen updated. Four hundred and fifty-one people had seen the post, one hundred and ten had liked it and fifty-one had interacted in some way. This pushed her post's influence rating up to thirty-four and her predicted Fluence rating up a point. Three minutes later it dropped by a point.

'Screen: public message to Opo. Babe. What's occurring. We having some nights out, boy?'

Two minutes later his response appeared. 'Girl. For certain. Gotta check out those that want some fun, eh? How about the Tagging Cellar?'

'Screen: respond: Opo ma boy, it's a date. I need some points.'

Her own personal charta was on the low tartan-covered table in front of the sofa. She picked it up, pressed her thumb to the corner and brought up the algorithm and database she'd been perfecting for the past year. When she'd bought it, illegally, it had been thirty percent accurate at predicting someone's Fluence rating. Step by step she'd painstakingly used the stolen data to improve it to an accuracy level of seventy-five percent. She could clearly see the patterns in the data that confirmed the obvious – the official algorithm tracked your activity and the amount of response to it.

And it tracked how many people at each Strata Level interacted with you. It was clear that it also factored in how much you inspired other conversations, either through direct interaction or by posting something that shifted trends. Slowly emerging from Amber's data were hints of it using your buying patterns – what you bought and where from – and where you took your holidays.

When she'd been mixing with the orange Strata, she'd heard stories of intelligent cameras using your hair, clothes and shoes to judge your suitability for a particular level. She couldn't find the patterns to back that up, but instinctively she believed them. Unlike Edith she didn't feel the need to constantly monitor and post because she knew from her own research that it was quality not quantity that mattered. She'd rather have a hundred people in quality interactions than a thousand simply reposting it. And it was even better if those that interacted weren't too prolific, making her one of their select few. She found this idea of quality over quantity an easy concept, but for some reason a lot of people didn't seem able to grasp it.

She searched the patterns for something new, but failed. She was agitated and wanted to be calm when Terence arrived home, so decided to bake a cake. The preciseness and control it required appealed to her and this small crumb of old-fashioned domesticity proved to her that she was capable of living the married life she'd chosen.

The view out of the kitchen window across what looked like a miniature film set of the London valley was wonderful. She took her grandmother's original copy of *Twentieth Century Cooking Revisited* from the shelf above the window. The pages were crumpled, some of the corners were turned over and favourite recipes were covered in food stains. The whole experience of using a dirty book, getting her hands dirty mixing the ingredients and handling dirty containers made her tingle deep inside with childhood memories. Hardly anyone she knew cooked anymore, choosing instead to watch professionals and buy ready-prepared meals. It had become voyeuristic with an edge of animalistic decadence and whenever she described the dirtiness of her cooking to Terence he got very frisky.

In the tall pantry was a box the cleaner had prepared and labelled as *Lemon Curd Butterfly Cakes, recipe #43*. Inside were two plastic containers. She carried the box over to the work surface and clipped the recipe book to a wire that ran along the wall at eye-level. It was a shortish recipe, but it still excited her. She followed it meticulously. She switched the oven to one hundred and ninety degrees and spooned the contents of the container labelled 'cake mix' into individual paper cases. The mixture oozed over the side. She couldn't wait to tell Terence that she'd had to wipe the mixture with her fingers and then lick them clean. She put the uncooked cakes into the oven and waited for exactly twenty minutes. The smell of cooking filled the kitchen and as soon as the alarm beeped she carefully moved them to the cooling rack of her latest gadget – a CakeEase. The beauty of the CakeEase was that it cooled cakes to the correct temperature within four minutes. It was a luxury, but Terence had agreed that she should have one because she enjoyed baking so much. She suspected it would boost her rating quite a bit as well. Once they'd cooled, she took a sharp knife and sliced the tops off, filled the middle with lemon curd from the other container – another messy job – and then artistically replaced the tops at a jaunty angle. Finally, using her ruyi, she updated her SMFeed to say that she'd baked some lemon curd butterfly cakes.

She was calm and ready for Terence to come home; ready to curl up with him and watch his favourite game show, *Other People's Ratings*. It was a mind-numbing game based on guessing the Strata Level of nondescript contestants. She professed to hate the show, but secretly enjoyed discussing it with him, voting and then teasing him when he got it wrong.

Her StrataScreen emitted a loud shrill and blanked.

She dropped her ruyi.

A message with the logo of an illegal app for transferring Corp-Card points appeared. 'I know what you're up to. How much is my silence worth?'

She grabbed her ruyi, hit the side of the screen with it and stood in silence while the message gradually disintegrated, pixel by pixel.

She felt sick, as if she'd been punched in the stomach.

'Ruyi: private message for Terence Huddson. Get home now. House: lock all the doors and windows.'

She ran up to their bedroom and waited.

.

FOUR

Martin's taxi pulled up outside of King's Cross train station. 'Much appreciated,' he said loudly to the driver. He leapt out and hurried across the concourse to the green bar. As he'd left the office, he'd registered his destination and roughly what time he wanted to leave, so the train operator could alert him when the train was ready to depart. If he was lucky he would have time for a quick pint.

The bar was an old-fashioned-looking place, a relic of the gastropubs that had blossomed at the turn of the century. They'd been designed to accommodate middle-class families, as they were known then, in their desire to have a real pub experience without the noise, the smell and the drunks. He checked his ruyi. The train was predicted to become economically viable in twenty minutes' time. Even if more people registered and it could leave sooner, NetCorp, who ran the trains, guaranteed fifteen minutes' notice. There was definitely time for one pint, maybe two.

'What's on offer today then, Jim?' he asked the barman.

'Hello, Martin. Good day to you too.'

'My most humble apologies. Good day to you. Would you be so kind as to serve me a pint of your finest guest ale, please?'

'Of course. It's a cheeky pint from our microbrewery. It's called "The Last Thursday" in honour of our looming Pay Day.'

'And tomorrow's will be "The Last Friday", I presume.'

'Exactly.'

Martin took his freshly poured pint and drank the first third in one gulp. He touched the designated spot on the bar with his RetailCorp card to pay and then strolled across to one of the high stools at the large window overlooking the train platforms. He twisted the end of his ruyi so he could speak to Sam back in the office.

'Hi, Sam. Martin here.'

'Martin. How's your day been?'

'Not bad. Yours?'

'Fine.'

'Do you have a nice evening planned?'

'Quiet night in.'

'I hope you have a nice time,' said Martin, taking a sip of beer and checking his ruyi. It was ten minutes before departure. 'You'll see I've filed a report.'

'Just the one?'

He took a gulp of beer. He hated this part of the day, having to account for his time in some mysterious competition with his peers. 'Yes. It was quite complicated.'

'I'm sure it was. Well done for completing it. But you really do need to do more than one a day. Especially this week.'

'It was complicated though. And we have to get them right, don't we?'

'Of course. The trouble is, Martin, I had to overrule your decision. It wasn't substantiated enough.'

'You took him off white?' asked Martin. He sighed heavily. He'd been so meticulous, so determined to make the right decision.

'Yes. Sorry, but I had to. I'll talk you through it in the morning. See you tomorrow, bright and early.' Sam hung up.

He downed the rest of his pint and hurried to the train. He rushed past the single red carriage that always had its curtains closed. The stripe along the side of the second carriage was orange. This carriage was laid out like a hotel lounge with armchairs at one end and a restaurant at the other. As usual, it was empty except for one or two solitary figures. The next few carriages were yellow striped and looked almost the same as his own except the seats were larger and made of fake leather rather than the grubby fabric of his green carriages. His ruyi vibrated, alerting him to their imminent departure, and he hopped on the train just in time.

He found a seat and made himself comfortable. There was a faint smell of perfume and a day's worth of sweat, slightly masked by the aroma of fresh tea and coffee. He sat back and imagined the other carriages. Further down the train it would be crowded with standing room only. And in the very last carriages there were no seats at all and it would be crammed full. He imagined the different smells as you made your way from the front to the back of the train, from the perfectly scented red to downright dank and disgusting violet. He liked this part of the day, this hiatus between work and home, this pause between his two different, but equally stressful, environments. He figured he'd be a happy man if he could stay on trains all his life, so long as the flow of alcohol never dried up.

His fellow travellers were all busy on their ruyi and he should have been too. He wasn't interested though and sat watching them for a few minutes instead, until the pressure got too much. He twisted it to SMFeed and thumb-typed: 'Pint of The Last Thursday at the station and now off to a well-deserved pint at the local. All is good.' He avoided looking at his FluenceRating, the lag of his pending requests and his CorpCard balances. Knowing them would only burst this interlude and let all the stress come flooding in. He put it away and watched the scenery morph from city to towns to villages and countryside.

At Cambridge station he unlocked his electric bicycle and set off on the thirty-minute journey to his village.

He propped his bike against the wall at the George and Dragon, his local pub and his last little bubble of solitude before home. He strolled in. 'Pint of your finest ale please, landlord,' he said in a mock posh voice.

'Very funny. You'll get what you're given,' replied a burly man in his mid-fifties standing behind the bar.

'Why do we do that?' asked Martin.

'Not sure. Bit of fun though, eh? Makes the visitors happy.'

Martin picked up his pint and turned to leave the bar.

'My good fellow,' said the landlord, 'haven't you forgotten something?'

Martin tapped the spot on the bar with his CorpCard and smiled. 'Payment is yours,' he said.

He sat down at his usual table for one in the bay window and sipped his pint. He wanted to delay the inevitable pressure his family was about to impose. His ruyi was poking out of his pocket, determined to make its presence felt. He gave in.

'Go on then. What have you got for me,' he said, as if the ruyi could answer.

The screen showed that his FluenceRating had fallen by two points and his lag rating – the weighted average of the time it was taking people to respond to his attachment requests – was extremely high, at two hundred and twenty-three thousand minutes, which he calculated in his head was about one hundred and fifty days. He was pinning his hopes on most of them replying positively before the week was out. Then he might stand a chance of staying green, but it was by no means a done deal and it might need something more drastic to stop his, and his family's, slide into blue.

He picked up his pint and paused to look at the barcode tattoo on his wrist. It reminded him of how carefree he'd been as a young man growing up in Hyver Hill and it still amused him. Scanning it with a RetailCorp barcode reader should order the delivery of a large gooseberry fool dessert from the supermarket. He'd chosen it back then because he'd often been single – a gooseberry – and his hacker name had been The Fool on the Hill. His thoughts drifted to his twenty-year-old layabout son, Maxamillion. Martin envied Max, although he'd never admit it to anyone.

He finished his pint and nodded an acknowledgement to the landlord as he left. He walked slowly along his street. This was his final five minutes of peace.

He stopped at his beautiful thatched cottage with its brick chimneys and porch covered in green foliage. He liked the way the traditional black painted window frames contrasted with the white painted walls. His home. His family's home. This was the reason he carried on struggling.

The small wooden foot bridge that led him over the village brook and on to his land creaked as he walked over it. This was the creak that signalled the end of his journey, the end of the hiatus and the end of the two most precious hours of his day.

Jenny was in the kitchen chopping onions on a large farmhouse-style wooden table. His daughter Becka was concentrating on her homework.

'Hi. How was your day?' asked Jenny.

'Fine. Bit of a tricky assessment, but I managed to complete it despite some interference from the office. I'm knackered. It really takes it out of me.'

'We appreciate it though. Don't we, Becka?'

'Sure,' said the monotone teenager.

'Is Max at home?' asked Martin.

Jenny looked at him. Her sleeves were rolled up and her hair was dishevelled.

'I don't know. He was here a little while ago. Go easy on him, Martin. Please.'

He slung his jacket over the back of a chair and took a couple of bottles of ale from the cupboard.

'And go easy on that too, please. What with it being Pay Day week,' said Jenny.

'Whatever you're cooking smells nice. Apple tart?'

'Yes. Did you hear me? Go easy on the beer.'

'Sure,' he said, copying Becka's monotone.

'How's the lead up to Pay Day going?' asked Jenny.

'Okay,' he said.

Becka raised her head from the homework. 'Are we nearly at yellow?'

'Touch and go, darling,' replied Martin. 'Touch and go.'

'Your dad's doing his best. We're all rooting for him, aren't we?' said Jenny.

'Not so sure about Max,' said Martin.

'He is in his own way, I'm sure. It would be great to be able to buy more things from BeWell rather than relying so much on GreenNet, wouldn't it?'

Becka nodded. 'Yup. Sure would.'

He popped open one of the beers, flicked the bottle top into the bin and left them to it. The ever present pressure to pretend that all was well, in fact the pressure to pretend that all was great, had started again. He touched the StrataScreen with his ruyi as he entered the room they called The Snug. It switched from Jenny's profile to his. He'd prepared a log fire that morning before he went to work and with one single flick from his pipe lighter, it lit.

He slumped into his leather armchair which was tucked into the corner of the room opposite the screen. He drank a long, slow swig of his beer and with a deep sigh took stock of his ratings. He had to digest what was happening and try to correct this downward drift before any of his family found out. If he lost his green Strata Level they would lose the house and everything that went with it. He was sure that his marriage wouldn't survive the stress of dropping to blue; the massive rift that would happen if Jenny ever found out how much he'd lied to her and their friends about how successful he was at the Bureaucracy, on top of losing the house, would destroy any respect his family had for him.

His rating was only twenty-six points from the bottom of the level. Forty-three of his attachment requests were still pending. They could make all the difference. He prodded twenty of them.

He twisted the ruyi. 'Update SMFeed: log fire, dinner on its way and a warm spicy bottle of bitter in hand.'

The screen updated. Martin's post had been seen by five people and reposted by nobody. Its influence rating was zero. The top trending posts, those with most influence, scrolled across the screen and were mostly about the end-of-year parties. Every now and again there was a flurry of journalists debating the merits, or otherwise, of the Pay Day system.

Responses to his prods started to come back. Twelve of them declined and eight accepted. His rating dropped another eight points. Those that had accepted were obviously lower down the pecking order than him and he'd lost the standard twenty percent of the difference in their points. Once again he'd misjudged things.

Becka came in with another beer. 'Mum doesn't know I've brought you it.' She smiled and left the room, luckily without catching sight of the content on his StrataScreen.

'Update SMFeed: Lovely daughter just brought me another beer. How fortunate I am.'

That one reached thirty people, but once again nobody reposted. He dropped a point.

'Update SMFeed: Sexy wife in the kitchen holding a chopper.'

Three hundred and twenty-one people reached. And, bingo, eighteen reposts. He gained two points.

'Update SMFeed: Sexy wife in the kitchen getting hot.'

No one reached and no reposts. He dropped five points. I don't understand this at all, he thought.

The door opened and in walked Max. Martin jumped up and tapped the side of the screen with his ruyi.

'Don't worry, Pop, I didn't see anything,' said Max.

Max's bohemian lifestyle, which he partly funded, was a constant thorn in his side. The handlebar moustache and the wacky haircut – shaved all the way round his head just above the ear line and then kept long on top so it flopped down over the shaved part – was the crystallisation of why Max invoked so much jealousy in him: he wanted to be that free.

'What fine things have you been up to today then?' he asked.

'This and that,' replied Max.

'This and that. Very grown up. While I've been making sure the country runs smoothly, you've been…?'

'Like I said, this and that. Actually, I'm getting lots of viewing activity on that surf-off vid. And on the back of it higher level folk are tracking me. Nice little earner as it happens.'

'Why can't you do normal things?'

'Like you? And then get pissed every night to forget? No thanks.'

'Max.'

'And how is the two-faced, Fluence-grabbing Amber?'

'Max. There's no need…'

'You were the one that kept on about her.'

Jenny joined them. 'You're not talking about her again, surely? What's she done now?'

Martin sighed. 'Nothing that's unusual. She's the favourite. She gets away with murder while I have every single decision questioned – even when I've followed her advice.'

'We know she's special,' said Jenny with a slight edge to her voice.

Max looked from his mum to his dad and to his mum again. 'She's a bitch, a scheming, lying bitch.'

'Max. Don't ever let me hear you talk about someone like that again,' said Jenny.

'She's what's wrong with the world. All spin and no substance. Her type should be brought down a peg or two.'

Martin stood up. 'Max, you're about to become an adult. Grow up, please. Jenny?'

'He's right. Listen to yourself. You'll be standing on your own two feet next week. It's time to accept the way things work and make the most of it,' said Jenny.

Max rubbed the back of his neck. 'Sure, I'll be given a dead-end green job and be expected to keep my head down and work hard.'

'Yes,' said Jenny.

'I don't see the point. I can earn enough with bits and pieces. I don't need a job.'

'It's more than a job though isn't it? Martin, tell him.'

'She's right. Just because you were born on April 1 doesn't mean—'

Jenny interrupted. 'Martin, for goodness' sake. Max, I know it's tough being a man and still having to rely on us, but that's the way it is. There's not enough work for everyone otherwise.'

'I can be a parent from next week. I don't need a lecture from you two.'

'Thank God they made you wait until now,' said Martin under his breath.

'Thanks a bunch, Dad.'

Jenny shrugged her shoulders. 'Both of you need to grow up.' She left the room.

'Max, can we talk?'

'Leave it,' said Max. He turned and walked away.

'Where are you going?' shouted Martin.

'To sell rare seeds to the gardening elite.'

'That's illegal.'

'Really? How wise and on the pulse you are,' said Max.

'Of course, son. You know best.'

Max shrugged his shoulders and left the room. Martin called through to the kitchen, 'Jenny, I'm off upstairs to work. I won't bother with any supper. Thanks.'

He picked up his last bottle of beer and with a slight wobble climbed the old wooden stairs that led directly to his study. Another StrataScreen hung on the wall and an old battered sofa sat in front of it. His desk was over by the window which perfectly framed the walnut tree in the front garden. That tree must have been there since the cottage was built in the seventeenth century and it gave Martin a sense of his part in the history of the village.

He switched the screen on with his ruyi, sat at his desk and took his charta out of the drawer. He pressed the corner with his thumb. Secreted in the depths of the system was his old hacker identity along with traces of his activity on the anonymous forums. They were run by left-leaning anarchists, trying to redress the damage their right-leaning counterparts had caused by backing the dismantling of the state and allowing the corporations to replace it.

'Fool on the Hill,' he said, and the charta logged him into the hackers' news page. He still kept up with the latest developments and contributed insights into how the Bureaucracy operated.

A message popped up on his screen. 'Hiya, Fool.' He stared out of the window, wondering whether to answer.

FRIDAY

FIVE

'Pass the coffee,' said Amber.

Terence passed her a coffee-tube which she held at either end and twisted. The grinder inside the tube whirred and steam created by the chemical reaction started by the twist was forced through the ground coffee. She poured the espresso into her favourite pure-white china cup.

'I can't believe you're still angry with me,' he said. 'I came straight home. And I haven't complained that we didn't have that special night you promised.'

'That's not the point, is it?'

'It's just a Pay Day prank. You're overreacting.'

'Exactly. You think I'm being silly. That was the word you used, wasn't it?'

'It's no big deal. You had a fright. That's all.'

'Someone knows what I'm up to. What have you been saying at work?'

'Nothing.'

Amber placed her cup on the kitchen table with precision, silently conveying her pent-up anger. 'They're too thick to understand anyway. Chopping away at bits of wood every day.'

Terence clenched his jaw. He knew she was deliberately trying to rile him and he didn't want to react, but he couldn't stop himself. 'We're craftsmen not bloody handymen. As you well know.'

'I know, I know. The last of the great carpenters and their eager young apprentices.'

'And what would I tell them, exactly?'

'That we're using stolen data to work out the algorithm.'

'Why would I do that? They're not thick, but they wouldn't be interested either. Maybe Sam's rumbled you? She's the one that has access to the charta logs. And she's the one that's all clingy and doesn't want you to leave.'

'Oh God.' She paused. 'No, Sam can't have found out. And even if she has, she wouldn't send a creepy message like that.'

'Talking of creeps, what about Martin?' Terence raised his eyebrows and smiled. 'He was a famous hacker wasn't he?'

'Very funny,' said Amber. She punched him playfully on the arm.

He pulled her close and hugged her tightly. He smelt of soap and toothpaste. On his left shoulder blade was the tattoo she'd designed for him – a bumble bee landing on a striped snapdragon flower – to symbolise his gift of passing on an almost forgotten skill. She kissed the tip of her finger and touched the tattoo.

'Time for work,' she said, rubbing her hand over his shaved and balding head. He kissed her on the bridge of her nose, which she'd broken playing hockey at school. This was their ritual. Their way of acknowledging they loved each other despite their imperfections.

Jenny passed Martin his eggs, bacon and toast. 'I know it's a special week, but do you really need to work until two o'clock in the morning?'

'Can't have it both ways, my darling,' he said, slurping his tea and pouring Jenny's home-made ketchup all over his breakfast. 'Either you want me to be successful or you don't.'

'It's not about being successful, is it? It's about providing the best start in life for the kids.'

'Of course. And that's what I'm doing. Although that layabout doesn't exactly make it easy.'

'Lay off him, Martin.'

'Yeah, lay off me, Pops,' said Max as he came sauntering into the kitchen. 'Mmm…nothing like the smell of toast in the morning.'

'Incredible. What on earth gets you up at this time of the day?' said Martin.

'Things to do, people to see.'

Jenny ruffled Max's hair as if he were still a naughty schoolboy. 'Max, don't tease him,' she said.

Max smiled at her and ducked away. 'Ripe pickings this time of year; the early bird 'n all that.' He took one of his performance-enhancing drinks out of the fridge, stole a slice of Martin's toast and left the room.

'You cheeky little…' Martin called out after him.

'Martin…' said Jenny.

'Well, why am I working myself to the bone for that?'

'You're the one that wanted the cottage. Wanted to live the country gentleman's life. Wanted his local village pub.'

'What? How can you say that? You're the one that wanted the farmhouse kitchen. Wanted the idyllic fresh air and fresh food. Wanted the wholesome kids, the perfect family.'

Jenny cleared away his unfinished breakfast. 'Go on. Piss off to work before I say something we regret.'

'Regret. What a laugh.' He looked out of the window. The morning mist was still hanging in the air and the sun was just managing to shine through the trees at the bottom of the garden. He picked up his ruyi. 'Message for NetCorps Trains: One green commuter from Cambridge to London at seven-thirty.'

He slammed the front door as he left the house.

They were gathered in one of the glass meeting rooms for their weekly team meeting. This was when Sam reviewed the week and sorted out any problems.

'Okay, folks. Five minutes to do your last SM updates and then we're meeting,' said Sam.

'Do we really need to?' asked Amber.

'Oh, I quite like these meetings,' said Martin.

Sam touched her watch. 'Yes, we do. Two more minutes and we start.'

There was a burst of frenetic thumb-typing. Amber was the last to put her ruyi on the charging mat and as she did she noticed that one by one the pixels of her StrataInfo were being replaced by a message.

'If you don't reply, it will cost you — the lag will cripple your chances of yellow.'

Immediately she looked at Sam and then at Martin. Neither of them showed any sign of sending it. Her stomach tightened and her hands trembled slightly.

Sam started the meeting. 'So, what's gone well and what hasn't? Anyone?'

Amber shook her head, trying to recover. Martin smiled, but didn't offer anything. The others stayed silent.

'Okay,' said Sam, 'I have some news for you which is also relevant to something I wanted to talk through. I've had a steer from above that we're over the quota for people on the white level. There's only so much funding the corporations will put into the Bureaucracy and they'd rather spend it on infrastructure than welfare. We must get people off white at every opportunity. Any questions?'

They all shook their heads.

'Martin, shall we talk through your assessment from yesterday as an example?'

'Sure,' he said, 'I went to see this old guy.'

Sam put her hand up to stop him. 'Actually, team, I only need Amber and Martin here for this. The rest of you can go. Martin, carry on.'

Martin waited while the others collected their things and left the room. 'Okay. I went to see this old guy,' he continued.

Amber interrupted. 'How old?'

'Seventy-five. Five years away from retirement. He'd been in security all his life. First as a bouncer and then as a night porter in a hotel. He's now in a wheelchair and he can't sleep properly.'

Sam nodded to Amber. 'Any thoughts?'

'What's been diagnosed?'

'He's still waiting for the results,' said Martin.

'If it's not diagnosed yet, I don't see that there's anything to think about. He's still considered fit for work, surely?'

Martin sat forward. 'The thing is though, he can't work. It's obvious. And he's done his time. I hope, if I was in that situation, I wouldn't be forced to work.'

Amber sat forward, mirroring Martin's posture. 'But he hasn't been diagnosed. For all you know he's pulling your chain. You can't let your emotions control your decisions.'

'It's common sense. It's common decency,' Martin said angrily.

'It's common sense that he could be trying it on and common decency that we don't have to pay for someone else's laziness,' replied Amber.

'Do you have a soul?' asked Martin.

Sam put both hands up. 'Stop. Enough. Martin, Amber's right. If there's no diagnosis we have to wait. You shouldn't have recommended moving him to white. And as we can only support a limited number of people we have to be tough.'

Martin opened his mouth to reply, but thought better of it.

Sam stood up. 'Thank you both. Now let's get on with the day. What have you got on?'

Amber stood up as well. 'I've got some routine visits, nothing special. And it's the same for you, isn't it?' she said, looking at Martin.

He nodded. 'There's still a couple of unallocated cases. An orange who's reported one of his employees and a white that didn't show up for his bi-monthly review.'

'I'll take the orange,' said Amber.

'No, I think it's best if Martin has that one,' said Sam.

Martin shrugged his shoulders. 'Doesn't bother me either way.'

'So I'll do orange then,' said Amber.

'No, I want you to do the white and Martin the orange. Thanks. Have a good day.'

Sam went back to her desk, leaving Amber and Martin together. Amber quickly picked up her things, shook her head and left the room. As she walked past, Sam said to her, 'Amber, do the white first. The sooner we reduce these numbers, the better.'

The taxi wasn't able to drive on to the estate so it dropped Amber off at the end of a narrow road of flats. Each block had street level garages and each garage was a hive of activity. Busy, dirty-looking men in overalls shouted and joked while they banged, pushed and coaxed their knackered cars back to life.

She walked past, looking straight ahead and trying to appear as nonchalant as possible. The smell of oil and home-grown dope hung richly in the air. A bead of sweat trickled down her back, making her even more self-conscious. When she'd got dressed that morning she was still feeling shaken by the blackmail threat and had needed something simple and classic to make her feel secure. But walking down that road she wished she was wearing something more casual and little bit sexy, something that would give her a boost of confidence so she could play the sassy girl slumming it in a no-go area. Sadly, the white silk blouse and jacket, the black and white dogtooth patterned shoes and the calf-length black skirt just didn't cut it.

One of the do-it-yourself mechanics stopped bashing away at his multi-coloured car. He leant back on the bonnet, put the paper-wrapped herb to his mouth and took a long draw. His hands were filthy. He patted the bonnet of the car. 'C'mon, baby, start for daddy,' he said, loud enough for Amber to hear. He stared at her legs and she realised that the full-length zip of her skirt was unzipped more than halfway, revealing her lower thighs. She walked as fast as her heels would let her, hoping she didn't appear scared. She'd often fantasised about being with a dirty manual worker and had even been to clubs where you could pay men to role play, but she wasn't finding the real thing sexy at all.

At the end of the road she opened her bag to check the charta. It directed her around the corner to the lift. She took off her long string of pearls, popped them into her bag hoping no one would notice and pressed the button for the thirteenth floor.

She stepped out of the lift and walked along a bland corridor. A lick of paint and a bit of carpet could easily have transformed it into the corridor of any low-grade hotel. She knocked on the door. One of the conditions of being supported by the Bureaucracy was that someone would always be at home, so her client hadn't been informed of her visit; there was no reason for all of a family to be out at the same time and if you lived alone you were expected to team up with a neighbour to stop you becoming isolated.

She knocked on the door again and a man in his late sixties

dressed in shabby jeans and a torn t-shirt put his head out of the next door along. 'Hi. Can I help?' He looked her up and down. 'From the government?'

'Amber Walgace from the Bureaucracy. I need to speak to Mr Franklyn.'

'What if he doesn't want to speak to you?'

'I will have no choice but to mark him fit to work. And promote him to the violet Strata.'

'I'm Harry Franklyn,' said the man. He unlocked his door and ushered Amber in to a small kitchen-diner with a battered Formica table in the centre. He pointed at the single chair. 'Have a seat.'

Yet again, Amber felt seriously overdressed.

'Mr Franklyn,' she said.

'Call me Harry, please.'

'Mr Franklyn.'

'You wanna play at formal? Okay. I know the drill, girl.' He put his mug of beer down. 'Nothing has changed. I still can't work. The dust from that packing factory did for my lungs something rotten. It's never going to change and it's got me so fucked up in the head I often lay in bed all day, too miserable to move.'

'So it hasn't got any worse since we last assessed you?'

'No. But that's not the point, is it. I can't work.'

'You didn't make your last appointment at the Bureaucracy. Why was that?'

'Honest answer, I forgot. And then once I'd remembered I didn't come in 'cos I couldn't face all the accusations and questioning. Just didn't seem worth it in the end.'

'You may regret that attitude, Mr Franklyn. I'm promoting you to violet, starting at the beginning of the new Pay Year.'

'That's not going to happen,' he said, slamming his fist on the table.

'It is. You can always appeal, but until your appeal is heard you're going back to work.'

Amber stood up, making sure he could see she was recording the interview on her charta, in case he was tempted to get violent.

'Good day to you,' she said and closed the door behind her. 'Charta: taxi and escort please. Straight away. I've just taken someone off white and I'm concerned for my safety.'

She took the lift to the ground floor and nervously stood next to a sign forbidding the use of StrataScreens. While she waited for her escort to arrive she reported her recommendation that Mr Franklyn should be promoted to violet and to expect an appeal from him. As she logged the report her ruyi informed her that Sam had awarded her a ten-point bonus for a job well done. The bonus increased her chances of becoming yellow, which gave extra weight to the doubt she already had about Sam being the blackmailer.

Two women dressed in the dark brown uniform of the Bureaucracy Security approached confidently from the same side road Amber had used to enter the estate.

'Ms Walgace. Come with us. We have a taxi to take you to your next appointment.'

They escorted her back along the road of mechanics to the waiting taxi. She climbed in and for once was relieved to smell the familiar mustiness of the well-used vehicle. Her rating had dropped thirty points, despite the ten-point bonus. The lag from the unanswered blackmail was dragging her down.

'Ruyi: public message to Opo. Tagging Cellar tonight. No ifs or buts, I have to get some serious points.'

Attached to the partition between her and the driver was a StrataScreen. She tapped its side with her ruyi.

'Tick Tock, Tick Tock' appeared for a few seconds before her real StrataInfo was displayed. She shivered. She could still feel the trail from the earlier trickle of sweat down her back. She shivered again.

SIX

Max stepped through a narrow door that led from the innocuous ground floor bar to a narrow set of stairs and down into a dark underground bar. A rat-like man chewing gum and looking as if he was wired for trouble took Max's ruyi, stepped to one side and with a swoop of his arm, invited Max into the room.

An announcement came from the empty stage. 'Attention, sports fans. Are you ready for this morning's entertainment? We have a splendid game for you. A race between five social-athletes.'

The illegal bar had a large multi-StrataScreen at one end of its long triangular space and was packed with all sorts of misfits. The corporations officially called them outliers and the media had labelled them the ColourLess. They preferred to be known as ColourFree.

The stench of stale smoke, stale alcohol and stale bodies hung in the dusty air. Old cinema seats, car seats, office chairs and battered sofas were arranged into small groups. He looked around for Dan, a man he only vaguely knew and who scared him a little. Dan and his associates were sitting in a semicircle on a matching set of old cinema seats. All four of them wore beige chinos, blue shirts and leather shoes. Unlike the other inhabitants of the bar – the dropouts and the violent criminals – Dan and his crew could blend into any level and any situation they chose. In fact if they hadn't been so obviously at home in the bar they'd have looked like a group of yellows having a lower-level Strata Experience.

Max pulled up an old car seat and sat down. A cloud of dust puffed out from the chair. He shook Dan's hand and nodded to the other three. Dan was clever and the one that Max dealt with. He knew less about the others except that one of them was called Machete because it was rumoured that this was his favourite form of intimidation. He'd heard the other man and woman were armed jewellery shop thieves.

'As requested,' Max said to Dan, giving him the shotgun shells he'd taken from Martin's stash. He presumed they were for the armed thieves.

'Thanks. We'll settle up later,' said Dan, placing them on his lap in full view of the bar. Dan's repertoire was broad – he bought and sold anything from cheap illegal food to the rare-breed seeds acquired from the higher levels. Max was a relative youngster in this outlier community and in awe of Dan.

The bar was somewhere to relax, somewhere you could do a bit of business without being hassled and only twice had Max seen any violent outbursts, which Dan had put down to small misunderstandings. He'd made it clear to Max that nobody here would ever consider using the CorpPolice to resolve anything; the unspoken rule was to sort it out yourself or not at all.

A tall black woman with a shaved head and strong muscular arms stepped on to the stage and spoke. 'Place your bet on whoever you think will gain the largest increase in fifteen minutes.' She stepped to one side of the screen and pointed with her ruyi. 'As I'm sure you know, their identities are protected. Man One, Man Two and Man Three. Woman One, Woman Two and Woman Three. The coloured border around their part of the screen denotes their Strata Level. We'll run their feeds for five minutes so you can acclimatise and then we take your bets. I promise you'll spend the whole of the fifteen minutes on the edge of your seats.'

Max checked his charta. It found the wireless connection he wanted – The SM Sports Bar. He connected using the code on the slip of paper he'd been given at the door and ran the app that would allow him to illegally transfer Fluence. He was ready to gamble.

He rubbed the shaved part of his head, something he did when he was excited or anxious, and snapped open his bottle of performance-enhancing liquid.

The six sections of the screen came to life. Two orange, one yellow, one blue and two violet. Man One, an orange, was obviously a minor celebrity, busy commenting on a party the night before and his irritation at being hassled by people who didn't even appreciate his art form – he was dropping. The other orange, Woman One, was in a four-way conversation about investments in 'dirt-cheap fodder' for white-level shops. She was slowly but steadily increasing. Woman Two, the yellow, was probably a professional philosopher and had posted her moral thought for the day, stimulating considerable activity. The influence rating of her post was increasing at a rate of about five points per minute. Woman Three, the blue, was silent but had been actively commenting late into the previous night on the recent episode of *Other People's Ratings*. During the five-minute lead-in she crept up a point. The two male violets were attached to each other and having a public and sexually intimate conversation. Max wasn't sure if this was social-media porn or amateur exhibitionism – either way their ratings were bouncing up and down rapidly, but overall they were steadily increasing by a point per minute.

'Ladies and gentlemen, it's time to place your bets. The odds are: Man One – evens; Man Two – one hundred and fifty to one; Man Three – fifty to one; Woman One – four to one; Woman Two – eleven to two and Woman Three – twenty to one.'

The punters thumb-typed frantically, placing their bets.

The room filled with disjointed announcements from each charta: 'This is illegal. If you are not placing a bet you need to leave now. Immediately.' A formidable-looking security man walked around the room, making sure everyone was logged on to the SM Sports Bar network.

The black female host counted down, 'Five…four…three… two…one… Place your bets please.'

Max liked the look of Woman One, figuring that she would probably spend the next hour catching up with her peers and there was an outside chance she'd let slip a nugget of info that only an orange would know. He bet on her.

'So,' said Dan, 'what brings you here so early on a Friday morning?'

'Nothing in particular. Anything you've got would come in handy, especially this week. There'll be lots of crazy behaviour from the Strata Straights the nearer we get to Pay Day,' said Max.

'Did you make that up? Strata Straights?'

'Yep. Good though, eh?'

'Has a ring to it,' said Dan. He pulled out a packet of seeds from his pocket. 'Take a look at these. Purple Stripe tomato. They grow dark green with deep purple stripes from top to bottom. And these Pale Caps grow white with a brown cap.'

'I can do something with those. Are they ancient stock or discontinued GM?'

'They're an ancient variety banned by the corporations because they look a bit weird, grow into strange shapes, are hard to transport and look a bit ugly. The taste though is out of this world.'

A loud groan filled the room. Max looked up. Woman Two had started an argument with one of her fans and her ratings were plummeting.

Max turned his attention back to Dan. 'How much?' he asked, pressing his thumb to his charta.

'Fifty Fluence for a pack of ten. Same payment method as usual.'

'Still safe?'

'Seems to be. Either the corporations aren't looking for us or that was a good hacking job you did.'

'Probably a bit of both.'

'Yeah. Probably.'

'The hack on the college system seems to be holding up too.'

'Are you still skipping college?' asked Dan as he raised his eyebrows.

'Logging on every day to join a forum of a thousand students isn't my idea of an education.'

'They must notice you're missing though, even with that many attendees?'

'Nah, I've set it up to piggyback on a few of the bright but not brilliant students and it either creates a hybrid of what they're saying or simply agrees with one of them. I seem like an averagely engaged, fairly intelligent participant.'

'You skip it every day?'

'Yup, I need Fluence. You know I can turn my hand to most things – I need whatever you can send me. And anyway, I'm twenty-one on Thursday – officially a fucking adult. Big deal, eh?'

'It means you can go legit. No more need for the likes of us.'

'No way! I want to stay on the fringes. I'm not becoming a Strata Straight.'

Dan nodded slowly. 'It's funny, upping the age to twenty-one might reduce the number of legitimate babies and the number of citizens that have the right to work, but it also encourages the clever entrepreneurs like you to step outside of the system. I wonder if they realise…' He paused, lost in thought, and then patted Max on the back. 'Of course, I'll keep sending things your way and protect you from the snoops. After all, your dad was one of the originals, wasn't he.'

Max tucked the two packets into a hidden pocket on the inside of his boot and relaxed back in his seat. A small burst of excitement came from the corner of the room. The minor celebrity had started to slag off one of his peers.

Max switched his attention from Dan to the screen to see if the ten Fluence he'd bet on Woman One was making him any money. He smiled. He'd been spot on. She was conversing with her peers about business deals and those conversations alone were pushing her ratings up faster than any of the others. He grinned at Dan.

The minor celebrity got very angry and in an attempt to redeem himself let slip some sleazy gossip about another minor celebrity. He bombed. His followers let loose a tirade of comments – they weren't interested in the other celebrity, but they were appalled by his blatant attempt to divert attention. A self-appointed moral watchdog had outed the two violet men as porn stars pretending to be exhibitionist amateurs. Activity around them was dying fast. *Other People's Ratings* was still causing a lot of interest but it was becoming more and more distant from the blue woman's posts.

She had increased for a while but her influence was quickly fading.

Their host stood up at the front and clapped her hands. 'Ladies and gentleman. That's it. Your fifteen minutes is complete. I hope you had a good morning and we hope to see you again soon. Your winnings, or losses, will be applied automatically to the accounts you provided. Thank you.'

Dan turned to Max. 'Cheers. See you again soon?'

'Actually, there's something I wanted to ask you about. Privately.'

'Sure. What is it?'

'Breakfast on me?'

'Okay. So long as it's somewhere in Soho. There's some people there that I need to be close to,' said Dan.

They left the bar together.

SEVEN

Martin stooped to speak into an intercom in the brick gatepost of a large detached house set back from the road. 'Mr Lenkan. Martin Brown from the Bureaucracy here. You reported one of your employees.'

The intercom buzzed, the gate clicked and swung open slowly. Martin loved coming to this sort of house. He loved the grandeur and potency of them. Back in the George and Dragon he regaled the locals with stories of these high-level meetings and forgot to mention the less glamorous parts of his job. He was really chuffed to have a new story for Pay Day week.

He strolled up the drive and paused to admire the Harley-Davidson trike.

A middle-aged man appeared in the doorway. 'Do you like it?'

'A replica?' asked Martin.

'No. The genuine article. Of course it's harder to come by the fuel than it was the actual trike. But where there's a will…'

Martin held out his hand. Mr Lenkan ignored the gesture and pulled his beige overcoat tighter. A strip of dressing gown and bare flesh jutted out from the bottom of his coat for a few inches before being swallowed up by his green wellington boots.

'Shall I come in? Then you can tell me all about it,' said Martin, stepping towards the door.

'No need for that. I have a favour to ask.'

'I'm afraid I'm here for the disability review you logged with us.'

'That was simply a way of getting someone from the Bureaucracy to come. I have an ulterior motive and as we are so near to Pay Day I'm sure you'll be very interested. I have a lot of Fluence to spend.'

Martin took out his charta and started to record the conversation as all Bureaucracy employees were taught to do when they found themselves in situations that were making them uncomfortable.

'No need for that, Martin,' said Mr Lenkan. 'I have a proposition. For someone who needs Fluence. For someone who'll think creatively to stay on their current Strata Level. In fact, someone like you, Martin.'

'You've lost me.' He was getting increasingly worried about being on this man's estate with no obvious way out except through the locked gate.

'I want you to find me a man who will subjugate for a day. My wife has particular tastes that I won't fulfil. And she shall have whatever she wants. I pay well. It could be a nice little earner for someone. If not yourself then I'm sure you come across plenty of people in your line of work that would be grateful for the opportunity so close to Pay Day.'

Martin had heard of subjugation days, when the rich bought a slave for the day. He'd heard that it could be quite lucrative and although it was demeaning it wasn't dangerous. The corporations turned a blind eye, making it semi-authorised and semi-policed.

'I've used your organisation before to source help of this nature. Why not go away for a couple of hours and give it some thought?'

Martin was about to speak when the gate clicked open behind him. He took a step backwards. 'Okay. I'll see what I can do.' He turned and hurried out into the street.

He looked at the map on his charta. He had some spare time because of the shortness of this visit and he was only two miles – a forty-minute walk – from the guy he'd seen the day before. He wanted to apologise for the overturned decision and if he walked then no one at the Bureaucracy would know he'd been.

At the end of the private road he turned left towards Hampstead Heath. The road was lined with a variety of ostentatious houses from different eras. Some were square and blocky and others were ornate and fussy. They were all built at the top of high slopes to get the best views possible. There were lots of cars whizzing by, but no actual people out on the streets. He turned into the road that ran alongside the Heath, which was lined with more ostentatious houses. His charta lost its signal, which was unusual. He guessed that one of the houses was a corporation-owned house that was blocking it for some reason. He passed the end of a gated road where children were playing. This was a new part of London to him and he was surprised at how similar to the countryside it felt. The houses stopped at the gates to the Heath where two men dressed in Corporation of London uniforms stood next to a van with a guard dog in the back. They checked the identity of some of the dog walkers passing through the gates. He carried on along a muddy path at the side of the road. To his left a scattering of young spindly trees stood erect amongst a carpet of bracken. As he walked along, the path got muddier and the trees became older and larger. The traffic died down and there were fewer roaming security guards and their dogs.

He paused and turned to look into the woods. The rich smell of mud and rotting leaves and the sound of birds chirruping in the trees made it even more like the countryside.

He stepped aside to allow a jogger to pass him and then turned to continue his walk. Up ahead was a traffic roundabout with a large pond in the centre. In the distance a church poked its spire above the buildings. He was on the top of the city and walking through what was affectionately known as the 'lungs of London'.

At the roundabout the traffic was constant and noisy and there were lots of couples strolling with dogs. This was where the orange area ended and no one was venturing into it, as if they were at the edge of an invisible barrier.

A man wearing headphones was drinking a can of beer and dancing around. Security guards were gently trying to move him along. He seemed oblivious to their presence which made them agitated. Jack Straw's Castle – a pub – caught his attention. He would have loved to stop for a pint but he couldn't. He was already off task and after his reprimand the previous day he had to be more careful.

He crossed the roundabout and the road dropped downhill dramatically. On the side of one of the houses was the most amazing tower with a spire at each corner and a large arched window in the middle. Somehow these buildings seemed old and interesting in comparison to the more gaudy and obvious orange houses. Halfway down the hill the houses were divided into flats, which was a sure sign of decreasing wealth.

A signpost on the edge of the Heath pointed to the Vale of Health. He took out his ruyi, took a photo of the sign and posted it along with the message, 'Vale of Health. On the Heath. And they say the youngsters can't spell nowadays!'

The City of London came into view, its odd-shaped skyscrapers rising out of the landscape below. He took another photo of a sign for a humped crossing. He posted it with the quip, 'Some of these country folk'll fancy anything!'

He crossed the road again as the pavement switched from one side to the other. He turned the corner and the smell of mud and leaves changed to the smell of cars and cafés. There was a sign for the World Peace Garden and it struck him that it was probably quite easy to think about world peace if you lived such a privileged life, but posting that on your SMFeed would be quite career limiting, so he didn't. Among the cafés were a few charity shops run by groups that were authorised to accept white vouchers.

He passed a woman dressed in a tweed overcoat talking to a man with an Irish Terrier. 'The new Dean's a really difficult woman you know.'

Academics and trendy dogs, definitely a yellow area, he thought.

The bustle of traffic and people increased. Tea rooms, pubs and restaurants lined the street, all overshadowed by the Royal Free Hospital. He crossed into a narrow road of tall terraced houses. Their hedges poked out and brushed the side of his head as he walked past.

In the next street the houses shrunk by a storey, the front gardens were in disrepair and an occasional motorbike or rubbish bin was wedged up tight to the front of a house. Buses were on the roads again and there were an increasing number of Food & News shops with people hanging around outside looking miserable. Buildings were encased in scaffolding covered in manky green netting. Row after row of four-storey-high concrete flats with graffiti-covered walkways imposed their desolation on the street. A steady flow of women shuffled along, weighed down with bags of shopping. They stopped every few yards to thumb-type into their shiny plastic ruyi. Other pedestrians typed into their ruyi as they walked, occasionally looking up to make sure their path was clear.

He passed a shop window with a few cheap and tacky things in it – paper plates and balloons mainly. A handwritten notice said it was bankrupt. Rotting rubbish was piling up in the doorway.

The area had the same spacious atmosphere as the Heath except instead of the bracken there was litter, the trees had become the bars of the railings and the birds were seagulls picking through discarded burger wrappers. He sensed the sinister undercurrent and mentally fidgeted, furtively looking around. He was uncomfortable and worried. He walked past a betting shop and a couple of pubs. Old furniture was strewn across the pavement outside a barber's shop from which a strong smell of cannabis leaked. A shop with flaking green paint advertising fishing tackle and bait caught his attention because he'd seen it the previous day when the taxi had dropped him off.

The gate from the street to the litter-strewn strip of grass in front of the flats creaked as he opened it. The flat was on the ground floor. Cautiously he walked along the path, conscious that he didn't fit in.

He knocked at the door. A neighbour popped her head out of her window. 'He's not there. Who're you?'

'I saw him yesterday and wanted to have a quick chat. I'm from the Bureaucracy.' He held his hand out. 'Martin. How do you do?'

'None of your business. And if I was you I'd scarper pretty sharpish. He's vanished. Here one day and gone the next. Some round 'ere might link your visit and his vanishing.'

'I had nothing to do with it. How do you know he won't come back?'

'Well, I'm sure you already know he couldn't walk? And there's been some smartly dressed official-looking types snooping around today. He's been vanished all right. Or done in.'

Martin didn't believe the Bureaucracy would stoop so low, but he didn't want to have to defend them to a gang of angry neighbours either, so he left her hanging out of her window and walked around the corner. The seagulls cooed as they picked their lunch from the discarded rubbish of the Malden Road street market. A dental practice named Maldent made him chuckle and feel a bit superior to the uneducated locals. He took a photo and posted it. 'Can the folk of Kentish Town speak French?' he thumb-typed.

At the end of the road he called a taxi for his next visit and waited. He hoped the big road-junction was public enough for him to loiter without anyone causing him trouble.

An old Land Rover slowed down as it drew level with him. He took out his charta, making sure that whoever was driving could see it. The engine growled as it turned the corner and sped off towards Hampstead.

EIGHT

'Did you hear what I just said?'

'Sure. You got another creepy message,' said Terence.

'And yet you sit there playing that stupid game with whoever you're online with.'

'StrataLife, is what it's called.'

'Game of no life, more like.'

'What's got you upset?'

'I'm losing points and I might have to stay green for another year. Some creep is threatening me and I could be made violet for twenty years. And my husband role-plays life rather than living it. I wonder what's up with me?'

Terence tapped the side of the screen. 'Okay, I'm listening. Nice flowers by the way.'

'Terence!' she shouted.

He patted the sofa next to him. 'C'mon, babe.'

She sat down. He kissed the bridge of her nose and she lent her head against his shoulder. 'I'm really worried,' she said.

He stroked her hair. 'I know. But would it be so bad if we had to stay where we are? I like it. I'm not sure I'd like yellow, I'm only just getting used to this – it's a big change from being blue, you know?'

'Of course I know. I've been there, haven't I?'

'Yeah. But somehow I doubt you really ever fitted in. Did you?'

'Not really. And I don't here either.'

'We agreed. It's where we can be together. What's with all the wanting to move up again?'

'I have to.'

'But what will it do to us? Maybe this blackmailer is a gift. Maybe you should stop the illegal stuff and stop trying to get somewhere you don't belong.'

'Terence! For fuck's sake! Are you for real?' She pushed his hand away from her head and stood up. 'I'm going out.'

He called after her. 'Babe! Amber!'

'House: I want music. I want it loud,' she shouted as she got to the bottom of the stairs. A heavy rock track fired up, the bass pumping and the guitar screaming as it followed her up the stairs.

She burst into the bedroom, tapped the side of the screen and flung open the wardrobe door. She needed to find something to wear that would help her evening quest for points. She manically flicked through the rails, not really paying much attention but using it to calm down after the bust-up with Terence. Why was he so stupidly passive? Why was he happy playing pretend life? And why did she ever think this marriage thing would work?

A message from Opo popped up on the screen. 'Hey Girl. Bad event. I gotta do some other stuff tonight. No choice. Can we slide the cellar visit to tomorrow?'

Shit, she thought, especially now she'd pissed off Terence. She'd have to think of somewhere to go alone. 'Message to Opo. Of course, hun. If you gotta slide you gotta slide. Better not let me down tomorrow though lol.'

She flipped through her charta's recommendations. An advert for a 'traditional dance with a twist' had been flashing up all day and it was also top of the list specifically tailored to her. It was a modern interpretation of border morris dancing with ruyi instead of sticks. It was an opportunity to meet people and if you wanted you could attach yourself to them for the evening through the knocking of ruyi – banging, as it was known. She touched the advert to add it to her SMFeed.

A message appeared – 'good girl, you got the hint' – and then disappeared.

She froze; she wanted to confront the blackmailer and she wanted to pretend it wasn't happening. It was her anger with Terence that made her choose confrontation. She sent Terence the details of the event, asking him if he'd come with her.

'No,' he replied.

She clenched her teeth. Fine, she thought. I'll go on my own.

She rifled through her clothes. She needed something that was a bit cheeky and a bit rock and roll. Something that would make people smile at the irony of rock and roll clothes at an ancient dance ritual. Something that would get her a better chance of attaching to higher rated people.

A new outfit caught her eye – a slightly see-through purple and black striped top, super tight black latex jeans with a zip from the ankle to the back of the knee, and black high-heeled boots with straps and buckles. Maybe, she thought and put the outfit on her bed. She carried on looking. She put another outfit next to it – a pair of heeled and pointed-toe cowboy boots with a flower-patterned frilly layered dress and a rose print leather jacket. She took out a shiny blue-black puffa jacket made of tiny crinkly plastic squares with a high stand-up collar and oversized cuffs and a matching mini-skirt and stockings. The skirt's hem flowed up and down like a wave. Finally, she found the outfit she'd worn to a heavy rock gig last year – a traditional leather biker jacket over a studded leather leotard with flat open-backed boots held on by a few straps and buckles.

She studied the outfits carefully. She wanted to make as many points as possible and first impressions would be vital. The leotard was too much, the latex jeans too obvious. It was a choice between the flowered outfit, as a nod to the Englishness of the evening, or the crinkly plastic as a nod to the urban grittiness of this modern version of morris dancing. The promo footage of the event had quite a dark edge to it so she chose the crinkly plastic puffa, mini-skirt and stockings.

She stripped in front of the mirror and then carefully checked every angle as she put on each piece of clothing. First, a black polka dot bra and knickers with tiny little pink bows drawing attention to her cleavage, her navel and her crotch. She looked over her shoulder at her bum in the mirror. That's okay, she thought. She pulled on a loose-knit sweater with a pattern of holes that resembled a skeleton, revealing her bra to good effect. She stepped into her mini skirt and pulled on the stockings. She loved the way the hem tantalisingly rose up and down revealing different amounts of flesh at the top of her legs and the way the crinkly plastic stockings gripped her thighs. She twisted and turned to see the full outfit. She was pleased. She hunted in the wardrobe for some shoes but settled on the flat boots with open backs and buckles. Finally, she added the oversized puffa jacket. Perfect, she thought.

She sat down at her dressing table to apply a Japanese style make-up of deep pink eyeshadow drawn up at the outside of each eye to meet black eyeliner that almost touched her eyebrow, creating the illusion that her eyes sloped up to form a V from her nose to the top of her ears. She didn't rub all of the blusher in, leaving it to highlight her cheekbones. She chose a vivid red lipstick and a clip-on lip ring. She was ready to go.

Downstairs, Terence was engrossed in his pretend life. She sat next to him and he put his hand on her leg, not taking his eyes off the screen.

'Please come with me,' she said.

'Where?'

'Camden Town. Modern morris dancing.'

'Not really my thing is it?'

'Could be. You might enjoy it.'

'You're only asking 'cos Opo dumped you. And you'll be so focussed on getting points you'll forget I'm there. And I'll get angry that you're not satisfied with what we've got here. It's not an attractive option.'

She studied him. He wouldn't blackmail me just to keep me here, would he? No, not his style, she thought. 'Go on. Let's have a night out,' she said. 'We could both get some extra points.'

'No thanks. Have a lovely time. I'll see you when you get back.'

She kissed him on his bald head and left the room. He called after her, 'Football tomorrow and then the pub with the lads.'

There was a queue of about fifty people waiting for the doors of the centre to open. In the distance she could see another huddle of people paying their respects at the shrine of Amy Winehouse.

She joined the end of the queue, looking around furtively for any sign of the blackmailer. It was a mixed bag of old and young. Some were obvious old timers and some obvious newcomers like Amber. She was nervous. On the one hand she wanted to meet her blackmailer, but on the other she didn't. The conflicting desires bubbled inside. She examined the queue. No one seemed to be paying her any attention; maybe it was a hoax after all. They were all carrying their ruyi. She twisted hers. 'Private message for Opo: Hey Boy, trust you're having fun. I need to talk about Terence. I think he might be blackmailing me to stay with him.'

Straight away her ruyi buzzed with a message from Opo. 'Ridiculous. Talk tomorrow.'

An athletic-looking man wearing a blue mask with white streaks painted on it, a half-sized top hat with feathers and a black jacket decorated with strips of material was working his way down the queue. The jaw and forehead of the mask jutted out like a gorilla. As he approached he took off his hat and tipped it in her direction. His hair was long on top but shaved around the bottom. 'Hi,' he said to Amber, 'you here for the morris dancing?'

'Yes. Looks interesting,' she said.

'You get all sorts here,' he replied.

'Do any oranges ever come?'

'Somewhere among this lot there'll be a few. No doubt you'll find out when we start banging. You'll need this.' He handed her a plain black mask and a long elaborate tassel of black ribbons. 'Attach it to your ruyi.'

'Thanks.'

'Maybe we'll dance together later,' he said and smiled a wicked smile.

'I hope so.' She watched him walk back up the queue. Lovely, she thought as he opened the door. The buzz of the queue increased in anticipation as it moved quickly.

Inside, the masked man was at the front of the room and everyone was facing him. 'Ladies and gentlemen. Tonight we have Ruyi Border Morris for you. If you're new we'll take you through the moves before we start. But first you need to form your groups.' He paused and looked around the room. 'We have about fifty people in tonight. Form into groups of five and one of us will join you to make the sixth. And don't forget that each time you bang your ruyi during the dance it's the same as tagging. Points will flow between you.'

Amber quickly searched the room. She had to make sure she joined a group of people on a higher level than her. People started choosing and they only had appearances to go on. She was relieved that she'd spent time on her clothes and make-up. Groups were forming. She scanned the room. A man asked if he could join a group of four women who looked as if they knew each other. They turned him away. She checked their clothes. She guessed they were orange and made her way across.

'Hello. I'm on my own. Mind if I join you?' Close up, she could see their ruyi were top quality. She'd made the right choice.

The one nearest to Amber glanced at her ruyi and her clothes. 'Of course,' she said, 'be our guest.'

'Amber,' she said and offered her hand. Her orange ruyi came in handy in these situations.

'Hi. I'm Xanthe. This is Joan, Holly and Nicole.'

'Hi,' said Amber, smiling.

The man in the blue mask clapped his hands. 'Jolly good. Does anyone need a quick lesson or are you okay to learn on the job?' Nobody said anything or raised their hands so Amber kept quiet. She'd learn as they went. 'Great. One of us will come and join you and then we can start.' He moved his head from left to right and then pointed at Amber. 'You're mine,' he said and swaggered across to her group.

'I don't know what I'm doing,' she said to him quietly.

'Put yourself in my hands and you'll have a great time,' he whispered.

NINE

An old Land Rover pulled up at the side of the road and Dan got out. He wiped his hands on his beige chinos and hoisted himself up so he was sitting on the bonnet. He tapped the windscreen. 'Here she comes,' he mouthed.

A small car pulled up outside the house opposite. The engine stopped. Dan and his crew watched as Sam leant back in the driver's seat and stretched. He jumped down and walked around to the back of the Land Rover. He poked his head inside and spoke quietly. 'Her charta's still switched on. Piggyback the feed so we can watch her inside the house.'

She gathered her things and walked slowly up the garden path. She fumbled in her coat pocket for her keys, found them and opened the door.

'Got it,' said a voice from the back of the Land Rover.

'As soon as she's inside switch the feed to the screen,' said Dan.

'Okay.' The windscreen became translucent and displayed the view from Sam's charta. The noise of keys jangling in her hand came through the sound system.

'Hi, Mum,' she said as she crashed her weekend bags through the front door.

'Samantha? What time do you call this?'

'The roads were busy and I didn't leave work until late.'

'As usual.'

'Nice to see you too. I'm just taking these upstairs and making a couple of work calls. I'll be back down soon.'

She threw her bags on the bed, pulled the armchair to the window and looked up at the dark open sky above the golf course and the beach. She twisted her ruyi to automatically upload her location. Her charta was cradled in her lap. She pressed it with her thumb and called Martin. 'Hi. Good day?'

'Not bad,' he replied, slurring his words. 'I'm in the pub relaxing for the evening. Anything I can help with?'

'Just checking today was okay. I had to travel down to my mum's which is why I'm ringing a bit late in the evening.'

'Okay. Sure. All is good.'

'How did it go with the orange?'

'False alarm.'

'Took a while to sort out?'

'Yeah, but all done now.'

'See you on Monday then,' she said and hung up.

Next she called Amber but got no reply. She left a message. 'Hi. Hope today went well. I'm down at my mum's. If you wanted a break from the city, come and join me.' As soon as she hung up she frowned and muttered, 'What on earth was I thinking? She's never taken me up on the offer of a weekend away and in this week it's even less likely.'

Her mum called up from the kitchen. 'Supper's ready.'

She quickly took off her work clothes and hung them up, ready for Monday morning. She glanced at her back and the elaborate tattoo of Ganesha – the elephant Hindu God. She dressed in her all-in-one pyjamas and went downstairs for supper.

'At last,' said her mum.

Dan touched the windscreen. 'Transmit the previous ten minutes,' he said.

Sam sniffed the air. 'Thanks for cooking. What is it?'

'Rice, smoky butter beans and chard. A good wholesome vegan meal. Such a shame you gave it up.'

'I became a veggie, Mum. There's not a lot of difference.'

'Tell that to the boy calves as they're murdered.'

'Okay, okay, enough,' said Sam. She sat down at the table.

'I still don't understand why you come to visit me so often. Haven't you got any friends to hang out with?'

'I come to make sure you're okay. And no, not really. Work is all consuming. I don't really have time.'

'You did until they all left you because of that Nabah.'

'Mum! You know he broke my heart.'

'It was always going to end badly.'

'Really? He was a lot of fun, actually.'

'Until he dumped you and went back to India.'

'He wanted me to go with him, you know.'

'I know, but they wouldn't let you immigrate. How ironic.'

'Thank you for that.' Sam tucked her blonde hair behind her ear and concentrated on eating.

'And you're pretty so I don't see why you don't have a boyfriend. You should get out and try harder.'

Sam nodded and scooped up the last mouthful. 'That was great. Thanks. Think I'll take a drink upstairs if that's okay. I'm done in.'

'I only say it because I care,' said her mum.

'I know. I know,' she said over her shoulder.

Dan touched the screen again. 'Start transmission.'

She sat down in a small, old and fraying armchair with a faded green checked pattern and tapped the side of the small StrataScreen hanging on the wall. She popped her charta into the bracket below and plugged it in, setting the screen to alert her if anything came up that she needed to know.

'Charta: three minutes of Victoria Wood, please.'

'Still Standing – Baby Boom' appeared, ready to play. 'Charta: play.' She breathed in, propped up the pillows on her bed and laughed along to the short ditty, especially the bit about getting to thirty-three years old before realising it was okay for women to move during sex. She played it a couple more times and gradually relaxed.

She unzipped her pyjamas a little. 'Charta: TagTease, please.'

A mix of young, old, handsome, ugly and plain men appeared in little square boxes on her screen. An option to review the female competition flashed in the bottom right-hand corner. She chose it.

'Charta: search for green, Amber, Walgace, Huddson, hazel eyes, bleached blonde, New Cross, Bureaucracy.' She quickly flicked through the women. 'Oh well,' she muttered, 'maybe one day.'

'Charta: search men. Intelligent, average looking, single, well-groomed and above average honesty rating.'

A selection of thumbnail images appeared and as she touched each one the charta played a brief profile description. She leant forward. 'Too creepy. Too vague. Too obvious.' She drew a tick on ten of the profiles, the maximum allowed at any one time.

Dan's ruyi buzzed. He twisted it. 'Yeah, got it. No worries,' he said and twisted it back.

The chosen men appeared on Sam's screen. She observed their public conversations while she waited for them to respond. A couple of the men stopped saying anything publicly for a few minutes and then disappeared from the screen, presumably because one of their private conversations had moved on to a different forum. Four of the remaining men said, 'Hi Sam,' in the public chat. The fifth sent her a private message. 'Hello. Loving the Dalmatian pyjamas. How are you?'

Sam checked his profile before answering. He was forty-five – only a little bit younger than her. He loved to flirt and tease but wasn't interested in anything more; he avoided physical contact with the opposite sex. He was good-looking with the same combination of blonde hair and grey eyes as her. 'Hi,' she replied, 'glad you like them. I'm just sitting here all cuddled up in bed having a last little flirt of the day.'

'And what a nice bed it is,' he said.

'Really? You think so?'

'Oh yes. You'd be surprised what you can tell about a girl from her pyjamas and her bed.'

'Do tell.'

'Well, let's see. First of all the exotic Indian drapes tell me that you're very sensual and well-travelled. Am I right?'

'It's a good start.'

'And the pyjamas tell me you're confident enough in your looks to come on here as a real person. They also tell me that you're a bit of a tease – the way you have them unzipped just enough to make me want more.'

'You want more?'

'Oh, yes please. If that's an offer?'

'Hold on. I do have something for you. Wait there,' she said as she got off the bed and walked over to the corner of the room out of his sight. She unzipped her pyjamas down to her waist and then moved back into view but with her back to the camera. 'There's a little piece of exotica for you,' she said and giggled.

'Wow. What a tattoo. Any more?'

'Now that would be telling.' She zipped her pyjamas back up but not quite as far as they had been. 'And I don't tell on first flirts,' she said and winked.

'There must be something I can do to get a better glimpse of those cute little freckles I can see adorning your tits.'

'Tits?'

'Sorry. Wonderful, curvaceous breasts.'

'Better. And you'll have to impress me first. There's not many that can say they've seen those.'

'You'll have to give me a clue on how to impress.'

'I like secrets. Big secrets that lock us together. If you trust me with secrets then I can trust you.'

They carried on chatting for a while, both making sure there was an undercurrent of flirtation. They touched on their radically different tastes in music – he liked the fast and furious dance music and she preferred the singer-songwriters of folk. She told him about the bullies at school who called her Creepy Crawley because she was a lettuce-eating vegan. He admitted to being a bit of a school bully himself and talked about how he'd grown up to regret it. Every now and again he pressed to see her freckles and she repeated her request for a secret.

Cautiously they began to talk about their jobs. 'I work for the Bureaucracy. Middle manager. Assessing disability claims,' she said. 'What about you?'

'For one of the corporations. Research,' he said and smiled.

'Interesting. Which one?'

'RetailCorp. And I could tell you a secret about them. About what I'm doing.'

She held the zip of her pyjamas. 'Go on then.' She winked.

'You wouldn't believe me.'

'Try me. You seem like a man I could trust.'

Dan's ruyi buzzed. He put it to his ear and twisted. He listened for a few moments. 'Of course, deleted as soon as it's said.' He drew his forefinger and thumb together across a small icon of a nuclear explosion in the bottom left-hand corner of his screen.

The man on Sam's screen spoke. 'I'm working on a genetic engineering project. If we succeed, then with one tiny change to your genes we can switch on and off your likes and dislikes for any food we want.'

'Why on earth would you do that? Why on earth would anyone agree to it?'

'The idea is that the poorer consumers can be aligned with the cheapest food available at the time. They're happy because they will get what their genes are telling them to like. And we're happy because we can predict and control demand.'

'That's horrible.'

'Really? Don't see why. If all the indigo and violet consumers had cravings for an affordable balanced diet that would be a good thing, surely?'

'It sounds disgusting to me.'

'I don't see how it's any worse than what you do? Anyway that's my secret. And it's commercial dynamite. So keep it to yourself.'

'Who would I tell?'

'No one, I hope.' He winked. 'Now, your turn.'

'Fair enough,' she said and did what she'd originally come online to do. She unzipped her pyjamas to reveal her breasts, making sure that the screen wasn't showing her face at the same time.

'Love the freckles,' he said.

She smiled, logged off and zipped herself back up. She was buoyant with self-confidence.

While she'd been flirting with him a message from her friend Beatrice had popped up. She took the charta off the wall and joined the forum for parents who were searching for their long-lost adopted children. Thumbnails of all those currently logged on came up and she could see Beatrice waving at her. 'Charta: Beatrice, please.'

'Samantha. Been a while,' said Beatrice.

'Busy time at work,' replied Sam. 'No luck finding Holly then?'

'No. I still don't even know what she's called these days. She was only a month old when she was adopted. How about you?'

'No. Thirty years is a long time. Not sure I'll ever find her.'

'Have to let them go, I suppose. Concentrate on the ones we do have.'

'Reckon you might be right. I won't make the same mistake again. I'd do whatever it took to keep hold of another one,' said Sam.

'Good for you,' said Beatrice. 'That's my gal.'

'I'm pooped. Think I'll log off for the evening. Bye.'

'Bye,' said Beatrice, and shrunk back to a thumbnail, waving goodbye.

Dan rapped on the Land Rover roof. 'C'mon then, let's do what we've been paid for.'

TEN

I t was approaching midnight and Amber had been dancing for hours. It was great fun, a lot more fun than she thought it would be. The blue-masked man had been amazing. He'd shown them all in turn what to do but each time he held Amber's hand he seemed to linger a little longer than with the others. She was still upset with Terence and Opo. They'd let her down on the one weekend she really needed them. Still, she was certainly not going to let either of them ruin her future and if they weren't interested in her then it was their loss.

'Glad you came?' asked the masked man.

'Absolutely. Totally amazing,' she replied. 'So,' she said, 'are you ever going to tell me your name? Or what you do in real life?'

'Nope. And that's the way you want it. Isn't it?' he said, leaning in close.

She could feel his breath tickling her ear. 'Maybe. Although it's hard to kiss through a mask.'

'Get a room,' said Xanthe in a loud whisper.

He grabbed Amber's hand. 'Come on.'

They left through a fire exit at the back of the hall. It led out on to a staircase. He kept hold of her hand and bounded up the stairs so fast that she was gasping for breath by the time they reached the top. He wasn't even breathing deeply. He's fit, she thought. He pushed open a door to reveal a small room with a sofa, a sink and a mirror covering a whole wall. 'Dressing room,' he said.

'Undressing room?' She giggled.

'How much of a risk do you wanna take?'

'Try me.'

'Let's bang,' he said. 'Ruyi, of course,' he added with a twinkle in his eyes.

74

'That is risky. I've no idea who you are. You won't wipe me out of points, will you?'

'That's a risk we both take,' he said, leading her to the sofa.

She paused before sitting down. The buzz of coming on her own, the dancing and the points she was sure to have gained from the orange women went to her head; she unbuttoned his thick fake-fur waistcoat and ran her fingers down his stomach.

He stopped her moving, pressing her hand gently to his body. 'Ruyi first,' he whispered. His blue eyes held her gaze. She moved her hand from under his and ran her fingers through his hair. She straightened a couple of the tassels on his jacket and stood up.

'Okay,' she said. In the mirror she could see his back, his shaved head, his golden hair and his cute little bum. She touched the scar on his chin. 'At least tell me about this.'

'Surfing accident. Annoying 'cos it stops me growing a full beard.'

'Surfing?'

'Yep. I'm a surfing celebrity, of sorts.'

'Tell me more,' she said, tucking her hand under his jacket to feel his shoulder blade.

He took a step back, smiling. 'Ruyi?'

She paused and then slowly removed her hand. 'Yes,' she said.

Martin put his pint down on the bar and hitched himself up on the stool. 'Fred, it's complicated. There's so much you have to take into account. People think it's easy. They think that because it sometimes goes wrong, it's run by complete numpties.'

Fred, one of four men sitting with Martin at the bar, popped a small roast potato into his mouth, took a swig of beer to wash it down and leant forward. 'You're the one that's bleating on about this bloody shed thing,' he said, through a mouthful of potato and beer.

'True, true,' said Martin. 'But that's just a silly rule made up by some idiot. It's not the same as the stuff I do.' He glanced at his ruyi and the others followed suit. It seemed the more they drank, the less inhibited they became in checking their SMFeed in front of each other.

Fred turned his ruyi face down. 'Tell me again, what do you do?' Martin's companions grinned and winked at each other.

Martin was too drunk to notice. 'I decide people's futures. And their children's.'

'By taking their livelihoods away from them?'

'No. Well…no. It's a fine balance. Too many relying on the corporations for handouts would cause a financial collapse, wouldn't it? I feel sorry for them though.'

'I bet you do,' said Fred, openly winking at the other three. 'And now they're going to take away your shed. Outrageous.'

'It's Jenny. She's got it into her head that Max'll leave soon and it's time to have a clear out. She's using this stupid, stupid Bureaucracy thing about spring cleaning and upcycling to get what she wants.'

'And how is the boy brat?'

'Max? As awkward as ever. Bit of a nightmare actually.'

Martin put his empty pint glass back down on the bar and almost slipped off his stool. He called down to the other end of the bar, 'Five of your best guest ales please, landlord.'

'Coming up,' came the reply.

'And how's the hacking?' asked Fred.

'Ha ha,' said Martin. They all checked their ruyi again. 'I still dabble a bit every now and again. How's the music coming along?'

'Slowly. I'm finding it hard to fit it in around the day job. Got some great little tunes in my head but it's as if they're being played the other side of a large field with the wind constantly changing direction – I can hear parts of them clearly and then other parts fade out and I can only hear every other note.'

'Sounds hard,' said Martin. 'And is anyone worried about Pay Day?'

They all checked their ruyi again. 'Not really,' said Fred, 'how about you guys?' The others shook their heads.

'Can't be arsed,' said Martin.

'You do realise it's midnight, don't you?' said the landlord.

'And since when did that bother you?' asked Fred.

'Look around. Not exactly heaving with punters, am I?'

'You got us,' said Martin, slurring his words.

'Mmmm,' said the landlord as he walked away.

'Quick. Put on the StrataScreen,' said Fred.

Martin slapped Fred on the back. 'What's got into you all of a sudden?'

Fred was agitated. 'Look,' he said.

They turned towards the screen.

Fred was pointing. 'It's been years since they did that.'

An announcement had been made that for the duration of the weekend all points gained and all points lost would count as double. The corporations were raising the stakes.

'Shit,' said Martin. Fred and the others nodded in agreement.

Amber and her mystery man emerged from the fire exit into the main hall. Her hair was scrunched up at the back. She tried to look nonchalant, but actually she looked a bit guilty and a bit pleased with herself.

The group of women had gone and there were only a few stragglers left. She straightened her skirt and checked her ruyi. There was a message from Opo. 'Have you seen the news? Damn, I wish I was out with you.' She twisted it to show the StrataInfo news, but was distracted by another message. 'Underage encounter. Penalty of fifty points. Doubled to one hundred.'

She dropped her bag on the floor and brought the ruyi to her mouth. 'Ruyi: explain that last message,' she said anxiously. The ruyi displayed another message. 'You have been Banging with a twenty-year-old and this is forbidden for your Strata Level. You have been penalised.' She checked her overall rating. At the end of Friday, at midnight, it had increased by forty points. After midnight it had dropped by a hundred points. Tonight had cost her sixty points.

'What the fuck is this?' she shouted. No one answered. She looked up. 'Where the fuck have you gone?' She spun round trying to find him. 'Oi! Mask man. Talk to me.'

He was gone. He obviously wasn't the good-time high-ranking

aristocrat having a bit of fun that she thought he was.

A StrataScreen was displaying the news that at midnight the corporations had introduced a double-points and double-penalties weekend. 'Ruyi: private message to Opo. I've been stitched up. I need tomorrow more than ever.'

Opo replied with a message. 'Sounds grim. Girl, I know you well. You'll have lots lined up this weekend. Don't sweat. Enjoy.'

Sometimes Opo really annoyed her. Yes, of course she had lots lined up but he was as bad as Terence for not realising what was at stake. And neither seemed to be taking the blackmail seriously, which after tonight she simply couldn't afford to pay. 'Ruyi: reply to Opo. The usual pedi and manicure – an outside chance of some gossip maybe? My geek entrepreneur meet-up – highly unlikely I'll get immediate points. And a night out with you!'

A reply came straight away. 'All have possibilities. Keep your chin up babe.'

She posted to her SMFeed hoping to capitalise a bit more on the first part of her evening. 'A ruyi banging night with the best – Xanthe, Joan, Holly and Nicole. Thanks girls.' They detached from her immediately, probably because they'd spotted she wasn't as orange as she'd appeared to be.

She walked from the hall to the station, hugging her jacket tight. The plan had been to catch a taxi home using some of the Fluence she'd gained from the evening, but she couldn't afford that any more. The streets were full of the carnage you'd expect on the Friday night before Pay Day. She hitched her stockings up as high as they'd go. Gangs of young lads and lasses huddled in doorways drinking cheap vodka. A flashing sign outside a TradeCorp shop advertised half-price fun for double-points weekend. A girl lay in the gutter frantically tapping her sugar-pink plastic ruyi, the stench of vomit rising from under her chin. Someone shouted, 'Posh girl. You come here for a fix?' Someone else added, 'A fix of dirty Camden Town?'

As she passed a group of young girls, one of them punched her on the arm as another tried to grab her ruyi. She wrenched her ruyi away and strode off, pretending not to be afraid. This was exactly why she'd worked so hard to escape her roots and exactly why she ached for the higher levels.

She reached the station just as a train was pulling in. She ran up the steps and leapt on. The doors closed behind her. A message from Terence arrived. 'Hey. Gone to bed – football in the morning. Missing you. Terry.' She hated it when he called himself Terry.

The train rumbled through the dark streets of London, heading east first and then south across the river and on towards New Cross. As she got nearer to home she gradually relaxed, breathing deeply and deliberately imagining the events of the evening fluttering away like tiny butterflies breaking free from their chrysalis.

The train pulled into New Cross station and her ruyi buzzed. It was the blackmailer.

'Enjoyable evening? Don't go forgetting me. You want me to stay silent don't you?'

Martin stumbled along the lane. He shouted to no one in particular, 'Fucking idiots. Why can't they leave us alone.'

The pressure from Jenny to make good use of the double-points weekend would be intense. All he really wanted to do was have a lie in, potter about in his shed, have a few pints in the evening, maybe do a bit of cooking and the weekend housework. In amongst all of that, how was he supposed to take advantage of the double points?

He crossed the footbridge carefully, trying his best not to creak. The downstairs light was on. Jenny was still awake. Or Max. He caught a glimpse of someone running across the fields. The moonlight reflected off their feet as they climbed the nearby stile and then they were gone, running fast and furious into the night. Probably Max, he thought.

'I can't perform bloody miracles,' he said as he opened the front door.

'What the hell are you on about now?' called Jenny from the kitchen. 'And quieten down. Becka's asleep.'

He bumped into the umbrella stand, almost knocking it over.

He caught it just in time. 'Oops,' he muttered. Jenny was sitting at the table reading a book on her charta. 'Sorry, my love,' he said. 'Bit tipsy.'

'Martin, my love. It's nothing new,' she said, not even looking up from the book.

He sat down opposite her. 'I can't do all this double points stuff that you want.'

'What are you on about?'

'I know you want me to make the most of it. But I don't want to. Don't see why I should. I work hard, you know. I deserve a little time off at the weekend.'

'I want nothing, Martin.'

'Yeah, right. I'm going upstairs. See you in bed soon?'

'In a while.'

In his study he sat and looked at the blank StrataScreen. 'No choice,' he said to himself, 'they all want a piece of something I don't have.' He found the card from the man in the posh house. 'Ruyi: private message to Mr Lenkan. I'll do it. I'll subjugate, but no sex.'

SATURDAY

ELEVEN

Amber hammered on the front door. Sam's mum opened it. 'What on earth? It's eight o'clock in the morning. Who are you?'

'Amber. I work with Sam.'

'Ah. You're Amber. I'm Sam's mum. What on earth are you doing here at this time of day?'

'Sam invited me. Can I see her?'

'She's still asleep and I don't really want to disturb her. Can I offer you a coffee and some breakfast until she wakes up?'

'I need to see her. It's extremely important.'

'I'm sure it'll wait a few minutes won't it, dear?' Sam's mum guided Amber to the kitchen and pulled out a chair. 'Now, what can I get you? Coffee?'

'Yes please, but I do need to see her.'

'Yes, dear. I got that. A few minutes won't hurt though will it?' Sam's mum poured the coffee from an aluminium pot on the stove. 'Soya or almond milk?' she asked as she handed the mug to Amber.

'Black.' Amber sat fiddling with her mug of coffee.

'You seem a bit stressed,' said Sam's mum. 'Anything I can do?'

'No. Not enough sleep probably. And I really need to see Sam.'

'I was just about to cook her breakfast and take it up to her in bed. It'll only take a few minutes. Peanut Butter Swirl Pancakes. Would you like some?'

'No thanks. But can I watch you? I'm learning how to cook.'

'Of course. Amazing how little you young things know about the basics of life.' She lined up the ingredients on the work surface, explaining as she went. 'It's vegan. Whole wheat flour, organic cane sugar, aluminium-free baking powder, little bit of salt, almond milk and banana as an egg replacement.'

Amber pulled up a stool so she could see what was happening.

'Now. We mix the flour, sugar, baking powder and salt together.' She tipped the ingredients into a bowl.

'How do you know how much to use?'

'Experience. Next we whisk in the milk and now the banana.'

'How long does this all take?' She looked towards the stairs to Sam's bedroom.

'Not long,' said Sam's mum as she took a clear plastic bag out of the fridge. 'This is peanut butter swirl batter.' She poured the milk batter on to a hot skillet and piped the peanut butter batter on top. 'You have to wait until the bubbles have formed and popped. Another coffee?'

'No thanks.'

Sam's mum took a tray from beside the oven and put a mug full of steaming coffee, a small jug of soya cream and a warm plate from the oven on it. She flipped the pancakes and let them cook for a little while longer. 'There. All done.' She slid the pancakes on to the plate. 'Shall we surprise her?'

Amber nodded and followed her up the stairs.

Sam's mum knocked on a door with a small wooden plaque announcing *Samantha's Room* in a swirly fairy font. There was no answer. 'Samantha,' she called. 'Time to get up.' Still no answer. She knocked again, a little louder. 'Samantha, darling. Breakfast.' There was still no answer. 'Hold this.'

Amber took the tray. Her palms were sweaty; she'd come here to confront Sam about the blackmail. She'd been up all night churning it over: was it Terence? Was it Sam? Was it Opo? Was it a client? Was it an old flame? Was it a random nutter? Was it someone from back home with a grudge or simply someone trying to make some quick Fluence? All of these possibilities had been spinning around inside her head and by the time it was morning she'd decided that Sam seemed the most likely. There was something a bit intense about the way Sam behaved around her and the message inviting her down for the weekend had tipped the balance, making Terence's suggestion that Sam was trying to stop Amber moving more plausible. She'd hired a Zip Car and driven down to confront her, face to face.

'C'mon, Sam,' shouted her mum. 'You can't stay in bed all day.' She rapped on the door. 'I've got a surprise for you.'

There was silence from the bedroom. She turned the handle. It twisted but the door wouldn't open. 'Sam. Have you locked yourself in? How old are you?' She put her ear to the door. 'I can't hear anything. Not even her snoring, which is usually quite loud.'

Amber put the tray on the ground and listened. 'Nothing,' she said. 'Maybe she's already gone out?'

'No. I'd have heard her. I was up at around five-thirty.'

'Can you feel a cold draught?' asked Amber.

Sam's mum put her hand in front of the gap at the bottom of the door. 'I think you're right.' She stooped down to look through the keyhole. 'There's no key in the lock and it looks as if the window's open. That's weird. Hold on.' She went into another room and Amber could hear drawers being opened and closed. 'Got it!' she called.

Amber picked up the tray.

Sam's mum came back with a key and unlocked the door. 'Samantha, darling. It's Mum and I've got a surprise visitor,' she called out before opening the door fully. There was a deathly hush from the bedroom. Sam's mum gasped. 'She's not here. Check in there.'

Amber put the tray down on the bed and popped her head inside the bathroom. 'No, not there.' The window banged against its frame. Sam's mum hurried over and closed it.

'Where is she? Tell me,' said Amber.

'What?'

'This is a sham. You know she was blackmailing me. Where is she?'

'What are you talking about? Stop being so silly.' Sam's mum opened the window again and looked down and then left and right. 'She's gone. But why would she leave through the window?' She checked the wardrobe. 'Her work stuff's still here.'

'Look. She's ripped the StrataScreen off the wall,' said Amber. 'Tell me now or I call the CorpPolice.'

'You're not going to do that, are you? You're making accusations of blackmail, you're extremely anxious and she's your boss.'

'Tell me where she is!' screamed Amber.

'Calm down. I'm calling the police. And I suggest you leave now.'

'I'll find her,' said Amber through gritted teeth.

'Piss off, young lady before I smack you in the face.'

Amber hurried out of the room, ran down the stairs and slammed the front door behind her.

Martin woke up, opened his eyes and took a long, slow look at Jenny. She was sleeping with her arm across her face, gently snoring.

He loved her. Even though at times the kids, the house and the job got on top of him and caused fights, he loved her. And them. He sighed. His head hurt a little, but not as much as it should after the previous night's drinking.

He was sad. He wished he could confide in her more. When they were first married they'd told each other everything, but then, as time passed, there were less opportunities to have long rambling conversations and gradually, almost unnoticed, they'd stopped asking each other what they were feeling, what their dreams were and what they were afraid of. Lying next to her he wished with all his heart he could tell her how afraid he was about the coming Pay Day, how much he wanted to opt out of this country life that was now a twisted version of what he'd hoped for.

She turned over. He studied her face. He was surprised that her thick brown hair was showing signs of grey – she normally kept it dyed, not allowing there to be any sign that she was ageing. She looked so peaceful with her arms tucked up under her pillow. Her hair was tied up in a bun and a single strand had escaped and was lying across her neck. He wanted to kiss it. The strap of the white vest – her habitual pyjamas – broke the long beautiful line of her neck and shoulders. He could see the fine hairs on her top lip. He wished that this moment could go on forever.

She opened her eyes. 'Morning. How's the head?' she said, smiling a crooked half-awake smile.

'Coming along,' he replied, touching her shoulder. 'You?'

'Fine. But then I wasn't quite as jolly as you.'

'Sorry.'

'Hey, forget it. What time is it?'

'Nine o'clock.'

'Wow. The kids are quiet. Are they okay?'

'No idea,' he said. 'Shall we forget them for now?'

'Mmm…nice idea. Not going to work though is it?'

'Guess not.' He got out of bed and pulled the curtains back. 'Nice day. Bit misty.'

He caught a glimpse of her bare bum as she pulled back the sheets and got out of bed. He called after her. 'See you downstairs soon.' He grabbed his ruyi and twisted. 'Ruyi: SMFeed. Naked bottom in the bed and mist on the fields. What's not to like?' Twenty people saw his post and one liked it, but its SMInfluence was zero. The news about the double-points double-penalty weekend was the only thing trending. A story about a couple who'd managed to amass a small fortune overnight by gambling all of their points was going through the roof. There were a few minor stories of people who'd spent most of their points in the sales and one particular quote was trending high: 'Life's short. You gotta make the most of it.'

'Ruyi: SMFeed. What's the point of a world of points?' There was no response so he swapped his ruyi for the charta on his bedside table. 'Fool on the Hill,' he said and the charta logged him into the hackers' news page. This was more interesting. There were rumours of hackers breaking into the Strata Database; the hackers' network publicly denied it, attributing it to Pay Day paranoia, but privately acknowledged there were traces of an attempted hack. Nothing changes, he thought. 'Charta: encrypt. Find me Sir Arthur,' he whispered.

Outside, the lower trunks of the trees at the bottom of the garden were showing as the mist started to clear. He smiled as he remembered the evening before, especially the mild panic when the double-penalty weekend had been announced. They all knew that there'd be surprises from the corporations before the week was finished, that's what happened every year, but they didn't know what or when. The charta buzzed. Sir Arthur was waiting.

'Any luck?' asked Martin.

'Not yet,' replied Sir Arthur.

'Nothing at all?'

'Nope. Not a whisper.'

'Okay. Can you carry on?'

'Sure. If that's what you want. I owe you.'

'Thanks. Yes, please. See what you can get.'

'Roger. Wilco. Out,' said Sir Arthur and disconnected.

Martin gazed at the misty garden. The vanishing mist revealed the fuzzy outlines of sheep brought in to the fields for lambing. Max appeared out of the mist, running towards the house. What the hell's he been up to now, thought Martin. He pulled on a musty old t-shirt and brown corduroy trousers. The mustiness reminded him of the contrast between the rustic weekend and the weekday sterility of the Bureaucracy.

'I see Max has deigned to join us,' he said as he walked into the kitchen.

'Martin,' said Jenny and sighed.

'I've just seen him running back across the fields. What is that boy up to?'

'Being a boy, probably,' said Jenny with an edge to her voice.

'Really?' he said, layering on as much sarcasm as he could manage.

'Martin, will you grow up!'

'Yep. 'Bout time you grew up,' said Max as he came through the door with a big smirk on his face.

'Listen to me, boy,' said Martin, 'you have no idea what I do for this family.'

'And you think you know everything there is to know about me, don't you?'

'If only.'

'You've no idea what I do for this family either,' said Max. He slammed the kitchen door behind him.

'Just bloody fantastic. Happy weekend to you too, Martin,' said Jenny. 'What a proud dad you must be.'

TWELVE

Amber sat on her sofa and scanned her algorithm, trying to understand the impact of the double-points weekend and to see what she could do to negate the underage encounter. As far as she could tell it had simply magnified people's behaviour. The lower levels were manically attaching themselves to each other. The already successful were still increasing their ratings, but at twice the speed, and the unsuccessful were dropping twice as fast.

A message appeared on her charta. She threw it on to the sofa as if it had burnt her or could read her thoughts.

She read the message out loud to an empty room: 'Time is running out, my not-so-young pretty strataclimber. Don't ignore me!'

She was shaking with the shock. Why the hell wasn't Terence here when she needed him? Why her? Who on earth was it?

She picked it up with her fingertips, closed the algorithm and the database and switched it off. She tapped the StrataScreen with her ruyi as she walked past.

Upstairs, she pulled her clothes back and forth, ransacking her wardrobe. There was nothing she wanted to wear. She threw herself face down on the bed. How could Terence be so selfish and play football on a day like this? she thought. The bastard wasn't living up to their agreement to look after one another, an agreement they'd made when they'd decided to get married against their friends' advice. Her ruyi buzzed with a message from Opo. 'Girl. Good night last night. Super good! I'm about to post an SMFeed. Be the first to track it. No more than fourteen minutes though. I promise you won't be disappointed.'

She wiped her eyes. 'Ruyi: track next SMFeed from Opo for fourteen minutes.' She tapped her StrataScreen and Opo's SMFeed refreshed. 'The next star of the *Red Time Traveller* is a woman. An actress you all know as a feisty trendsetter with a massive brain. I know, she told me last night.' Opo's rating rocketed and she was getting five percent of his success. Her tracking automatically stopped and disconnected her. One minute later a public message from NetCorp appeared. 'Violation of copyright: penalties will be applied equally to all.' Everyone that was still connected was fined a hundred points; only Opo and Amber made a net increase. 'Ruyi: private message to Opo. You are my number one boy!'

She straightened the bedclothes and scooped up her pyjamas. Lying on top of the dirty clothes inside the laundry basket were the knickers she'd left for Terence the day before. He must have tidied them away. She dropped her pyjamas on top and went to shower. As she washed away the previous evening, night and morning, she thought about the past twelve hours. She was being blackmailed and the threats were getting worse. She'd been unfaithful and lost a lot of points along the way. She'd accused her boss of being a blackmailer and her boss had mysteriously disappeared. If she didn't get her act together, she'd drop rather than rise a level.

She rifled through the piles of clothes spilling out from the wardrobe and chose a shortish black skirt that hugged her nicely, snug but not stupid tight, and a red gingham top that stood high on her neck with a single strand of black ribbon tied in a bow, puff shoulders and a lace bib. 'Ruyi: private message to cleaner. Can you come in and tidy the bedroom.'

She held the top of the left cowboy boot and banged her foot on the floor to push it into the boot. She did the same for the right foot, grabbed a padded denim jacket and closed the bedroom door behind her. Stopping briefly on the middle level, she sniffed the air to create a memory of the flowers that the cleaner would throw away.

Out on the doorstep, she glanced from side to side and curled her shoulders in, making her appear slightly stooped. She half expected someone to leap out from behind a hedge and confront her about stealing data or for an unmarked van to appear and kidnap her.

'House: triple lock.'

At the bottom of the steps she stopped and searched frantically for the Bureaucracy charta. I should record my movements just in case, she thought. She thumbed the charta. 'Tracer on. Feed to Amber Walgace's staff record.' She walked along the street, looking over her shoulder less and less as she settled into a rhythm. 'Ruyi: private message for Opo. If anything happens to me check my staff record.'

She chastised herself for being weak; the only way she was going to get through these next few days was to behave as if she truly belonged on the yellow Strata. There was every possibility that cameras were recording the behaviour of anyone likely to get promoted and the slightest hint that she wasn't of the right calibre would be spotted straight away. She pulled her shoulders back, popped her wireless headphones into her ears and strode along as if she owned the world.

The *Best of Female Country and Western Music* lifted her spirits. She pumped the pavement to the sounds of Dolly Parton, Reba McEntire and Shania Twain. She watched her ruyi as she walked. The double points announcement was still trending high, but apart from that the only other theme was the huge weekend parties competing for top position and encouraging people to join virtually if they'd not managed to get a ticket. Bars were attaching themselves to their chosen party, promising an equally good night with a live stream from the actual event.

'Ruyi: SMFeed. Party, party, party. Off for the pedicure and manicure of the year. Look out London.' Her rating moved up five points. She twisted the ruyi to camera and took a photo of herself. 'Ruyi: upload photo. SMFeed. Off to the Tagging Cellar tonight. What should I wear?' Her rating moved up another twenty points, but there were quite a few lurid comments about being naked and one or two about wearing fetish gear. She smiled. 'Ruyi: public reply. Tag me and find out what might be possible.' An avalanche of comments followed and her rating shot up by forty points.

She strolled, mouthing along to Dolly Parton singing *Jolene*, thinking about her seduction of the young masked man and

91

wondering what the coming night might bring. She stroked through the comments. One of them stopped her dead. She stared at it. 'Hello, my not-so-young pretty strata climber' had been posted by Androgynous. She threw the ruyi in her bag and scurried to the beauty salon.

The clean, fresh smell of the salon hit Amber like an invisible shower. 'Cobra. How are you?' she said.

'Amber, how lovely to see you,' said a woman dressed in a stiff full-length dress patterned with large mustard-yellow and pure white four-inch squares. Her long brown hair spiralled down to her chest, perfectly framing her junkie-style make-up. 'We're good, splendid. And busy today.'

Amber put her bag down and noticed that Cobra was wearing one yellow and one white shoe to match the dress. 'Busiest day of the year, I guess?'

'Close run thing between today and next Saturday when everyone's celebrating. The usual?'

Amber nodded. She followed Cobra across the floor that sparkled as if it were made of glass and past the chairs in front of full-length mirrors and highly polished sinks. At the end of the room was a mesh curtain of fine transparent slivers of plastic. Cobra held the curtain to one side and waved Amber through into a dark room with two rows of eight sheepskin-covered armchairs. At the foot of each chair was a tank of blue neon-lit water and inside each tank was a shoal of genetically engineered fish. Each armrest had an equivalent smaller tank.

'This is Asp. Ask her for whatever you want. Enjoy!'

'Hi,' said a young girl wearing a black and white striped dress with hoops from the waist up and stripes from the waist down. Her hair was a messy tousle and looked fabulous. Amber began to relax, soaking up the opulence of the salon and the gorgeous people that inhabited it. Asp pressed the lever on the only empty chair with her silver slipper-boot and the armchair reclined. 'Would you like me to explain about the fish?'

'No thanks. I've been here lots of times,' said Amber.

'I know. We have to ask though, for legal reasons.'

Amber nodded and smiled. She took her charta out of her bag and lay back on the chair. Asp pulled off her cowboy boots, pressed a button next to her head and an angled block of perspex lowered from the ceiling. Amber put her charta on it. Asp took a combined headphone and microphone from the side of the chair, carefully placed it on Amber's head and gave her the thumbs up. Amber returned the gesture and settled back to enjoy the pescecure.

A dedicated fish for each finger and each toe licked the polish from her nails and then nibbled to get rid of the dry skin. It tickled slightly, but she loved it. As they started to chew away the rough edges and push back the cuticles, she commanded her charta to open up the database. She stepped through the data, line by line, studying the algorithm. There was something new emerging that she couldn't fathom out. She ran a comparison of the current data against past data. Instinctively, she knew there was something, but it eluded her, staying on the periphery of her brain, close but out of reach. She homed in on the six records that showed the greatest changes and it became obvious. The higher you climbed, the lower your loyalty to any individual or group became. She looked at the data as a whole, to test the theory. It seemed to hold true. She was excited; this was a valuable insight into how to behave. She focussed again on the six records, hoping for more revelations.

'What the fuck?'

Amber looked up. Asp was standing there staring at the charta, her fashionably bloodshot eyes wide open.

'Hi. Data for work,' said Amber.

'I saw you looking at that last time you were here. And I told him.'

'Told who?'

'My brother. You're looking at him.'

'Your brother?'

'Yes, look. Mark. There,' she said, pointing at the charta.

'It's Bureaucracy data. He must have been in touch with us recently.'

'Nah. Ages ago he lost an arm in an accident and you assessed him, but then he took out a loan for a prosthetic arm and he's been fine ever since.'

'Oh, that would explain it. I'm just archiving some old records.'

'But why were you looking at it that other time as well?' Asp stepped back and put her hands on her hips. 'He was mightily pissed off when I told him last time,' she said.

'What are you accusing me of?' said Amber with a raised voice.

'Not sure. But something isn't right, is it?'

'Cobra!' shouted Amber. 'Cobra!' she shouted again.

The mesh curtain swept aside and Cobra hurried over. 'What can I do for you?'

'This girl is accusing me of something which she won't name. And she's been sneaking a look at confidential Bureaucracy records.'

'Asp, is that true?' asked Cobra.

'No, not really,' said Asp, looking awkward and rubbing one of her silver-covered feet over the other.

'Not really?'

'She's got data on my brother.'

Amber took her hands out of the tanks and signalled for them to stop talking. 'I don't want to cause a fuss. I think it's best if I leave and let you sort this out,' she said to Cobra.

'If you're sure? There'll be no charge.'

'I'm sure,' said Amber, taking her feet out of the tanks.

'Asp. Please finish Amber's treatment as quickly as you can.'

Asp took a towel from the side and knelt down. She looked at Amber through her tousled hair with the ferocious look of a trapped animal. Silently, she dried Amber's feet and hands and helped her on with her boots.

Amber stepped out of the salon. All of her internal organs felt as if they were floating around inside her and she wanted to be sick.

Her ruyi buzzed. 'That was a bit tricky, wasn't it? I know what you're up to. Don't ignore me!'

She puked.

THIRTEEN

Martin and Jenny got out of the car. 'We won't be long,' said Jenny to a surly Becka.

'Sure,' she replied. Her attention was on the charta as she busily flicked her finger tips across the screen. 'Dad, can I play StrataLife?'

'Junior version only,' replied Martin, 'and don't forget it's the Bureaucracy charta so no funny business.'

'Okay. Thanks.'

'You indulge her,' said Jenny.

'And you indulge Max.' He pressed the trolley release catch on the side of the car and waited for the small wheels to touch the ground. When the green light came on, he pressed the button again. The trolley section detached from the back of the car and he pulled it out. 'Come on then, Jen. Let's get the shopping.'

They walked alongside each other in silence as they did every Saturday morning. Neither of them wanted to be there and neither of them was willing to take the risk and speak in case the fragile situation cracked. At the entrance to the GreenNet supermarket, Jenny paused and looked across at an open market area for yellows run by the BeWell corporation. She sighed. Martin echoed her sigh, but instead of being wishful like Jenny's, his conveyed impatience.

'C'mon,' he said.

Jenny pressed her thumb to her charta to transfer their shopping list to the store and then popped it into the slot in the front of the trolley. They wandered around in the same daze as all the other weekend shoppers. Every time they passed an item on the list the charta buzzed and the item lit up. They had done this so many times they knew exactly how fast they could go with two of them taking items off the shelf. Every now and again the charta buzzed with a slightly different sound to bring their attention to an item they might like or that was on offer. As usual, Martin picked the extra items, Jenny huffed and he let her put most of them back.

The checkout girl placed their charta on the flat bed of the till, Martin swiped his thumb across it and the Fluence was deducted from their account.

'NetCorp wish you a happy Pay Day,' said the checkout girl as she handed back the charta.

At the car, Martin pushed the trolley into position and clicked the safety catch.

They smiled at each other, relieved to have finished, and got in the car.

'Becka, will you help me unload when we get home?' asked Jenny.

Becka nodded.

'Answer your mother properly,' said Martin.

Jenny pressed herself back in the seat to allow the safety belts to tighten. 'Martin, she's fine.'

'Thanks a bunch,' he said under his breath. He drove them home in silence – Becka was engrossed in StrataLife and Jenny was busy on her ruyi.

He parked the car in front of the house, detached the trolley and wheeled it to the front door. 'I'll do the housework while you two unpack.'

He liked this part of his week. He liked the sense of order that he created and he liked being a part of the family. It made him feel useful and that he belonged somewhere. He put the robot vacuum cleaner on the floor and switched on the flying robot duster. No matter how often he did this, he chuckled at the thought of Mary Poppins and her magical cleaning. The vacuum cleaner and the duster moved efficiently around the room, the vacuum changing course to avoid his feet and the duster to avoid his head. He straightened the cushions and was about to take out the bag of rubbish he'd filled from the bins when the vacuum beeped – it needed to be lifted on to the curtains. He paused it so he could lift it up. In the silence he overheard a conversation in the kitchen.

'He's such a loser. Why do you put up with it?'

'Max, stop that,' said Jenny.

'I know you agree.'

'You know nothing, young man.'

'Oh come on. I see the way you flinch when he tells a stupid joke. Or when he's pissed. You're embarrassed by him.'

'No, I'm not.'

'Well, I am.'

'Max, you're horrible,' said Becka. Martin smiled at the thought of his daughter sticking up for him.

'Shadap, squitch,' said Max, but he softened his tone. 'I just want you to be happy, Mum.'

'I know. It's complicated though isn't it? This life we have, it's not cheap you know.'

Martin crept across the room to look through the gap. Max was sitting on the floor next to the fridge with yet another bottle of performance-enhancing drink. No wonder he was so wired all the time. Becka was sitting at the table peeling potatoes and Jenny was making a pot of tea. This should have been a picture of perfect bliss, but overhearing the conversation had stripped away the veneer, revealing the difficulties they faced as a family. If only I could get a promotion, he thought, or maybe just more points.

He pushed the door open with the rubbish bag. 'Hi, how's it going in here?' he asked with a fake country accent. 'Life's a game. Ain't that right, Becka?'

'Sure is. A game of snakes and ladders,' said Becka, replying with her childhood bedtime routine. 'Watch out, Dad, you're about to step on a snake.' She laughed.

Martin jumped and laughed too. 'Thank you, number one daughter. Now watch me climb the ladder.'

Max stood up and kicked his heel against the fridge. 'Fucking unbelievable.'

'Max!' said Jenny and Martin at the same time.

Becka chuckled.

Martin tilted his head towards Jenny, poured a cup of tea and left the room.

Upstairs in his study, he sat on the sofa and stared at the StrataScreen. He was not doing well in the ratings. He was only a few points away from blue. The SMFeed was trending parties, double-point promotions and a bit of sport. He was scared to interact and he was scared not to. It seemed that every time he tried to join in he lost points and he still had attachment requests pending which were also dragging him down.

Wafts of baking bread and frying onions drifted up the stairs, making the anxiety he felt about losing his home and family more acute. 'StrataScreen: prod all twenty pending requests.' He crossed his fingers and waited, but nothing happened. 'StrataScreen: public post. The wife's hot and sizzling and kneading again. Happy days.' He gained a few points and one of the pending attachments confirmed. He sat a bit straighter. 'Might need to grab her buns later.' Two more pending requests attached. 'And spread them with soft butter.' Immediately, the three new attachments cut their link and his rating dropped just below where it had been a few minutes before. He punched the arm of the chair. 'Shit!' he shouted.

'Martin?' called Jenny.

'Nothing. Stubbed my toe,' he called back.

He opened the window. Out in the garden, Max was playing tennis with Becka and she was bossing him around. 'Not like that. Hit it straight. There's no point playing if I can't hit it back, is there?' Max obeyed and hit the ball straight to her.

All of this wonderful life was in jeopardy.

'Charta: encrypt. Find me Sir Arthur.' He carried on watching Max and Becka until the charta beeped.

'Sir Arthur,' it said in the voice of Kirsty Watson, the movie star. 'You are speaking to Fool on the Hill.'

'Anything?' asked Martin.

'This isn't something you just order from a corporation, you know?'

'I know. But you've had quite a while. I'm desperate. I'm on the edge of a meltdown.'

'You will pay the outstanding fee, no matter what?'

'Of course. No problem. But I do have a bit of a cash flow issue. Any idea how to make some Fluence quickly?'

'You're making me nervous.'

'Hey, have I ever let you down?'

'You expect me to answer that?'

'You know what I mean. I'm good for it. Not forgetting you have my bike as security.'

'True. Okay, let's think about making some quick Fluence. Legally, you could use a Pay Day loan but the interest rates are extreme, or you could make short term investments in other people. Both are high risk though; the repayment rates are crippling and investing in others is a bit hit and miss. There's a bit of a legal grey zone around gambling and subjugation. And then there's different forms of prostitution, all of which are illegal. Any of those take your fancy?'

'Probably. I'll need to think about it. Gambling maybe, or a loan.'

'I can put you in touch with some people tomorrow at the outlier festival. I'll send you the location, but keep it secret.'

'Martin!'

'Thanks. Must go, the wife's calling.' He bounded down the stairs two at a time.

'What are you feeling guilty about?' she asked as he walked into the kitchen.

'Nothing.'

'Yeah, right. Running down the stairs like that. I'm not daft you know. Anyway, when are you going to finish the cleaning?'

'I thought I had. Sorry, I got distracted watching Max and Becka playing in the garden. He can be sweet if he wants, can't he?'

'Sometimes,' she said. 'Sometimes you can too.' She kissed him on the forehead and carried on preparing the dinner.

The cleaning robots were both sitting in the middle of the room, idling. He'd been sure he'd finished off all the cleaning. After all, it was something he really enjoyed and earned him a guilt-free rest in the afternoon with his feet up in front of the reality soap opera. The current favourite of the nation was about a housing estate of violets trying to set up their own hospital. They hadn't a clue what they were doing and were so naive it was hilarious and addictive. He picked up the robots, moved them to The Snug and set them off on their tasks while he sat back to watch the soap.

The background noise of the robots was comforting, but he couldn't settle. The realisation that he was so stressed he'd forgotten to finish his favourite household job and that his rating was still slowly dropping, made him jittery.

Jenny came in and sat next to him. 'What are we going to do?' she asked.

'About?'

'Us. The kids, the house, the whole thing.'

'I thought you liked it. Needed it.'

'I love it. I love them. I love you. But something's wrong.'

'I don't know what you mean. It's just the stress of Pay Day.'

'Martin. Don't shout at me or get angry.'

He switched off the screen. 'Okay…' he said.

'I borrowed your ruyi to look at your rating…'

'You did what?'

'Sorry. I had to know. I was worried.'

'And…'

'We're in trouble, aren't we?'

'Not at all. I've been investing loads of our points ready for Pay Day. You wait and see.'

'Martin, you can trust me.'

He took hold of her hand. 'Sure. I know.'

The back door burst open and in tumbled Max and Becka laughing. They shouted at the top of their voices, 'I won. I won. I won.'

'We have to involve the kids,' she said.

Martin dropped her hand. 'Involve them in what?'

Jenny stood up. 'Max!' she called.

Max came lolloping in with yet another enhancing drink in his hand. He looked at Jenny and then at Martin. 'What's he done now?'

'We need to talk to you and Becka,' said Jenny in a voice that Martin suspected she hoped sounded calm but actually sounded as if she was about to fall apart.

Martin stood up. 'I'm sorting it,' he said quietly to her and walked away.

'Martin. Please!' she shouted after him.

'Mum, when will you learn? Don't rely on him,' said Max, loud enough for Martin to hear as he left the house.

FOURTEEN

Amber steadied herself on a parked car outside the salon. The piercing shrill of its alarm snapped her out of the fear about the data and into a fear of being arrested. She ran down a side road, stumbling as she tried to put as much distance between her and the car as possible. At the entrance to the Nunhead Cemetery she stopped, checked that she wasn't being followed and then stepped inside. Before they were married, Terence had often taken her there for afternoon walks and a bit of canoodling. In front of her was the familiar chapel, its arched entrance forming an A and its two elongated turrets forming an H. Terence had joked that it stood for Amber Huddson and that one day he'd buy it for her.

She sat down on a shiny marble gravestone, leaned back against the stone obelisk, twisted her ruyi to camera and took a photo of the chapel. She spoke quietly, 'Ruyi: public message for Terence Huddson. Still waiting!' She sat staring at the screen, urging it to display a reply, but nothing came. She slumped her head and closed her eyes. She needed to gather her thoughts. Every minute or so she checked. Absolutely nothing. The initial comfort from the familiar place – their place – slowly evaporated. She slapped the gravestone, stood up and spoke. 'C'mon, girl. Get a grip. There's still plenty to play for.'

To get to the meet-up in a Shoreditch coffee shop that afternoon was a fifteen-minute walk followed by a fifteen-minute train journey. She set off, regaining her composure with each minute that passed. On the train she checked her ruyi. There was a private message from Xanthe. She opened it cautiously. 'Hi. Feeling bad about detaching. I thought you were great fun the other night. I've treated you to an hour of tracking me. You'll get twenty percent of my rating. Maybe we'll meet up again at the dance?' Amber relaxed a little, watched the rows of blue and green houses pass by and started to dream of being yellow again.

The Saturday afternoon coffee-shop buzz of animated conversation hung in the air, as if it was coating the room with its thick, warm softness. She shouted over the noise to the head barista. 'I've come for the GeekPlus meet-up.' He pointed to a heavy wooden door at the back of the room. 'Thanks,' she said and winked. He winked back.

On the door was a handwritten sign. 'GeekPlus meet-up – females only.' She pushed it open. The fifteen ambitious and technically minded women that she'd been meeting up with for the past year were sitting at two round tables. They'd agreed to keep their number to a pleasing sixteen and to only invite others if one of them couldn't come. She was the last to arrive and sat down at the empty space.

'Welcome,' said Madeleine. 'I think you already know that we're going to discuss data standards. I'm sure I don't need to remind you that everything that's said here is private and stays here. But, of course, feel free to take the ideas and make something of them. Okay?' Everyone nodded. 'Great, you should have received a briefing paper for the discussion, so let's start. Amber?'

Amber pressed her thumb to the charta. 'We're looking at five attributes of a data standard, aren't we? Who can use it? What is it we want it to show? How might collecting it affect society? What fields might force a certain world view and to what extent can it evolve?'

Madeleine nodded enthusiastically. 'Good summary, Amber. Are we all agreed that these are the main issues to discuss?' The others nodded. 'Let's take the first of those.'

'Before we start, can I ask why we're looking at this?' asked a woman with bright red hair who Amber didn't recognise.

Madeleine touched the woman's arm. 'Everyone, this is Victoria. I asked her to join us this afternoon to make up the numbers. Victoria, this is Olivia, Lily, Tamara, Imogen, Laura and Amber.'

'Hi. Call me Vicky,' she said, joggling her hand back and forth in a miniature wave. 'Sounds fascinating, but I'm not sure why you're bothering.'

Amber was irritated at being interrupted and especially irritated at having to justify herself to an outsider.

Madeleine pointed to each of them in turn. 'One day all of us will be in positions of power. We need to sort out the mechanics of being in charge so we're ready when the day comes. One thing's for sure, there'll be a lot of data at our disposal and we need to know how we're going to use it when the time comes. That's why we discuss things that appear to be out of our reach.'

'An old girls' network in the making?' asked Vicky.

'If you like,' said Madeleine.

Olivia and Imogen chuckled. 'Indeed,' said Laura.

'Carry on, Amber,' said Madeleine.

Amber put her charta on the table. 'The first question then, of any data, is who can use it.'

'Surely that depends on who owns it?' asked Lily.

Amber turned her charta face down. 'Not necessarily. The data can be owned by someone, but made publicly available. The question then becomes, "How easy is it for the woman in the street to use it?"'

'Surely the corporations own all the large datasets? And they're not going to make those available are they? It'd be commercial suicide,' said Vicky.

'Not necessarily,' replied Amber. 'That's part of what we're thinking about. Let's park the question of how the corporations might react until the end, okay?' They all nodded. She continued. 'There's an argument that says the data is so complex it can't be used unless someone technical interprets it first. There's a counterargument that says you could turn it into lots and lots of simple sets of data that are relevant to everyone. Making the wider connections and doing the deeper analysis could still be done by anyone with the ability to join the data together.'

Takara put her finger in the air. 'At least that way there's less chance of skewing what the data's telling us. It's more transparent.'

Imogen leant forward. 'Rubbish! Do you really think anyone is bothered about all this data? What on earth would they use it for? It seems to me that we should start with a different question – who wants to use it rather than who can.'

'I would,' said Amber, with some force.

Madeleine stared at her.

Amber was a bit thrown, but carried on. 'It links to the second question of what we want it to show us. Depending on your perspective, and even on your Strata, you'd want to know about different things.'

Madeleine raised her eyebrows. 'Maybe Lily's right and there is a question of who owns the data? Amber, what do you think?'

Amber faltered. 'It's complicated,' she said and at the same time was thinking, what does she know?

'Go on…'

'With any data there's always the big question of who it belongs to. Often that's a tussle between the subjects and the collectors of the data. I think we should answer that question by deciding who we want to use it.'

'And that links to the question of what the effect of collecting it has on society,' said Laura.

'Takara?' said Madeleine.

'Exactly. I've been thinking about what the possibilities might be if all of this data was collected for your local community instead of being centralised and analysed at a national and global level as it is at the moment.'

Lily interrupted. 'It's analysed by Strata Level, isn't it?'

'Sure, but maybe that makes people feel isolated. Their sense of local community is eroded, but if the data could be used to bring communities together that'd be very powerful. It'd change the way it's collected and what becomes important is where you live, not your Strata Level or some other corporation construct.'

The others shifted uncomfortably in their seats. 'Maybe we should think about what data it would be useful to have,' said Madeleine, diffusing the tension.

They talked around the subject until Madeleine brought it to a close. 'We're out of time. When we next meet we can return to the questions of how data promotes a certain world view and the extent to which the data could or should evolve.'

Vicky sat back in her chair. 'Wow, thanks, that was fascinating.'

Madeleine stood up. 'I must stress that no matter what we say here, the corporations own all data and we must remember that for our own safety. Agreed, Amber?'

'Errr...agreed,' stuttered Amber.

The rest of them stood up and performed the ritual banging of ruyi as a sign of trust and as a symbol of their linked futures. Amber left the room first, trying to leave as fast as she could without appearing rude or flustered. Outside she checked her ruyi. She'd increased by a few points and the trending SMFeed was still about the parties. 'Ruyi: public message to Terence Huddson. A couple of hours to spare, shall I join you?'

She sheltered from the wind in the entrance of a RetailCorp FluenceShop. A strange mix of people were queuing at the checkout, reinforcing that this was one of the few areas that was home to multiple Strata Levels. There were even whites living in what was known as the Shoreditch Rainbow, living happily side by side with the orange, yellow, green, blue, indigo and violets. Her ruyi buzzed. 'Sorry. Bit tricky at the moment. Boys only, I'm afraid xx.' She kicked the door with the back of her heel.

'Oi! What the fuck?' shouted the wrinkled old woman from behind the counter.

'Ruyi: reply. Thanks a bunch.'

She set off to the train station to go and confront him. A bus pulled up at a stop at the same moment as she was passing. I need some time to calm down, she thought and got on. As soon as the doors closed she regretted her decision. A smell of putrid puke wafted from the back of the bus, causing her to gag. There were a few passengers and they all stared at her. One of them muttered, 'Spoilt brat.' She climbed the stairs, bouncing against the side of the bus as it swung and swerved its way along the road. As soon as her head emerged she scanned the upper deck. There was only one passenger and he was an old man. She sat down in the front seat and sighed. The sting of ammonia bit into her nostrils. She looked down. There was a pool of fresh piss slopping around on the floor. The old man chuckled. She moved back a few seats, wishing she was behind him and could see him, but not wanting to walk past him to get there.

At each stop the bus announced its location and after a few stops the old man sauntered past her saying, 'Cutie,' under his breath.

'Piss off,' she replied.

'Again?' he said and cackled.

She ignored him and settled back into her seat, watching the houses and shops pass by. Every now and again she'd get a waft of urine, but she didn't want to go back downstairs and face the other passengers so she stayed where she was. She got off the bus at Highbury and strolled across the park, contemplating what to say to Terence.

The pub was typical of a London pub. It had rows of wooden trestle tables outside which were mainly occupied by families. The ground floor was painted a dark green with two brick storeys of flats above it. A loud roar burst out through the doors which were propped open by two men who were smoking. Every time they exhaled they turned their heads away from the door and blew into the street. They smiled and the smell of smoke from their breath hit her as she inched past them.

Terence was sitting with his friends in the far corner. She apologised to the afternoon drinkers as she pushed her way across the room. Jonno spotted her first. 'Hey, Terry. Guess what?'

'What?' asked Terence without turning around.

'You got company.'

'Eh?'

'Look behind you, you plonker. It's a surprise.'

'I bloody hope it is,' said Keefy. 'Not allowed on a Saturday afternoon.'

Terence glanced over his shoulder. He stared at her. 'I thought I told…'

'Sure. I know, but I was close by and I've got time for a couple of drinks. No harm, eh?'

'For fuck's sake,' said Keefy.

'Tricky,' said Jonno and laughed.

Terence put his pint down and strode across the room towards the door. She followed.

'What on earth?' he said, once they were outside.

'I needed you.'

'What for?'

'I'm really scared about this blackmail.'

'You're not still on about that are you? For goodness' sake, Amber, get a grip.'

'Up yours,' she said and stormed off.

FIFTEEN

'House: let me in. Now!' Amber slammed the door behind her. 'House: music. Loud. Heavy. Trash Glam.' She stomped on the first stair. 'Fuck.' She stomped on the second stair. 'You.' She stomped on the third stair. 'Husband.' Her anger didn't dissipate as she slammed a cowboy boot on every stair to the first floor lounge. The pungent smell of rotting flowers filled the empty room. 'You lazy bitch!' she screamed and kicked the vase. It shattered. A pool of stale water formed a dark stain on the carpet. Dying flowers lay across it as if they'd been scattered at a funeral. She banged the screen with her ruyi. 'Public message to cleaner. Get your arse over here and finish your work. Now!'

Her rating dropped by ten points. 'Shit!' she shouted. An advert popped up. 'Three thousand trackers for five Fluence.' She hit the side of the screen. 'Fuck. Off,' she shouted. Her ruyi buzzed with a private message from Terence. 'Sorry, babe, but you know how it is.'

Her back scraped on the wall as she slid to the floor. 'Ruyi: reply to Terence. In what way is that an apology?'

She cried and cried and cried.

The front door opened. 'Hello,' called the cleaner. 'Are you there, Mrs Huddson?'

Amber scrambled to her knees, pushed herself up and called back. 'Up here. You didn't clear the flowers.' She ran up to the bedroom and called down, 'Let yourself out when you've finished.'

She threw herself on the bed and pulled the pillow over her head. The music was muffled and soothing. She lay there unable to think of anything other than the stupid argument with Terence. When she'd first met him she'd loved the way he hung out with his mates, the way he was so loyal to them and the way he knew exactly where he fitted in. These were all the things she lacked and were the exact same things that she'd come to hate, despise and resent about him. She should be the most important thing in his life, no matter what else was going on. Her mum and her sister had always said Amber was the spoilt baby and she wondered if she would have been different if she'd been the eldest. She yanked the pillow off her head, wiped her eyes and sat up. Right. Tonight's the night, she thought. 'Ruyi: message to Opo. Babe, come and help me choose what to wear. You know you want to.'

He replied immediately. 'Hun. On my way. What a fabulous idea.'

'Ruyi: reply to Opo. I'll be in the bath, let yourself in when you arrive.'

The roll top copper bath sat in the centre of the bathroom. She stroked the inside of it, running her hands along the wonderfully smooth and cool tin coating. As it filled with piping hot water she poured in a large dollop of her specially formulated dermatological foam bath and some lavender infused salts. For a bath to be totally indulgent she needed to feel completely naked. She removed her make-up. She opened the drawer beneath the sink and took out her wedding present from Terence – a set of six tiny robot insects that removed unwanted hair. She set them free and watched in the wooden framed oval mirror standing in the corner as they crawled their way over her body. The sensation was extremely pleasant and the thing she liked most was being able to watch her body be cleaned without having to make any effort herself. She took out the other robot that he'd bought her – a masseur in the form of a rabbit – and let it follow the insects, massaging her body by rubbing its paws over her flesh. It was heavenly. The bath detected it was full and at her specified temperature. The taps switched themselves off. When the robots finished she carefully placed them back in the drawer and slipped into the hot foamy bath. The scent of lavender filled the room. She inhaled and exhaled deeply.

'House: music. Classical violin concertos. Screen: SMFeed and music video.' The StrataScreen was hanging from the far wall, at an angle so you could see it easily whilst lying back in the bath. It sprang to life. In the middle of the screen was a video of an orchestra playing Bach's 'Double Concerto in D'. The image was partially transparent so you could still see the StrataInfo behind it. The conductor lifted his arms and jerked the violins into their punchy opening phrases. The mellow sounds of the solo over the top of the stretched notes of the other violins weaved its way through her head, down inside her limbs and then out again through her muscles as if it were trying to touch the water to make a warm hammock of bubbles; of sound and smell. Her thoughts drifted along with the music and the trending SMFeed. She concentrated on the feeds about parties, about uplifting stories of pets being rescued and on the offers from the corporations for the new Pay Year. A haunting solo filled the room – the beginning of a Sibelius Violin Concerto. She writhed in the bath along with the music and her thoughts turned to the evening, to the Tagging Cellar.

'I'm leaving,' shouted the cleaner. 'Your friend is here.'

Amber grinned. Her freshly pampered body made her feel great and the haunting violin sent sensual shivers down her spine.

'Hey,' said Opo as he strolled into the bathroom. As always he was dressed in his own dandy style – tight brown fake-leather trousers splattered with black spots and the occasional snake skin print, a black studded belt and a black shirt covered in a fern motif that looked as if it was made from gold-leaf. His wool jacket was a brown and black check with neon-blue cuff buttons. Finishing it all off was a massive chocolate brown silk flower emerging from his top pocket and a sky-blue hat with a white motif of tiny birds sitting on thin branches. He looked fabulous.

'Hey,' she replied. 'You look brilliant. Love the hat – genius.'

He grinned, showing his perfectly shaped and stunning white teeth.

'I need you to do my make-up though. A sort of mean and moody look.'

'You're looking good too,' he said, eyeing her up and down. He laughed.

'Of course. You know it's yours if you want it,' she said, wiping the foam off her arms.

He sat down on the Victorian armchair next to the bath, rested his hands on the edge and leant in close to study her naked body.

'No hair,' he said, 'no smell.' He kissed the top of her breast. 'Too soft and squidgy.'

She sighed. 'I know. Don't want to try a girl? Not even once?'

'Nope.'

'You'll still do my make-up, won't you?'

'Of course. Who could refuse cheekbones and lips like that? Now what's with all this hassle over the past few days?'

'I'll tell you in a bit. First, I want you to help me choose an outfit for tonight.'

'Why not tell me while you're in the bath. You'll find it less stressful.'

'Okay.' She pulled herself up straight and sponged off the remaining foam, revealing the top half of her smooth, freshly groomed body.

He twisted one of the three long strands of hair that hung down the side of his face from his otherwise short cut and hitched himself into the chair so he could sit cross-legged. The violins were reaching their peak and the brass was pounding alongside them. It finished and the audience clapped and cheered.

He chuckled, mischievously. 'They appreciate your efforts,' he said, pointing at her.

'Naturally, I'm the perfect specimen,' she said, pushing her arms close to her side to accentuate her cleavage.

He took off his hat and his jacket and placed them carefully on the low table next to the chair.

'I had the most awful row with Terence. I needed him and he didn't want to know. This blackmail is really nasty. I got thrown out of the salon 'cos some kid saw I had data on her brother and the woman who runs the meet-up went all weird on me. Oh yeah, I also went to see my boss 'cos I thought she was the blackmailer and she's vanished into thin air.'

'Woah, slow down, babe. Start at the beginning.'

'Okay. Last Thursday—'

He interrupted. 'This only started two days ago?'

'Yeah. Feels like a lot longer though.'

'Babe. I didn't realise you were so freaked out. Tell me.'

'I told you!' She slid down into the bath to warm up a little. 'Be a darling and run some more hot water for me.' He leant over and turned the tap. 'Thanks, sweetie,' she said.

'What's freaking you out the most?' he asked.

'I'm not sure. I guess it's the blackmail. Terence, Sam, Pay Day, the salon, the meet-up are all horrible, but somehow I can handle those. I'm sure at least one of them is connected to the blackmail, that's why they're all freaking me out.'

'Take me through it slowly.'

'I can't talk about this in here.' She stepped out of the bath. 'Can you rub me down?'

He winked. 'Thought you'd never ask.'

'Don't. Not funny. Especially as I have.' She winked back.

He took a large thick white towel off the warm rail and wrapped it tightly around her. 'Come on then.' He rubbed her arms, her back and her shoulders vigorously. He nudged her legs apart and dried the inside of her thighs, working his way down her legs to her ankles. 'Lift,' he said, pulling her left leg into the air. He rubbed her foot and in between her toes. He wrapped her in the towel again, took a smaller one off the back of the chair and dried her hair. He patted her bottom. 'Now, you can do the rest. I'll be in your bedroom.'

Why are all the good ones gay, she thought as she dried all the intimate places he'd carefully avoided. She put the towel back on the rail and went to join him.

'So perfectly stripped and scrubbed,' he said, as she walked through the door.

'Yup. Just the way I like it,' she replied.

He was standing at the window. She sat on the edge of the bed and faced him. 'On Thursday I got a message saying that they knew what I was up to and asking how much my silence was worth.'

'What did you do?'

'Nothing. Apart from lock the house and tell Terence to come straight home.'

'Did he?'

'Yeah. But he wasn't very sympathetic. He thinks it's just an end of Pay Year practical joke.'

'But you don't?'

'No. The only thing I can think of is that it's to do with me stealing all that data.'

'Possibly. Go on.'

'On Friday, just after I'd been to see a client and taken him off white, my ruyi was interrupted with a simple message that read "Tick Tock Tick Tock" and then disappeared. I got another message on my way home in the early hours of this morning telling me not to forget. That scared me a lot. I got it into my head that it was my boss so I went to confront her and guess what? She'd done a runner through her bedroom window!'

'Do you really think it was her? What's her name?'

'Sam. Terence thinks it's either her or Martin.'

'Is he the creepy guy you had a crush on last year?'

'Hardly a crush, but yeah, that's him. I told Terence about him and about Sam being too clingy and he's convinced it's one of them.'

'What do you think?'

'I don't know. I did wonder for a while if Terence was trying to stop me getting promoted. He doesn't want to climb the ladder at all.'

'Who else might it be?'

'At lunchtime the girl in the salon caught me looking at her brother's data and was angry. She mentioned she'd seen me looking at it before and that he was pissed off when she told him.'

'You really are in a bit of a muddle, aren't you?'

'And then this afternoon there was Madeleine, the woman at the meet-up. We were discussing data – who owned it and stuff – and she kept looking at me oddly.'

'Did you ever think it was me?' he asked.

'No.'

'Anyone else?'

'There's a whole load of people I upset last year when I was yellow. There's old flames. There's people from my childhood who resent my promotions. All I know is that I'm terrified.'

'What does the blackmailer want?'

'I haven't asked.'

'Why not?'

'I don't want to answer them. It'll look as if I've something to hide, but the trouble is that each minute that passes without me answering I lose points.'

'Why?'

'Somehow they've set it up so it looks as if they're waiting for me, as if it's a pending request.'

'You have to ask them exactly what they want.'

'But then I'm admitting guilt.'

'The alternative is worse. You've no idea what they might do next.'

'I don't know what to say.'

'Keep it simple and ask them what they want.'

'Okay. Screen: reply to pending message. What do you want from me?'

SIXTEEN

Martin sniffed as he walked down the dirt track that ran alongside the field at the back of his house. His hayfever was getting worse each year. It seemed to be increasing in its intensity as well as its duration. There were rumours in the pub, started by some of the less successful local farmers, that more allergies was the price that had to be paid to grow their bumper crops all year round. After all, what was a bit of snuffling compared to national food security? There were hackers on the anonymous network that suggested it was another tool in the corporations' armoury to unsettle the population and make them grateful for something they didn't understand; if food security was such a big issue that their health had to be sacrificed then they'd be relieved that someone was looking after them. Martin didn't pay much attention to the rumours; he was either too preoccupied with his own predicament or too drunk to care.

He kicked a shrub that was growing across the path and set free a cloud of pollen, sneezed and immediately regretted it. He jogged along, panting heavily. Each step fell heavier and heavier. 'Whatever happened to me,' he muttered. He slowed to a fast walk and then slowed again to an amble. He sat on the two-foot-high mound that surrounded the field, looked around to make sure that no one was watching and took out a cigarette and a hip flask of brandy. He'd told the Bureaucracy that he didn't smoke and his pension was dependent on his answer being true and if he was caught he'd be dropped to indigo with no chance to appeal.

The spring sun warmed his face and with each lungful of smoke his stress wound down a notch. He finished the cigarette and carefully buried the stub in the soil and took a long slug from the flask. The brandy burned his throat, making him choke a little, but then warmed him from the inside. The sun wrapped his skin in its heat and the brandy cuddled his internal organs. Bliss.

'Ruyi: find an encrypted channel for Sir Arthur. On speaker.'

The voice of Kirsty Watson spoke through the ruyi. 'Fool, give me a chance.'

'I need to see you.'

'Why?'

'I have some big decisions to make. I need to see what you've got so I know what to do.'

'Really? Are you sure you're not just being impatient?'

'I only have six thousand minutes until Pay Day.'

'Five thousand nine hundred and ninety-nine. Wait. Hold on. Ninety-eight.'

'Very funny. Look, it's important. Isn't that enough?'

'No, but for old times' sake I'll break protocol and show you what I have so far.'

'Thank you. Where?'

'Do you know Big Bruce's place?'

'The illegal brewery?'

'Yes. Meet you there in an hour.'

'Okay.'

He walked briskly back to the house.

Max and Becka were outside playing tennis again. Jenny was sitting watching, and sipping a gin and tonic. His heart strings twanged for the second time that day; he had to do whatever he could to protect his family. It was his job, it was his duty, it was his life.

He crawled along on his hands and knees behind the hedge that separated the lane and his garden, hiding from his family and their inevitable questions about where he was going. Once he was past the hedge he stood up and dusted himself down, crept into the garage and wheeled his bike quietly out on to the road. He pedalled to the end of the street and then switched on the engine.

The main road was empty. He let the bike take over, keeping him to a steady thirty miles per hour. The fields glowed in the setting sun and he sat back to enjoy the long orange horizon. He didn't hear the car approaching from behind until it was alongside. He wobbled in its aftermath. He checked the dashboard – he'd forgotten to switch on the proximity sensor. He flipped the switch, relaxing in the knowledge that no car could come any closer than the stipulated three feet without its engine cutting out. Ahead, on the brow of the hill, he could see the row of stumpy trees that lined the unnamed road that led to Bruce's. The bike's engine revved to get up the hill and as he reached the top he leant over and swung the bike into a sharp right turn. He leant to the left, then to the right and back to the left as the road twisted and turned before straightening out into a long stretch of tree-lined tarmac. The road was so narrow that he had to turn off the sensor. He rested both feet on the handlebars and held his arms in the air to balance. Memories of childhood flooded in – his own and Max's.

The ruyi in his back pocket buzzed to let him know it was out of signal range. He stopped and carefully put the bike down on its side, scrambled up the grassy verge and walked through to the other side of the trees. He lit his second cigarette of the day. Perfect, he thought as he gazed at the ramshackle arrangement of fields. Bruce refused to sign up to the corporations' requirements for regularised farms, choosing instead to trade with the outliers. He ran the risk of being stripped of his land if he didn't comply and Martin was impressed with such a brave decision. The corporations had already imposed trade sanctions on him, forbidding him to use Fluence – the outliers knew him as Black Market Bruce.

Martin smoked the last cigarette in his pack. I hope Bruce had a good crop, he thought. He buried the stubs, checked the road for cars as he emerged from the trees and climbed back down to his bike. It was starting to get cold. He put on the many-times-repaired gloves that Jenny had knitted him for their first Christmas at the house and headed off to the illegal brewery and black market heaven.

Bruce's farmhouse was at the end of the long stretch of road. He was standing outside his steel front door. 'Hey, Fool. How the devil are you?' he shouted.

Martin propped the bike against the side of the house. 'Good thanks. You?'

'Real good. I've got some pretty cool things on offer at the moment. You picked a good time to come by.'

'Is Sir Arthur here?'

'Downstairs already. He's picking through my cannabis crop, trying to find all the seeds I imagine. You'll need to get a move on if you want any.'

'Just cigarettes for me. Could you make me up twenty?'

'Of course. I've a fresh batch of tobacco, cured and aged especially for the connoisseur.' Bruce slammed the steel door behind them and pulled the levers to slide six heavy duty locks into place. 'Down there. You know the way,' he said, pointing to a trapdoor in the kitchen floor that was propped open with two logs from the pile next to the hearth.

Martin swung his leg on to the ladder and stepped down into the basement.

'He's round the other side,' shouted Bruce, 'around to the right, down the end and then left.'

Martin's right foot touched the sawdust floor, followed quickly by his left. He paused, waiting for his eyes to adjust to the low light. There were long rows of orderly shelves in a large underground store. The shutters on most of the shelves were closed, but occasionally he glimpsed a shelf of bottles or seeds or local cheese as he walked towards Sir Arthur. He turned the corner and there was the old man bent over a long bench covered in leaves. He was shuffling them, separating out a small pile of seeds.

'Hi,' said Martin.

Sir Arthur didn't look up or stop shuffling. 'Hello. Give me a minute, I'm almost finished. It'd be a shame to waste such an opportunity.'

'Sure,' said Martin. He sat down on an old wooden church pew that was pushed up against the wall. The air smelt slightly musty, despite the highly sophisticated ventilation system that was keeping each shelf of produce in the precise conditions it required.

Sir Arthur picked up the pile of seeds, popped them in a paper bag and weighed them on the electric scales in the centre of the bench. He pressed a button and the machine printed a label. He stuck the label on the bag. 'This way,' he said. Martin followed him back along the corridors and up the ladder. 'Bruce?' he called.

'Use the small bedroom,' replied Bruce from somewhere else in the house. Martin followed Sir Arthur up the stairs. Inside the room a StrataScreen covered an entire wall. 'Decommissioned StrataScreen,' called Bruce. 'No need to worry about anyone finding out what you're up to.'

Sir Arthur placed his charta on the rack below the StrataScreen and sat down on a pile of cushions in the bay window.

Martin sat next to him. 'So, what have you got for me?'

'Some footage of his activities. He's clever though. This wasn't easy.'

'That's my boy,' said Martin, polishing his finger nails on his shirt. 'Learnt from the best.'

'If you say so,' said Sir Arthur. 'This'll give you an idea of who he's hanging around with and might give you a clue about what he's up to.'

'Do you know what he's playing at?'

'Not yet, but I know where he goes, who he's with and what he does.'

'I guess that's a start.'

Footage of Max approaching a bar appeared on the screen. The door was opened from inside and he walked through. 'That's an illegal outlier gambling bar. Look at the time. Gambling early in the morning is unusual unless you want to trade on the black market at the same time,' said Sir Arthur. He moved the footage back an hour. Four young men dressed in chinos and blue shirts knocked on the door. 'They're notorious outliers that can get you anything. And will do anything for a price. Nasty bunch if you get on the wrong side of them, or if someone pays for you to be on the wrong side of them.'

'So he's gambling in a bar where some dodgy types hang out. Can't say I'm surprised,' said Martin.

'Wait.' Sir Arthur moved the footage forward. Max and one of the outliers left the bar and walked off together. 'That's Dan, the brains. It looks as if they're sharing more than the same bar.'

Martin nodded. 'What else?'

'There's this.' Sir Arthur twisted the data-stick in his hand and the footage changed. Max was walking along the street holding a blue mask. Sir Arthur moved the footage forward. A man wearing the same blue mask was strutting up and down a queue of people. He stopped at a woman wearing a shiny blue-black puffa jacket.

'That's Amber,' said Martin. 'Is that Max in the mask?'

'Yes.'

'What's he doing?'

'He's running a morris dancing club.'

'Cool.'

'I'm not sure what happened that night, but she comes out alone, a long time after everyone else, and she doesn't look good. Look.' Sir Arthur flicked the data-stick. Amber was leaving the club hugging her jacket tight. She looked frightened.

'Fuck,' said Martin. 'Anything else?'

'One more.'

Dan and his crew were standing beside a Land Rover smoking. 'Bruce's tobacco?' asked Martin.

'Of course. There's very few outliers that smoke anything else.'

'Illegal, but I don't see the connection to Max.'

'There might not be. Except they're standing across the road from your boss, Sam. Too much of a coincidence?'

'What do you think?'

'Maybe. She disappeared during Friday night. From her bedroom.'

'Fuck! You think these guys were involved? You think Max was involved?'

'If I had to put money on it, I'd say yes.'

'Little shit!'

SEVENTEEN

Amber laid a floor-length skirt with tight pleats on top of the bed. It shimmered. The black and red cloth seemed to flash with specks of gold, even though there weren't any. Next to it she placed a jacket made of the same cloth. It only had one fastener at the very bottom, just below the belly button, and its padded shoulders accentuated the plunging neckline. 'What about this one?' she said.

'Is that made from tagging material?' asked Opo.

'Yup,' she said, adding a three-inch black leather belt and a pink-tinted perspex necklace that looked as if it was sculpted from two semi-circular icicles. 'Cool, eh?'

'Let's see all the choices before we choose though, shall we?'

'Okay.'

'How many do you have?'

'Another three.' She leant into the wardrobe and took out a pair of white sandals with zigzag five-inch heels and calf-high straps. She put them on the bed. She held up a white stretch-jersey mini-skirt which was ruched at the front and a belt made from the waistband and front pockets of a pair of frayed white jeans.

'Nice,' said Opo. 'Which jacket?'

She slipped on a beaded white cotton jacket.

'Love the rhinestone cowboy look,' he said.

She took it off and threw it on top of the skirt and belt. She stood there totally naked and laughed. 'This is cheering me up. Thanks.'

He bowed. 'My pleasure. Cinderella, you shall have some balls.'

'Opo!' She punched him playfully.

'Strip boxing?' he said, pretending to undo his trousers.

'Look at this one.' She waved an ochre-yellow toga around.

'With this,' she said and held up a pale brown leather belt that was so large it looked more like the bottom half of a corset. Its three sets of silver buckles and silver brooch of leaves glinted in the light. 'One more,' she said and threw the toga on the bed alongside the others. She put her arms in the air, revealing her smooth polished armpits. 'This one's so sexy. Put it on for me.' He took an olive green dress and slipped it over her head. It only covered the top half of her buttocks. She twirled. On the back was an intricately embroidered set of butterfly wings.

'What do you wear with this then, babe?'

'A nice pair of knickers.' She laughed. 'Look, there's even a clip for a ruyi.'

'Shall we do the make-up and jewellery after we've chosen the outfit?'

'Of course. How on earth could you do anything else. Opo, you're losing the plot.'

'I'm losing the plot says Ms Paranoia.'

'Fuck off.'

'Just teasing. Come on, let's choose you something.'

'I love them all.'

'But, which one do you want to be rubbing up against your tagging buddies?'

'What do you think? Classy or slutty?'

'Ooh, you could never be slutty,' he said and grinned. 'Except when it gets you what you want.'

'Will you do my hair too?'

'Of course. For you...anything.' He took her hand, walked over to the bed and kept hold of it while they looked at the clothes. He squeezed. 'White mini-skirt looks great, but maybe a bit too naughty virgin cowgirl?'

'Agreed.'

'Butterfly wings. Great in a club, but it makes you look too desperate for attention. Toga – just wrong.'

'This one then?' she said as she pointed at the black and red skirt and jacket.

'Gets my vote. Depending on what you wear under the jacket. You are going to wear something aren't you?'

'Of course. I've got a black polo neck pullover with no shoulders and the bottom two-thirds of the arms and body cut off.'

'Babe, sounds perfect. Let's get you dressed.'

'Hair, make-up and bling first.'

'That icicle necklace looks great. How well does it hang?'

'It rests perfectly across my collar bones and between the neck and the body of the cut-off pullover.'

'Use that then.' He let go of her hand and opened her jewellery drawer. He took out a curved piece with deep-purple glass beads hanging from it. 'Does this fit over your ear?'

'Yeah. It's fabulously perfect isn't it?'

'Absolutely.'

She shoved him to the side. 'Let me look.' She foraged around in the back of the drawer and pulled out a piece of tarnished silver chain mail and slipped it on her hand like a glove. The chain links covered her wrist and up to the knuckles and the shield shaped petals covered most of the rest of her fingers. 'This can tag as well.'

'Wow! You have to.'

'I want my hair piled up high to make me look stern. When I flirt I want it to be a surprise.'

'Your make-up will need to be quite austere then. With a hint of playfulness, otherwise they won't even come near.'

'Brilliant. I love you.'

'I know.' He tried to disguise his pleasure, but failed.

She sat down at her dressing table and let him work his magic. Her mind wandered – should she give into the blackmail, should she try harder with Terence and should she get rid of the illegal data? She checked her ruyi to see if the blackmailer had responded. They hadn't. And neither had Terence. The data was worth keeping, worth the risk. It might reveal a key piece of information in the last few minutes of the Pay Year. She decided the decisions about the blackmailer and Terence could wait. Opo cupped her breast and gave it a little squeeze. 'All done, squidgy.'

'Why?' she asked.

'What?'

'Why do you do that? It's as if you get off on the fact that I fancy you. Some sort of power trip maybe?'

'Woah! Just teasing.'

'Really? Well, you better not this evening. Seriously, this is my last chance to get some massive points.'

'Okay, sorry.'

She stood up, kissed him on the cheek and admired his handiwork in the mirror. The bright pink lipstick and vivid green eye shadow outlined with the same pink as her lips was the perfect contrast to the sharp eyebrows and straight lines of the hair pinned on top of her head. 'Bring me my clothes, my good man. Dress me.'

She stepped into the skirt and he zipped it up. She put her arms in the air. 'Bra?' he asked. She shook her head. He pulled on her polo-neck. He held the jacket for her and she put her arms in. He fastened the single button. From behind he put the belt around her waist and buckled it, giving her a quick hug once he'd finished. Lastly, he clipped the perspex necklace and the ear cuff in place. 'There,' he said, 'all done and wonderful.'

She touched the silk flower in his top pocket with her jacket sleeve. 'The first tag of the night,' she said. They brushed lips in an exaggerated kiss.

Opo took two ruyi tassels out of his pocket. 'Tickets. One for you and one for me.'

'Green and orange? Did you have to be so obvious?'

'Sorry, hun, they insist you have the colour of your Strata.'

She attached the green tassel. 'I'll add some orange strips. For humour.'

'Girl, you're outrageous. Love you,' he said and kissed the air.

'House: order a taxi to the Tagging Cellar. Come on, let's go party.'

They stood on the front step, holding hands and looking up and down the street.

'Opo, thank you so much. I'm so excited. You have no idea what this means to me.'

'I think I do,' he said and squeezed. 'C'mon, Mr Taxi. We got a party to go to.'

Amber had a look at her SMFeed. 'Nothing from Terence. Typical.'

'What are you expecting?'

'Anything really. It'd be nice to hear from him, I guess.'

'What else is happening?'

'It's all about tonight. There's rumours that the corporations are about to make another announcement, something that'll make double points look like a mere gesture.'

'Oh my God, what next,' he said and laughed. 'How fabulous.'

The taxi pulled up with three female passengers already on board. Opo placed his charta on the pad behind the driver's seat. 'Tonight's on me,' he said to her.

She sat back and looked at the others who were all dressed in smart but gaudy dresses. Opo had been spot on about what she should wear and she was proud to be seen out with him. We'll turn some heads tonight, she thought.

The taxi weaved its way north and then west through the London streets, past groups of all ages queuing outside a multitude of venues – some with bright lights, some with spotlights sweeping the sky and others with plain unmarked doors. She lowered the window. The streets were buzzing with the sound of the chattering crowds. A mix of frying garlic and grilled meat filled the air as they drove slowly along a street lined with restaurants. The taxi stopped and two of the passengers got out. Fifty yards on it stopped again and two men dressed in dinner suits and white bow ties got in. They looked Amber up and down and glanced at Opo. One of them casually placed the charta on the pad. The other took out his ruyi. 'Mind if I take a snap?'

Opo straightened. 'Of course not, go ahead.'

'I meant your girlfriend. Is that okay?'

Amber put her hand on Opo's knee. 'He's my best friend, but

I'm not his girlfriend. Why would you want to take a snap of me?'

Opo laughed. 'Just let them. Stop fishing for compliments. It's so crass.'

'Where are you going?'

'We're off to the Tagging Cellar. You?' asked Amber.

'I'm not sure I can say.' He took a photo of her.

His friend huffed. 'Private party next door. No tagging, just good food, good wine and good company. Private.'

'Johnny! Behave. You could join us if you wanted.'

'No thanks,' said Opo.

Amber put her finger to her lips to hush Opo. 'Who would I ask for?'

'Lord Balfour,' said his friend.

'Really? Red?' said Amber in a slightly quieter voice.

'Ignore him,' said Lord Balfour. 'Shall we bang? Maybe meet up later?'

She held out her ruyi. He gently knocked his against hers. 'Later, gorgeous.'

The taxi stopped at the end of a gated road of six large detached houses. Each one must have had at least ten bedrooms and a garden the size of a cricket pitch. Opo took hold of her hand and walked towards the gate. He touched the gatepost with his ruyi tassel and then with Amber's. The gate opened. Behind them Lord Balfour and Johnny waved at the camera and waited. A young woman dressed as a geisha opened the door of the first house and bowed to them. 'Jules, that's perfect,' said Lord Balfour as they strutted past Amber and Opo. 'See ya later, greeny.'

Amber's ruyi buzzed with a message. She read it out loud to Opo. 'Private message from Lord Balfour. I will find you!'

'Wow, a real red. It's your night, I can feel it,' said Opo.

As Amber and Opo approached the entrance to the Tagging Cellar's driveway, a line of photographers began shouting: 'Over here. Pretty boy, look this way. Hey, blondie!' They stood and posed. The cameras were flashing and the photographers were all shouting at the same time. Opo had a smile so big that Amber thought he might stay there all night, but after a few minutes he turned away and took her with him.

'I know it's an exclusive party, but I thought it was going to be a bigger place than this,' she said.

'Aha. It's deceptive. Underneath these houses are interconnected basement complexes. Some of them are three floors deep and they all extend under the gardens. It's massive once you're down there.'

'All of the houses?'

'Yup. But don't get too excited. You need a special invite to get into the red's house.'

'Don't know what you mean,' she said and blew him a kiss.

The driveway looped around a lawn in front of the house. A trapdoor was propped open in the centre and a woman in raggedy clothes sat beside it. As they approached Amber could see that she was holding a metal bowl. Opo dipped his ruyi into the bowl and stepped on to the stairs. Amber followed. 'There's no SMFeed once you're inside,' he said as he skipped down in front of her.

She checked her ruyi. 'Terence. Please,' she whispered.

'Opo,' called a woman dressed in a translucent peach-coloured dress. He waved and went to greet her.

Amber's ruyi buzzed and she read the message to herself. 'I'll tell you what I want. Before Pay Day I want you to quit your job, hand back the data to everyone you've stolen it from, make a public apology and pay me enough points to make you drop to the bottom of green. You're going down, and not in a good way.'

She swallowed a mouthful of vomit that had leapt into her mouth. 'Opo,' she called, but he'd gone.

EIGHTEEN

n the centre of the large room and surrounded by a crowd of onlookers was a group of six actors dressed from head to toe in black robes and with bare feet. They stood still and silent. On a dusty wooden stand was a copper bowl melted by acid to resemble a piece of post-apocalyptic junk. It was filled to the brim with clear mints. In the centre of each sweet was a single delicate leaf made from gold. Amber popped one into her mouth.

A naked girl with matted armpit hair, an unruly mass of pubic hair and wearing only a cat mask with two-foot wide whiskers grabbed Amber's tassels and led her across the room. The cat-girl meowed loudly and the crowd parted. She passed the tassel to one of the actors and knelt down on her hands and knees, pretending to lick a bowl in front of her. Two actors stood on either side and rolled her whiskers in their fingers.

The actor led Amber into the centre, pointed at her mouth and stuck his tongue out. She smiled. He gently prised her lips apart, tilted his head and moved in close, trying to see inside her mouth. She opened wide. He beckoned with his finger and pointed to the tip of his tongue. She complied and he took the mint from the tip of her tongue and showed it to the crowd.

He pretended to put it in the cat's mouth but stopped just short and instead dropped it into her bowl. He passed her a small toffee hammer. She cracked the mint into small pieces and licked the gold leaf. It stuck to her tongue. She stood up and he put his arm around her and around Amber. They formed a circle with their backs to the audience and she passed the leaf to Amber's tongue and snapped her own back into her mouth. He nodded to Amber and she did the same. He spun all three of them around to face the crowd. The actors all showed their tongues at the same time. All of them had gold leaves. The cat meowed and put her finger to her mouth. The crowd hushed.

'Welcome to the Tagging Cellar. Follow a gold leaf and see where it leads,' said a disembodied voice.

The six black-robed actors pulled up their hoods. Each hood had a different number of dots embroidered on it – the six sides of a dice. They parted and left by different exits. The crowd split and followed.

Amber tucked the gold leaf in her jacket pocket and followed number five. At the exit he dropped his robe to the floor and continued, naked. She was shocked, but didn't want to show it. Instead, she concentrated on his beautiful buttocks as she followed him out of the room. He walked faster and faster, but she kept up with him through small rooms, corridors and the occasional doorway. His other followers were close behind. He paused, looked over his shoulder and waited a few seconds for them to catch up. On the wall next to him was a live StrataScreen showing people arriving. He placed his hand flat against it and pushed. The screen clicked into the wall and a door-sized section shot up into the ceiling. They followed him into a wide corridor.

He ran and Amber walked as fast as she could without looking flustered. The others fell behind. She turned a corner into a long corridor. At regular intervals stood a naked person – boy, girl, boy, girl. She slowed down a little. She walked past the first boy and looked at him out of the corner of her eye. He stared back. It was the same with the second, the third and the fourth. The fifth boy grabbed her ruyi tassels and pulled her close. He plucked one of them, put it in a wooden bowl at his feet and waved her through the low gap in the wall. She knelt down and crawled through.

Before she could get her bearings, a hand grabbed her under the armpit and helped her up. Someone from behind blindfolded her. She was led across the room and gently lowered on to a padded chair with armrests that smelt of mothballs. A woman with a throaty voice spoke. 'Ladies and gentleman, boys and girls. We are here for your pleasure. Sit tight and enjoy the anticipation. All will be revealed. Soon.'

The silence was suffocating. She touched her blindfold, but before she could undo it someone steered her hand back to her lap. She sat and waited.

Gradually her hearing and smell took over from her sight. She could hear the shuffling of someone sitting either side of her. Someone opposite was muttering, but she couldn't hear what they were saying. The room smelt of expensive polish and a mix of subtle perfumes, the sort that weren't available to greens. She fiddled with her ruyi, fiddled with the gold leaf inside her pocket and fiddled with her ear cuff. She was biting her lip; she winced when she realised she'd betrayed her anxiety. She sat on her hands to stop herself fidgeting. She thought about Terence and about the morning they'd spend together the next day. She relaxed. Where's Opo gone? she thought. He shouldn't run off like that.

There was a loud click followed by the whirr of a motor. Her blindfold was removed just in time to see the door sliding into place. They were in a sealed room lined with dark wooden panels and an olive green carpeted floor. Twelve of them sat in a circle – male, female, male, female.

A naked man, perfectly formed and completely stripped of all his head, body and pubic hair stood in the middle. 'Now, why were you chosen?' he said. He bent over, grabbed the bowl and tilted it away from his body. Still bending, he moved round slowly, showing everyone in the room the contents. Amber's was the only green tassel among the other yellows and oranges. He lifted the bowl above his head. The cat crept towards him from behind, cautiously taking a step and then pausing before taking another. Each time he turned around she darted out of his sight. The twelve onlookers sat rigid. All of Amber's thoughts were now concentrated on what was happening in the room, wondering what would happen when the cat finally reached him.

The closer the cat got to him the more vigorously she wiggled her bottom. When she was close enough to touch his buttocks she squatted down behind him

She leapt into the air and grabbed a tassel from the bowl.

They all gasped and let out a communal sigh of relief. She dashed to the edge of the room and laid the tassel down on a silver tray with handles moulded in the shape of a snake. She repeated the slow stealth dance back to the man with the bowl and snatched another tassel. She crept back to the tray, placed it next to the first one and twisted her whiskers. She repeated her dancing and leaping until the twelve tassels formed six carefully laid out pairs.

The cat walked around inside the circle, close enough to be touched. She stopped in front of Amber. The intimate smell of sweat and a faint odour of stale piss flooded Amber's nostrils. The cat lifted her arms and stroked her armpit hair. She held her fingers under Amber's nose. She opened her mouth to show the gold leaf on the tip of her tongue. Amber's stomach tightened. The cat smiled and leapt, turning around while she was in the air. She landed, wiggled her bottom at Amber and ran to the door, which slid open in time for her to disappear through it. It slammed shut.

The man was squatting in the middle with the tray. Attached to one of his fingernails was a gold extension. He stroked the first pair of tassels – one yellow, one orange. He looked at his golden fingernail, scanned the room with it and then looked again. He pointed to a woman wearing an all-in-one white trouser suit with a yellow tasselled ruyi in her lap. He beckoned her. She looked at the others and after hesitating stood up and walked quickly to him. He pointed to a woman wearing a perfectly frayed high-fashion blue pinstripe skirt and jacket. She smiled, her super-white teeth beaming, and bounded over to him. He took their ruyi and banged them together. The orange woman's smile vanished. The door slid open and he motioned for them to leave. The door closed behind them.

Amber looked at the tray. She was paired with an orange. Shit, she thought, that's going to piss someone off.

He slowly worked his way through the pairs until only Amber and a middle-aged man wearing nondescript clothes remained. I'm not bothered about him, thought Amber. They stood up and walked to the man with the tray. He banged their ruyi. Amber let the middle-aged man go ahead of her and as he left the room the actor put the empty tray on the floor. He pressed the wall and the door closed before Amber could leave. She was locked in a room with a superbly attractive naked man. He stuck his tongue out and on its tip was a gold leaf. He tapped his cheekbone, pointing upwards to his eye. The door slid open.

Amber left the room. Wow, she thought, I can't wait to tell Opo. There was a little niggle at the back of her mind about Terence and what he would make of all this, but she ignored it.

One of the black-robed actors ran past her. It was number five again. She ran to catch up. At the end of the corridor was a sharp right turn. She turned the corner too fast and slammed into the wall. He was standing at the bottom of an escalator. He lifted her on to it. She looked over her shoulder; he was standing watching her. As she neared the top, she stretched to take a peek. There was a small empty room with a single low stool in the middle and six steamed-up glass doors around the edge. The doors were identical except that they were numbered one to six in the same dice format as the black robes. She sat on the stool and caught her breath. She checked her ruyi, but as Opo had warned her, there was no signal. 'How am I supposed to choose a room?' she said.

An old-fashioned loudspeaker on the wall crackled and made her jump. 'As with most choices, it's the people you're with that make the difference,' said a female with a Russian accent. Part of the wall turned into a screen and displayed a glimpse of the faces inside each steamy room. She spotted Opo in room four.

The door led through to a small antechamber where a naked woman was waiting for her. 'Please,' she said.

'Please?' said Amber.

The woman took Amber's hands and lifted her arms. She unbuttoned Amber's jacket, took it off and hung it up. She did the same with the polo neck pullover. Amber stood there topless and worried. 'It's best to go with the flow,' said the woman as she put a t-shirt on. She was now dressed in the exact opposite way to Amber – wearing a top and nothing else

'Sure,' replied Amber. 'Of course.'

The woman detached the ruyi from Amber's belt, finished undressing her and then pulled her own jeans on. She gave Amber her ruyi and opened the door to the steam room. It took Amber a few seconds to adjust to the heat. Everyone in the room was naked except for a couple of waiters. She saw Opo sitting next to an older man with a droopy moustache. Opo was over-flirting. She headed over to him.

He waved. 'Hun! Over here!'

NINETEEN

Opo tucked the man's hair behind his ear, stroked his moustache with his thumb and kissed him. He held his ruyi out and the man banged it. 'Let's sit over there,' he said to Amber.

They sat on an empty bench. 'Bloody hell. He was red,' whispered Amber.

Opo grinned. 'Cool, eh?'

'Babe, you're outrageous. And scrummy. No wonder he couldn't resist.'

'We're the perfect tagging couple.'

'What I don't get…'

'Go on…'

'You can tell by the tassels what strata everyone is?'

'Yup…'

'So why would anyone tag with a lower level?'

He held his head in his hands. 'Hun, I'm so sorry. I forgot to say – we all got a batch of points when we entered. Admittedly, the exact numbers are based on our Strata Level, but that's what we're gambling with. Well, for the first two hours. Then they're added on to our real-life points. But by then who knows what points anyone else has.'

'You sure?'

'Of course. If you look like you're winning, you'll attract interest.'

'Cool.'

Opo stood up and flung a towel over his shoulder. 'C'mon, let's go find some points.'

Amber followed him through a door with a graphic of a person with a penis and breasts. A tall woman wearing a short skirt, a tight t-shirt and a little too much make-up was waiting. She rubbed their tassels against a panel on the wall. 'Your threads are on their way,' she said in a deep voice.

Opo kissed her on the cheek. 'Perfect,' he said and patted her bottom.

'Opo,' said Amber and chuckled.

'C'mon, let's get dry,' said Opo and pointed to a small cubicle off to the side. He pulled Amber in with him. 'Close your eyes.' Bursts of dry hot air blasted them from every angle. Amber giggled. 'Keep them closed,' he said and spun her round and round. He stopped her. 'Stand still. Legs open,' he said and pushed her calves apart. He grabbed her elbows. 'Arms up,' he said and tickled her. 'Wiggle your toes. All dry?'

'Totally.'

They stepped out of the dryer and found their clothes laid out on separate chairs. The woman spoke in her deep voice. 'Honey, this is so crucially embarrassing. We seem to have misplaced your knickers. Can you describe them?'

Amber laughed loudly. 'Opo, tell her.'

'Tell her what?'

'You know.'

'Know what?'

'I didn't bring any.'

The woman smiled. 'Go get 'em, gal.' Amber kissed her on the lips. 'Sweetie, a different time and place and who knows,' said the woman.

'Time to get dressed,' said Opo. 'Let's get those points.'

'Will you dress me?' asked Amber.

The woman and Opo both said, 'No,' at the same time and laughed.

Once they were fully dressed and about to leave, Opo picked up the ruyi from the woman's pile of clothes that she'd been taking off as they'd dressed and banged it with his. 'I'm sure we'll see you again,' he said.

'Thank you, my bad man,' she replied.

They stepped out into the corridor they'd left an hour or so before. 'Did you see her, his, her...'

Opo nodded. 'This way,' he said and looped his little finger in hers. 'Let's get away from this Zone of Titillation.'

They danced along the corridor.

Opo stopped outside a glass door. 'Look,' he said, 'Speed Tagging.'

'What?'

'You have one-hundred and forty characters to convince the other person to tag with you. Fancy it?'

'If you want to...I'm easy.'

'We all know that,' he said and pinched her bum.

'Go on then. For a few minutes.' She pushed the door and stepped inside. The smell of freshly brewed coffee floated around the room amidst hushed intense bursts of chatter. She accepted a cup from a formally dressed waiter and made her way over to a man standing with his back to a full-length mirror. He was wearing riding boots, white breeches and a red coat – an old-fashioned fox hunt leader's outfit. He smeared Amber's face with a riding crop. She gasped. The crop had left a red smear across her face.

'It'll fade when you leave,' whispered Opo in her ear. 'It shows it's your first time and that you're registered; you're approved.' He touched his own cheek and strutted across the room to an empty seat opposite a young man looking starry eyed at the approaching Opo.

A girl who looked a few years younger than Amber was chewing gum and fiddling with her ripped checked shirt. Amber sauntered over, trying to give off the air of someone in control, but in reality she was nervous. She scraped the plastic chair away from the table and sat down with an aggressive bump.

'Novice,' said the girl, still chewing. She grinned, lifted a bare and slightly dirty foot on to the table and fiddled with the frayed edges of her cut-off jeans. She stared at Amber. 'Press that,' she drawled, pointing to a small cube in the middle of the table. 'To start.'

Amber did as she was told.

'Now tell me why I should tag with you,' said the girl.

'You should tag with me because I'm on my way up and I can help you along the way. No that's rubbish. See him?' She pointed at Opo. 'He is my best friend, he is coo…' The cube hummed and joggled around on the table.

'That's it,' said the girl. She folded her arms across her chest. 'Not a great first attempt.'

Amber sat forward. 'I'll…'

The girl frowned. 'You've had your chance.'

'Quiet,' said the cube.

The girl unfolded her arms, touched Amber's red streak, pressed the cube and stared Amber in the eyes. She didn't blink. 'Tag with me because you know you want to,' she said quietly and pushed the chair on to its back legs. She winked, folded her arms and grinned.

The cube glowed. 'Amber, do you want to tag?' it said. The glow faded.

Amber hesitated. She didn't know the Speed Tagging etiquette and the girl was giving nothing away. 'I'd love to,' she said, unsure if she really meant it.

The cube glowed again. 'Ashley, do you want to tag?' It faded.

'Sure, what the fuck. Why not? She's kinda cute.' The cube became transparent. Ashley put her hand inside the top of her shorts and pulled out a ruyi with red tassels. She stroked the cube with it. 'Touch it with your ruyi,' she said.

Amber did as she was told.

Opo appeared at her side. 'Hun, how's it going?'

She stood up. 'I'm no good at this,' she whispered and looked over her shoulder at Ashley, who sat there picking her toes.

'How can you say that? You just tagged a red.'

'Only 'cos she was bored and wanted to make me squirm.'

'Maybe.'

'Can we get out of here?'

'Yeah. I know the perfect place. It's the highest risk and hence the highest reward spot in the cellar. Are you up for it?'

Amber swallowed. 'Okay. Let's do it.'

'It's quite a way. Stay close and don't get distracted.'

'If you say so,' she said and saluted.

'I mean it, there's some weird shit in here.'

'I know.'

'You don't. And hopefully you never will, my sweet, sweet Amber.'

'Opo, you're creeping me out.'

'Good. Follow me.'

They dashed along corridor after corridor. Some had doors, some had frosted windows and some had only walls. Every now and again they'd stop and Opo would check the small piece of paper that Amber guessed was a plan of the cellar. On a couple of occasions he pressed the wall and a door opened to reveal an escalator which they used to change floors.

As they passed a door with the red cross of a hospital on it she felt him tense and speed up a little. 'What's in there?' she asked.

'Nothing.' He squeezed her hand tightly.

'That hurt,' she said. 'How much further?'

'Almost there.' He slowed the pace a little.

'What's in this high risk place?'

'No idea. We're in the gambling part of the cellar. I heard that it's the place to get the most points. To take the biggest gamble, but I don't know any more than that.'

'Should I be scared?'

'Probably, but nothing ventured...' He stopped and consulted the plan. 'Here.'

'I don't see anything.'

He touched the floor and a screen appeared under their feet. He knelt and tapped in a code, checking each character with his piece of paper. The floor started to slide back. He jumped to the edge, dragging Amber with him. The floor stopped moving. In front of them was an escalator into a pitch black basement. The smell of damp soil and rotting vegetables filled the air. He turned his head to face her and nodded. She nodded back and stepped on to the moving staircase. As soon as their feet touched the metal, the floor began to slide back into place, cutting out all the light. She clutched his arm and they descended in silence.

The escalator dropped them gently and then without warning scooped them back up again. It got faster and faster as it climbed and then dropped again. Amber's stomach jumped into her mouth and then, as it eventually settled back into place, they started to climb again. A hole appeared in the roof and the escalator took them through into an amphitheatre.

Sitting on tiered seats around the sides were at least five hundred silent people watching them emerge. The sun shone through the tiny fragments of glass that made up the roof. Amber blinked several times in rapid succession to adjust to the light.

A woman covered from head to toe in a lion's skin appeared out of the ground. The crowd cheered and clapped. 'Amber. We are so pleased you could join us,' she said.

Amber turned to Opo. He shrugged, gave her the thumbs up and sat down in the front row. For the first time she noticed the crowd were all wearing togas.

'Do you accept the challenge?' asked the woman.

Amber glanced at Opo. 'What is it?' she asked quietly.

'Speak up,' shouted the woman.

Amber pulled her shoulders back. 'What is the challenge?' she shouted back.

'Our resident champion will take your ruyi and by analysing your posts to Terence she will attempt to pass herself off as you. If she can get him to reveal a secret she wins, if not you win.'

Opo shouted from his seat, 'She accepts.'

Amber moved her head with small nods. 'I accept,' she said.

'Louder,' said the woman.

'I accept,' shouted Amber. The crowd erupted. 'Amber, Amber, Amber,' they shouted.

The floor opened and the girl from the Speed Tagging emerged. Amber gasped. 'Ashley?'

She bowed and held out her hand. The woman took Amber's ruyi and gave it to her. She paraded it around the arena, waving it at the crowd and then crouched down to read it.

A few people slow handclapped and gradually more and more joined in. Ashley seemed oblivious. Amber stood in the middle of the baying crowd with her hand in her pocket, fiddling with the gold leaf as if it could protect her. Ashley sprung to her feet and signalled the crowd to stop. They immediately fell silent.

'Ruyi: private message to Terence Huddson. I hate falling out.'

She held the ruyi in the air and as soon as it buzzed she read from it. 'Me too. Where are you?'

Someone in the crowd laughed and the woman in the lion skin pointed at them and shook her head.

Ashley spoke again. 'Ruyi: private message to Terence Huddson. Missing you. I'll be back in the morning. Will you be there?' She paused to make sure the crowd knew the next time she spoke it would be the reply from Terence.

She spoke. 'Are you still fretting?' She waved the ruyi in the air. 'Ruyi: private message to Terence Huddson. Tell me how to stop and I'll try.'

The crowd clapped. 'Silence,' shouted the woman.

Ashley held the ruyi close to her face and read the next message. 'It's just a prank. Ignore it.' She looked at Amber and licked her lips.

Amber cringed.

Ashley inclined her head to the left. 'Ruyi: private message to Terence Huddson. Are we talking about the same thing?' She inclined her head to the right. 'I presume so. I'm worried about you.' She inclined her head to the left. 'Ruyi: private message to Terence Huddson. If you're so worried then spell it out. What are you worried about?'

Amber took a step towards Ashley who tilted her head again. 'Babe, why are you being so weird?' Amber took a step back. 'Ruyi: private message to Terence Huddson. I'm not being weird. I need to know that you really understand what's worrying me.'

'Amber!' shouted Opo.

Ashley waved the ruyi at Opo and read from the screen. 'I'd rather not post it, no matter how secure it's meant to be. Unless you really want me to.'

Amber leapt across and snatched the ruyi from Ashley. 'You win,' she said.

Ashley bowed and whispered into Amber's ear. 'It wasn't real. It's a computer simulation. Intrigued by the blackmail though.' She bowed again and was lowered out of view.

Amber held her head in shame as she walked across the arena to Opo.

TWENTY

'Head up. Back straight,' said Opo as he led her across the arena.

'I need to find her. Find out what she meant.'

'Okay. Get ready to do exactly what I do.'

The floor opened up as they approached the spot where they'd arrived. He took her hand. 'Bow,' he whispered.

The crowd shouted, 'Amber, Amber, Amber.'

'See? They still love you,' he said as they stepped on to the escalator and disappeared into the ground.

Back in the corridor, Amber sat down on the floor and pulled her knees up to her chin. 'I need to see her. She knows about the blackmail.'

'What about Terence? Shouldn't you contact him?'

'She told me it was a simulation.'

Opo jumped up. 'Let's find her.'

'How?'

'Let's go to that red party your lord invited you to. She's bound to show up.' He unfolded his piece of paper against the smooth white wall and traced a path with his finger. 'We're close,' he said. 'This way.'

They ran along the corridors and every now and again Opo stopped, consulted his piece of paper and then ran again. Amber followed. She was churning over Ashley's comment about the blackmail, wondering how much she could have possibly picked up from a few minutes on the ruyi. Did she know what the blackmail was about? Did she know who the blackmailer was? Did she intend to hand Amber over to the corporations?

'Here,' said Opo and nodded towards a geisha girl outside a door with an old-fashioned key protruding from a lock. They walked casually to the girl. Amber's heart was pounding with the physical exertion and the emotional turmoil.

'Hi,' said Opo.

'Hi,' said the geisha to Amber.

Opo showed her his piece of paper. 'Can we come in?'

'That is a map, not an invite.' She turned to Amber. 'I believe you have an invite though?'

'Do I?'

'I believe so.'

'Lord Balfour invited us, if that's what you mean.'

'It isn't. You have a physical invite. And the invite does not include him,' she said, pointing at Opo.

Amber held his hand. 'It's both of us or neither of us.'

'Don't be silly,' said Opo, pushing her a little closer to the geisha.

'Come with me,' she said to Amber and poked out her tongue. On it was a gold leaf. 'Pop yours in your mouth.'

'I want Opo to come too,' said Amber. The geisha stood there with her tongue out, not moving a muscle.

'Go,' said Opo. 'I'll catch up with you later, hun. You can't afford to miss out on this.' He turned and left.

The geisha touched the key. It turned with a loud mechanical clunk and the door squeaked open.

'Enter and enjoy,' she said.

Amber stepped into a room of floor to ceiling paper books. The decadence hit her like a punch to the stomach. The door squeaked shut and locked with the same mechanical clunk. There was a faint mustiness in the air and a dusty tingle in her nostrils. There was no key and no other way out of the room. She touched the door with her gold leaf, but nothing happened. She knocked, but nothing happened. She kicked, but nothing happened. She was trapped.

She sat on the floor and stared at the books. This was the most physical wealth she'd ever seen in one place. She could have traded any one of these on the black market for enough points to rise a whole level. As the shock of being locked in and the sheer magnitude of the wealth slowly subsided, she took a book from the shelf and held it, feeling its weight. The cover was smooth and cold and the sides were rough and tickled a little as she ran her hand along their paper edges. It smelt clean and fresh and yet there was a background earthiness as well. Her mind drifted to her childhood and the one battered book, a copy of *Lord of the Flies*, that her mother had owned before she'd traded it in during the one-off offer – Books for Points. Amber remembered being equally fascinated and repulsed by the wild barbaric Jack and his longing for total power. That same year her mother had given her a pile of dirt from the yard as a Christmas present. 'To remind you how dirt poor we are,' was all she'd said as Amber unwrapped it.

A section of bookcase opened, snapping Amber from her daydream. She tucked the book behind her back as if she was a naughty schoolchild. 'Tada!' shouted Ashley as she jumped through the newly revealed door and threw her hands in the air. 'Surprise!'

'You?'

'Yes, me. Who did you expect? Lord Balfour?' she asked, with a wicked grin on her face.

Amber put the book back on the shelf. 'Actually, yes, I did.'

'Sorry to be so disappointing.'

'I thought he invited me. That's all.'

'He did, sort of. You'll see him tomorrow if all goes to plan.'

'Plan?'

'More of that later. First we need to talk about this blackmail. Don't we?'

'Do we?'

'Yes.'

'Okay…'

'Do you want to start from the beginning?'

Amber folded her arms. 'Not really. Why don't you tell me what you think it is you know?'

'They said you were smart…ish.'

'Who?'

'Not important.'

'So what is it you think you know?'

'Slow down, no need to rush. We have all night and tomorrow. Enjoy the ride.'

'The night must be almost over and I'm spending the day with Terence. So get on with it.'

Ashley laughed. 'Spunky. I like that. No knickers – that's cute too.'

Amber blushed. 'Not my best idea, but I was expecting a very different evening.'

'Power is not all about sex, you know. Real power lies in the ability to set the mood; to control their hearts and minds without getting involved. To make them thirsty and then let others lead them to the water.'

'What's power got to do with anything?'

'That's why you came, isn't it? To get enough points to rise a level and gain more power.'

'Sort of.'

'We can help you. If you help us.'

'Who are you?'

'I'm Ashley. I'm red. And that's all you need to know at the moment.'

'So, what do you think you know about me?'

'You're being blackmailed for stealing data from the Bureaucracy. You've no idea who is blackmailing you. You're scared by their threats. You're caught between doing as they ask, which will mean you drop a level, and calling their bluff in the hope of rising a level. And in the background to all of this is the fragility of your marriage. Not to mention the disappearance of Sam.'

'Go on,' said Amber.

'Sofa,' said Ashley. A three-seater, draped in red woven material with a coat of arms depicting a roughly dismantled ruyi, slid out from the wall. 'Take a seat,' she said.

Amber kicked off her sandals, hitched up her dress and sat with one leg under the other. Ashley sat cross-legged at the other end. 'We can help,' she said.

'With what, exactly?'

'Your predicament.'

'Which is?'

'As I explained.'

'Go on.'

'We can stop the blackmail.'

'Do you know who it is?'

'We can find out, easily.'

'And what do you want from me?'

'We want some passwords, that's all.'

'Passwords?'

'Yes. Passwords to the Bureaucracy systems.'

'I thought you were the all-powerful ones.'

'As I said, we just set the direction, we don't get involved in the actual mechanics.'

'So why do you want the passwords then?'

'I can't tell you until we're convinced of your loyalty.'

'And I can't give you them until I'm convinced of your sincerity. Stalemate?'

'Stalemate? Of course not. We'll take things step by step. Okay?'

'Try me.'

'In a nutshell – we've been slightly scuppered by the corporations who are getting too big for their boots. For us to steer the ship we need to be able to analyse the data correctly. They feed us data, but won't tell us the purpose it was originally collected for and so our analysis is potentially flawed. And we've no idea how fresh the data is either.'

'Interesting, but I don't see how I fit in.'

'You've already stolen data and with guidance you're capable of knowing what's important and what's not. You're one of our routes into the Bureaucracy.'

'What would you need me to do?'

'Sam's disappeared, hasn't she?'

'Was that you?'

'No, but it's convenient and we'll take advantage. You'll replace her on Monday and that'll give you the level of access to the system that we need.'

'I'm not stealing large amounts of data for you.'

'Really?'

'Yes. Really.'

'Anyway, that's not what we're asking. We'll need some passwords and some network details, that's all.'

'And then what? I thought you didn't get involved.'

'We work with the outliers. You'll meet some at a festival tomorrow.'

'I'm spending the day with Terence. I have to get back on track with him or we might break up.'

'True. But I think you'll choose this. It's your one opportunity to rescue yourself from the inevitable downwards spiral of being arrested for stealing that data.'

'That's blackmail.'

'No, it's a choice we're offering you. I'm stating the alternatives. Not blackmail, just facts.'

'You mentioned proving my loyalty.'

'Later. First steps first. Will you come to meet the outliers tomorrow?'

'I'm not sure,' said Amber as she stood up and began to walk around the edge of the room, running her fingers along the spines of the books.

'You know you want to,' said Ashley and winked.

'Can I contact Terence first?'

'Yes, if you agree to come to the festival.'

'Okay, I'll come, but I want to let Terence know I'm not going to be home until later tomorrow.'

'Great. You can contact him from here.'

Amber unclipped her ruyi and spoke. 'Ruyi: message to Terence Huddson. Something important has come up. It's a great opportunity for both of us. I'll be home later tomorrow. Miss you babe x.' She sat and waited, but there was no response.

'Ready to meet your chaperone?' said Ashley.

'Chaperone? Bit formal.'

Ashley smiled and took Amber's hand. 'This way. It's a nice surprise.' They left through the same door that Ashley had entered.

It was pitch black and Amber stumbled. 'Can we have some light?'

'No. Security, sorry. Can't afford for those darn cameras to identify you from your body temperature, pulse and whatnot. Secret mission.' She laughed.

Amber held on to Ashley's shirt as they sped along in the dark. Suddenly, Ashley stopped and Amber bumped into her. 'Sorry,' said Amber.

'No worries. I nearly always miss this door.' She dusted the wall with her tassels and there was a distant whirring noise. 'This way,' she whispered and pulled Amber with her.

The whirring stopped. A faint glow lit up the floor of a swimming pool.

'Hi,' a voice shouted from the dark.

'Who's that?' asked Amber.

'It's your Lord Balfour,' said Ashley. 'Have fun.'

'Hi,' he called again.

Amber knelt by the side of the pool. 'Hi,' she called back.

'Come in, it's fantastic.'

'What are you doing here?'

'I'm your escort to the outlier festival. Cool, eh?'

'Yeah. Guess so.'

'Come on in. Don't be shy. I've seen it all anyway on the cameras.' He laughed loudly. 'Hope you don't mind. You've a lovely body.'

'Thanks,' said Amber. She undressed and dived in. 'Wow, this is fabulous,' she shouted across to him.

SUNDAY

TWENTY-ONE

'Shit,' said Martin, as he opened his bleary eyes and realised he was still at Bruce's. 'What happened?'

'A bit overindulgent with Bruce's finest offerings. That's what happened,' said Sir Arthur.

Martin stretched and massaged his neck to try and relieve the ache. His head felt heavy and his mouth was dry. 'Shit. Jenny's gonna be mightily pissed off with me.'

'We told her you wouldn't be home last night.'

'You did what?'

'We sent her a message.'

'She knows I was here? What did she say?'

'She didn't reply.'

Martin scrabbled around on the floor. 'Shit! Shit! Shit! Where the bloody hell is my ruyi?'

'You're out of signal.'

'Shit and shit again.'

'You can use Bruce's setup if you want?'

'No. That would be a red rag to an already angry bull. I'll have to get going straight away.'

'But what about Maxamillion and his various transgressions?'

'Shit. It's coming back to me now. We're going to the outlier festival aren't we?'

'Yes.'

'Do you really think we'll find out any more about what Max is up to?'

'I can't think of anywhere better to try. Can you?'

'No. It's just that...Jenny thinks I've left it all behind.'

'She'd want you to look after Max though, wouldn't she?'

'I guess so. These days it's a bit hard to know what she wants.'

Bruce called up the stairs. 'You guys ready to roll?'

'On our way,' called Sir Arthur. 'C'mon. Let's find out what that son of yours is up to. Once and for all.' He handed Martin his ruyi and cigarettes and headed down the stairs.

Martin followed. He stepped out of the front door and laughed. 'You are kidding?' he said to Bruce, who was sitting on a chestnut-brown horse and holding the reins of two others. 'I haven't ridden for years.'

'It's the quickest and least traceable way to get there. We don't want the bureaucrats knowing where we are, do we?'

'Or Jenny,' said Sir Arthur as he slapped Martin on the back.

Bruce and Sir Arthur were still laughing as they rode into the woods.

The morning air was cold and crisp. The horses' hooves stirred up a rich earthy smell as they trotted along and each time he brushed a tree the sticky sweet smell of pine filled his nostrils.

They came out of the wood into an open meadow and broke into a gallop. The cracked and faded leather bag with his ruyi and cigarettes bashed against his leg with the same rhythm as the horse. They charged across the fields, jumping hedges and shouting with joy. He forgot all about Jenny and Max. He forgot all about the forthcoming Pay Day and he forgot all about Amber and Sam. He was focussed on making sure he stayed on the horse, with the occasional thought about how much Becka loved to gallop across the fields.

They approached another wood and Bruce signalled for them to slow down. At the edge, Bruce leapt off and stood with his arms in the air and his legs apart. The other two did exactly the same. Martin chuckled. 'We must look like scarecrows trying to ward off the evil wood spirits.'

Bruce turned his head sharply. 'Be quiet.'

They waited.

And waited.

Martin pointed at a tree stump. 'It moved.'

'Quiet.'

'Sorry,' he whispered.

A periscope rose from the centre of the stump and inched its way around in a circle. It returned to the three horsemen and stopped. Martin coughed. Bruce lowered both arms and held out his hands, palms up, to the steel-encased eye. They waited.

The ground shook a little and spooked the horses. Bruce tied them up. The ground shook some more and a six-foot narrow slit appeared. Bruce beckoned them to follow him down the ramp and into the tunnel.

At the far end was another slit of light with a ramp leading up to it. Along the walls were flickering oil lamps casting stars and moons on the ceiling. They walked along in silence, looking from left to right at the graffiti stick-men with slogans below them – *Choose your colour carefully, you could be in it a long time* and *Nothing is compulsory, merely a compromise.* Bruce led the way and Sir Arthur followed. Martin was lagging behind, partly captivated by the slogans, but also a little cautious of what they were getting themselves into.

As they emerged, they were hit by the sound of hundreds of people talking, singing and laughing. The festival was covered by a canopy of woven branches and leaves through which sunlight filtered, giving the festival a green tinge. The smell of coffee and frying bacon drifted across from an open-fronted tent. 'Hi. What can I get you?' shouted a muscular woman from behind the counter. She was wearing a blood-stained apron with *Rare Breed Pigs for All* handwritten in neon pink paint. Martin's stomach cramped with hunger, but as he was about to go and purchase his breakfast he noticed a high wall of screens up ahead.

'StrataScreens? Here?' he said to Sir Arthur.

'Seems odd, I agree. Let's investigate.'

The wall was ten screens high and ten screens wide, forming a forty-by-sixty-foot entrance with a two-screen-high gap in the middle – the entrance to the festival. Three images cycled round on the screens. The first was the familiar white of the broken StrataScreen, except these were covered with a web of cracks. The second was the five corporation logos burning at the base of a tall pole with LEDs displaying the word outliers at the top. The third was the slogan from the tunnel – *Nothing is compulsory, merely a compromise.* The effect was terrifying and inspiring.

'Impressive,' said Martin.

'Welcome to the outlier festival,' said Sir Arthur. 'Shall we wander?'

'Sure. Where's Bruce?'

Sir Arthur laughed. 'Lost him already? He'll be up to no good, of that I'm certain.'

Beyond the screens was an avenue of sculptures. They paused to look at a six-foot-high ruyi made from soiled sheets and used toilet paper. There was a tank of fish that slowly changed colour through red, orange, yellow, green, blue, indigo, violet and finally white before they exploded into tiny pieces which, when they hit the bottom of the tank reformed into fish which reversed colour back to red. A group of kids, no older than Becka, were inhaling gas at the base of a statue of a giant rat eating people of all shapes and sizes and defecating identical spheres with eyes and nose, but no mouth.

The end of the avenue opened up into a market square of covered stalls. 'Shall we get something to eat?' asked Martin.

'Splendid idea,' said Sir Arthur. 'Anything in mind?'

'Nope. Let's see what's on offer.'

Inside the square the stallholders were all shouting out their wares, competing for trade. Martin stopped at a stall selling apples. Instead of the usual two types on offer at GreenNet or even OrangeNet, there was a plethora of varieties. 'What are all these?' he asked.

The stallholder smiled and offered him a slice. 'This one is out of circulation for anyone other than the reds. And outliers, of course.' He chuckled. 'It's a Joanneting, also known as the St John the Baptist because it's ripe on the twenty-fourth of June. But we accelerate its growth. This was picked yesterday and needs eating today for the best taste. What do you think?'

Martin popped the slice in his mouth. 'It's sweet and crisp. So much more alive than the usual ones.'

'Those aren't apples that you buy in the shops, they're conveniently sized balls of nothingness,' said the stallholder.

At the next stall along Sir Arthur picked a couple of taster slices of Gloucester Old Spot pork, cured in cider and then smoked over applewood. He passed one to Martin. 'Try this.'

'Wow, that's good.'

'Shall we get some?'

'Let's see what else is on offer first.'

They went from stall to stall sampling the goods. They tried slices of pears, spoons of different plum jams and a dollop of the most wonderful cherry and black pepper chutney. They tasted a tiny slice of pork pie, a sliver of dried beef and a small lump of roast lamb. They ate half slices of oatmeal bread and cottage loaf and a spoonful of bread pudding.

'Is this how the reds live every day?' asked Martin.

Sir Arthur shrugged his shoulders. 'No idea, but I guess they could if they wanted.'

'It's amazing. I think I'll have roast lamb with cherry and black pepper chutney in an oatmeal sandwich; the breakfast of kings. How do I pay?'

Sir Arthur put his hand in his pocket. 'My treat,' he said.

Beyond the market square was a sprawling mass of activity gathered into areas of similarity. They walked through an area where you could have anything repaired from clothes to technology. 'Isn't fixing a ruyi expensive and dangerous?' asked Martin.

'Not when the corporations aren't in control of the spare parts and so long as you know what you're doing.'

Next came the mundane, the essential everyday items. These were the alternatives to the corporation supermarkets that outliers couldn't use because of their refusal to accept a strata and hence points and Fluence.

Up the hill, just below the tree line, was a twenty-carriage, three-storey train. Martin pointed. 'What's that?'

'That, my friend, is where we're heading. That's where we'll find Dan and his crew. That's where we'll find out what Max is up to.'

'I'm not sure I really want to know,' said Martin as he slowed down.

Sir Arthur grabbed him by the elbow and dragged him forward. 'Yes, you do. Come on.'

They pressed on, past groups sitting on blankets with small fires cooking exotic-smelling foods of the most amazing array of colours. It was as if Bruce's basement had been multiplied hundredfold and distributed among the crowds. As they neared the top, he could see the carriages more clearly. They were divided into two halves. The left-hand side was divided again with queues at each of its three windows – Drugs, Documents and Data. Outside the other half was a veranda with tables, chairs and individual parasols. Waiters took orders and either ran down the hill to a stall or sidled over to the drugs counter, jumped the queue and returned with their narcotic parcel. Two men stepped out of the end of the far right-hand carriage. One was dressed in a black jacket decorated with strips of material and carried a blue mask. He ran down the hill with his back to them. The other, in beige chinos and a blue shirt, sat down at a table.

'That's Dan,' said Sir Arthur. 'Let's go and talk to him.'

'Up there in the carriages, they're reds aren't they?' asked Martin.

'Yes, mostly. Why do you ask?'

'Why are they at an outlier festival? Don't we need to be careful?'

'Let me do the talking. Otherwise, you're going to drop us right in it. We could get into some serious trouble; this has to be dealt with carefully.'

Out of the corner of Martin's eye, he spotted the blue mask running towards the morris dancing arena. 'Max?' he said under his breath.

TWENTY-TWO

'Dan.'

'Sir Arthur,' he replied and tilted his head towards Martin. 'One of your knights?'

Sir Arthur faked an exaggerated laugh. 'Ha ha. Very jocular.'

'I aim to please.'

Martin held out his hand. 'I'm Martin, Maxamillion's father.' Dan ignored him.

'Martin, we'll come to that later,' said Sir Arthur. 'So, Dan. How are you? Looks like a good festival?'

'It is good. I'm good. Are you good?'

'As good as I can be,' said Sir Arthur and grinned.

Dan waved his hand in the direction of his table. 'Take a seat.'

'Thanks,' they said in unison.

Dan took a deep breath, held it and then exhaled with a loud sigh. 'Contentment, that's what that is,' he said. 'Look at all that down there. It makes you glad to be alive.'

Martin put his elbow on the table and rested his chin in his hand. 'It's illegal though? Right?'

'Depends on whose laws you recognise, I guess.'

Sir Arthur coughed. 'Martin. Too many questions so early in the day. Dan, Martin here was one of the original hackers, but he's not so active now. You must forgive his impatience.'

'He's fine.' Dan paused. 'Martin. This, all of this, is a secret. Can you keep a secret?'

'Of course.'

'Even from your bosses at the Bureaucracy?'

'How did...'

'It doesn't matter how we know. It's enough that we do.'

'And what about the reds that are here?'

'Martin!' snapped Sir Arthur. 'Enough, please.'

Dan stood up. 'Let me show you inside. I'm sure we can trust you, Martin, can't we? Given everything we know about you.'

Martin didn't respond. As he got closer, he realised that the train had a semi-permanent wooden structure built around it. Dan gestured for him to go first. The door was made up of two parts – an outer door with an insect screen and an inner metal door. Inside it resembled an old wooden house more than a train. The floorboards were long polished planks and the wooden walls were rough. A small round table stood in the middle of the first room with an open book of photographs showing the story of the renovation. In its centre was a bowl. 'Drop your ruyi in there, please,' said Dan as he stepped past them and continued into the next compartment. They followed and as the door closed the room became dim. Two darkly covered antique high-backed sofas sat opposite each other. A portrait of Mao Tse-tung hung on the wall. Opposite hung an oil painting of a sea storm with a stuffed goose attached to the top as if it were flying out of the painting. A lamp from the original train cast a shadow of the bird across the sofa. The single female occupant – a woman in a dark green silk dressing gown with her hair piled high on her head – looked up from the leather-bound book she was reading. She glanced at them, nodded at Dan, picked up a metal pipe, inhaled and went back to her book.

The next carriage was brighter. It had skylights and windows that let in the faintly green sunshine. 'This is the kitchen and dining room. Although it's rarely used,' said Dan. To their right was a glass room full of people lying on sun loungers. 'We won't disturb them,' said Dan, noticing Martin's attention drifting that way.

He guided them through three more rooms covered in paintings, stuffed animals and brightly coloured rugs. Books were scattered everywhere. Silent and engrossed people sat in wooden armchairs. In each carriage, the occupants glanced up and acknowledged Dan before going back to what they were doing. A wooden spiral staircase rose from the corner of the third room and Martin stepped on to the bottom stair. 'No,' said Dan. 'Let's go to my office and talk.'

They worked their way back through the rooms until they came to the dividing door to the other half of the train. Dan picked up Martin's ruyi from the bowl and handed it to him and Sir Arthur retrieved his own. Dan stroked the door with the palm of his hand and it clicked open.

They stepped through and were met with a cacophony of shouting and laughing. It was such a sharp contrast that it made Martin feel sick with nervousness. 'This is where we trade,' said Dan.

Sir Arthur's whole body seemed to grow a few inches and he grinned with pure joy. 'This is more like it,' he said.

'I thought you'd like this,' said Dan. 'This is the real action. That's simply a glorified gentlemen's club next door, but the reds get off on it so who am I to refuse?'

'I presume they like the implicit danger? The feeling of being outside of the Strata Levels?'

'Seems so. Although the reality is that they're always above the Strata Levels, no matter where they are or what they're doing.'

'A strange mix, but it seems to be working for you.'

'So long as they pay, we'll keep giving them what they want. But don't be fooled, we can survive perfectly well without their patronage. We've opted out of their constructed world totally. They come here to pretend to opt out but only for a weekend or two.'

'And now we're in the outliers trading part of your operation? Am I right?'

'Yup. Here we trade the three most sought after things from the Strata World: pharmaceutical drugs, documentation to operate within the Strata World and black-market data which the hackers hunt and gather to trade with each other to build wider, deeper and more sophisticated datasets. It's those datasets we trade with the reds; we help them control their world and they help us live outside of it.'

As they passed through each carriage, Dan stopped for a few minutes and talked to the traders. Martin had heard about these festivals; in fact he was convinced that he'd been at the first one, which was now legendary. It had been a small gathering of hackers swapping bits and pieces of illegal code.

'My office is on the middle floor,' said Dan as he stepped on to an identical spiral staircase to the one they'd not been allowed to climb. 'Let's talk.'

His office stretched the entire length of the train. The roof and the walls were one-way mirrors so he could see out but nobody could see in. It was open plan, but divided into defined areas. A cylindrical pillar through which the other staircase ran was covered in mediaeval tapestries. At the far end was a dark oak hot tub with steam rising from the surface. A faint smell of rubber, custard and jasmine wafted across the room. A large four poster bed with old English protest songs woven into its drapes stood proudly next to the tub. An untidy, heavily used kitchen came next, a sunken seated area surrounded by StrataScreens after that and finally, a round table with twelve high-back chairs. 'That's why I have a soft spot for Sir Arthur, a knight of the realm,' said Dan as he touched the table. He laughed to himself. 'Shall we talk?'

Sir Arthur sat down. 'He was the King, not a knight.'

'Whatever,' said Dan.

'What do you know about Max?' asked Martin with an undercurrent of accusation in his voice.

Sir Arthur turned sharply. 'Martin, please.' He turned back to Dan. 'We're keen to find out what Martin's son is up to and I think you have some dealings with him.'

'Think?' said Martin under his breath.

Sir Arthur carried on. 'We're worried about him.'

'Why?' asked Dan.

'He's young and may be in over his head.'

'I've come across him.'

'At last!' said Martin.

Dan leant across the table to Sir Arthur. 'Does *he* have to be here?'

Sir Arthur nodded, but with an apologetic look.

'Very well,' said Dan. 'I think our paths have crossed.'

'Can you remember where or when?'

'Isn't he the guy that's at the forefront of this morris dancing craze?'

'He certainly has something to do with it. Is that the only thing you know about him?'

'What's with the twenty questions?'

'Like I said, we're worried.'

'Should I be worried? Maybe I should ban him.'

'No need for that. It's just a father's worry, not yours.'

'Then come clean. You know more than you're letting on. You wouldn't bother me unless it was more serious than an errant son playing at being the dance master.'

'Okay. This must be kept quiet. Only between us?'

Dan gave them a look which managed to silently convey that he was offended they thought there was any possibility he would break a confidence.

Sir Arthur pursed his lips and then smiled. 'I have some footage of you coming out of a club one morning with Max. I also have footage of you and your friends outside the house of Martin's boss, who then disappeared. Coincidence?'

'Must be.'

'C'mon, Dan. Within these walls.'

Dan stood up and ran his fingers along the edge of the table as he slowly walked around it. Sir Arthur and Martin watched and said nothing. Halfway round, he twisted a chair to face outwards and sat down, resting his chin on its back. 'Samantha? Right?'

'Sam, that's right,' said Martin.

Dan stared at the ceiling, seemingly lost in thought. 'Aren't those gargoyles fantastic?'

'Sure,' said Sir Arthur. 'And Samantha? Max?'

Dan stared at Martin and then at Sir Arthur. 'Okay, let's talk. Yes, we were asked to find Samantha, but not by Max.'

Martin jumped up. 'For fuck's sake.'

Dan snorted. 'The Fool on the Hill – appropriate. Sit down, please.'

Martin sat back in his chair.

'As I said, we were asked to locate her, which we did. Max had no involvement.'

'And what about that old man that disappeared after I'd visited him? The description his neighbours gave me fitted you perfectly.'

Dan chuckled. 'That's better, Mr Fool. Now you're getting somewhere. We did help him move to a better place.'

'A better place?'

Dan smiled.

'Why?' asked Martin.

'Honestly?'

'Yes.'

'Max asked us to. He felt that you'd made such a huge error in judgement that although the Bureaucracy had overturned your decision there would still be some major implications for your career. He wanted to move the story on and away from you.'

'How the hell did he know what I'd been up to?'

'He asked us to keep an eye on you.'

Martin put his head in his hands. 'Bollocks.'

'What? I didn't catch that,' said Dan.

'Nothing,' he replied.

Sir Arthur patted Martin on the back. 'Why did he ask you to keep an eye on his dad?'

'He wouldn't say.'

'And you do everything he asks?'

'No, but I did owe him a couple of favours and there seemed to be no harm in it.'

Sir Arthur grinned. 'Will you do anything I ask for?'

'Of course not.'

'Maybe you should reconsider that answer, young man.'

Dan pushed his chair to one side. 'What, old man?'

'Don't forget how long and extensive my memory is.'

'Is that a threat?'

'Yes.'

Silence filled the room. Martin fidgeted. Sir Arthur adopted the pose of a monk at prayer with his hands on the table, his fingers intertwined and his body relaxed. Dan was rigid.

No one spoke.

Slowly, Sir Arthur unravelled his fingers and pointed at Dan. 'Anything else you want to share with us?'

'Not really.'

'Dan. Don't make me...'

'Can you guarantee this won't get back to Max? Not even from him,' he said, glancing at Martin.

'Agreed. Martin?'

'Yeah. Agreed.'

'Okay, there is one other thing. We've been assisting Max in some blackmail.'

'You've been what?' shouted Martin.

'Calm down,' said Dan in a mock soothing voice.

'Fuck you,' he muttered.

Sir Arthur interrupted. 'Explain.'

'Max wanted to freak someone out so he asked us to help.'

'Who?' said Sir Arthur.

'Is that important?'

'Depends. Tell me and I'll let you know.'

Dan turned his attention to Martin. 'His colleague, Amber Walgace.'

Martin gulped.

'His colleague? Why? What's the connection? What's he up to?'

'Dunno. He knew some things about her and asked us to set up the tech to hack into her stuff so he could blackmail her.'

'You must have some idea what he's doing?'

'None at all. To be honest, it's best if I don't. Max is a good guy, I trust him.'

Martin roared with laughter. 'You what?'

'I trust him and so should you.'

'Not much chance of that.'

'Whatever,' said Dan. He put his hand on Martin's arm and squeezed hard. 'Don't forget. This is just between us.'

'I guarantee it,' said Sir Arthur. 'Martin, let's go. We're done here.'

TWENTY-THREE

Amber was standing by the window. 'Unbelievable.'

'What?' asked Lord Balfour.

'I've seen someone I work with.'

'Why is that strange?'

'Balfy. Don't be so stupid. We're at an outlier festival and I've seen someone from the Bureaucracy.'

'You're here. You're from the Bureaucracy.'

'Sure, but I'm on this exclusive top floor. Although I think he may have been with that guy we met from the floor below.'

'Dan?'

'Yeah.'

'Now that is interesting. Who was it?'

'Martin Brown.'

'The Fool.'

Amber smirked. 'You could call him that. Do you know him?' she asked with a rising pitch to her voice. 'Why would you know him?'

'I know everything and everyone.' He grabbed her hand and tried to pull her towards him.

'Oh, Balfy. I said no, didn't I?'

'I apologise, my beautiful green Amber.'

'And so you should.' She gave him a quick kiss on the lips and pinched his bum. 'I'm married.'

'Happily?'

'So. Remind me why we came here.'

'To get you the promotion you deserve.'

'And you get what you want?'

'Of course. I always get what I want.'

He moved towards the bedroom and tried to take her with him.

She resisted, but the dusty smell of the old oak panels, the sense of history and power and the sheer luxury of the surroundings made it difficult. The large bed covered in off-white fake fur and the jet-black sheepskin rugs on the wooden floor promised a sumptuous setting for the passion he'd proposed as they'd swum around the pool. Beside the low bed was a small hand-carved table with legs in the shape of ruyi. On it was a red hookah pipe. 'Can I tempt you?' he asked.

'Always. But never successfully.' She turned him around to face the rest of the room. There were four large wing-back armchairs each covered in a different tartan and placed symmetrically around a glass-topped table with a church candle at either end. To the side of the fireplace was a taller semi-circular table with antlers wrapped around its single leg to help balance it against the wall. At the far end a grand piano was framed by windows that ran from the floor to the ceiling. Beyond, Amber could see a steel balcony with hammocks gently swinging in the breeze. In the centre of the ceiling, above the glass-topped table, was an amazing chandelier made from six sets of antlers knotted together with leather straps. Several animal skins were scattered across the floor in sharp contrast to the reflected shine of the highly polished floorboards. It was almost too much of a cliché to be real.

He kept quiet while she took it all in. 'The ultimate in glamp-ing?'

'Absolutely.' She sat down on the edge of the bed and fiddled with the hookah.

He smiled. 'Sure I can't tempt you?'

She put it down quickly and stood up. 'Very funny. Let's talk.' She walked over to the armchairs and sat down – carefully; it had been fun to be without knickers the night before, but in the cold light of day being dressed in a posh frock with no underwear was disconcerting.

He sauntered over to join her. 'Let's talk.'

'Please.'

'I can't tell you much because it's not my area of expertise—'

She interrupted. 'What is your speciality then?'

'Hospitality.'

'Escort,' she said and laughed.

'That's cruel…'

'Sorry. Only kidding. You're a very good host.'

'I'd like you to meet our data expert. She can explain what we're after.'

'Okay.'

He pressed a pad on the arm of the chair and part of the floor slid back to reveal a spiral staircase. A pale-skinned woman appeared. She was wearing a white t-shirt with blue hoops and a pair of battered jeans tucked into biker boots. Amber couldn't take her eyes off the antenna that looped up from behind and across the top of her head. The woman touched it. 'Part of my built-in ruyi,' she said. 'Linked to these.' She touched the hearing aids which sat discreetly inside each ear. 'They pick up the images, the sound and the text that's travelling the airwaves and translate it directly into my brain.'

Amber stared even harder and said nothing.

'Impressive?'

'Yeah.'

The woman opened the palm of her hand to reveal a screen implant. 'Normally I only have to think of the response and it's sent, but when that doesn't work I use this.'

'She can intercept any non-secured transmission. Any ruyi conversation that's passing through her space,' said Lord Balfour.

Amber clasped the arm of her chair. 'Wow.' She looked from Balfy to the woman and back again. 'Wow, and is the antenna yellow for a reason?'

'Of course. That's my Strata Level, but with the help of Lord Balfour I'm expecting to rise quickly.'

Amber fixed her attention on Balfy. 'You want to do this to me? Is that why I'm here?'

He laughed. 'No. No. No. Mildred's also our data expert. That's why she's here.'

Amber relaxed.

'Mildred. Can you explain the background to Amber, please.'

She picked up a stool and hurried across the room, slipping slightly on one of the animal skins. 'Fucking poncey room,' she said under her breath. She slammed the stool down next to Amber. 'How bright is she?'

Lord Balfour chuckled. 'Bright enough.'

Amber straightened her back. 'Don't let these fool you,' she said, waving her hand up and down her party clothes.

'Fine,' said Mildred. 'The key things to remember about good data is that it needs to be fresh and generally the people trying to hack it are smarter than the ones trying to protect it. If you can access large amounts of data, or better still own it, the leverage you have against society is massive. If you can then create specific small datasets you can identify individuals and then you've got them cornered for whatever purpose you like—'

Lord Balfour interrupted. 'To control the corporations and spot talented individuals, like Mildred here.'

'I don't understand why you're working with the outliers.'

'Amber, all will become clear. But you're right to ask. We do have different agendas. Mildred, carry on.'

'There's always a tension about who owns the data; the law isn't clear, although the way it's interpreted will always favour the corporations. There's an old saying that possession is nine tenths of the law and that's such a perfect rule of thumb for data. The outliers are wholeheartedly behind shifting the paradigm so that individuals store their own data, even the centralised data like StrataPoints. Ideologically the reds want that too, but they also recognise the need to make sure that all the data is still available to them so they can maintain their upper hand.

'The outliers believe that if someone has a dataset that's larger than their own individual set or have done some analysis it should be shared; if someone has it, everyone should have it. The implicit danger is that data collected for one reason and repurposed for another can be misleading at best and extremely dangerous at worst – mistakes are bound to happen. Their solution is to punish these mistakes with consequences of a similar scale to the impact on the victim; if someone cocks up and you lose all your points then so should they.' Mildred turned towards Lord Balfour. 'Is that enough background?'

'Don't forget that we include passive data as well.'

'What's that?' asked Amber.

Mildred replied, 'It's the data that's captured as you go about your daily business and without you knowing.'

'Like what?'

'Mostly camera recognition of your face, your body signature – heat, pulse and the like. In some locations it even records your conversations. The most sophisticated can interpret your underlying feelings, desires and unspoken responses using your body language and with a large enough dataset it can truly see into people's minds and souls.'

'And manipulate them accordingly...' said Lord Balfour, trailing off towards the end of the sentence.

'Okay. I get all of that. What I still don't get is why you're interested in me and what you want.'

'Maybe now would be as good a time as any?' asked Mildred.

'Sure,' said Lord Balfour. 'As I mentioned, we need to control the corporations and we're not convinced they're sharing all of their data with us. Actually, we're convinced they're not. If you do what we ask and tap into the Bureaucracy then we'll have our own copy. Information is power and all that.'

'Knowledge and understanding that comes from information,' said Mildred.

'I stand corrected. Anyway, my point is that we've spotted that you're a bright, ambitious person who's already a tad corrupt.'

Amber looked shocked. 'Corrupt?'

Mildred shifted her stool slightly. 'Yes. Corrupt. Do you deny that you're already stealing data? You're being blackmailed for goodness' sake.'

'Piss off.'

'Very grown up.'

'Says the woman with the antenna sticking out of her head.'

'Stop it, you two. Amber, don't get defensive. It's not a crime. Well, it is but we're not worried about it. And Mildred, more emotional intelligence please.'

'Okay,' they both said at the same time.

'The point is that we need more data so we can steer the ship in the right direction and you're in the perfect position to help.'

'If I do…would you crunch my data so I can figure out how to get to yellow and then orange?'

'We could…but wouldn't it be better if we just moved you?'

'You can do that?'

Mildred and Lord Balfour glanced at each other. 'Of course,' he said, as if it was the most natural thing in the world.

'And you'd only want me to tap into some data for you?'

'We'd need some proof that you can be trusted, that you wouldn't try any funny business.'

'Funny business?'

'You know. Like trying to blackmail me, leaking stories to the corporation press – that sort of stuff.'

'I wouldn't, but how can I prove it?'

'We have some ideas. First though, let's have that smoke.'

'Not for me, thanks,' said Amber.

Balfy banged his pocket-watch against her chain-mail glove. 'Join in.'

There seemed to be no option so she followed them over to the bedroom and sat on one of the sheepskins. Balfy loaded up the bowl of the pipe with an organic substance. 'Smoking through the highest quality vodka – it's the only way to start the day,' he said as he poured a clear liquid into the base. He lit it with a chrome lighter and the air filled with the smell of burning cannabis and lighter fuel.

Amber sniffed. 'Reminds me of my mum's cigarettes.'

Balfy passed her the hose and lay back on the bed. She inhaled, coughed, and inhaled again. The room started to spin a little. Mildred leant over and took the pipe. Amber lay on her back and studied the wooden ceiling. It was intricate and beautiful. She focussed on one of the panels. It had six horizontal sections with the grain of the wood flowing in alternating directions, left to right, right to left, and so on. At the edge of the panel was a chamfered beam with a swirly grain that wouldn't stay still. The flow of the wood prompted thoughts about the fact that she and Terence had come from opposite directions. The beam surrounding the panels reminded her of the fence Terence had built to trap her. The fence of convention, of apathy and of mediocrity.

A spider's web filled one of the corners. Its creator sat motionless, waiting for breakfast. Doesn't that sum up my life perfectly, she thought. Feeding off the mistakes of others.

The warmth and softness of the rug made her feel as if she were floating on a cloud. Her skirt felt uncomfortable. She bent her legs so her knees were in the air and hitched it up. Balfy passed her the hookah. His eyes wandered. With a lazy grin and blatant lechery he made sure she knew he could see up her skirt.

'For fuck's sake,' said Mildred.

'What?' he said.

'What?' said Amber.

'We need her to prove her loyalty,' said Mildred.

'*I* need her to prove her loyalty. It's not really any of your business, is it?'

'No. Sorry.'

'Amber. Mildred's right. We do need you to prove yourself.'

'How?'

'We'll support you if you do three tiny things for us.'

'Sure – what are they?'

'Steal the data…'

'No worries.'

'Have sex with one of your clients.'

'What?'

'We'll tell you who.'

'What?'

'And leave Terence behind.'

'What?'

'Get a grip,' snapped Mildred.

'What?'

Balfy moved his gaze to her face. 'Amber. Are you being really stupid or are you completely wasted?'

'Both,' said Mildred.

'You heard what I said. Three little things to fulfil your life ambitions. How easy is that?'

She pulled her skirt down and sat up. 'What the fuck are you talking about?'

TWENTY-FOUR

Max stood in the foyer of the building where they developed enhancements; Dan had tipped him off that there was good Fluence to be made if you were prepared to take part in a trial.

'Proof of identity, please.'

Max pressed his fingers and thumbs against the wall. The violet-uniformed security guard clicked a small sphere in the palm of his hand.

'What's that?' asked Max.

'Scans your body signature, sir. So the building can recognise you and let you move about freely.'

'Is that really necessary?'

'Of course. BeWellCorp doesn't inconvenience you unless it has to.'

'Okay.'

'Thank you, sir. Could you press each eye against this, please. Left first and then right.'

Max rested his left eye against an eyepiece attached to the guard's charta. And then his right eye.

'Thank you. Lastly, some DNA.' He passed Max a swab.

Max swabbed the inside of his cheek and passed it back. 'All yours. Do I pass for human then?'

'Very funny, sir. It's simply a precaution against commercial espionage. You're cleared.'

'Phew. You had me worried,' said Max as he wiped his hand across his brow.

The guard smiled. 'Through there and to your left, sir. Follow the yellow line.'

The smell of disinfectant, of bleach and of stale air that was slightly too warm reminded Max that this was a clinical establishment. The doors opened automatically as he wound his way along the route laid out for him by tiny pinprick lights in the floor.

'Welcome,' said a woman who walked awkwardly towards him.

She could do with some enhancement, thought Max. He smiled.

'I'm Susan, Doctor Bravn. Take a seat and I'll fetch you the information and consent forms.' She disappeared for a few minutes and then returned with a charta. 'Please read this and then when you're ready, thumbprint the consent form. If you have any questions, I'm here to help.' She hobbled back to her chair. As she sat down she uttered an inelegant groan that echoed around the bare room.

'It says here that you are going to use a variety of methods. Can you tell me what they are?'

'Of course. We'll use some biotech, some brain training and some pills.'

'Do I have to do all three?'

'Yes. If you want to get paid.'

'That's my other question. How do I get paid?'

'At the end.'

'No. What I mean is, what will you pay me with?'

'You're off-grid?'

'Not exactly, but it helps to be paid under the radar. If you know what I mean.'

'We can use AltFlu if you like. Are you part of that blockchain?'

'Yes, that's perfect. How risky do you think the trial is?'

'Perfectly safe. Are you ready for the screening examination?'

'Yeah. Fire away.'

'If you could strip and step into the scanner.'

He hesitated for a second and then walked boldly to a booth that looked remarkably like a shower cubicle. He took his clothes off, left them in an untidy pile on the floor and stepped inside. A padded seat with a bar across the front was at the back of the cubicle. It was similar to the old-fashioned fairground rides that spun you round and round and that could still be found at the outlier festivals.

'All tucked in nicely?' called Doctor Bravn.

He pulled the bar into place. 'Yes, thanks.' A loud staccato alarm filled the tiny space. Each burst of sound accentuated the slight panic he was experiencing. 'How long does this go on?' he shouted.

'Five minutes,' she shouted back. 'We'll flash some images on the walls. You don't need to do anything except look at them. Okay?'

Images streamed in front of him in time with the rhythm of the alarm. Images of war, of children, of people in pain and of people laughing. Occasionally the cubicle was bathed in one of the colours of a Strata. A live feed of different people's StrataInfo appeared sporadically. Segments of film from the violet, indigo, blue and green areas of London were woven into the montage. His emotions were on a roller-coaster ride. He felt despair, he felt elation and he felt nothing. He felt joy, he felt sadness and he felt anger. He felt overwhelmed, he felt distant and he felt contempt. He felt envy, he felt hate and he felt confusion.

The images and the noise stopped. The cubicle doors opened. 'Okay?' asked Doctor Bravn.

Max stumbled out. 'Yeah. Probably. I better get paid a decent amount for this.'

'You will. And you'll be helping change the moral fibre of the human race.'

He snorted. 'You really believe that, don't you?'

'Yes, I do. Don't you?'

'A little, I guess.'

She gave him a wristband. 'Wear this. It'll continue to monitor you.'

'All the time?'

'Yes. For the next three thousand minutes. That's not a problem is it?'

'Nope.' He took the device, wrapped it around his wrist and snapped it shut. 'Am I ready for the outside world then?'

She handed him the charta. 'Swipe this and you can go.'

His ruyi buzzed. It was a message from one of his old flames. 'We're nearby. Fancy a quick slug of liquid enhancement?' He laughed out loud. 'Ruyi: reply to Nova. Perfect timing, I'd love to. It seems to be enhancement day today.' He dressed in a hurry, waved goodbye to the doctor and jogged out of the building.

'Hiya, lover,' called Nova from the other side of the road. She was still as sultry as ever, still had the same lazy posture and still wore the same half-sized top hat covered in Victorian brooches with a peacock feather sticking out of the top. Her blonde hair with its purple streaks framed her angular face and she'd painted large dark bags under her big almond shaped eyes. Nova and Max had been on and off lovers for six months when they were in their last year of school and had become close friends since. Amaia was with her. His affair with her had not been as serious or as long, but it had been more vibrant and edgy. He was pleased to see them both.

'Hiya,' he called back. 'How about a cocktail in there?' he said, pointing at an underground bar that had once been a Victorian toilet.

They sat at the bar and ordered their drinks. 'What's that?' asked Amaia.

'Yeah, what's that?' Nova twisted the wristband and brushed his wrist with her fingers.

'Girls…'

'Boy…answer the question,' said Amaia. She grinned.

'It's part of a medical trial.'

Nova let go of the wristband. 'A medical trial for what, exactly?'

'To increase empathy. To see if it's possible to change the way someone reacts to a situation.'

'What are they trialling then?'

'A mixture of things. Some biotech implants, I think. Some neuroscience stuff to change your brain patterns. Oh, and I get pills as well.'

'What if you empathise with the wrong people?'

'They told me it's targeted towards a certain type. A good type.'

'How?'

'I'm not sure.'

'You must be mad.'

'Sounds kinda cool to me,' said Amaia.

'Thank you,' he said, tilting his cocktail in her direction.

Nova sipped her Espresso Martini, carefully placed it back on the bar and put her left hand in Max's right hand and her right in Amaia's left. 'I read an SMFeed about this the other day. They were saying that if you accept it's a lack of empathy that causes people to do bad things and they can't control what they do, then you can't reward or punish behaviour. If you accept we're not in control of what we do then everyone would stop trying to be good; they have the ready-made excuse that it's just the way they're made.'

Max shifted his hand. 'I read that as well. Didn't it go on to say that it undermined the notion of free will?'

'Yeah. And that free will is an illusion anyway.'

'It also said that if we find a way of fixing a lack of empathy then it increases our free will because once you're corrected you no longer have the excuse of not being able to stop yourself.'

'That's right. Once you're normalised and have the same empathy levels as everyone else you really can do what you truly want. You have free will.'

'And you're responsible for your actions.'

'Are they going to give you Oxytocin?' asked Amaia.

'Probably.'

'Wow, that's cool. Can I have some?'

Max stroked Nova's hand. 'Maybe the three of us—'

Nova interrupted. 'We said never again.'

'True… But…' said Amaia with a twinkle in her eye.

'No,' said Nova.

Max finished his drink. 'Guys. I gotta skedaddle. My train home is leaving soon. Let's catch up after Pay Day?' He looked over his shoulder as he left the bar. They were holding hands and watching him leave. He waved.

He stepped into the house and was about to slam the door behind him when he heard his mother. 'Well, Martin, it bloody well matters to me.'

He could smell the tiny particles of roasting meat and boiling vegetables drifting through the kitchen door and filling the house like an invisible culinary fog. The screech of grunge folk music flowed down from Becka's room, intermingling with the aroma of supper. There were times when he liked his family and his family home and this was one of them. The cocktails had helped of course and it was possible the clinic had given him something that also helped. It wasn't important to him why he was in such a good mood, it was enough that he was.

'Well, Martin, what have you got to say for yourself?'

'I didn't plan to be out all night.'

'And then all day as well?'

'No. I didn't plan that either.'

'Well, Martin, that makes me feel a lot better. Don't you get it? I was worried and Becka was frantic. She was convinced you'd been hurt.'

'That's below the belt. Bringing the kids into it.'

'They're already in it, you stupid man. They're as worried about Pay Day as we are.'

'Jenny. Max is an adult and he's not worried about my Pay Day.'

'He is.'

'I really don't think he is, you know.'

'What makes you so sure?'

Max moved a little closer because their voices were getting quieter.

'I just think we've raised an independent, self-sufficient young man. There's more to that boy than meets the eye.'

'Will you leave him alone then? Will you stop prodding and poking and needling him?'

'I'll try.'

'Good, but don't think that by distracting me I've forgotten that you stayed out all night and then all day. With only a stupid message from those degenerates to explain where you were. Although how they thought a message that said "He won't be home tonight" was of any help I don't know.'

'I knew you'd be upset…'

'You know you're pathetic, don't you?'

'I…'

'What, Martin? You're sorry? You're going to make it up to me? You're a fucking waste of space?'

Max was feeling increasingly agitated by the way his mum was treating his dad. He'd only stayed out for a night – where was the harm in that? And so what if his old mates were a little on the fringes; at least it made him more interesting than a Monday to Friday Strata Straight.

Jenny started again. 'You make everything so fragile. This house, this home, this family. Us.'

'Is that really what you think? Don't you see me going to that job every day? Worrying about points? Worrying about Pay Day? Worrying about the kids?'

'Becka.'

'Both.'

'Honestly?'

'Honestly.'

'No. I don't.'

'Well, I do. I worry night and day.'

'No, you don't. If you did, you'd be different.'

Max's feelings for his dad were welling up. He slammed into the kitchen. 'What the…' He stopped. They were holding hands and tears were trickling down both of their faces. They looked at him and he was sure they squeezed each other's hands before letting go.

'Max,' said Jenny.

'Mum. Dad.'

'What's that thing on your wrist?' said Martin.

'Eh? Oh, this,' he said, touching the wristband.

'Yes, that.'

'It's medical research.'

'It's what?'

'I'm part of a research programme.'

'Why?' asked Jenny. 'Are you okay? What's wrong?'

'Nothing's wrong, Mum. I get paid and it helps towards the greater good.'

Martin stepped a little closer. 'Prostitute.'

'Martin. Stop.'

'Dad?'

'You heard. Selling your body to the corporations.'

'Martin. Apologise.'

Martin grabbed the wristband. 'It's obscene.'

All the warmth for his dad evaporated and turned to frustration and anger. He pulled away. 'It's obscene is it? And yet every day you suppress yourself. You put on your office uniform, you neutralise any sense of self and you go to that filthy factory of misery. That's obscene.'

Martin exhaled. 'I'm going to check on my points. Remember those? Remember how your education was paid for?' He stomped up the stairs.

Max and Jenny sat at the table fiddling idly with the crockery.

Martin came back down the stairs slowly.

Jenny looked up. 'What?'

'Only one point before I drop to blue.'

Silence; no one spoke.

TWENTY-FIVE

Amber stepped on to the platform at Deptford Bridge Station and self-consciously straightened her skirt. She was sure that everyone was staring, knowing that she'd been out all night; on the train she'd seen people out of the corner of her eye nudging each other and averting their eyes immediately as she turned her gaze on them.

The drugs were wearing off, but there was still a lingering sense of otherness, a sense that she was slightly askew from the rest of the early Sunday evening crowd. A teenage lad snapped her photo and banged his ruyi with his mate's, sending the image soaring out across the world.

She slowed down as she approached her house. She was thrown by how unchanged it was. Her whole being was in turmoil and yet here she was at her front door, a door that was exactly the same as when she'd left it. How could the world be unaltered?

She pressed the lock and the door clicked. The familiar smell of fresh flowers greeted her in the hallway. Terence's dirty football socks were peeping out of his bag. 'Hi, babe, I'm home,' she shouted.

'Hi. I'm up here,' he called from the lounge.

She took off her shoes and holding them in her hand she took each step of the stairs slowly, eking out every last second of her adventure.

She could hear the StrataScreen streaming one of his favourite football matches. The one where he'd scored the winning goal. This was his comforter. He would play it over and over again if he was feeling depressed or thoughtful – neither of which he found easy to cope with.

She stopped on the last step and waited for the goal; she knew each minute of the match by heart.

'Go on, my man. Go on...' he whispered. 'Yay! Nice one,' he shouted as the ball rocketed past the keeper and into the back of the net. 'Amber,' he yelled.

She steadied herself against the wall. 'Coming.'

'I love you,' he shouted.

She stopped, not daring to breathe.

'Hey? Honey?'

She heard the clink of a glass being set down on the table.

'Amber?'

'Yeah. Here,' she said as she walked in. 'You're keen.' She laughed, but it was a hollow laugh.

'Nice dress. Bit crumpled.'

She dropped her shoes on to the floor and perched on the corner of the sofa. 'Hi. How was football?'

'It was good. Better than lunch with Mum and Dad.'

She flinched.

'Where were you? They kept asking and I couldn't answer.'

'Terence...'

'You don't need to tell me. I've been really worried though. What happened?'

'Terence...'

'No. I promised myself I wouldn't ask.' He stretched across the sofa towards her and she moved a little closer, holding out her hand for his.

They touched and he tugged gently, pulling her closer still. 'I know I was a pig,' he said.

'Terence...'

'No. Let me finish.' He kissed the tips of his fingers and touched the bridge of her nose. 'I'm really sorry I didn't take this blackmail more seriously. I was telling Mum—'

'You told your mum?'

'I was explaining why you weren't there. I had to tell them something.'

'Why?'

'Look. Amber. I was freaking out about where you were, what

might have happened to you. I thought you'd been kidnapped. Or that you'd left me.'

'I can't believe you told your mum.'

'I'm sorry.'

'Sorry for being an unfeeling arse or sorry for telling your mum I was being blackmailed?'

'Both.'

'You didn't tell her what it was about, did you?'

'No. Not exactly. I said you'd nicked something from work and someone had found out. I was missing you so much I couldn't keep it to myself.'

She kissed the tips of her fingers and touched the top of his bald head, returning the intimate gesture.

'Come here,' he said patting the sofa. She didn't move. 'Please?' She didn't move. 'Pretty please?'

She moved across the sofa, he put his arm around her and she cuddled up beside him. 'We've got a lot to talk about,' she said.

'I said I'm sorry.'

'I know, but we have to talk about Pay Day.'

'How about we cook first? I think the cleaner has left us a mix.'

'Terry…'

'Yes…' He waited nervously; this was the first time she'd ever called him Terry.

'Can we… Can we start from scratch?'

'How do you mean?' he said, failing to hide his anxiety.

'You know…buy the ingredients and mix them ourselves.'

He let out a nervous giggle. 'Of course.'

'Thank you,' she whispered.

'Coffee cake?'

'Yum. Shall I get the recipe book?'

'I'll get it. You rest,' he said. 'Would you like a drink?' he asked as he left the room.

'Some wine would be nice.'

A few minutes later he was back with a bottle covered in drops of condensation, a stainless steel wine bucket half full of ice and the old recipe book. He poured two glasses, handed one to Amber and raised the other. 'To us.'

'To the future,' she said, unable to look him in the eyes.

He flipped through the pages until he came to the recipe he was looking for. 'Wow, this looks a bit complicated. Do they even sell all this stuff?'

'What stuff?'

'We need self-raising flour, salt, butter, caster sugar, eggs and coffee. Why don't we just get a mix? It'd be a lot easier.'

'Don't you even want to see if we can make a cake from basics? Come on, we need to push ourselves. Don't you want to try new things?'

There was a pause. 'Of course,' he said. 'Let's do it.'

'Give it here then,' she said, pointing at the book. 'Who do you think is most likely to sell this sort of stuff?'

'Good question. I never did this as a kid, did you?'

'No.'

'Probably a yellow or even an orange thing. They'd get their cooks to make old-fashioned cakes, I guess. Maybe we won't be able to do it after all?'

'Don't give in so easily. I've set my mind to it now. Ruyi: order the following from OrangeNet for immediate delivery.' She scanned the ruyi across the recipe.

'You can't do that.'

'Why not?'

'That's for orange strata only.'

'Says who?'

'Err...everyone.'

'Live a little, my timid husband.' She stroked his head.

'Very funny. This is hardly the high life though is it?'

Amber rested her hand on his chest. 'It's symbolic. And important to me right now.' She snuggled in tighter and ran her fingers across his shirt. 'Terry...do you like me calling you Terry?'

'It's a bit strange coming from you, but I think so. Amber, what's changed?'

'StrataScreen: Amber Walgace,' she said.

Terence shifted her hand. 'I wish you'd use Huddson.'

'Not now. Don't spoil things.' She put her hand back to where it had been, undid one of his buttons and then another. She let out a yelp of excitement. 'Terry, look at my points! I'm in yellow!' She put his hand on top of hers. 'Don't you see? We're on our way up.'

'Babe. You're on your way up, not me.'

'You can come with me if you want. I'm sure to get more before the week's out. We can share. How many have you got?'

'Last time I looked I was about middle.'

'Look, if we add them together we've just enough for both of us to get in.'

He smiled and touched her nose. Her ruyi buzzed, letting her know the delivery had arrived. She unravelled herself. 'Let's bake,' she said and punched him playfully on the leg.

'Okay. Can I mix?'

'Depends how good you are at it.'

They raced each other down to the kitchen, picking up the delivery on the way. They tore open the box and spread the contents across the table: a dozen self-greasing bun tins; one hundred grams of self-raising flour; a small twist of salt; a hundred grams of butter; a hundred grams of sugar; two eggs; and a coffee-tube. Terence propped the book up against the wall and turned the oven to one hundred and eighty degrees.

'What about the CakeEase?' asked Amber.

'If we're gonna do it, let's do it properly. Empty the flour and salt into this bowl.'

She grabbed the bowl from him and tore open the flour bag. Clouds of white dust mushroomed into the air. She laughed. He laughed. She wiped her finger in the settled dust and drew a white line on his nose. He retaliated by taking a nick of butter and smearing it across her shoulder. 'Stop! Stop!' she screamed. 'I'll have to shower if you carry on like that.'

'Good,' he said and winked.

She ran her dusty finger down the page of the recipe. 'It says we have to cream the butter with the sugar until it's light and fluffy. Any idea what that means?'

'None. Charta: show me what creaming butter means.' The charta asked if they wanted to include adult material. 'Fantastic, it thinks we're being naughty,' he said.

A video started – a woman was cutting butter into cubes, putting them into a bowl and then pouring the sugar over them. With the back of a wooden spoon she pressed hard on to the butter and sugar, mixing it together. 'Make it nice and fluffy,' she said. 'You can't over cream it.'

Amber and Terence giggled. 'Do we have a wooden spoon?' she asked.

He slid open a drawer that neither of them had ever looked inside. Neatly laid out were rows of wooden spoons and silicone spatulas. He smacked Amber on the bum with a spoon.

She tried to tickle him, but he moved out of the way. He started to work on the butter and sugar, pushing and pressing the mixture against the sides of the bowl. 'Here, let me,' she said, making a grab for the spoon. After a few seconds she handed it back. 'Men's work,' she said.

'Can you make the coffee while I do the mixing?'

'Sure.' She took the coffee-tube, twisted and waited. He added the eggs to the mixture, beat them vigorously with the spoon and then poured in the coffee. Finally, he stirred in the flour and salt. 'Can I scoop it into the tins?' she asked.

'Of course,' he said and kissed her on the tip of her nose.

She took the wooden spoon and filled each of the tins carefully. 'There's some left. What do we do with that?' He dipped his finger into the bowl, collected some of the mix and popped it into her mouth. 'Is it safe?' she asked.

'Depends what you want to be safe from.'

'Getting ill, silly. What did you think I meant?'

'Well, I saw it on a movie once and it led to all sorts of interesting things.'

'Terry!'

'Amber!'

'Terry!'

'Amber. Don't pretend you're so innocent.'

'But I am.'

'Quick, get the buns in the oven.'

It wasn't long before the warm smell of baking filled the kitchen. They sat in silence, drinking the rest of the coffee and enjoying their natural companionship.

The timer pinged and the oven door opened automatically. A cloud of hot sticky air escaped, filling the room with the cooking smells. 'Perfect,' he said as he moved the cakes to the cooling rack. 'Coffee cakes for madam?'

'In bed?'

'If that's your desire.'

She followed him up the stairs and into the bedroom.

TWENTY-SIX

t was midnight. Martin and Jenny were still sitting at the dining room table. Max had left and Becka was upstairs playing music. Martin was fiddling with his ruyi, scrolling through other people's SMFeeds, people he didn't even know. Jenny was pretending to organise the food for the week ahead. Occasionally one of them would make a comment on what they were reading or planning, but they met each other with silence.

Martin was thinking about his situation. He was on the verge of dropping a Strata Level, which almost certainly meant losing the house and most probably Jenny. Becka would be devastated and lose all respect for him. And then there was Max. What was Max really up to? Blackmailing Amber, sneaking around and prying into Martin's private life. Maybe a shock to the system was what they all needed, but he couldn't bear the thought of losing any one of them, let alone all three.

The StrataScreen switched itself on and a disembodied voice spoke. 'Attention please. This announcement is so critical that the five corporations have agreed to set aside their competitive differences and make it as one entity. Citizens…'

Terence and Amber lay in each other's arms. The bed was covered in cake crumbs and they were euphoric and exhausted, as if they'd run a long-distance race. In the background, the StrataScreen silently displayed the trending SMFeeds. They were dozing, sporadically waking up and lazily watching the screen with little or no focus on what was passing across it. Amber was thinking about the past few days, especially Balfy's offer and its conditions and how the previous few hours with Terry had been the best they'd ever had.

A voice from the screen started to speak, making them both

sit up abruptly. 'Attention please. This announcement is so critical that the five corporations have agreed to set aside their competitive differences and make it as one entity. Citizens, as you know the past year has been a difficult one economically and so it's with great regret that entry to each Strata Level has been increased by two hundred points. This will be difficult for us all, but without this change the fabric of our society will fail. We hope the remainder of your weekend and the days leading up to Pay Day are pleasant and fruitful.'

The screen blanked and a timer appeared, counting down the minutes: 4 3 2 0...4 3 1 9...4 3 1 8...

MONDAY

TWENTY-SEVEN

'What are you doing up so early?' asked Jenny.
'Must get to work. Need to find out what's happening,' said Martin. He kissed her on the forehead.

She was barely awake. She stretched her arms, scratched her leg and shook her head vigorously, shaking off the layer of sleep that was stopping her understanding what was happening. 'What time is it?' she asked.

'Four-thirty.'

'What! Martin!'

He kissed her again and crept out of the room, hoping she'd not managed to shake off enough sleep to come after him. He listened at Becka's door; it was quiet. Max's StrataScreen was announcing surf conditions around the world. Martin was scared. He was worrying, as he had been all night. He needed a minimum of another two hundred points to stay green. He knew it was desperate, but he didn't know what to do. Outside he stopped and looked at the house, the garden and the village twinkling in the early morning light. He clenched his muscles as his stomach threatened to expel itself and soil his trousers. He ran to the hedge and puked.

A bedroom window opened and Max stuck his head out. 'Pop, what on earth?'

Martin put his finger to his lips to silence him. 'Dodgy beer,' he mouthed. Max sneered and closed the window.

Terry walked into the bathroom as Amber was brushing her teeth. He hugged her from behind, winking at her in the mirror. 'I don't understand why you're so calm. You've been frantic all week and yet now, when you've got something to worry about, you don't seem at all bothered.'

'I'll wait to see what the day brings. First though, I need to get to work. Can't afford to mess up at this late stage, can I?'

He kissed the back of her neck. 'Do you have to go in today?'

She smiled at him, locking eyes with his reflection. 'Nope, guess I could take the day off and hang out with you.'

He pulled her tighter. 'Could you?'

'Don't be daft. Now let me finish in here.' She pushed him towards the door. 'Alone, please.' She flipped her dirty underwear at him and blew a kiss.

'Amber, I wish you wouldn't. I find it a bit weird.'

She shut the door and sat down on the toilet. Tears were falling from her eyes, a new one forming as the last one reached her chin; the evening and the night had been delicious, but now reality was biting. She had to make some big decisions and she was so worried that she couldn't even relax enough to relieve herself.

'Hey, you gonna take all day?'

'Just coming.' She flushed the unused toilet, rinsed her face and stepped confidently into the bedroom. 'All yours.' She dressed hurriedly in the clothes already laid out – a pair of black Chelsea boots and black ankle socks, a calf-length skirt in four vertical sections of black and cherry red, a stiff white shirt, a black Edwardian tailcoat and a bowler hat with an inch-high felt spike.

'Bit dressy for work,' said Terry.

'Well, now they've upped the limit I might need to go out point-hunting straight from the office.' She finished her make-up, not bothering to turn around and face him.

'Sure. Whatever,' he said and left the room. She knew she was being frosty towards him, but her head was in such turmoil that she couldn't find the room to be gentle. She blew on her wet moss-green fingernails, adjusted the collar of her jacket and ran down the stairs. 'Bye!' she called, slamming the door before he could respond.

The StrataScreen in the reception area of the Bureaucracy was showing a heightened security level. Sam had no idea what that meant, nor did she care. She wheeled her weekend bags across the hallway and into the lift. Being first into the office on a Monday was almost sacred to Sam; it gave her the time to prepare and without it the whole week felt chaotic. She'd fallen out with her mother earlier that morning and it'd unsettled her, especially as it was the last few days before Pay Day and so, more than ever, she needed to plan her week carefully. Everything in the office was as the weekend cleaners had left it – the chairs had been pushed neatly under the desks, each and every charta docking-mat was in place, the tops of the cabinets had been cleared of the half-empty boxes of biscuits and the bins were empty and smelled of bleach.

Sam sat at her desk, took out her charta and began to flip through the day's cases.

She heard distant voices and looked up. Amber, dressed as immaculately as ever, was one step ahead of Martin, tilting her head slightly to speak to him. In stark contrast, Martin's clothes were crumpled, his hair was dishevelled and his shoes were smeared with mud. The banal tone of the conversation drifted across the otherwise pure and silent space. Strange, thought Sam, neither of them have been early before.

Their voices grew clearer. 'Usual stuff…bit of cooking, bit of shopping. Nice and easy,' said Amber over her shoulder.

'Yeah. It's good to spend a bit of time at home. Jenny and the kids played tennis, I went to the local pub on the Saturday…'

Amber's step faltered. 'Sam! I didn't expect—'

Sam interrupted. 'Amber, let's catch up later shall we? Martin, you look a little rough today. Is everything okay?'

Martin tried to smooth the front of his shirt and straighten his tie. 'Sam?' he said. 'How lovely to see you.'

She looked at him quizzically. 'Lovely to see you too, Martin.' She focussed back on her charta.

Amber chose a desk where Sam couldn't see what she was up to and Martin sat down next to Sam, stealing sideways glances every now and again.

They sat in silence

Once Sam had completed allocating the cases for the day she

spoke. 'There's been a big increase in self-referrals since they made the announcement. We've got a busy two days ahead of us, I'm afraid.'

'Oh God, they're not the only ones that have problems,' moaned Martin.

Sam put her hand on his forearm. 'Do you need to talk?'

He hesitated, but then shook his head. 'No, I'm fine. It's just a bit early on a Monday morning, that's all.'

'Good. Amber, shall we have that chat?'

Amber lifted her charta off its docking-mat. 'Sure. In one of the booths?'

'Probably best,' said Sam.

Martin mumbled. 'Do you need me?'

'No,' said Sam.

Amber picked up her ruyi and followed Sam into one of the glass booths set aside for casual meetings.

Sam sat down on one of the comfy chairs. 'You won't be needing those,' she said.

Amber sat opposite her, tucked her ruyi into her jacket pocket and put the charta face down on the low table between them.

'Anything you want to say?' asked Sam.

'Such as?' replied Amber.

'Anything about Saturday morning?'

'Ah, that...'

'Yes. That.'

'Well, I was freaking out a bit – lack of sleep probably.'

'You were freaking out? Do you know what you did to my mother?'

'What I did? You were the one with the locked door and the open window. What on earth was that all about?'

'Don't push this on to me. You came to my mother's house accusing me of blackmail.'

'Yeah. Look, I'm sorry. I've had a whole weekend to reconsider. I was wrong.'

Sam leant across and tucked Amber's shirt collar into her jacket. Amber flinched.

196

'What made you come banging on my door at such a ridiculous hour? Is there anything you need to talk about?'

'No. It's all sorted. Honestly.'

'Okay. I'll believe you, but if you need to talk at all, just ask. Won't you?'

'Sure.'

They both relaxed a little into their seats and Amber rested her hand on the pocket with her ruyi in. 'So what did happen to you?' she asked.

Sam needed no further encouragement. She checked nobody was listening outside the booth and leant forward to whisper. 'I was whisked away to paradise.'

Amber shifted in her seat. 'Really? To paradise?'

'Really,' said Sam, hoping she was being suitably mysterious to raise Amber's curiosity levels high enough for her to be genuinely interested. 'Two men came to my window with a ladder.'

'Really?'

'Really. They'd been sent by someone I'd just met. Someone who turned out to be quite wealthy.'

'And what did they want?'

'Me,' said Sam and chuckled. 'Me.'

'That's nice.'

'Shall I tell you what happened?'

'Sure,' said Amber in a bored monotone.

'Well. I was lying on my bed in my pyjamas – you know those all-in-one types – when there was a knock at my window. Two dishy young men were tapping on the glass, beckoning for me to come closer. How could I resist? I slid the window open and they told me that Frank, the man I had just been flirting with, had employed them to find me and persuade me to join him for the night. "Nothing intimate," they said. It seemed plausible; his profile had mentioned that he was only into flirting and didn't want physical contact. We'd got on well via the screen. Oh, I almost forgot, they pulled the screen off the wall to make it look as if there'd been a struggle. The idea of a romantic adventure was thrilling, although I must have looked hilarious climbing down the ladder in my pyjamas.

'I felt so special, being escorted by these smartly dressed men in chinos and nice shoes to their fabulous battered old Land Rover with large areas of rust forming a sort of camouflage across its dark green body. Oh my, they're sexy aren't they? It only had seats up front so I had to squeeze in between the two of them. My heart was racing, I can tell you.'

'Wow,' said Amber, flatly.

'It sure was. We sped along and I kept sliding into them as we spun round corners and hit bumps in the road. We headed out towards the disused nuclear power station, past the old lighthouse; it's completely flat, you can see for miles. It was spooky. We bumped over a little bank on to a beach and driving across the shingle was like having a massage of tiny little vibrations. I could feel the blood pounding down there, you know…all turned on. We stopped at the most wonderful brown house with orange window frames and a high corrugated tin roof. In front of it was a sparse garden lit up so you could see the occasional pure white stone circles surrounding a bush. He was sitting there, just in front of the house, in full evening dress at an old wooden table. "Hi, fancy some supper?" he called. I can tell you, I was impressed.'

'Was he handsome?'

'You bet. He was one of the most handsome men I've ever seen. He pulled my chair out for me and when I sat down he gave me a gorgeous yellow flower he'd picked from one of the bushes. We ate Whitstable oysters on a bed of salted samphire and drank half pints of Spitfire real ale. I was in heaven.'

'What did he want in return?'

'Nothing.'

'Nothing? That's hard to believe. And did you…'

'Oh no. He was true to his word. Although we did do something quite shocking – I'm not sure if I should tell you.'

'No worries if you'd rather not.'

'Okay, I will. After supper we went into his house and he showed

198

me his computer room full of screens and keyboards and stuff. In the corner was a sofa which he asked me to sit on. He said I was so pretty and sexy that he'd like me to unzip my pyjamas in the same way I'd done online.'

'What?'

Sam blushed. 'Sometimes I use those flirting sites you recommended.'

Amber coughed and shifted in her seat again. 'And, did you?'

'Did I?'

'Unzip your pyjamas.'

'Yes. It was electric… I unzipped them down to my waist and then he asked me to pull them down to my ankles.'

'Did you?'

'I loved it.'

'And did he make a move?'

'Not once.'

'Nothing?'

'Well. He did have a fiddle with himself, if you know what I mean. But hey, that's fine. It's sort of what I expected.'

'Don't you mind?'

'A little, but not too much. He was such a gentleman.'

'How did you get home?'

'He drove me back himself.'

'Will you see him again?'

'Who knows, but I doubt it. So, what do you reckon? A pretty far out and wild weekend, eh?'

'Very wild.'

'What about yours? What did you get up to?'

'Oh, just a couple of parties and a bit of time with Terence.'

Sam grinned. 'Don't tell anyone else, will you?'

'Of course not.'

TWENTY-EIGHT

Martin closed the door of the Bureaucracy taxi. It sped off, leaving him on the side of a road that could accommodate six lanes of traffic, but was only occupied by gusts of wind and the occasional bus or rickshaw. He was in one of the run-down areas of London to see a new client who claimed he could no longer work because of a medical injury. A flock of plastic bags were being blown around. He grabbed one as it skimmed across his face – it had been reused so many times it was almost transparent.

A group of three girls were leaning against the railings of a scrapyard piled high with redundant technology being stored in the hope that a way of extracting the precious metals would be found. They were laughing and passing a cheap brightly coloured ruyi between them. They tensed as Martin walked towards them. One of them took a step forward. 'Hey, whiskers. What brings you round here?' He ignored them and carried on walking past. 'I said, what brings you round here?' she repeated. He smiled, but said nothing. 'What you smiling at, mister?' They laughed. He gave them a single nod of acknowledgement. She passed the ruyi to her friend. 'What you looking at?'

'Nothing,' said Martin.

'Oh, nothing are we? Guess that makes you something, eh?'

'Not really.'

'Word of advice. Be careful, we don't like strangers around here. Especially creepy old men.'

'Okay,' he muttered.

'Babe, take his photo in case he's one of them perverts,' she said to her friend with the ruyi.

Martin kept walking with his head slightly bowed, cursing the cuts introduced that morning that now restricted the taxis from spending those extra few minutes to drop them off outside the actual location. He turned into his client's crescent, which was a grand name for a row of late Georgian houses that looped back round to the main road. The four-storey houses were visibly crumbling; chunks of masonry lay on the pavement and most of the window frames were rotten or the windows boarded up. The smell of decaying food and stagnant water hit him. Wild dogs foraged in piles of loose rubbish in the gutter and babies screamed from metal cages hanging from some of the windows, cages that extended the cramped living space.

The girls were following him a few steps behind, still filming him and providing their own commentary. 'He looks like a fish out of water, but don't be fooled. That's how the perverts want you to see them. Then they pounce. Look at his shoes. They're covered in mud. Now where did he get covered in mud around here? He didn't. It must be from hiding in bushes and spying on young girls in their bedrooms. Pervert.' They ran around in front of him. 'Look at his clothes. All crumpled. Lives alone. Pervert alone. Sad, sad man with his creepy whiskers. If this man gives you any grief, alert the Guardian Girls. We're signing off now, but remember…we'll take care of him, with pleasure.' They sauntered off, leaving Martin alone with the dogs.

He found the house he was looking for and pressed the doorbell. There was no sound and nobody came. He banged the door knocker as hard as he could. A couple of the dogs barked and strolled towards him. Someone called down from the third-floor window, 'Who're you?'

'I'm looking for Mr Vickers.'

'Who are you?'

'I'm from the Bureaucracy. Martin Brown. I'm here to see Mr Vickers. He called us.'

'You come to assess me?'

'Are you Mr Vickers?'

'Who are you?'

'I just told you. I'm Martin Brown from the Bureaucracy.'

'What do you want?'

'You called us.'

'You here to assess me?'

'Are you Mr Vickers?'

'Who are you?'

'I've come to assess you.'

A key on the end of a perfect length of string flew from the open window. Martin opened the door and the string was quickly withdrawn. 'Third floor, room fourteen.'

He stepped over a couple sleeping in the hallway under a blanket of the transparent bags and climbed the stairs, carefully avoiding the occasional sleeper or drunk. He accidentally stepped on a pile of rags on the second floor landing and from underneath a woman of indeterminate age poked her head out, snarled and waved a battered ruyi at him.

'Sorry,' he said.

'Fucking perv. Those girls should have chopped your cock off there and then, not made a fucking film.'

He hurried up the next flight of stairs. The door to room fourteen was open. The man inside was muttering, but Martin couldn't hear what he was saying. He tapped on the door and stepped inside.

The room was sparse, but immaculately tidy and smelled slightly acidic; on the table was a bottle of white vinegar and a rag for cleaning glass. On either side of the open window were matching wooden crates turned upside down. On one of them sat a man Martin presumed was Mr Vickers.

'Who are you?' said Mr Vickers.

'Martin Brown from the Bureaucracy. You called.'

'You here to assess me?'

'Yes.'

'Good. I got problems.'

'Do you want to tell me about them?'

'I'd love to, but I might leave gaps. Tell me if I miss something out.'

'Okay. Do you mind if I record it? It means we can guarantee an accurate assessment.'

'Sure, I'd like a copy though.'

'Of course. Now, tell me what the problem is.'

'Well. It's like this. My brain keeps getting full and then things drop out of it.'

'Tell me about it. That's age I'm afraid.'

'No, it's bloody well not. It's those sodding drugs.'

'Drugs?'

'They gave me drugs.'

'Who did?'

'Who are you?'

'Martin Brown from the Bureaucracy. I'm assessing you.'

'Drugs. They gave me experimental drugs.'

'What drugs? Who gave you them?'

'The clinic.'

'Your doctor gave you experimental drugs?'

'No. No. The clinic that pays you to be experimented on. The drugs were supposed to enhance my ability to memorise things. Look.' He passed Martin a scrap of paper. 'I wrote it down.'

Martin read the scribblings. 'Drugs to increase the brain's capacity to memorise facts over long periods of time. Possible side-effects on short term memory.'

'Bloody drugs have knackered my brain. Can't do anything now. Can't go out and certainly can't work.'

'Your file says you've asked to be made white. Is that correct?'

'Who are you?'

'Mr Vickers! I'm Martin Brown from the Bureaucracy. I'm here to assess you. You've asked to be moved to white. Is that correct?'

'Yes. Look at the state of me. I can't work, can I?'

'That's not really the assessment I'm here to make, I'm afraid.'

'Eh?'

'There's more to it than being able to work. I also have to assess whether you've knowingly made yourself unfit.'

'Who are you?'

203

'Are you taking the…?'

'I'm buggered.'

Martin sighed. 'Mr Vickers. You took a risk and it went wrong, but you knew what you were doing. I can't move you to white. And even if I did, they'd just bump you back up again. You're going to have to work, I'm afraid.'

'What? For fuck's sake, have some humanity.'

'It's the law. I don't make the laws, do I?'

'You're their ears and eyes though. You interpret them.'

'It's no use. I can't do anything for you.' Martin stopped recording the interview. 'You could always try the outliers,' he whispered.

The door squeaked. The Guardian Girls were standing in the hallway. 'He'll be fine with us. Now piss off, you pervert, before we slice your tackle off and feed it to the dogs.'

'I'm just doing my job.'

'That's what the last one said. Now piss off.'

Martin scurried out of the room, down the stairs, out of the house and ran to the end of the street. He crouched down on the side of the wide empty road and began to cry. 'How did it come to this?' he whimpered to himself. 'How did I become a corporation enforcer? Is this really the only way I can keep my family?'

His charta buzzed and Sam's voice announced, 'Complaint lodged by Mr Vickers. Inappropriate advice to join the outliers given during assessment visit by Martin Brown.'

'Fuck!' He wiped his face on his tie, stood up and walked towards the row of shabby shops that formed the ground floor of the neighbouring tower block. Two women sat gossiping in the launderette and a man was slumped outside the off-licence. The second-hand ruyi shop was closed, but its cheap and gaudy reconditioned ruyi were displayed behind the bars of the window. There was a long queue of people waiting to buy their bargains at the counter of the One Point Store and there was a steady stream of customers flowing between the pub and the bookies. Beer, bargains and bookies – the staple consumption of the displaced class. Martin smiled, remembering Sir Arthur getting agitated one evening as he'd explained that this was no different to the upper strata with their love of a good wine, getting a good price on an antique and their investment funds. He was tempted by the bookies and the pub, but managed to keep walking until he came to a Pay Day loan company. He stopped. On offer were easy to get loans at only one percent interest. The two hundred points he needed would cost him two points in interest. He knew that Pay Day loans were for the desperate, which he was, but the deal didn't seem too bad.

'Hi. I'm after a loan,' he said through the grille in the shop window.

'You're not from around here, are you?' replied a female through the intercom.

'Does that matter?'

'No, just making polite conversation. If you have your ruyi we can arrange whatever you'd like.'

'I need two hundred points until Pay Day.'

'That's not very long to pay it back, sir.'

'Is that a problem?'

'No, but we'd recommend you take it out until the following Pay Day. That way you've got just over a year to pay it off and it means you don't start the new year already below your Strata level limit. What colour are you, sir?'

'Green.'

'Can I see your ruyi please?'

He slipped it under the grille.

'Thank you, that's fine. So you want a loan of two hundred points for three hundred and sixty-eight days. Is that right?'

'Yes. It says the interest is one percent.'

'That's correct. One percent per day. So it'll only cost you two points a day. And you can pay the interest daily so it never builds up to anything too big to handle.'

'And I can pay off the loan in one lump sum in a year's time?'

'Yes, that's fine.'

'Okay. I'll take the loan please. I presume I can set up an automatic payment rather than having to come here?'

'Sure. I can use your ruyi to set it up now, if you'd like.'

'How else can I pay?'

'That's the only option really. It's how we manage to offer loans so fast and with so little paperwork. Shall I set it up then, sir?'

'Yes please.'

His ruyi was slipped back under the grille and he quickly checked his rating. He'd been credited the two hundred points and, to his amazement, fifteen of his pending requests had responded and increased his points by a further ten. He did a little dance of joy and called for a taxi to take him to his next appointment.

TWENTY-NINE

Ashley sat there with her chair tipped back. 'C'mon, sit down,' she called out, seemingly oblivious to the pedestrians walking close by on the pavement. 'You know you want to,' she drawled.

Amber took a step closer, but stayed standing. 'No thanks. I haven't got long.'

'Oh! Don't be a spoilsport.'

'I'm supposed to be out on a case. Where's Balfy? He said he'd be here.'

'Am I not good enough for you? I can do everything he can… well, almost…'

'Stop messing around. What do you want?'

'I want you to share a pot of tea with me.'

'You what? I don't even have time for a coffee.'

'What's the rush? I thought you were on your way up. Lord Balfour's new assistant…'

'I've agreed to nothing.'

'Maybe…'

'Certainly.'

'But you're here, aren't you? Take a seat, Amber. Let me tell you the good news.'

Amber fiddled with the edge of her charta, tucked her hair behind her ear and sat down.

'That's better. Now, Lady Grey or Lapsang? I do like the idea of a lap that sang.'

'Coffee.'

Ashley raised her eyebrows and tapped the side of the teapot. She placed a saucer, then a cup and finally a silver spoon in front of Amber.

207

'Earl Grey,' said Amber as she picked up the spoon.

'Only girls here I'm afraid. Lady G it is then.'

Ashley twisted the metal pipe in the centre of the table. 'A pot of Lady Grey and mixed sandwiches for two, please.'

'I can't eat here. It's filthy and it stinks.' Amber grimaced.

'It's fine. It's just the smell of a city at the height of the day and a bit of outdoor dust.' Ashley stroked the side of Amber's face. 'Delicate, are we?' She laughed, revealing the chewing gum in her mouth.

'This is so…so…lower level.'

'Don't be so…so…green. It's fun.'

Amber looked around. The street was lined with market stalls selling food, jewellery and clothes. The stall next to them was selling picture frames and quirky animal statues made from upcycled egg cartons. Smells of pastry and grilled meat weaved their way in and out of the background smell of the city. A canopy of noise rose and fell as the sounds of the street pulsed. On the corner a crowd of people were banging their ruyi, laughing loudly and generally having a good time. Amber felt uncomfortable in her work clothes. She was an outsider observing, which was accentuated by Ashley who was dressed all in black, but still managed to look as if she could be on her way to an illegal underground party or a high class fashion shoot. She was wearing an ankle-length white speckled black coat made from soft carpet, the smallest of shorts made from the same material, a torn flimsy t-shirt, thigh-length black soft leather boots and a cowboy hat. Her eyebrows, eyes and lips were heavily defined with thick black make-up. She was striking.

She sucked on her e-cigarette and blew an extravagant cloud of vapour towards Amber. The metal pipe lowered into the table and a circular tray appeared with a pot of tea and a slice of lemon. Ashley lifted them off and poured Amber a cup of Lady Grey. The sweet perfume mingled with the smells of the street. She squeezed the lemon and its acidic sharpness cut through the air, cleaning the back of Amber's nose. She twisted the tray a little and it lowered. When it returned a few seconds later it was laden with sandwiches piled high on a three-tiered stand of china plates decorated ornately by tiny red roses with delicately hand-drawn ants crawling across them.

'High tea. At high noon.' Ashley chuckled.

'I'm sure this is all very lovely if you're someone who can laze around all day. I can't.'

'Very well. But don't forget, you become as you behave.' Ashley put her gum on the edge of the saucer and popped a whole quarter salmon sandwich into her mouth.

Amber could smell the fish being chewed and sat back a little. 'Please, tell me what you want. Or rather what Lord Balfour wants you to tell me.'

Ashley swilled her mouth with the remainder of her tea, swallowed and deposited the gum back in her mouth. She took a long drag of the e-cigarette and leant forward. 'He wants you to have this.' She slid a small brass cube across the table.

'What is it?'

'A data-bug.'

Amber frowned. 'A what?'

'A data-bug. It eats and excretes data.'

'Oh. Thanks. I'll be on my way then.'

Ashley smiled. 'Okay. Off you go then.'

'For fuck's sake. What does it do?'

'It sits inside fibre-optic cables, taking data in, copying it and then passing it on as if nothing had happened.'

'And why do I want one of those?'

'You promised to steal for us.'

'I didn't.'

'But you will, won't you?'

'Maybe. But this won't work 'cos the Bureaucracy is all wireless.'

'Really? So those intelligent fridges on every floor – how do you think they get their intelligence? How do they know what food and drink to order?'

'They're connected to the main reception, I guess. Logging who's arriving and who's leaving.'

'Smart girl. But they're not connected to the wireless network.'

'Well, we don't have a physical network so they must be. Miss Smarty Pants.'

'Oh yes you do. It's the mains electrical wiring. That's how they plug into it.'

'So you want me to put this data-bug into a fridge?'

'Yeah. Why not? If you wanna piss us about. And see how quickly we bust you down to violet.'

'Okay. Enough. Tell me what you want. I really must be going. We're being scrutinised more than ever this week.'

'You still don't get what he can do for you, do you? Just do as he asks and you won't need to worry about points ever again.'

Amber picked up the cube and put it in her pocket. 'Okay. What do I do?'

'Good girl. Unplug the fridge on your floor. You'll need this.' Ashley passed her a small screwdriver with an octagonal tip. 'Place the cube next to the open wall socket and twist the top half clockwise. Wait ten seconds and then plug it back in.'

'That's it?'

'That's it.'

Amber turned and walked away as slowly as she could; the excitement of the weekend was back in her veins, racing faster and faster and setting off surging pulses of adrenalin in her brain and in her stomach.

A faint beep and a single strobe of light from the scanner in the Bureaucracy reception caught Amber's eye as she walked briskly past security on the way to her team's section of the building. It was early afternoon and the entire floor was empty – people were either in meetings or out and about visiting cases. There was a real push to clear backlogs and to make sure new cases were dealt with rapidly. They had to have an empty caseload for the start of the new year, partly as all Strata Citizens would be assessed and begin the Pay Year on their newly assigned level but also because even if you didn't move levels you might be moved to a different job. The team dealing with these types of case would be different on Thursday morning.

The fridge was in an alcove along with the hot and cold water dispensers, the rapid cookers and a few tables and chairs. This was an area designed to help staff stay in the office for as much time as possible. There were rumours that the higher levels had showers and beds as well.

She wasn't used to being there during the day; it was considered bad practice and seriously frowned upon if you weren't out closing as many cases as possible. She paused. The air was fresher than normal and the low hum of the air conditioning was soothing. Her tension subsided a little. She put her things on a desk in her area and strolled around to the kitchen alcove. She took a mug from the cupboard as a decoy in case anyone asked her what she was up to. She knelt down in front of the fridge. She looked to the right and to the left but couldn't see any cables. She stood up. Nothing above either. She lay on her front and checked underneath. Still nothing. She opened the door and moved the contents around so she could see right to the back. Nothing there.

'Hi.'

She tensed. A young lad with an empty glass was approaching.

'Hi,' she said.

He filled his glass from the tap. 'See ya.'

'Bye.'

She closed the fridge door and leaned on the edge of the sink. What a stupid idea, she thought.

She noticed a cable running out of the back of the rapid cooker and into the wall. She carefully edged the fridge out and there it was – the cable she'd been searching for. After checking that nobody was coming she pulled the fridge out a little more and crawled in behind it. The air was thick with the stench of old dirt and grease. She pressed the screwdriver into the eight-sided hole just below where the cable disappeared into the wall. It rotated automatically. The cable loosened and she pulled it out. She tried to get the cube out of her pocket but the space was too tight. She crawled out backwards.

'Hi,' said the same lad. 'You okay?'

She froze. 'Yeah. I dropped something. I'm fine.'

'Can I help?'

'Thanks, but I've got it now.'

'Okay,' he said and walked away.

She took the cube from her pocket and crawled back in. The cube fitted the hole perfectly and once it was in place she twisted it. It buzzed for a few seconds. She slipped it back in her pocket and lined the cable up ready to push it back. This time the screwdriver rotated in the opposite direction and secured the cable.

'Hi,' said a familiar voice. 'Problem?'

She dropped the screwdriver and shuffled out. 'Sam. What are you doing here?'

No answer. Sam stood there silently with her hand out and a stern look on her face. She extended her hand a little further, offering it to Amber, who took hold of it. Sam helped her up.

'I dropped something,' said Amber.

Sam turned her back, stormed off into one of the glass booths and sat there staring. Amber joined her. The silence was oppressive.

'I dropped something,' repeated Amber.

'What?'

'My ruyi.'

Sam remained stony-faced. 'Why were you here in the first place?'

'I forgot my ruyi so I came back for it in-between cases.'

Sam snorted and half closed her eyes, leaving no doubt that she thought Amber was lying.

'Really? And what cases would they be?'

'I haven't logged them yet. How did you know I was here?'

'Security alerted me.' Sam folded her arms across her chest. 'Don't fuck about, Amber. I can't protect you.'

Amber raised her eyebrows. 'Fuck about? How?'

'I'm just saying.'

'Okay.'

'There's an urgent, number one priority case just come in. I'll assign it to you and let's both assume you came back to collect the background information for it. Okay?'

'Okay. What is it?'

'It's a bit strange. It seems to have been referred to us from somewhere else in the Bureaucracy. It's a successful thirty-year-old man in Kensington who has suddenly become catatonic. He just switched off. His referrer, a Lord Balfour, reported that the pressure of Pay Day was too much and he closed down. Can you check it out?'

Amber pinched her leg under the table, a habit she'd developed as a child to stop herself from saying something she shouldn't. 'Sure. What about all my other cases?'

'I'll reassign all of today's cases to the others. This might be a test, so we have to get it right and you're the best. Don't let me down.'

'Of course not. You can trust me.'

'And whatever you were doing with that fridge, please stop and focus on the task. This isn't the time for practical jokes. Got that?'

'Absolutely. Sorry.'

THIRTY

'Put those on and wait there,' said Mr Lenkan, as he dropped a pile of clothes on to a chair. 'She'll come to collect you when she's ready.'

The outhouse filled with the roar of the trike as it kicked into action and crunched across the drive. It gradually faded as it took Mr Lenkan away from his wife and Martin's afternoon of subjugation.

He rifled through the clothes to see what he'd been asked to wear. It was a policeman's uniform. He undressed, dumping his already crumpled and dirty clothes on a bench in the corner. As he pulled on the trousers of the uniform he shivered with worry that his stipulation of no sex had been ignored; he felt more like a male stripper with each article of clothing he put on. He was about to complete the outfit with a peaked cap when the door connecting to the main house opened. A naked woman walked in. Her shoulder-length light-brown hair framed her olive-skinned face. She wasn't pretty but there was something special about her. She oozed confidence and wealth. The healthy colour of her face extended across all of her body, almost hiding the loose skin of her stomach. Her upper arms and the bags under her eyes hinted at her age and Martin struggled not to stare at her breasts, which although they'd sagged a little were surprisingly well shaped.

'Er...hello,' said Martin. He put his cap on and saluted.

She stood and stared.

He took his cap off. 'Did Mr Lenkan mention the "no sex" part?'

She reached up to take something off the shelf, revealing that she was a woman that didn't believe in shaving – anywhere.

'What would you like me to do?' he asked.

'I want you to give me a word that you will use if, when, you want me to stop,' she said in a beautifully rounded Spanish accent.

'A word to stop?'

She was silent, waiting patiently and at ease.

He'd heard of this sort of thing – a safe word in case things got out of hand. He didn't like the fact that he needed one. 'Seems a bit unnecessary,' he said.

She stared at him.

Martin was flustered and uncomfortable with being stared at by an attractive naked woman. 'Motorbike,' he said and laughed a nervous laugh.

'Thank you. Hand me your watch. Now, please wait,' she said and left the room.

He sat on the edge of the bench and waited. And waited. And waited.

After what seemed like twenty minutes he started to have a look around the room. He took an old shoe box off the top shelf and opened it.

Her voice came through the ceiling. 'Put that back and wait as you were told.'

He was startled, but carried on looking in the box. On the top of a pile of papers was a beaten-up red and white teddy bear. He took it out.

'Put that back. Now. Unless you want to do this the hard way?'

He put it back, closed the lid and put the box back on the shelf.

'Good. Now do as I asked and wait.'

The room was small so he could still see its contents clearly without moving. He turned his head to the left. On the bottom of floor to ceiling shelves was a brand new table-tennis kit of two bats, a ball and a net. Next to it was an unopened children's playhouse and an inflatable paddling pool.

'Eyes to the front.'

He did as he was told and waited. And waited. And waited.

This might be a bit weird but it's an easy way to earn some points, he thought

The connecting door opened again. She was wearing an elegant fawn suit with a knee-length skirt and a high-necked sweater under a thigh-length jacket. An intricate lace skirt was layered over the skirt of the suit, echoing the elaborate patterns on her three-inch-heel patent fawn leather shoes. A simple necklace of black Tahitian pearls sat perfectly around her neck.

'Don't speak,' she said.

'Er…'

'Quiet,' she said and put a finger to her lips. 'I will tell you when to speak. And when I do, you will address me as Cima.'

He nodded. She dumped a pile of crumpled clothes in a dirty wet patch on the floor in front of him. 'Put these on.' Her voice was harsh but her eyes were soft and she smiled before leaving the room.

He undressed to his underwear and picked up the musty indigo overalls.

The ceiling crackled again. 'Get rid of what you're wearing, completely. Everything. And fold that uniform.'

He did as he was told. He searched the pile on the floor for underwear but there wasn't any so he pulled the overalls over his naked body, pulled on the socks and laced up the steel-toecap boots.

Cima returned. 'Follow me.'

The vulnerability he already felt was heightened by the contrast between the luxury of her outfit and the grubbiness of his own. The lack of underwear added to his feelings of insecurity. He followed her into the yard, round the corner of the house and in through a large sliding glass door. The kitchen was spotless. The work surface was bright pink and so smooth it reflected the designer room as if it were a mirror.

'Natural quartz with pink resin pigments,' she said and held up her finger to stop him answering. 'Over there.' She pointed to the corner. 'The pipe in the cupboard underneath the sink is faulty.'

He knelt down and opened the cupboard door. A bucket was catching drips from a leaking pipe.

'Block the pipe with your fist.'

He looked up at her and she stared back. He unscrewed the pipe carefully and pushed his fist inside.

She removed the plug from the sink. 'Good. Wait there.'

She took another bucket and left the room. Grimy water was finding its way around his fist and dribbling down his hand and into the bucket. A few trickles were working their way down his arm and he dried them on his overalls as best he could. After a few minutes of kneeling and wondering what she was doing, he heard sporadic bursts of liquid hitting the bottom of her bucket and then splashes of liquid on liquid as it filled.

'Stay there and don't move,' she said as she came back into the kitchen. She pointed at him and smiled. 'You're doing well so don't spoil it.' She tipped her bucket into the sink and he felt warm liquid against his fist. A little escaped and rolled down his arm. He gagged and opened his mouth to object.

'Stop. Stay there until I say different,' she said. Her heels faded slowly as she disappeared behind him and left the room.

He knelt, not moving and trying his best not to think about what was inching its way across his hand and down his arm.

'Good. I'm pleased,' she said through a speaker in the wall above the sink.

He waited.

His knees were hurting and his legs were aching. The warm piss against his fist had turned cold. He considered using the safe word and calling it a day, but he needed the points. It wasn't too bad anyway; nothing that wouldn't wash off and be forgotten after a beer or two. He looked over his shoulder at the kitchen. It was so different to the farmhouse style of home and a prick of nostalgia for the conversations he'd had with Jenny about what sort of home they wanted tickled his brain. It was a long time ago; they'd both changed and drifted apart but he was sure that once Pay Day was over they'd find the magic again.

'Let it drain into the bucket,' she said through the wall, startling him. He removed his fist and the pale yellow liquid drained into the bucket. He swished the sink with cold water, put the plug in its hole, turned on the hot tap and picked up a bar of soap from the back of the sink.

'No washing.'

He ducked his head a little lower. 'Seriously?' he said to the wall.

'Be quiet. You're doing well.'

He put the soap back in its place and stood rigid, waiting for his next order.

'You'll find a different set of clothes in the outhouse. Put them on and wait.'

He wiped his hands on his overalls. On a chair in the outhouse was the blue uniform of a dental nurse – a short-sleeved smock, trousers and rubber shoes. He untied his boots, put his socks inside them and neatly positioned them by the side of the chair. He slipped out of his overalls. Underneath the smock was a pair of boxer shorts which he quickly put on. The smock, the trousers and the shoes all fitted perfectly and in the pocket of the smock he found a face mask which he looped over his ears and set in place across his mouth.

'Perfect. Come to the surgery – through the white door next to the walk-in pantry. Quickly now.'

At the far end of the kitchen was a large walk-in cupboard with a bronze plaque on the door announcing *Our Pantry*. His hand hesitated on the door handle and then with a boldness that overcompensated for his nervousness he burst through the door. In the centre of the pure white surgery was a grey plastic-coated chair; one of those that reclines so you can lie flat on your back while the dentist digs around inside your mouth. Cima was standing next to it, still wearing her suit but with a long see-through apron over the top and wearing protective latex gloves on her slender hands. She was holding a metal implement with a hook at either end.

'Please. Take a seat and make yourself comfortable,' she said, patting the back of the chair.

He stumbled a little as he walked towards her.

'You may ask one question,' she said.

'Are you qualified?'

'Address me as Cima when you speak.'

'Cima, are you qualified?' he asked again in a quiet, apologetic voice.

'You can trust me,' she said and flashed him her winning smile.

He sat down and she lowered the chair so he was lying horizontal. She put a pair of goggles over his face and wiped the beads of sweat from his forehead.

'Now, what seems to be the problem?'

He raised his eyebrows, not sure if he was allowed to speak or not.

She patted his head. 'You may speak but keep it brief and to the point.'

'Nothing.'

She folded her arms and stared at him.

'Nothing, Cima.'

'Better. But you need a full cleanse, don't you?'

'Yes, Cima.'

'Good. I'll be very happy to oblige.' She picked up a pair of scissors and cut his face mask in half, slowly. She clamped his upper and lower lip and pulled them apart, forcing him to open his mouth. He winced. She smiled. A high pressure jet of water blasted his bottom front teeth, causing his gums to ache. 'Keep your head still,' she said. He nodded. 'I said keep still.' She held his hair and continued to blast the inside of his mouth. The intense pain worked its way around his gums and every now and again she pulled his head to the side and made him swill with mouthwash.

'There, that's better,' she said as she put the jet down and relaxed her grip.

His breathing was shallow as he tried to internalise the pain and concentrate on not thinking about what was coming next. She grabbed his hair again but this time she clamped it so that his head was held tight against the clammy plastic chair. She tested the lip clamps to make sure they were still gripping him tightly and picked up the metal hook.

'Right,' she said and smiled.

THIRTY-ONE

Amber stood on the opposite side of the road to the house where Sam had sent her. Behind her was a private park lined with trees and protected by the railings she was leaning on. The street of near identical large white houses curved away to the left and to the right. This was a level of privilege she'd never encountered before. She took a deep breath and crossed the road. She paused in the driveway to admire the sleek curves of a convertible e-type jaguar with an embossed licence plate – BAL F1 Y. The tree in the front garden was reflected in the immaculate bronze paintwork. She ran her hand along the curve of the back of the car and almost giggled with delight. The five perfect steps up to the old oak front door were flanked by six-foot-high pot plants of green and purple bushes.

She pulled the cord and bells jangled inside the house. A beautiful young man opened the door. 'Miss Walgace. We've been expecting you,' he said in a voice that purred. He stood to one side to let her pass.

'Ms,' she said.

'Of course. My mistake. First floor, top of the stairs and straight ahead. They're expecting you.'

She raised her chin a little to hide how small she felt and gave a tiny nod in his direction. 'Thank you. I can look after myself from here.'

He gave an almost unseen bow with the side of his head and pressed a button to his left.

The wide staircase was long and straight with balconies along each side of the first floor. 'Hi,' called Balfy from the far end of the left-hand side.

She waved and quickened her step.

'Shoes off,' he called and disappeared.

She took off her shoes and swung them back and forth. The soft pile of the carpet caressed her between the toes like the soft sand of a beach. This was the sort of house she wanted, the sort of house where she could wrap herself in luxury and hide away with Terry, never having to deal with the outside world ever again. She wiggled her toes and thought about the previous evening they'd spent together at home.

Only one of the many doors along the corridor was open and inside was a large bedroom with a magnificent globe chandelier throwing golden sparkling light around an otherwise pure white room. In the centre and directly underneath the chandelier was a circular bed with a low headboard all the way round it. A scraggy bearded man in red silk pyjamas sat propped up facing a window overlooking a terrace and a long garden.

Balfy sat beside him, holding his hand and talking quietly. He beckoned her to come and sit on the bed with them. She pulled up a stool and sat nearby.

'Am I at work?' she asked.

'Yes. Most certainly, but it may be a little unorthodox.' He winked. 'No need for any forms today,' he said, looking at her charta. 'Put it away.'

She tucked her charta back in her bag and took out her ruyi. 'Just need to check this and then I'm all yours.'

'Come here,' he whispered.

'Hold on,' she said and twisted her ruyi.

He bounced across the bed and banged her ruyi with his. 'There. That'll keep you in points for a while. Now pay attention. Please!'

'I want to see if Terry's been in touch.'

'Amber...you're pushing your luck...'

She dropped the ruyi into her bag and turned to face him. 'So what's wrong with...'

'Hugo.'

'What's wrong with Hugo?'

'It's a mystery. One minute he was fine and the next he closed down. He's been like this ever since.'

'And you want me to register him as white?'

He let out a huge guffaw. 'Why would I want that?'

'If he can't function, I can move him on to support – make him white.'

'He's red. He'll always be red. We don't ever change colour – didn't you know that?'

'Err…not sure I did. Is that true? Wow, that's cool. What, never?'

'Never. We look after our own.'

'So why am I here?'

'I wanted to see you.'

'Is that all?'

'I'd like you to help me get him out of this state. Remember we talked about the things I wanted you to do for me. So that I could help you? This is one of them.'

She touched Hugo's leg. No reaction. 'I wouldn't know where to start. I'm not a doctor. Do you have any ideas?'

'A few. Shall we start with some music? Isn't that what they do for people in comas?'

'I think so.'

He grabbed his ruyi and leapt off the bed. 'House: music. Chopin. Nocturnes.' The tinkle of a piano playing single notes floated across the room. One by one, other layers were introduced, creating a melody over a rolling undercurrent of wonderfully precise music.

She clasped her hands together. 'Awesome.'

'Hugo's favourite.' He took hold of Hugo's hand and moved it around in time to the music. 'Amber. You have a go at cajoling him back to life.'

'Sure.' She climbed on to the bed. Hugo now had Balfy holding one hand and Amber holding the other. Between them they moved his arms as if he were conducting the pianist.

He stared ahead. Not moving a muscle.

Balfy sighed. 'I know a different tune. It may be a bit tacky, but we loved it at school.'

'What?'

'Wait and see. House: Flight of the Valkyries.' The music entered the room with the strings whipping up the atmosphere and the brass slowly inching their way from the back to the front until they took over with those five famous notes.

The skin on Amber's neck prickled; so many films and adverts had used this refrain that it was now inextricably linked to power and danger.

Hugo showed no sign of life whatsoever.

'You choose,' said Balfy.

'Me?'

'Yes, you!'

She rubbed her temples trying to think of something that would get through to Hugo.

'Classical, I presume?'

'Yup. It's all he listened to.'

'What was that wonderful theme tune to the film about the creation of the United Kingdom?'

'Do you mean Beethoven's Moonlight Sonata?'

'Not sure. Let's see. House: Moonlight Sonata.' A slow haunting piece of piano music drifted across the room. 'Yes, that's it.' She lay back on the bed, still holding Hugo's hand, and rocked gently. She looked dreamily towards Balfy. 'I could sink into this and be swallowed whole, never to return.' She whispered in Hugo's ear, 'It's so cosmically erotic.' They lay on the bed either side of Hugo and let the music wash over them. As the sonata ebbed and flowed she tightened and loosened her grip on Hugo, encouraging him to feel the life bursting out from the piano in the same way that she was feeling it.

He showed no reaction.

As soon as the music had finished Balfy sat up. 'We're going to have to try a different approach. Maybe some poetry would help He loved that new stuff, what's it called? Fib, that's it.'

'Never heard of it.'

'It's like Haiku but based on the Fibonacci sequence – 1 1 2 3 5 8 syllables.'

'Wow, love it. Do you know any?'

'No, but I can make some up.'

'Go on then.'

'*Sleep*
Death
Dying
Still sleeping
Hugo wake up please
I need you awake now or else.'

Amber chuckled. 'Brilliant. You're a genius.'

'Now you.'

'Okay.'

'*Moon*
Stars
The sun
Fluffy clouds
A sharp clear blue sky
It is waiting there for you, us.'

Balfy punched the air. 'Loving it…you've got talent.'

They both looked at Hugo – nothing.

'Let's play Ruyi Twister. That'll make him laugh.'

'What's that?'

'I'll show you.' He pulled a box out from under the bed and laid out a mat covered in coloured circles. 'So…you spin the spinner—'

Amber interrupted. 'I know how to play Twister, but you said Ruyi Twister.'

'It's almost the same except you hold your ruyi in your mouth and at the same time as moving your hands and feet you also try to bang ruyi. The colours you're on affects who gains and who loses points.'

'Okay. Sounds fun but I don't see how it's going to help Hugo.'

'Let's move the mat so he can see. It'll appeal to his sense of humour, I'm sure.'

They dragged the mat into Hugo's line of vision. Amber spun first and put her right hand on an indigo circle. Balfy spun next and put his left foot on a violet circle. Next Amber had to place her left foot on orange and he placed his right foot on green. The close contact with him was making her a bit giddy and a bit guilty; Twister was a game that Terry had always wanted to play and she'd always resisted, considering it too infantile and lower level. And yet, here she was happily playing it with Balfy.

In her peripheral vision she saw him moving swiftly and before she could do anything about it he smacked her lips with his.

She dropped her ruyi on the floor. 'What the fuck?'

'Do you know how to play?' he asked.

'Sure. It's not that complicated is it?'

'So what's the problem with me banging you? You're the one on the higher level spots so I'm the one that'll gain the points.'

She smiled, not letting on that she hadn't really understood the game. They put the ruyi back in their mouths and she spun again. This time she landed on violet; he spun an orange and she spun a yellow. They giggled and giggled as they intertwined their limbs into infeasible knots. He'd been on much higher colours than her for a while before she plucked up the courage to try and bang him. As she moved her right leg around his left and their faces came close she gave him a full-blown kiss and banged his ruyi. He dropped the ruyi from his mouth and tried to kiss her back.

'Woah,' she said.

He winked. 'Do you know what, I wonder if kissing Hugo would bring any life back to him. Fancy it?'

'Only if you do,' she said, confident that he wouldn't.

He unwrapped himself from her, jumped on the bed and snogged Hugo with a long, lingering kiss. She could see his tongue exploring the static opening of Hugo's mouth. 'You next,' he said as he licked his lips.

'That's creepy.'

'Men can kiss men.'

'Not that. Kissing someone who has no idea what's happening.'

'Try it. You never know, it might get through to him. He might love it or loathe it, but hopefully he'll react.'

She edged her way on to the bed. 'Can't hurt, I guess,' she said and gave Hugo a peck on the lips.

'C'mon. He won't even know that happened. You've got to give as good as I did.'

She held her breath and with a silent apology to Terry she gave Hugo a long, lingering kiss, making it look as if she was pressing her tongue into his mouth but in reality she went no further than his teeth.

'Good girl,' he said and clapped. 'Now, let's try bathing him to see if that'll do anything.'

'Bathe him?'

'Yeah. Take his clothes off, get him into the bath and wash his body. It's one of the most intimate things you can do.'

'I'm not a nurse.'

'Oh shut up and help me carry him to the bath.'

They stripped him, pulled him to the edge of the bed and then dragged him to the bathroom. Balfy filled the elaborate bath with warm water – not too hot and not too cold – and they lifted Hugo in, propping him up against the tall back rest. Balfy passed her a bar of soap that smelled of cannabis although it was actually lime, basil and mandarin. They took an arm each and worked their way down each side. Hugo remained passive and silent. They soaped his legs and washed his feet. Balfy put his arms under Hugo's and lifted him so he wasn't sitting down.

'All yours,' he said smiling.

'Do you mean…'

'We've got to wash him all over and I don't think he'd thank me for being so intimate with him.'

'And I don't think he'd thank me either.'

'I think he would,' he said and smirked.

'Well I'm not going to. It's disgusting.'

'It's what he would want.'

'He can fuck off.'

226

'Good point. Maybe you could fuck him instead.'

'You can fuck off too.' She slammed out of the bathroom, picked up her stuff from the bedroom and stormed out of the house.

'Ruyi: public message to Terence Huddson. You're mine and don't forget it.'

THIRTY-TWO

Martin was sitting in the outhouse dressed as a Catholic priest and waiting for Cima's next instalment. His gums were sore, but he was relieved and impressed with how gentle she'd been. It was as if the threat of inflicting pain was more interesting to her than the actual pain itself.

'Upstairs, first floor, second door on the right,' she said through the ceiling.

He did as he was told and left the room, walked through the kitchen and into the hallway. At the top of the first flight of stairs were four identical doors. With trepidation he opened the second door on the right. The room was empty apart from what looked like an ornate yellow wardrobe split into two sections divided by gold-painted corkscrew pillars and each with a closed dark-green curtain. Burning incense filled the room, creating a mystical atmosphere. He drew back one of the curtains. There was a wooden chair and a slatted grille to the adjoining section. It was a confessional box. He sat down inside and closed the curtain.

The floor of the box creaked as someone sat down on the other side of the grille. She coughed and mumbled a few words. It was Cima. 'I confess to Almighty God and to you, Father, that I have sinned. My last confession was one year ago. Since then, I have committed no mortal sins.'

'Er, okay. Do you want to tell me what they were?' He fidgeted on the chair, feeling uncomfortable and unsure of his role. 'My child,' he added.

'It was thirty years ago today. A cold and sunny spring morning. He was three months old and I was going out for the first time since he'd been born. I'd arranged to meet friends in a café for Almuerzo, for lunch. I'd met them hundreds of times before so in some ways it was no big deal, but this was the first time with the baby. It had been a difficult morning, washing and drying clothes; I didn't live in a big place like this back then. I was exhausted from night after night of crying and feeding, but I remember clearly the excitement I felt in the simple fact that I was going to meet my friends and have some adult conversation. I'd even cut back on the grocery bill that week so I wouldn't have to worry too much about money. The effort of getting him ready to leave the flat was exhausting and by the time we were leaving I wasn't sure it was worth it. And I was late.

'As the bus made its way slowly along the busy streets I managed to calm down and look forward to the afternoon. I was expecting it to be long and lazy, chatting about what was going on in the world, gossiping about friends and maybe even an amble around the park. As I got off the bus I accidentally bumped a man with my pushchair and he shouted at me, accusing me of being stupid which threw me back into my bad mood. I struggled to get into the café and negotiate my way around the tables, furious that people just stared rather than offering to help. Finally, I reached the table and was devastated to see they were already eating; I was only thirty minutes late, which was minor when you consider the difficulties I'd faced to get there. As soon as I sat down they explained, one by one, that they could only stay for an hour – half of which had already gone. I was still waiting for my food to arrive when they had to leave so they gave me their money and disappeared. I ate alone and angry.'

He interrupted her while she took a breath. 'That's understandable.'

'That's not my sin, you stupid man.'

'Please continue, my child,' he said and suppressed a giggle.

'When I got back to the flat, the mess, the dirty dishes and the wet washing hit me like a thunderclap – that was my life. Every time I tried to tidy something away or wash something the baby cried. I'd feed it or change its nappy, but it still kept crying and crying. The tension built and I had no way of stopping it. He cried and cried. I shouted at him to stop and he cried louder. I smashed

229

the dirty plates against the wall. I shredded his nappies with a pair of scissors. I screamed at him to stop. He wouldn't. I picked him up and shook him. I slapped him across the face, but still he cried. I punched him on the arms and on the legs. He screamed. I grabbed his throat and held it tight, squeezing until he stopped crying.'

Martin gripped the seat of the chair. 'Should you be telling me this?' he asked quietly.

'Address me as Cima when you speak to me.'

'Cima. Do you want to tell me this?'

'Be quiet and listen. That's all you have to do.'

'Okay, Cima.'

'I let go of his throat and he started crying again. I was on the verge of killing him. I punched and punched him and then I called the police, gave them my address and left him there on his own. I never saw him again.'

He could hear her sobbing, but kept quiet as instructed. He waited. She took a deep breath and spoke softly. 'Ralph found me on the streets and we fell in love.'

The curtain swished open and the sound of her heels quietened as she walked away.

He sat still and waited. He wasn't sure if the story was true or a fantasy. He wasn't sure what reaction she was expecting and whether he should do anything about what she'd told him. If this was a confession then she'd probably admitted to murdering her young child, but what could he do about it? She'd said that it'd happened thirty years before and that she'd been to a confession since so it couldn't have been the first time she'd told anyone. He concluded that it must be a fantasy, maybe something she'd wanted to do when her children were small.

Cima spoke through the wall. 'Meet me on the top floor.'

At the top of the stairs was a door leading into a tiny attic room. The walls, the floor and the ceiling were all covered in fake rabbit fur. Two orange towels lay folded on the floor. Cima came in behind him. She was naked again. 'Strip,' she said in a matter of fact voice.

She watched him as he undressed clumsily; he wasn't used to the priest's robes and he was nervous. He stood there naked and she stood and stared at him. There was nowhere to sit so he had no option but to stand and be stared at. He covered his genitals with his hands.

'No,' she said.

He uncovered them.

'Good.' She passed him one of the orange towels. 'Put this on,' she said and wrapped herself in the other towel. 'On the other side of that entrance, all you have to do is enjoy yourself. Understood?'

'Understood.'

She looked at him angrily.

'Understood, Cima.'

She smiled. 'Follow me.'

She ducked as she stepped into the next room and Martin followed. The door closed behind him with a soft thud. The scent of warm pine and dry heat filled his nostrils. In the centre of the sauna were two young women wearing orange bathrobes standing beside two massage tables. He followed Cima across the rubber mats that covered the tiled floor. 'I think you should have Gina,' she said and smiled softly at him. One of the women, Gina he presumed, rolled out an orange towel on the table and beckoned him to lie down on his front. He put his head in the hole at the top of the table so he was lying perfectly flat. 'Don't forget, this is all about enjoyment,' said Cima. She chuckled. 'I like you,' she added. The other table creaked as she lay down.

The heat had built up enough to make him sweat which eased the movement of Gina's hands and she pressed hard on his muscles as she rubbed up and down his legs. She moved up to his arms and his back, taking her time to make sure each and every part of him was pushed and stretched. She held each of his fingers one by one and, holding them tightly, she pulled from their base to their tip. On the other table Cima was letting out little sighs of delight. He relaxed a little in response.

Gina silently rolled him over and he tilted his head so he could

see Cima. She was already on her back and facing him. She winked. 'This is the luxury of the orange strata. I trust it is to your liking?'

He nodded. 'Yes thank you, Cima.'

'Good. Now relax while the girl works her magic.'

Gina held his head and worked her thumbs time and time again across the back of his neck. She moved on to his temples and pressed them gently but firmly. She picked up a cloth from a bowl at the side of the table and he closed his eyes as she laid it across his face. The attention to his head and the warmth of the cloth relaxed him even more. She stopped massaging him and he could hear her moving around the table. A tangy citrus aroma cut through the heat. She encased his right foot in both hands for a moment and then massaged the sole of his foot and then each toe. It sent ripples of soothing tingles up his entire body. She placed his foot back on the table carefully and gave his left foot the same treatment. He felt her remove the towel and replace it with a smaller one that only covered the middle part of his body. She replaced the cloth on his face with a cool one that had a faint hint of mint.

'Look at me,' said Cima as Gina removed the cloth from his face.

Cima was lying on her back with a small orange towel covering her from the top of her thighs to her hips. He glanced at her breasts and she grinned. He looked away.

'Enjoy,' she commanded.

'Yes,' he mumbled.

She stretched her arm out towards him with her hand open, inviting him to hold it. He mirrored her and with his arm outstretched he locked his fingers into hers. The masseurs moved around the tables and massaged the shoulders and arms that led to the interlocked hands.

The pine door slammed open and Mr Lenkan stepped in. He looked at Martin and then at Cima and then at Martin again. He shook his head with minuscule movements. 'What the hell is going on here?' he asked in a quiet, cold voice.

'Mr Lenkan,' said Martin.

'Shut up,' said Cima.

'Shut up, you little shit,' said Mr Lenkan. He turned his head so that it was facing Cima. 'Well? I asked you a question,' he said in the same cold voice.

'What would you like to be going on here?' she replied.

'Bitch,' he said.

Martin shuffled off the table, grabbed a towel and walked towards the door.

'Stop,' said Mr Lenkan.

'I did what you asked,' said Martin.

'Really?'

'Yes. I want my Fluence. Please.'

'Let me give you a word of advice. In your line of work you should always ask for the payment upfront. That way you avoid being disappointed in the way you are now.'

'Disappointed?'

'I'm not paying you. Leave this house immediately and if you breathe a word of this to anyone I'll destroy you and your little family. Got that?'

'That's not—'

'Got that?' shouted Mr Lenkan.

Martin left the room without replying. Behind him he heard Cima say, 'Ralph, you saved me. Again.'

He hurried down the stairs to the outhouse, got dressed and left the house.

TUESDAY

THIRTY-THREE

Terry kissed Amber on the bridge of her nose. 'Morning, gorgeous. You were all loved up last night.'

She pulled back the duvet and stretched, still half asleep. He kissed her throat, her cleavage and her stomach. 'You too,' she said and kissed the top of his head. A loud beeping noise came from the bathroom. 'Shit, that's the shower alarm – time I was getting ready.'

'Stay?'

'Love to. But we're only two days away from Pay Day.' She picked up her ruyi from beside the bed and hurried through to get washed. In the bathroom she quickly checked her points. They hadn't changed much overnight. There was a slight increase but not the dramatic rise she'd hoped for from Balfy. It wasn't surprising given the way she'd stormed out on him, but she'd done a lot of what he'd asked and she'd hoped for some recognition. Thankfully, there were no more blackmail threats.

The hot clear water hit her head and dribbled down to her feet. She faced one way to symbolise the option of another year with Terry creating the home she'd always craved and then the other way to symbolise the life as yellow or even orange that Balfy was offering. She was certain there was no possibility of having both; Terry had no ambition beyond green and Balfy was not going to compromise. She felt a waft of cold air as the bathroom door opened and Terry walked in. He was fabulous and sexy and hers.

'Hey, I gotta go to work too. Stop hogging the shower, you naughty, naughty girl,' he said and pinched her bum.

'Cheeky. Pass me the towel.'

'Max, your dad didn't come home again last night. That's twice in one week. It's not like him.'

Max put his coffee on the table and his hand on her arm. 'Mum, it's 'cos he's a complete shit. Selfish, stupid, lying shit.'

She put her hand over his. 'He isn't though. Yeah, he's an idiot and a tad self-obsessed, but he genuinely did all of this for us.'

Max lifted her hand off and stood up. 'He lies, Mum. He's created a myth around himself. He's not honest with any of us.'

'It's his past. It makes him wary of letting people know the truth. One day he'll tell you about it, I'm sure.'

Max let out a shallow, sharp breath. 'His past? It's not that dramatic. He just plays it up to make sure you still find him interesting and so he can wander off without explanation.'

'That's unfair and you don't know as much about him as I do. He's a good, slightly misdirected man. And I love him.'

'I love him too, but I won't turn a blind eye to what he's really like. You should wise up, Mum.'

'I'm really worried about him, Max. I'm really worried that he's on the verge of a breakdown. We have to help him, it's our job. We must be there for him when he needs us – that's the least we can do.'

'I should be out having fun not babysitting my own dad.'

'Max!'

'Okay, okay. For you.'

'And him?'

'And him.'

As usual, Sam had arrived at the office first. She waited for the others to arrive, thinking about how they would take the latest news.

Amber arrived first, spectacularly dressed in gold stilettos, high-waisted white linen trousers and a ruffled peach shirt with a coral-pink sparkly bib that faded to white just below her breasts. The left-hand side of her bead necklace was black and the right-hand side was cherry red.

'Amber, you look stunning. What's the occasion?' asked Sam.

Amber smiled. 'No occasion. Is it too much?'

'Only you could get away with wearing it to work. You look great.'

Martin arrived next wearing the same clothes as the day before, only more crumpled. His stubble was now three days old.

Sam sat next to him and spoke quietly. 'Martin. What on earth is going on? You look rough. Is everything okay?'

'Not really,' he mumbled.

'Do you want to talk about it?'

'Not really,' he mumbled again.

'Why don't you go and tidy yourself up as best you can? We'll be meeting in fifteen minutes.'

'Sure.' He shuffled back along the office towards the gents.

One by one the other members of the team arrived.

Martin sauntered back having attempted to straighten his clothes and having used the shaving cream provided to dissolve his stubble from an emerging beard to a mere shadow. He followed the team into the meeting room and sat on the last available chair.

'Morning,' said Sam. She waited for them to respond before she carried on. 'It's two thousand three hundred and forty minutes before Pay Day and for those of you that won't be at tomorrow's meeting, this is the last time we'll see each other. I'd like to thank you all for the hard work and dedication you've shown over the past year. It's not always been easy, but you've been professional and I'm proud of the work we've done together.' She glanced at Martin and pulled a sad face. 'There's some important HR news for you this morning and we have someone joining us in a while to explain it and to answer your questions – either as a group or individually. While we're waiting I'd like to tell you my exciting news. I was chosen to represent GreenNet last night on *The Feed*. Did anyone see it?' They all shook their heads. 'I'll show you.' She turned to the front of the room. 'Screen: corporation cook-off.'

The studio had six differently coloured cooking areas with the corresponding corporation logo hanging above them. RetailCorp was violet, PowerCorp had chosen indigo and TradeCorp was blue. NetCorp was using its GreenNet and OrangeNet logos for green and orange and BeWellCorp was yellow. Sam was standing in the GreenNet area.

'Can you see me?' she asked. There were a few nods around the room. 'I had to choose a recipe and then shop for it in the GreenNet store. The catch was that I didn't know what they had in stock so it was a real gamble. I chose to cook *Truffled and Brandied Field Mushrooms*. And guess what? They didn't have any truffles so I had to use porcini mushrooms instead.'

Martin coughed and Sam looked across at him quizzically. 'Can't see it working, that's all,' he said.

'That's all part of the fun though. Trying to compete using the best ingredients you can find.'

'If the higher up the ladder you are the better the ingredients you're allowed to use, it's hardly a fair competition is it?'

Amber laughed. 'Martin, it's an incentive to climb the ladder. And some people need a bigger incentive than others.'

Sam interrupted her. 'It was a bit of fun.'

'Who won?' asked Martin.

'OrangeNet.'

'What a surprise.'

Amber sat upright. 'Martin, what's your problem? They won because they're orange and they're orange because they're the best. It's a fact of life – get over it.'

Martin slumped back in his chair and kept silent. The cook-off continued on the screen and they all sat and watched in silence. The host of the show was commenting on each of the contestants and making witty comments designed to belittle them, especially the lower levels. Whenever it was Sam's turn to have the host's caustic honey applied, her eyes skittered around the meeting room and she giggled at the mistake or the sarcastic commentary. Her team were visibly uncomfortable watching Sam's humiliation.

A middle-aged woman in a beige suit walked into the meeting room and Sam commanded the screen to stop. All attention was now on this bland but important visitor.

'This is Jean from HR,' said Sam.

'Hello, everyone. Sorry to keep you waiting; it's been quite a busy morning what with one thing and another. Anyway, I'm here now.' She pulled her charta from her bag. 'Does everyone here have their charta with them? Good, nods all round.' She gave Sam the thumbs up. 'What a compliant team you've created. That's to your credit, Samantha.'

Sam winced at the use of her full name, but then smiled. 'Thank you.'

Jean shuffled in her seat, increasing the tension in the room by making them wait a little longer. 'I bet you're wondering why I'm here. Unless Sam has already spilled the beans?' They all shook their heads. 'Good. Let me recap our position. I'm sure you'll be aware of most, if not all, of it but I find it's always helpful to make sure we're on the same page.' She tapped her charta. 'We're two thousand and three hundred minutes away from Pay Day. The corporations have run a double-points weekend to help those that are helping themselves. Sadly, the economy is such that they've also had to increase the levels by two hundred points. The Bureaucracy has been keen to react accordingly to these events without risking further economic problems. The Board met late yesterday and came to an agreement on how it wished to proceed and overnight we in HR have been number crunching the outcomes of that agreement. Any questions so far?'

Martin raised his hand.

'No need to raise hands, we're all grown-ups here. Mr?'

'Martin Brown.'

'Martin. What's your question?'

He put his hand down. 'Actually, I think you've already answered it. Sorry,' he said quietly.

'Okay… Any more questions?' She looked around the room and held each one of them with her gaze for a few seconds. 'The great news from yesterday's Board meeting is that they've decided to award bonuses this year.'

There was a communal intake of breath; this was unprecedented.

'I need each one of you to get your charta ready to accept the outcome chit with your individual bonus. I must warn you upfront that the amounts are to be kept confidential, to you and you alone.

Any breach of that instruction and the bonus will be removed and a fine of the same amount applied. This is non-negotiable and will be instigated without warning and without exception. Understood?'

They all muttered their agreement.

'Place your charta in front of you please so I can connect with you.' She stroked and tapped her charta and one by one they received the bonus chit. 'I'm more than happy to answer any questions either now or with you individually afterwards.'

Amber received hers. 'Great but hardly going to change the world,' she said and laughed.

Jean shot her a look of contempt. 'Quiet unless you want to be fined,' she said sharply.

Martin dropped his head into his hands. 'Fucking fine me then,' he said through an exasperated exhalation.

'Martin!' snapped Sam.

'What? Fining me nothing is hardly going to kill me is it?'

'It's not the only repercussion,' said Jean.

'There's very little left that you could do to me. I'm finished.'

Jean reached out and picked up his charta. 'If you break the confidentiality agreement, we can find something to respond with. I can assure you.'

'No doubt,' he said and left the room.

Sam turned to Amber. 'Are you okay?'

'Sure. It all helps, I'm sure. Did you decide who got what?'

'No. It's the first I've heard of it.'

Jean rapped the table. 'In case any of you are in doubt, these bonuses are based on your past year's performance as described by Sam. And on the number of cases you've resolved in line with the Bureaucracy's strategy. Thank you for all your effort and please enjoy your privilege day off tomorrow and don't forget to make the last two thousand two hundred and eighty minutes profitable.'

THIRTY-FOUR

'Max, I need to talk to you about this blackmail thing you've got going,' said Dan.

'Yeah, I need to chat about that too.'

The bass from the dub reggae in the main part of the club pumped through the walls, softened by the rough concrete and the steel door. The club was still full of punters winding down after a night of intense sounds, forming a useful barrier between the illegal back-room trading and the outside world.

Max leant close to Dan's ear. 'I've not sent any blackmail threats since Saturday. These drugs I'm trialling have done some strange things to me you know.'

'Later,' said Dan.

Max nodded. 'Let's trade,' he said loudly.

A middle-aged man with a full neat beard and a tiny tattoo of an upside down cross beneath his right eye tapped the podium with an auctioneer's gavel. His attention roamed around the room. He took off his checked brown suit jacket and placed it carefully on the high stool next to him. 'Welcome to AltStrata, the place where it's what you can do that's more important than who you know. Here you'll be able to trade your skills for the skills of others without the fake layers of the corporations. Here you'll be able to look each other in the eye and trade as equals without needing a go-between. Here you'll be able to trust your own judgement and not be forced to rely on a third-party to tell you who is and who isn't up to the job.'

Dan offered Max an e-cigarette. 'Can I tempt you?'

Max was surprised. 'Here?'

'It's fine.'

'Okay. Thanks,' he said and accepted the gift.

The auctioneer smoothed his greased hair across his head and banged his gavel again. 'Are we ready?' he called.

The hundred or so people in the room quietened down and an expectant hush fell.

'Good. Let's begin.' He shuffled a pile of micro-thin sheets. They'd gone to great lengths to explain to Max when he arrived that although he needed to enter the skills he wanted to trade on to one of these sheets they were not charta and were not connected to any wider networks that could trace him.

'First up we have Ms Sharpe. Raise your hand, Ms Sharpe.' A slightly nervous young woman in overalls raised her hand. The auctioneer clapped his hands twice. 'Good. Ms Sharpe is a plumber and she is offering one hundred and twenty minutes of her time. She's a level three plumber who can work with complex domestic plumbing systems. What am I bid?'

'Thirty minutes of live violin music,' shouted a scruffy man at the back. Ms Sharpe held up one finger.

'Three hundred minutes of cleaning,' shouted a small woman with a heavily wrinkled face. Ms Sharpe held up three fingers.

'One hundred and twenty minutes of mathematics tuition.' She held up three fingers.

'Thirty minutes of investment advice.' She held up one finger.

'Any more bids?' said the auctioneer. He waited, making sure he was watching all parts of the room. 'No? Well then…it's between the tuition and the cleaning. Any advance?' He held his hand out to the cleaner first, inviting her to increase her offer. She shook her head. He turned to the maths tutor, who raised his hand.

The auctioneer began again. 'One hundred and eighty tuition bid, now three hundred and thirty cleaning, now three hundred and thirty cleaning, will ya give me three thirty cleaning?' The old woman raised her hand. 'Three thirty cleaning bid, now two ten tuition, now two ten tuition, will ya give me two ten tuition?' The man raised his hand. 'Two ten tuition bid, now four hundred cleaning, now four hundred cleaning, will ya give me four hundred cleaning?' The woman shook her head and looked down at her lap. 'Closing at two ten tuition. Going once…going twice…gone!' He banged the podium with his gavel. 'Ms Sharpe, you have traded one hundred and twenty minutes of level three plumbing for two hundred and ten minutes of mathematics tuition. Next up we have Mr Cadborn, an undiscovered actor offering thirty minutes of children's party entertainment.'

Max touched Dan on the arm and pointed to the bar. 'A chat?'

'Sure,' said Dan.

They walked to the bar and sat down, sandwiched between the rumble of the reggae and the rhythmic rant of the auctioneer. The smell of the freshly cleaned floor and the polished beer pumps hung in the air.

'Sod this,' said Max and handed Dan a slender but real cigar. 'Shall we?'

Dan opened a small branded box that he'd picked out of an ornate china bowl on the bar. He struck a match and Max leant forward, inhaling short bursts until his cigar caught light. Dan did the same. They sat puffing, contented and watching the room in the mirror behind the bar.

Max was the first to break the silence. 'I know I asked you to get some dirt on Amber Walgace and to find out what my dad was up to…'

'Yes…'

'And I appreciate all you've done. It's just that…I'm no longer sure it's such a good thing.'

'You mentioned drugs?'

'Yeah. I'm on some drug trial and they're testing empathy. Ever since I started I've been uncomfortable with the spying thing.'

'Why?'

'I'm not sure. It feels wrong. I'd go ballistic if someone did it to me.'

'I thought the point was that you needed to protect your dad and you can't do that unless you know what he's up to and unless you have some control over those that want to hurt him.'

'I know. I'm torn. I really do want to help him. In fact that desire increases minute by minute. And I'm pretty sure that bitch of a strata climber is undermining him and making sure she gets all the glory.'

'So what's the problem?'

'I don't know. I think he'd do the same for me. That's another thing I'm more sure of as each day goes by. And I'm also sure he needs help. He's a mess and it's not really his fault. Well, not entirely. But blackmail? It's so nasty. It's so crude. It must be making her life hell.'

'You told me she deserved it.'

'I did. Can I confide in you?'

Dan nodded.

'I'm really struggling. I'm sure it's the drugs. I'm getting more and more aware of how some people must be feeling. It's only a few people, but sometimes it's chaos inside my head and I feel as if I'm losing all sense of myself.'

'Stop the drugs then, surely?'

'I need the Fluence.'

'Can't you rise above the chaos?'

'I am, but only just and it's getting harder all the time.'

'What do the trial people say?'

'I haven't told them. I'm due back later today. Do you think I should tell them?'

'Why wouldn't you? Isn't that the purpose of the trial?'

'I guess so, but I don't want them to take me off it. Like I said, I need the payment.'

'You must be fairly well off though? You've got so many income streams and you're still strata levelled according to your parents, aren't you?'

'Not for much longer. I'd be doing all right, if it was only me I was concerned about. I have to help him stay up at green, otherwise we lose the house and I'm sure my mum will ditch him. He'll fall apart. He might be a sad, good-for-nothing loser, but he's my dad.'

'Fair enough. Let's see what you can get over there then,' said Dan, pointing to the auction.

'Thanks. Did you say you needed to chat about something as well?'

'It can wait until after the auction.'

They clipped the burning end off their cigars and wandered back to the main part of the room.

The auctioneer tilted his head to one side and made a point of waiting for Max and Dan to sit down. 'Welcome back to the auction, Mr Brown. You're next.' He spread his arms out to regain the attention of the room. 'Mr Brown – you may know him better as Maxamillion – is offering one hundred and twenty minutes of indoor surfing lessons, co-starring with you or the person of your choice in a twenty-minute stunt-surfing film. I'm sure I don't need to remind you that Max here is the star of that famous battle with the surf-master. If you win you'll get to surf with one of the best and get some niche fame by association. So what am I bid?'

'Five sixty-minute grooming sessions,' called out a handsome well-dressed man in his fifties. Max held up one finger.

A famous underground artist that was the darling of the SMFeed and needed no introduction called out next. 'A portrait.' Max held up three fingers.

Two men in the middle of the room raised their hands. 'A whole pig, butchered. From me and my friend.' Max held up two fingers.

'Three hundred and sixty minutes of level eight cognitive therapy,' said a woman at the front. Max held up four fingers and tapped his leg with the index finger on his other hand.

Dan raised his hand. 'Twenty miles of solo travel in a luxury car.' Max held up four fingers.

'Any more bids?' asked the auctioneer. He waited. 'No? Good. We have two bids on the table, the solo travel and the therapy.' He pointed at the therapist. She raised her hand. 'Four twenty of therapy bid, now thirty miles of travel, now thirty miles of travel, will ya give me thirty miles?' Dan raised his hand. 'Thirty miles bid, now four fifty of therapy, now four fifty, will ya give me four fifty?' She nodded. 'Four fifty bid, now forty miles, now forty miles, will ya give me forty?' Dan nodded. 'Forty bid, now five twenty, now five twenty, will ya give me five twenty?' She held up eight fingers. 'Eight hundred bid, now one hundred, now one hundred, will ya give me one hundred?' Dan nodded. 'One hundred bid, now nine hundred, now nine hundred, will ya give me nine hundred?' She raised her hand. 'Nine hundred bid, now one hundred and fifty, now one hundred and fifty, will ya give me one hundred and fifty?' Dan shook his head and broke eye contact with the auctioneer. 'Closing at nine hundred. Going once…going twice… gone!' He banged the podium with his gavel. 'Mr Brown, you have traded one hundred and twenty minutes of surfing lessons plus co-starring in a twenty-minute stunt-surfing film for nine hundred minutes of level eight cognitive therapy. Congratulations.'

Dan tugged Max's sleeve. 'C'mon,' he said, stood up and walked back to the bar.

'What is it?' asked Max.

'I don't quite know how to put this.'

'Say it as it is then.'

'You have to stop the blackmail. Immediately.'

'I told you I haven't done anything since Saturday.'

'I mean more than not doing anything. You have to tell her you're stopping. And give her a reason she'll believe.'

'I can't do that.'

'You have no choice.'

'Are you serious?'

'Deadly.'

'I won't do it. She'll go ballistic, drop my dad in trouble and he'll get busted down to blue. And now I've got him that therapy, in another year he might be well enough to fend for himself. My plan's coming together. And when she admits to stealing that data the entire wrath of the Bureaucracy will fall on her and they'll be distracted away from my dad.'

'You have no choice.'

'Dan, stop repeating yourself. Explain.'

'Some extremely powerful people, one in particular, have told me to stop you blackmailing Ms Walgace. You must tell her that she doesn't have to quit her job or hand back the data or make a public apology or pay you any points. Max, these are reds, you can't fuck about with them.'

'What's their interest in her?' asked Max, curious to know if there were any more levers he could use.

'I've no idea, but what I do know is that this guy was serious. Serious in a way that leaves no room for doubt, no room for disobedience and no room for trying to be clever and outwit him. I was told to make it clear that if you don't obey then the consequences for your dad are dire. Do you get what I'm saying?'

Max nodded. 'Okay. You told me. You've done your bit.' He turned his back on Dan and walked away.

THIRTY-FIVE

Without Martin realising, Max had followed him from outside of the Bureaucracy to a desolate part of South London, to the infamous Peckham Rye 'Friends on the Fringe' market. Small bonfires surrounded by rusted wrecks littered the approach road to a five-storey disused car park. A steady stream of people filed in and out of the ground floor entrance. A sign declaring that CCTV was in operation had been torn off the gateway and discarded against the wall. The cameras it warned of were dangling from their housing like the entrails of roadkill.

Max kept enough distance to blend into the crowd and follow Martin without being seen. At the top of the first ramp was a booth. Sitting with their backs against it and their feet propped up on anti-riot helmets was a man and a woman dressed in full protective Kevlar body armour. They were checking passes, waving through those that showed them and selling them to those that didn't. Martin joined the queue.

Sunlight streamed in through long horizontal gaps in the walls only to be deadened by the low concrete ceilings and the rough concrete floor, creating a sense of oppression and danger; there were no soft options in this particular market.

The crowd moved slowly upwards, flowing around groups of sitting, squatting and standing people absorbed in whatever activity it was they were sharing. It reminded Max of a colony of ants working their way to and from a common destination.

Whenever Martin stopped, Max stopped and pretended to listen to the nearest group, but in reality he was focussed solely on Martin. On the fourth floor, Martin walked over to the sunlit gap, leant on the chest-high wall and lit a cigarette. Max stood the other side of a couple who were laughing loudly and holding hands. The skyscrapers – the middle fingers of the corporation beasts – littered the skyline. Martin flicked his cigarette butt into the Peckham streets below and rejoined the stream of human ants.

On one corner of the roof was a large red canopy held up by a wooden A-frame secured with wires attached to poles set at a sixty-degree angle. Smoke from the cooking fires gathered in the roof of the canopy until it reached sufficient volume to escape and billow out into the sky. The smell of burning meat, coffee and baking bread grew stronger the nearer they got. Martin knelt down to talk to a group of nine women and one man – all of them appeared to be on edge. They were sitting on a circle of old toilets that had once been glossy white but were now covered in brown webs of dirt that filled the cracks of wear and tear. A black bag was attached to the back of each toilet. Martin looked as if he was likely to be there for a while so Max wandered across to a nearby group of teenagers.

'Care to join us?' asked one of the girls.

'Sure,' he said. Under normal circumstances he would have found her long red hair framed by a sky-blue hood and the tattoo of three red stars tracing a line from her cleavage to her throat extremely attractive, but all his emotions and longings were focussed on his dad.

'Give us your ruyi then.'

'Why?' he said, distracted by Martin waving his arms around in an animated conversation.

'So we can rejig it,' she said and smiled. 'You do know what we do, don't you?'

'Err…no, not really.'

'We rewire them to randomise the points and the status and then play Ruyi Russian Roulette.'

'What's that?'

'Whoever has the highest score obliterates the other and sucks up all the points.'

Max shook his head in dismay. 'No thanks.'

She rested her finger on the lowest of her star tattoos. 'It's fun,' she said in a husky voice.

'I'm sure it is, but I need to watch that man over there. Can you pretend I'm playing?'

She giggled. 'Why are you watching him?'

'It's no big deal. I just need to watch him. Okay?'

'Sure.'

Max moved to the other side of the group so he could see Martin without having to turn his head. 'Isn't this game a bit stupid?' he asked.

She banged her friend's ruyi and then checked the result. 'Damn,' she shouted and threw it into a cardboard box piled high with discarded ruyi. 'I lost again.' She laughed.

'Lost again?'

'Lost again,' she repeated.

'If it wipes you out, how can you lose more than once?'

'I have more than one.'

He shrugged. 'Even with illegal and multiple accounts it's a high risk to gamble your life away like this.'

'What do you mean?'

'If you lose all your points, you're fucked.'

She laughed and pointed at him. 'Did you think...' She laughed again. 'They're not mine.'

'So who do they belong to?'

'We steal them. We're gambling with the lives of their owners, not ours.'

He chuckled. 'Fair enough. Guess they shouldn't be so careless.'

'Exactly.' She smiled at him. 'You're kinda cool, aren't you?'

'Kinda,' he said.

One of the women from Martin's group was returning with a large jug of cider, four fist-sized steaks of meat and a chocolate cake. She placed the feast in front of him. He drunk half the cider in one go and then rammed alternate pieces of meat and cake into his mouth. The group watched in fascination. He washed down the last of the cake and meat with a final slug of cider and then knelt in front of the toilet. He lifted the lid and put his fingers down his throat. Max could hear retching. Brown vomit erupted into the toilet and the black bag began to swell.

The girl groaned.

'What's going on over there?' Max asked.

'They're bulimic. Ex-bulimic. They pay to see others gorge and puke.'

The woman handed Martin a data-stick.

'Fucking idiot,' said Max under his breath.

'You what?' she said.

'Nothing. I gotta go. Nice to meet you.'

Max got up and followed Martin out of the car park.

The crowd surged forward as the bus approached, holding their ruyi above their heads so they didn't accidentally bang. They pushed and shoved their way through the narrow doors. Halfway up the second flight of stairs, Martin stumbled. Max was close behind so he stopped and turned sideways to allow people to pass, hoping that Martin wouldn't spot him.

The top deck was rammed full and the sweaty smell of cheap genetically modified garlic hung in the air. The buzz of people frantically touching and talking to their ruyi filled the space and was amplified as it bounced off the metal shell of the bus. Max squatted on the edge of a seat that was designed for two but already occupied by four teenagers chatting away even though their eyes were fixed on their ruyi. Martin was standing with his back to Max and with his hands in his pockets. His whole body was slumped as if part of his insides had been removed.

One of the teenagers put her fingers either side of another's ruyi and held it. 'Look, I'll show you,' she said.

'Go on then,' said the boy, letting her take it.

The girl stroked and swiped. 'There, that's him. You know him, don't you?'

The boy nodded. 'Bao McCrour.'

'He's completely off-strata.'

'He's always provoking, making trouble.'

'Precise. He poured his heart out the other day. Told me deep stuff.'

'Bao?'

'Yeah, Bao.'

'Expand.'

'He's dead inside. Can't see the point. Wants to die. Too pale to do it so he goes out at night, riding the buses and provoking. Hoping to ping someone who has a knife and who'll do the job for him.'

'You're feeding me?'

'Straight.'

'Don't go banging with Bao then.'

'Precise.'

'Precise.' The boy took his ruyi back.

Out of the corner of his eye, Max saw Martin moving and turned away. 'Show me his face, this Bao,' he said to the boy.

'Not happening.' The boy shifted slightly so Max couldn't see.

Martin passed behind Max and down the stairs.

Max followed him off the bus and on to the desolate high street. He was walking slowly and the other passengers drifted past, heads down to their ruyi yet somehow aware enough not to bump into each other. Martin dragged his feet slightly as if he was being drawn towards somewhere he didn't want to go.

Makeshift barriers of old pieces of plastic surrounded large potholes and washing flapped on racks hung from the windows of flats above boarded-up shops. Illegal plants – cannabis, tomatoes, carrots and beans – grew among orange and yellow French Marigolds in window boxes balanced precariously on *For Sale* signs bolted to every building. The shops were covered in ornate and colourful graffiti created by spraying the walls with minuscule organic lights that attached themselves and glowed constantly. The narrowness of the street and the height of the buildings kept sunlight at bay, allowing the glow of the lights to be more prominent. In its own way the street was beautiful.

Martin took a left turn. Max glanced discreetly as he walked past. It was a narrow street piled high with rubbish and littered with the corpses of stray dogs. At the far end, Martin was shuffling through the entrance to an estate of tower blocks. Max jogged to catch up, worried that he would lose sight of him in the walkways and underpasses.

A group of girls flanked Martin, chanting, 'Bureaucracy Man, Bureaucracy Man, Bureaucracy Man. Fuck off.' Martin ignored them and shuffled along with his head hung low, deflated. The people in the launderette and outside of the off-licence looked up casually as Martin and the chanting girls passed by. He stopped to look in the window of a second-hand ruyi shop. The girls pushed and nudged him along. 'Move along, move along, you can't stop here,' they shouted at him, inches away from his face, and then resumed the original chant of 'Bureaucracy Man'. People spat on the ground as he shuffled past the One Point Store and the bookies. The girls joined the crowd outside the pub and stopped chanting. The chatter died down to a hushed murmur. Martin carried on to the Pay Day loan company next door.

A loud voice broke the muted atmosphere. 'What can we do for you?'

Max ducked into a doorway close enough to hear what was happening; the volume of the voice from the other side of the grille gave no privacy to those unfortunate enough to be using their services.

'I've come to pay my first instalment,' said Martin.

Max was shocked. Had his dad taken out a Pay Day loan? Surely he wasn't that stupid? Or that desperate? He listened carefully.

The voice from behind the grille spoke again. 'And you are?'

'Martin Brown.'

'Ah yes, the man from the Bureaucracy. What do you have for us?'

'Some Fluence.' Martin slipped the data-stick from the bulimic woman under the grille.

'Are you kidding? That's not even worth the cost of processing. Come back when you can pay us something worthwhile.'

'Please, it's not much I know, but every payment takes a bit off the loan doesn't it?'

'Seriously, Mr Brown. If we take that tiny amount it'll cost you more in charges than the actual payment. Take my advice and save up first. It'll cost you less in the long run.'

'But in the meantime you're piling on the interest.'

'You knew the deal when you signed.' There was a loud click and the grille closed.

The girls were standing guard at the exit of the estate. They slow hand-clapped Martin as he shuffled past them.

As Max drew level with them, they blocked his path and taunted him.

'Hey, freak.'

'Weirdo.'

'Who cuts your hair? Your mum or your gran?'

'Don't you look a picture, all dolled up and no place to go.'

Max grabbed the ringleader's pink ruyi, dropped it on the floor and stamped on it. It shattered.

She hissed through her teeth. 'You…'

Max took hold of her earlobe between his thumb and forefinger and pulled her head to one side. 'If you want the wrath of the outliers to descend on your petty piss-ridden estate, keep hassling me. If not, walk away quietly and we'll say no more about it.' He let her go.

She kicked the remains of her ruyi. 'You don't scare me,' she said.

He shrugged. 'You don't look that stupid to me.' He pushed his way through them and sauntered off the estate.

THIRTY-SIX

Amber was in a Bureaucracy taxi driving from West London to East London, to her next client. 'Ruyi: message to Terence Huddson. Still in Camden Town?'

'Reply: Yes.'

'Message to Terence Huddson: Late lunch and a stroll?'

'Reply: Splendid. Give me thirty minutes. Where?'

'Message to Terence Huddson: The tree on the narrow bridge.'

'Reply: Okay.'

She knocked on the partition between her and the driver. 'Can you drop me off here, please?'

The unseen driver replied, 'Not really, Ms Walgace. Your journey is already in the system.'

'Change of plan. Here's fine.'

'I need authorisation.'

'Can I do that from here?'

'It's highly irregular.'

'Pay Day emergency.'

'Very well. I'll amend your journey. Pass your charta through to me.' Amber slid her charta through the narrow gap. The taxi sped along the special lane reserved for the Bureaucracy and the corporations. Buses filled the rest of the road, inching forward with their horns blaring as they battled to beat each other to the queues of potential customers. A few people ran across the road, weaving in and out to find their bus before it filled up.

The charta reappeared. 'Highly irregular,' repeated the driver.

The taxi stopped in the middle of the road. 'Thank you,' said Amber. She opened the door cautiously, checked that there were no speeding taxis coming up from behind and dashed across to the pavement.

The road to Camden Town cut through the half-built HS2 complex that had been abandoned by the corporations as commercially unworkable once government funding had stopped. It had been repurposed into an immigration processing area surrounded by high fences topped with razor wire. This is where you were stored if you couldn't immediately convince the corporation border controls you had sufficient disposable income.

Amber hurried along the road as dogs barked from behind the fences on both sides. The low hum of poorly maintained generators hung over the compound. Young children waved at her from the top of the poles that connected the generators to the spotlights. She held the bottom of her shirt and wriggled to straighten it. The fence rattled, startling her, and a dog snarled as it tugged at the wire with its teeth. Her gold stilettos were splattered with dirty puddle water – this was not a road that was often walked along. She held on to her black and cherry-red necklace, twisting it between her fingers as she scurried along as fast as she could.

A bus pulled up a few feet in front of her. She ran to catch it and pushed her way on to the lower deck. The passengers were crammed in but still found the space to use their ruyi. Amber jostled her way to a small gap near the middle of the bus and held on tightly. A baby was crying. The father patted its head occasionally while still absorbed by his ruyi and his SMFeed. The crying turned to screaming. Everyone, including Amber, turned their heads the other way until the stench of baby shit exploded into the air. Amber turned. The father was kicking the dirty nappy under the seat with the back of his heel while pulling up the baby's trousers. Amber was almost sick.

The woman next to her muttered under her breath, 'Disgusting, shouldn't be allowed out with a baby.'

He smiled. 'He can't help shitting himself, can he? What's your excuse, you old witch?'

She opened her mouth to reply but thought better of it and dropped her gaze back to her ruyi.

The bus drove over the small canal bridge and stopped. Amber squeezed her way to the exit, stepped on to the pavement and squirted some sanitiser gel on to her hands, rubbing them together until it dried. Terry was waiting over by the tree, leaning against the railing and waving nonchalantly. She strolled across, trying to regain her composure.

'Babe, you look exhausted. Hard day?'

'Charming,' she replied and rubbed his head.

'This was a surprise. Are you okay?'

She took his hand and pulled. 'Let's walk along the canal, shall we?'

'Sure.' He smiled and blew her a kiss. 'Do you remember this tree? That night?'

'Of course, that's why I chose it.'

Hand in hand they strolled across the bridge, down the steps and on to the tow path that weaved its way along the side of the canal. Gangs of old people and gangs of young people were gathered along the path, chatting and drinking. A gang of wizened old men who gave off a sweet acrid smell hushed as Amber and Terry approached. Terry nodded. 'All right, gents?' he said.

'For sure, young man,' said one of them.

Amber put her arm through Terry's and moved a little closer so their shoulders touched. 'My hero,' she whispered.

'My lady,' he said and bowed.

She chuckled.

They walked along in silence, past a family of four pushing the lock gates open to allow their boat to drop thirty feet to the canal below as it meandered east. An apartment block with curved sides in the shape of a ship stood on the opposite bank. The residents sat on their balconies overlooking the canal. The only access to their homes was through the OrangeNet store attached to their block. They were isolated and safe.

She squeezed his arm. 'That'd be a nice place to live wouldn't it?'

'Bit boring, I'd have thought.'

They carried on walking. The canal curved to the left under a low bridge and they had to move even closer together to avoid bumping their heads on the arch of the brick roof. 'We should do this more often,' said Amber. Terry kissed her cheek. The crisp spring sun was shining and bouncing off the water along with the reflection of another top-level strata apartment block that had once been a warehouse. A group of orange-level children were playing among the trees and bushes on the opposite bank.

Terry put his arm around her. 'Cute.'

'Cute?'

'Kids.'

'Oh,' she murmured and put her arm around his waist.

The wall to their left was covered in old-fashioned painted graffiti and someone had planted shrubs and flowers in the soil at its base. Amber pointed to a row of houses above them on a narrow street overlooking the canal. Victorian street lamps fitted with cameras to keep watch over the residents stood like sentries. 'I bet that's a nice place to have a family,' she said.

'Expensive,' he replied.

They came to another bridge and moved closer again. 'I'm sorry,' said Terry.

'Sorry?'

'Yeah. The blackmail. I didn't realise how freaked out you were. I'm sorry.'

'What's brought that on?'

'This walk. Hanging out together. Feels more normal than all those parties and posh restaurants.'

She stopped and turned to face him. 'What exactly are you saying?'

'That I'm sorry.'

'And…'

'Tell me what's happening with the blackmail. Can I do anything?'

'It stopped.'

'Just stopped? With no explanation?'

'Yes, just stopped.'

'Strange. Do you think it was a hoax then?'

'I don't know. Maybe someone else sorted it out for me.'

'Someone else?'

'Sam or someone. Who knows.'

'That's great then, isn't it?'

'Terry. What if it starts again?'

'That's unlikely. Sounds like whoever was playing the prank got bored.'

'Do you have any idea what they were asking me to do?'

'Hey. It's over.' He held her shoulders, pulled her towards him and kissed her on the lips.

She stepped back. 'Terry. Are you listening? They wanted me to quit my job, hand back the stolen data, publicly apologise and then pay them enough points to make me drop to the bottom of green.'

'Nasty. Great that it's all over then, eh?'

She stormed off.

He caught up with her. 'Babe, what's wrong? It's good news, isn't it?'

'Yes,' she said. They walked on in silence, lost in their own thoughts.

A couple of men with long nets were fishing plastic bottles out of the canal, trying their best to avoid the ducks that kept pecking at the poles. Loud rock music blasted from a flat and a group of teenagers sat with their feet dangling in the water, engrossed in the SMFeeds on their plastic ruyi.

'I'm sorry,' said Amber.

'No. I'm sorry.'

They kissed. 'Get a room,' shouted one of the boys.

Terry took two long steps and lunged towards him. The boy leapt to his feet and Terry grabbed him by the elbows. The boy stood rigid with a defiant expression. 'Go on then,' he said.

'One day, little boy, you'll have a beautiful wife and you'll want to kiss her as much as possible. And, mark my words, no snotty kid'll stop you.' He patted the boy's cheeks. 'Until then, enjoy your paddling pool.' His friends laughed and clapped their hands.

Amber smiled at the boy and hugged Terry tight, giving him a long and luxurious kiss. 'C'mon,' she said.

At the next bridge Amber's ruyi buzzed with a message.

'Who's that?' asked Terry.

'A friend.'

'Do I know him?'

'Her, and no you don't. I met her, Ashley, at a party this weekend.'

'Ignore her. This is too nice to share.'

'Let me see what she wants.' Amber read the message and then looked up to the bridge. Ashley was standing there next to Balfy's car. 'Too late I'm afraid, she's up there.'

He touched her hand. 'Amber... Please don't go.'

'Let's see what she wants. You can come too. You'd like her. She's a proper red.'

'That's why you ask how high when she says jump.'

'Terry... Don't spoil things.'

'Me?'

She pulled him towards the steps. 'Yes, you,' she said and squeezed his hand. She bounded up to the road and, reluctantly, Terry followed.

Amber glanced at Ashley's cigarette, trying her hardest not to stare. 'You can't do that in public,' she whispered.

'Really? Why not? Who's to stop me?'

'It's illegal.'

'Oh, that old cliché.'

Terry hovered in the background, pretending to be using his ruyi.

'Is that him?' asked Ashley.

'Yeah. Terence,' replied Amber.

'Hot.'

'Hands off.'

Terry put his ruyi in his jacket pocket. 'I *am* here,' he said.

'You most certainly are,' said Ashley. She flicked her cigarette butt near his feet. 'Amber's bit of rough.'

He ground the butt beneath his foot. 'Yeah, Amber's bit of rough. And her husband.'

Ashley opened the car door. 'Whatever... Amber, look at this.'

She held up a see-through short white silk dress with six-inch capped sleeves held in place by wire sewn into the fabric. A white collar formed a V down to the waist, designed to accentuate the breasts through the see-through top. A large white bow was attached to the waist, designed to hide the knickers, so long as you were looking from above.

Amber laughed. 'That's outrageous.'

'But you like it…'

'I love it. Terry, what do you think?'

'I can't really tell until it's on,' he mumbled.

Ashley laid it on the car roof and put a bracelet of thinly sliced pearl on top. 'I've got one for you too, hot and handsome husband.' She leaned into the car and took out a brown wool and cashmere suit with sky-blue pinstripes, a light-blue dress shirt with chocolate brown buttons and a pair of dark brown brogues with deep-blue eyelets. A mini ruyi was stitched into the lapel.

Amber touched the suit. 'Terry, it's fantastic. You'll look fabulous.'

Terry shuffled his feet. 'Why?'

Amber looked puzzled. 'Why what?'

'Why is she giving us this stuff?'

Amber turned to Ashley. 'Why give us the presents?'

'They're from Lord Balfour. He also sent these.' Ashley handed her two micro-sheets. 'VIP invites to ZeitFeast.'

Terry took one. 'Who's Lord Balfour? What's ZeitFeast?'

Amber snatched it back. 'Terry!'

Ashley picked up the clothes. 'If you don't want them…'

'Of course we do,' said Amber. 'Terry, it's the most exquisite fashionable underground restaurant in the world.'

'Where is it? I've never heard of it.'

'It's invite only and it's never in the same location twice.'

'What's so special about it then?'

'If you're invited, you get to vote on a whole range of incredible ingredients and the menu is created from the most popular. The more of the ingredients they use that you voted for, the more points you get. It's the Zeitgeist feast – ZeitFeast.'

Ashley coughed. 'So my little sex pots, do you want the invites? Do you want the clothes?'

'Of course we do, don't we, Terry.'

'Well…'

'He does, but he's too shy to ask. Hand them over.'

Ashley gave each of them their clothes and invite. 'By the way, it's all made from tagging material – have fun.' She jumped into the back of the car and it drove off.

Terry looked at Amber angrily. 'So, who is Lord Balfour?'

THIRTY-SEVEN

Max was getting dressed after another session with Doctor Bravn and her cubicle. The images had been the same as the time before but the feelings of elation and despair had been much more intense. He was exhausted.

'Maxamillion. Come and take a seat. I have some options for you,' she said.

He slung his jacket over his shoulder and strolled over to the desk. 'Susan, I can call you Susan can't I?'

'Of course.'

'Susan. Do you enjoy your job?'

'Why do you ask?'

'Curiosity, plain and simple.'

'Really?'

'Really.'

'Well…yes, Max, I do.'

'Good.'

'Shall I explain your options?'

'Go ahead.'

'As you know, the trial is complete. It was only ever a short three-thousand-minute trial—'

Max interrupted. 'Did I pass?'

'There's no pass or fail. You know that. Are you deliberately being awkward?'

'No…I don't think so.'

'Okay. You have the option to continue with the trial through to the next stage.'

'I passed then?' He smiled.

She smiled back. 'Very funny, Max.'

'Gotcha,' he said and laughed.

She shuffled the micro-sheets on the desk. 'Max. You are a receptive participant and can carry on with a much bigger test if you want. Or you can stop now.'

'Carry on at a higher rate of AltFlu?'

'Yes. It's in two stages. In the first you'll inhale some smart dust that lodges itself in various places around the body and triggers certain neural drugs and then monitors your reaction. The second stage is more intrusive – we embed smart dust into your brain, into your cortex, and it sits there stimulating and monitoring.'

'Or I can stop now, get paid and walk away with no side-effects?'

'You can stop now, if that's what you really want. Side-effects... we're not a hundred percent sure.'

He put his hand on top of the micro-sheets to stop her fiddling with them. 'Susan,' he said and paused. 'Susan. You're not sure? You're not sure? How can you be...not sure?'

'Max,' she said and took his hand off the pile of case notes. 'You signed the disclaimer. You knew what you were signing up to. And anyway, the results show a real increase in empathy which gives you a real edge on others. You should be grateful, not upset.'

'Sure. I think I'll stop now and take the payment though. I've got a lot to do before Pay Day and that other stuff sounds a bit too full on.'

She slid the micro-sheets into a leather slip-case, swiped her hand across a panel in the desk and stood up. 'Security will see you out.'

As she left the room a female security guard arrived and patiently waited for her to pass. 'This way, sir,' said the guard, pointing along the corridor to a revolving door.

Outside, he stretched his arms and legs, preparing his body for some gruelling physical exercise to shake off the feeling of being trapped that had descended on him in the lab. He pulled the band off his wrist, threw it on the floor and set off to find Dan. He jogged along, enjoying the fresh air and the looseness of his limbs. He checked his ruyi to see what time it was – four o'clock. Dan would be in the park supplying the corporation administrators with their daily fix of gambling. 'Ruyi: distance – current to Victoria Tower Gardens.' It was three miles which would take him fifteen to twenty minutes and the route was simple – down to the river and along the Chelsea Embankment and Millbank.

The river was crowded with small boats chugging up and down, transporting reds and oranges from one part of the city to another. They darted between the large barges stacked high with containers either destined for the supermarkets or for export. At Chelsea Bridge he crossed the road to distance himself from the armed guards patrolling the nearby exclusive hospital. The tall, shoddy, crumpled-looking metal and glass towers of the Battersea Power Station Estate overpowered the skyline in front of him. He ran past Tate Britain – the Museum of Marketing – which, when all publicly owned art had been sold to private individuals, had become the home of the definitive history of the corporations' brands. The RetailCorp flag fluttered on top of the thirty-three-floor Millbank Tower, emphasising how much profit there was to be made from the poor violet Strata.

He stopped to breathe in the river air. The background smell of the sea and the grandeur of Lambeth Palace on the other side conjured up thoughts of a different era; the Church was one of the few remaining voices that occasionally criticised the corporations even though they were usually silenced with a leaked story of some scandal or other. He thought it was ironic that compared to the outliers the Church had so much more power and yet because of its holier than thou stance on a multitude of insignificant issues it was vulnerable to attack in a way that the outliers would never be.

Further along the path, surrounding the statue of *The Burghers of Calais*, was a group of grey-suited young men. Dan moved amongst them, offering a wide range of illegal gambling activities. They were typical of their blue strata – cocky and proud. Max enjoyed the irony of them gathering around a statue that commemorated the selfless sacrifice of six senior leaders. Behind them, the Palace of Westminster, formerly the home of Parliament, was where the corporations debated and negotiated their trade and price agreements;

it stretched into the sky, casting a shadow of power.

The eight chimes of Big Ben striking the half hour echoed around the park and the young men dispersed, hurrying back to their offices for the last part of the working day. Dan was leaning against the plinth rapidly moving his fingers across the surface of his outlier-hacked charta.

Max jumped up on to the plinth and sat next to him. 'Dan. Can we talk about my dad?'

'What's changed since earlier today? You weren't exactly in a chatty mood when you stormed off, were you?'

'I'm sorry. I've had a bit of time to think since then.'

'Okay. Give me a minute,' he replied, still stroking the charta screen. 'I need to finish this and get it logged. Then, I'm all yours.'

The park was emptying as the sun began to set and the river turned a reddish purple. Dan tucked his charta into his inside coat pocket and buttoned it up. 'I've been seeing a lot of you lately,' he said.

'Yeah, is that okay?'

'I suppose so. What's on your mind this time, young man?'

'The blackmail and my dad mostly.'

'Spill the beans – what's bothering you?'

'What you said about the blackmail. I've changed my mind. It's not fair to punish her.'

'Good. Will you do as the red asked?'

'What, tell her that I'm sorry and explain why I did it?'

'You only have to give her a reason she'll believe. The red wants her to be convinced the threat has truly disappeared.'

'Okay, but what can I tell her? Any ideas? I'm not going to tell her I did it to get back at her for the way she treated my dad.'

'Why not?'

'Because then I'd have to tell her what I know about him and about them.'

'What do you know about them?'

'She enticed him into an affair.'

Dan punched Max's arm. 'Silly boy. They didn't have an affair.

She was intrigued by his past and he enjoyed the attention. That's all that happened.'

'Really?'

'Really.'

'So why is he so weird and secretive about her?'

'He's intimidated by her youth, her ambition and her intelligence.'

'How do you know so much?'

'You asked me to find out. I know some of his old friends from the hacker days. He confides in them.'

'Okay…I guess I believe you. He keeps all this locked up inside his head; I wish he had the confidence to admit it openly.'

'He does.'

'I mean to his family, to us.'

'So you'll tell her the blackmail is over?'

'Yeah. I'll tell her. I'll make something up about feeling guilty and wishing I'd never started it. Do you think she'll buy that?'

'Probably, but if she smells guilt she might turn the tables on you and demand compensation. Either that or she'll ask for more details about why you started in the first place.'

'Okay. I'll tell her that I was wrong and no longer believe she's been stealing data. I'll apologise and ask her to forget I was ever in touch. How does that sound?'

'Not as convincing as the first idea. Why not say that you've been persuaded to see the error of your ways?'

'Why would she accept that?'

'It's true, isn't it?'

'I guess so.'

'Trust me, she'll accept that explanation willingly.'

'Can I use your charta so I'm not traced?'

'You don't have your own blockchain encrypter?'

'At home.'

'Do it there. What will you say?'

'Tick tock, tick tock, it's over. I've been persuaded to drop the threat. The End.'

Dan nodded and patted Max on the back. 'That's good.'

'My dad?'

'What about him?'

'Are you still watching him?'

'Of course. You asked me to.'

'Can you stop?'

'Not that easy.'

'Why?'

'You're not the only one that asked me to keep an eye on him.'

'Who else?'

'I can't say, but they're very influential.'

'More influential than whoever asked me to back off the blackmail?'

'About the same.'

'Here's the deal then. I'll stay away from blackmail if they persuade the others to stop tracking my dad. Deal?'

'Not my call, but I'll ask. Don't you want to know what we found out about him?'

'Yes…'

'There's some sort of low-level trolling of his SMFeed going on. It keeps dragging him down. It's hard to detect, but if you know what you're looking for and you look long enough, you'll see it.'

'Shit, who's responsible?'

'I didn't get that far, but I think I know who can stop it.'

'Who?'

'I can't say.'

'What would they want in return?'

'They'd want something and probably something from you. They see you as the up-and-coming hopeful.'

'Me?'

'Yes, you.'

'Can you ask them?'

'Leave me alone for ten minutes and I'll see what I can find out.'

Max walked back to the river. The undercurrent of deep history that flowed with the Thames and with many of the buildings along its banks helped him gain some perspective. His dad obviously needed help and had obviously upset some powerful people. He didn't like the burden he felt as the one that could do something about it. After all, he had a life to lead as well. It wasn't fair that he should get into debt so his dad could be free. But wasn't that what family was about? No judgements, unconditional love, rallying to the coat of arms when it was needed? He had to consider his mum and Becka as well. He was being offered his manhood and it was up to him to take it, whatever the consequences.

A boat of day-trippers chugged past, its happy tourists waving to him as if they didn't have a care in the world. And assumed he didn't either.

It was hard to imagine what these acquaintances of Dan's might ask in return for freeing his dad from the hook they'd so expertly caught him on.

He waved back – he didn't want to spoil their day out.

Dan joined him. 'They'll do it. They'll make sure he's freed from the troll.'

Max sighed, anticipating the weight of the next part, the part where Dan told him the price.

'They want something in return though.'

'I guessed they would. What?'

'They need loyal people in high places. They want you to work for a corporation, preferably RetailCorp, and rise to the top of the organisation ladder. They'll give you whatever assistance you need and you'd be orange within fifteen years. It's a good offer.'

'I sacrifice my life for his.'

Dan put his hand on Max's shoulder. 'Yes, in effect that's what it boils down to.'

'Let me think about it.'

'You've got until midday tomorrow.'

'Why so soon?'

'They need twelve hours to make stuff happen before Pay Day.'

'Okay. I'll let you know.' He turned and jogged away, leaving Dan and the river behind.

THIRTY-EIGHT

'You look gorgeous,' said Amber as she brushed the lapel of Terry's new suit.

'I don't like it,' he said and pulled away.

'How can you not like it, silly? It's so completely wonderful.'

'It's like I'm wearing someone else's clothes.'

'It's a present. Enjoy it, there could be many more.'

'Eh? What do you mean?'

She pressed her finger to his lips. 'Shush,' she said and kissed him.

'Let's stay in.'

'Terry…' There was a knock at the door. 'Here's our car.'

'Our car? What the—?'

'Enjoy. Please. This is such a fabulous opportunity, don't spoil it. Please?'

'Okay.' He kissed her on the nose, straightened his jacket and led the way to the front door.

Balfy's limousine was waiting outside and as Amber bounced down the steps the chauffeur opened the rear door for her. She stepped into the car as gracefully as she could in such a short skirt and giggled. 'Good job there's no paparazzi,' she said, tugging the bottom of her skirt. The chauffeur smiled non-committally, closed the door and walked around the back of the car to hold open the other door.

'No need, I'm fine,' said Terry and took hold of the door handle, practically shoving the chauffeur to one side.

'Terry, don't be so rude,' said Amber.

He leant towards the driver, 'Sorry, mate, didn't mean any offence.'

'None taken, sir.'

'This is so exciting,' said Amber as they sped through the city streets. 'I wonder where it's going to be!'

'Hasn't your Lord Wotsit told you?'

'No. And don't be so horrible or we're not going to have a very nice evening, are we?'

'Sorry. It's this suit – it makes me feel awkward.'

She kissed him on the cheek and they sat back in silence watching the streets go by and wondering about the evening ahead.

The car pulled up in front of a church with four tall columns either side of white stone stairs leading up to tall wooden doors. At the base of each column was a flaming vase and four ushers – a butcher, a baker, a farmer and a beekeeper.

Amber gave her ticket to Terry. 'Can you do the honours?'

A butler swapped their tickets for a small round red disk with an elaborate '1' embossed in gold. 'Your table is at the front,' he said and gestured towards a young waitress. 'Sally will show you the way.'

They followed her through a maze of circular tables to a single table on a raised platform with a centrepiece of a goldfish bowl with a red and black flower sitting majestically in the base and a spiralling green leaf reaching out of the top. Two couples already occupied four of the seven seats. Two men wearing full white-tie evening dress sat next to each other with their little fingers entwined. Next to them an older man and woman sat stony-faced. 'Hi, I'm Amber and this is Terry,' she said as they approached. She caught Terry's eye and inclined her head towards a chair. Terry returned her nod with a quizzical look. She gestured again and he looked more puzzled.

'I think she wants you to pull the chair out for her, dear,' said the woman. Her husband couldn't take his eyes off Amber's dress; it was catching the light and showing off her bra-less breasts. 'Quick, before he has a heart attack,' said the woman and smiled at Terry. 'You're not so bad yourself, young man. What a fun evening we're going to have. I'm Poppy and this is Harold.'

The younger of the two men coughed. 'I'm Andrew and this is Peter. How did you get your ticket?'

Amber sat down. 'Compliments of Lord Balfour.'

'Who's he?' asked the old man.

'Darling, you remember him. That cocky little lord that drives that awful car. We met him a few weeks ago at Freda's shindig.'

'Did we?'

Andrew coughed again. 'So, Amber, you know Balfy?'

'Yup. Do you?'

'We've had our encounters,' he said and winked at Peter. 'And, Terry, how do you know Balfy?'

'I don't. I'm just the sidekick,' he mumbled and immediately looked away, scanning the room.

'What's that?' asked Amber, pointing at a bowl of yellow dust with a small silver spoon in it.

'That's tonight's intoxicant,' said Andrew. He took a spoonful, lifted it to his nose and sniffed. 'A genetically modified variant of cocaine wrapped in pollen husks excreted by honey bees.'

'Honey bee poo?' asked Poppy.

'Makes an excellent drug delivery system,' replied Peter.

Terry sniffed a spoonful and offered one to Amber. She shook her head. He sniffed it himself and sat back with his arms folded. 'How's this voting thing work then?'

Andrew passed him a micro-sheet. 'Here's a list of ingredients for you to vote on. The chef then creates a menu from the highest votes.'

'And if you vote for the most popular you get StrataPoints,' added Amber.

'Do you? How quaint,' said Poppy.

Terry read from the menu. 'Whipped jacket potato. Celeriac. Python carpaccio.'

Poppy held Terry's hand. 'I like the sound of the celeriac, how about you?'

Peter handed each of them a micro-sheet. 'You're not allowed to confer.'

'What a spoilsport,' said Poppy and nudged Harold, who was staring at Amber's top again. 'Eyes down.'

'Where are you from, young man?' Harold asked Terry.

Amber spoke before Terry had a chance. 'The Brighton coast.'

'Hastings,' said Terry. Amber frowned.

'And what do you do to keep yourself out of mischief?'

'Sport. Football mainly.'

Amber interrupted again. 'He owns his own business.'

'Carpenter and a bit of whatever else is needed,' added Terry.

'Don't be so modest,' said Amber.

He sniffed another spoonful. 'I have a posh wife, go to posh restaurants and talk bollocks.'

They all turned their attention to the micro-sheet menus.

Poppy broke the silence. 'Harold, you've got two minutes to decide. Shall I help?'

Harold held Amber's forearm. 'What do you think I should choose, my dear?'

Amber moved her chair nearer to him and scrolled his menu up and down. She wrapped her hands around his skinny biceps. 'What do you fancy?' she asked and giggled.

'A little bit of everything. And then a little bit more,' he said and shot Terry a quick glance.

Poppy clamped her hands around Terry's biceps. 'What's she like, eh?'

Terry pulled himself free. 'I need the toilet,' he said and rushed off.

The room fell silent as the chef came out on to the stage directly in front of their table. He bowed and the crowd clapped and clapped until he lowered his hands, palms down, to signal that he wanted them to stop. An expectant hush descended and everyone's focus was on the micro-sheet in his hand.

There was a crash at the back of the room. Amber turned around. Her worst fears were coming true – Terry was making his way through the tables, apologising loudly and causing people to scrape their chairs on the floor as they moved to let him pass.

Peter squeezed her hand. 'Bit out of his depth, is he?'

She smiled back.

When he arrived at their table he shot Peter a filthy look and sniffed another spoonful of powder. 'Sorry, babe,' he said. Amber ignored him and fixed her stare on the chef who was standing like a teacher pretending to wait patiently for a disruptive pupil to stop talking.

'My lords, ladies and gentleman: eyes down for the ZeitFeast results. In the starter category you have chosen...yellow peas, duck eggs and Marmite. For the main course you have chosen...salsify, Jerusalem artichokes and verbena and for pudding...espresso coffee, ground almonds and whipped blue cheese. What a challenge you've presented me. A challenge to which I shall rise.' He looked around the room from left to right and from front to back. 'It would be crass to ask who chose the most popular ingredients, you know who you are. I hope you enjoy the result of your votes.'

He paused.

Amber slid her micro-sheet in front of Terry. 'Look, seventy-five percent correct, that's got to be worth a few points.'

The crowd waited in anticipation for the chef to speak.

'Okay, I think I have a meal that will blow you away.' He pointed at Terry. 'Are you sitting comfortably?' Terry nodded and took another spoonful of powder. 'Watch closely and whet your appetite.'

Four camera drones floated in from the side and began filming; the images were displayed on large screens above the stage.

'Isn't it great that we can see him without the screens?' Amber whispered in Terry's ear.

'Yeah. Amazing,' he said with thick sarcasm.

'Terry!' she said quietly through clenched teeth.

'Sorry, babe, just a bit wired and this bloody suit doesn't help.'

'Please enjoy yourself – this is what our life could be like after tomorrow.'

He ignored her and sat on his hands, concentrating on the chef busily preparing the food.

'My lords, ladies and gentlemen: in the kitchen, my five-star chefs have been preparing an identical meal for you which will now be served,' said the chef.

He left the stage to a standing applause and circulated around the room shaking hands and signing charts. As he got closer Amber kept an eye on where he was, so she wouldn't miss out.

Once he'd been to every table except theirs and was enjoying another round of bowing and applause, Amber grabbed Terry's sleeve. 'Don't let him escape,' she whispered.

'Wouldn't dream of it.'

The applause died down and the chef took a final bow. He stepped on to their platform and sat in the empty seat. Amber let out a little screech of excitement.

Terry sighed. 'Oh, fucking brilliant,' he said under his breath.

'Hi,' said Peter. 'Splendid evening so far. Are your chefs able to match your genius though?'

'Yes. Absolutely. But there is a slight hitch.'

'What a surprise,' said Terry.

'What?' asked Amber.

The chef took off his red hat and tucked it under his chair. 'The problem is…you get to eat my food, not theirs.'

'That's fabulous,' whimpered Amber.

'Excellent,' said Poppy. Harold nodded.

'Yes, excellent,' said Andrew and Peter in unison.

The chef turned down Terry's offer of powder with a look of contempt.

'Well I'm bloody well going to have one,' said Terry.

'Ruins the palate. And the desire,' said the chef.

'But helps the evening along.' Terry laughed.

'Please excuse me,' said Amber as she stood up. 'I must check out the little girls' room so I can truly appreciate your magic.' She weaved her way through the tables, her short skirt swishing around her thighs, her breasts moving seductively, catching the attention of most of the male guests.

In the lobby she slumped down on a sofa, exhausted by the effort of holding her head up high during her walk of shame; she vowed she'd never forgive him. 'Ruyi: call Opo.'

'Hun. You want to speak? Not message? It's extremely expensive. What's the problem?'

'Terence is a complete jerk. I can't believe what he's just done to me.'

'Tell me. Did he hurt you?'

'We're at ZeitFeast and he's off his face and being stupid, trying to be the alpha male but without anything that makes him alpha. He's ruining the whole evening.'

'Poor you. Hun, it's only one evening though.'

She started to cry. 'It's not though, is it? If I pull off my promotion, which might even be to red, then this is our life and he can't fit in.'

'Or doesn't want to?'

'Opo. It's such a mess.'

'Chin up. Let's chat tomorrow. Is that okay?'

'Of course. Sorry. What are you up to?'

'Now that would be telling. Which I will tomorrow.' She heard a deep female voice in the background. 'Yes, I'm coming.' He laughed. 'Talk tomorrow.'

WEDNESDAY

THIRTY-NINE

Martin was sitting halfway across the footbridge to his house, slumped against the fence and holding his head. His shoes and trousers were covered in mud and a low rhythmic moaning was coming from somewhere deep inside of him. He hugged his knees tight to his chest as Jenny slammed the front door and marched across the lawn. He groaned louder and louder with each footstep until she was standing next to him.

'You stupid, stupid man. What have you been up to?' she shouted at him.

'I can't cope,' he spluttered through bursts of sobs. 'I'm finished.'

'Can't cope? Can't cope with what?'

'This.' He sobbed uncontrollably.

'This? Us? You? Life?'

'Yes.'

'Martin. Pull yourself together, you're a complete mess. Where have you been for the past two days?'

He sobbed quietly, hugging his knees even tighter.

'You're unbelievable. It's the day before Pay Day, you've probably wiped out any chance we have of becoming yellow and you wander off into some sort of woeful self-indulgent misery. Did it ever occur to you that we might need you here? That *I* might need you here?'

He looked up at her with a deep longing, as if he was reaching out and trying to answer with words that kept evaporating. 'I need you,' he said quietly, as if he hoped she wouldn't hear.

She grabbed his arm roughly, yanked it away from his knees and pulled him to his feet. He obliged, docilely. 'Come inside, you pathetic man,' she said with a hint of tenderness. 'Let's at least get you cleaned up.' He shuffled along behind her, into the house and up the stairs.

'Go into the bathroom, take off your clothes and give them to me.'

He sat on the edge of the bath and fumbled with his wet and muddy shoelaces. He gave up and took off his jacket and shirt and placed them carefully in the bath. He pulled at his laces again. 'Jenny,' he called.

'Yes, what now?' she said as she walked in. She took one look at him struggling with his laces and burst into tears. 'Martin, how did it come to this?'

He shrugged and frantically tried to pull his laces apart. He tried to pull his shoes off with the laces still tied. He tried to lever his left shoe with the heel of his right. He failed in every attempt. He punched the mirror and it shattered over his family's toothbrushes.

Jenny stopped crying. 'Enough,' she said firmly. She lifted a pair of scissors from the glass-covered shelf, cut his laces and pulled off his shoes. She undid his trousers and pulled them down, taking his socks with them as she eased them over his feet. 'You can do those,' she said, nodding towards his underwear. He took them off and stood naked in front of her, waiting for the next instruction. 'Shower, then shave,' she said and left the room.

He sat down at the kitchen table.

'You look much better. How do you feel?' she asked.

'Battered, but a bit better,' he said and forced a smile.

'What the hell happened?'

'I don't know. It all got too much. I wandered for hours across the fields trying to make sense of it all. I'm so sorry. I'm lost. I'm a loser.' He folded his arms on the table and lay his head on top of them. 'I know you need me to go. I understand. It's just that... I don't want it to be real. I can't stand the thought of letting you all down and having to let you go.'

'Martin...'

'No. Hear me out.' He sat up and looked her in the eyes for the first time since she'd found him on the footbridge. 'I can't keep us at green, let alone take us to yellow. I tried really hard, but I'm not cut out for it. It doesn't make any sense to me and the more I try to play the game the more I realise I don't even understand the rules.'

'Martin…'

'Jenny, please listen. That's what I've been thinking about for the past two days. You're better off without me. I know it'll be tough on Becka but it's for the best. I'm holding you back and there's no way I can give you what you want or what you deserve.'

'Martin! Will you shut up and let me speak.'

'Sorry,' he said and rested his head back on his arms.

'First and foremost, you don't get to unilaterally decide what's best for me and the kids. We made this home together and we decide its future together. Secondly, and never ever forget this, I love you. Yes, you're a frustrating man, a failed man in some ways and a fragile man in many other ways. But you're my man, the man I chose and the man I want to grow old with. Do you hear me?'

He shrugged his shoulders which bobbed his head up and down. 'Jenny? You don't have to—'

'Shut up, you annoying man,' she said and held his hand. 'We'll work this out. We're stronger than you give us credit for. And we most certainly love you more than you're allowing yourself to believe.'

'I did have one idea,' he mumbled.

'Go on…'

'I'm not sure you'll like it and I was only really thinking of it for me. And maybe for Becka. I'm not sure I should say. You'll probably be really angry. I think it's what I want though. I've thought about it a lot and it seems like the perfect solution. If you wanted to come along too then it could be the answer.'

'Martin, please tell me what it is before I scream.'

'Let's drop out. Become outliers.'

'What?'

He lifted his head. 'Hear me out. It could work.' He stood up and walked to the fridge, giving himself time to compose his thoughts. 'I can't play the corporations' game and I'm always going to lose or at the very best struggle to stay afloat. They imposed it on me, I didn't choose to join in. The only response to someone who's forcing you to play a game you can't win is to opt out. Stop playing. It's so simple that most of us miss it. We can simply refuse. I want to opt out.'

'Do you realise what you're saying?'

'Yes, I do. If Becka wants, she can come too. Will you come with me?'

Amber was sitting in an old-fashioned café sipping coffee and enjoying a skinny blueberry muffin, one tiny piece at a time. It was her way of counteracting stress – to get up early and leave the house before Terence was awake. The place was empty which was one of the reasons it was her favourite place to take time out. On the counter was a small replica of the Palace of Westminster that the corporations had flooded the market with when they'd been handed control. You could slot your ruyi into it and it would automatically add a message to your SMFeed with the detail of your location and your purchase. Although they'd not caught on and had gradually disappeared from all but a few deliberately retro places, she delighted in its quaintness and used it without fail.

Her table looked out on to the small garden at the back of the café. Terracotta pots with plants and herbs she didn't recognise stood in a line along the low wall around the edge. A single tree with a narrow trunk and bare branches stood as a solitary sentry over the rusty table and chairs. It reminded her of the backyard of her childhood, of the scavenged furniture inside and outside of their home. There was a part of her that yearned for those simpler days, for the security of knowing your place in the world and the freedom that came with not having to strive to climb the ladder. But it was a false memory, she knew that. Her mother had struggled each and every day to find enough cleaning jobs to put food on the table and a roof over their heads. She wouldn't have understood the decisions Amber faced but she would have agreed that hard choices have to be made to survive; unhappiness and a lack of satisfaction wasn't only for the privileged mid-level strata.

Every time she tried to decide between Balfy's offer and a life with Terence her mind wandered, refusing to make the choice. She checked her ruyi. It was predicting that she would be high enough to become yellow but not by a large enough margin to take Terence with her. The SMFeed was bubbling with news that the corporations had legalised gambling on other people's rise and fall in points. Every five minutes the runners in another points race were announced, bets taken and the race run. The buzz across the feed was massive. The other competing news story was that the annual protest against Pay Day was under way and a handful of the disillusioned were setting up camp outside each of the corporation headquarters. The trending SMFeed was vitriolic in its glee over the destroyed losers of the points races and in its hate for the protesters who dared to question the status quo of the strata structures. The corporations were awarding points to these trend leaders, which further stoked both fires.

She ignored the bell above the door as it tinkled and announced another customer. 'Ruyi: message to Opo. Where are you?'

'He's no good for you.'

She turned round. The masked man from the morris dancing was standing behind her.

'Can I sit down?'

She looked around at all the empty tables. 'Here?'

'I'd like to talk to you. If that's okay?'

She shrugged. 'Free country.'

'Free to choose their chains,' he said as he looked over her shoulder at the trending SMFeed.

'Whatever.' She turned her ruyi face down on the table. 'I'm not in the best of moods so be careful. And don't for one minute think I want to talk about it.'

'That's not why I'm here.'

'Did you come here especially to talk to me?'

'Yup. Do you mind?'

'Depends on what you want to say, doesn't it?'

'I suppose it does. I was watching you from over there. You look sad and lonely.'

'I was having some private time. Or at least I was trying to.'

'Okay. I'll get to the point.'

'Good.' She inched back a little, conscious that she still found him extremely attractive and that she might not be able to refuse the comfort of his advances. 'Get on with it then,' she said with a little more snappiness than she'd intended.

'It's hard for me to say, especially as you look so sad. It made me realise how unforgivable my actions have been.'

'It was a one-off, don't overinflate its importance.'

He looked puzzled. 'Oh, I wish that was all I had to feel guilty about. Can I get you another coffee?'

'If you don't blurt it out soon I'm going to leave. What are you blathering on about?'

'The blackmail—'

She interrupted. 'What blackmail? What on earth are you talking about?'

'You're being blackmailed for stealing data.'

'No, I'm not. Piss off and get out.'

'I know it's true and I know how much pain it must be causing. I hate myself for it.'

'Hate yourself for feeling my pain? What planet are you on?'

He chuckled. 'Planet empathy, it would seem.'

'I can do without this. Look, if you've come to see if you can get a repeat performance of the other night the answer is no and will always be no. Stop wasting your time and my time. Move on.'

He took hold of her hand and she moved away, but not entirely. 'I've been made to see the error of my ways. Persuaded to back off.'

'What?'

'I was the blackmailer and I've been told in no uncertain terms to stop.' He let go of her. 'I was going to stop anyway,' he added. 'You've got to believe me.'

'Why would you do it?'

'My dad.'

'Your dad?'

'Martin Brown.'

'Martin? Brown?'

'Yes.'

She stood up and rushed out of the café, knocking over chairs and bashing into tables as she fled.

FORTY

Terence kissed her on the nose. She pulled away. 'Terence, please don't.'

'You're calling me Terence again.'

She shrugged.

'What happened to Terry?'

'Terence feels right. Do you remember when we first came here?'

'Of course. I promised to buy you that chapel. And I will.'

'Full of promises,' she said quietly.

'Let's walk and talk,' he said and stood up. He took her hand and helped her to her feet. She held his hand limply. They walked along in silence. The morning sky was a cold crystal blue and the air was light and refreshing with a hint of soil and grass. The birds were singing and an occasional mourner was laying flowers on a grave.

'What is it you want?' he asked.

'Same as ever. To be comfortable, secure and enjoying life.'

'I can give you that.'

'Your idea of comfortable and secure is very different to mine.'

'Is it that different? Really?'

'You have no ambition. You're happy to plod along taking what life gives you.'

'And you'd rather take from life, I suppose.'

'Yes. It's the only way to guarantee you get what you want.'

'I thought you had what you wanted. You even dropped a level to be with me. What's changed?'

'You.'

A couple with their young children walked past in the opposite direction. The boy ran up to Terence and stood staring. He bent down and patted him on the top of his head. 'How's things, young lad?' He cocked his thumb towards Amber. 'She's angry with me.

Can you do something to cheer her up? Maybe pinch her bum?'

The boy ran off laughing and shouting to his mum and dad, 'He told me to pinch her bum.'

'Oops, time to make a quick exit,' said Terence.

They hurried down a side path into the woods. Twigs crunched under their feet and unseen animals scurried away into the undergrowth. He stopped at a clearing where the sunlight was breaking through the canopy as if there were spotlights in the trees pointing down on a green moss stage.

'Isn't this wonderful?' He stepped behind her, held her shoulders and gently lifted her hair. He kissed her earlobe and she sighed. He rolled his tongue around the grooves and ridges of her ear. She stood still and silent. He pressed the tip of his tongue into her ear. She moaned with pleasure. 'Amber,' he whispered and flicked her earlobe with the tip of his tongue. 'We can be so happy if you'll let us.' The tip of his tongue was licking and probing, slowly turning her on.

'Terence,' she whispered back.

'Yes,' he said with shallow breath.

'Not now. Not when there's so much at stake.'

'That's the best time. Relax and enjoy.'

'I can't.'

'Try. We could spend the rest of our lives like this.'

'That's the problem,' she whispered.

He spun her round. 'The problem?'

'You don't know what I need.'

'I think I do,' he said and lifted her hair again.

'Stop.'

'C'mon, babe. It's the day before Pay Day. It's time to live a little.'

She wrenched herself free and ran off. The branches scratched her arms and the twigs stabbed her legs as she pushed her way through the wood. She took a sharp left and half ran and half clambered up an incline, grabbing hold of low branches to help. The undergrowth slid and slipped beneath her walking boots. A nettle stung her hand as she grabbed a branch and she squealed.

Terence was close behind, deliberately not catching up with her. 'For fuck's sake, Amber, stop running. You'll hurt yourself,' he shouted.

She ignored him and with a final pull reached the top of the slope. She was crying. She ran off again and he followed close behind. At the edge of the wood he ran past her, turned and blocked the gate back into the cemetery.

'Explain,' he said through gritted teeth.

She stood with her hands on her hips and her legs placed firmly apart as if she were a sumo wrestler getting into position. 'Fancied a run,' she said.

'I said, explain.'

'Out of my way.'

'Not until we've sorted this out.'

She pushed against his chest with every ounce of her strength. He didn't budge. She pushed again and this time he grabbed her wrists. 'Amber. We have to sort this out.' He checked his ruyi. 'Seven hundred and eighty minutes to go.'

She held his face and kissed him on the lips. 'Let me go, I'm no good for you.'

'You're perfect.'

'No. I'm really not perfect. You have no idea.'

'So, tell me.'

'Please, Terence. Do us both a favour and admit defeat. Leave me. Please.'

'You want me to be the one that ends it all? You want me to be the one that lies alone at night tormenting myself for leaving you?'

'I want you to be the one that's strong.'

'No. If you want to leave, you have to be the one that says it.'

She kissed him again. 'I'll see you at the house later this afternoon,' she said as she walked around him and into the cemetery.

He turned and watched her walk away with her head bowed down. 'Ruyi: private message to Amber Walgace. Babe, I haven't given up. You told me not to forget that I belonged to you. We're meant for each other.'

He pounded the pavement with his running. It was giving him the chance to expend all the excess anger that had built up during the chase with Amber. He loved her and would fight to keep her but she was so damaged by her past and by her upbringing that it was hard to make her see sense. She'd never be happy until she stopped striving for something that was an illusion. He had to find a way to help her see the folly of falling for the corporation dream of promotion and see the reality of the corporation nightmare – the lie that made you feel as if you were missing out on something, no matter what level you were. He could see it so clearly but Amber just couldn't get her head around it. No matter how many times he tried to help her see what was obvious to him she couldn't. She was as blinkered as a racehorse hurtling towards the finish line for the benefit of its owner.

A car swerved on to the pavement in front of him and screeched to a halt. He ran into the side of it, banging his knee on the front passenger door. Instinctively he crouched down to take the weight. The door opened, pushing him against the wall. He was trapped in a triangle of wall, car and door. Four women stepped out and walked slowly around to him. They were dressed in identical green camouflage trousers and jackets with black balaclavas that only revealed their eyes and their mouths. The bright red lipstick and the long mascaraed eyelashes gave them a particularly sinister look.

'Terence Huddson,' said one of them.

'No,' he replied.

'It wasn't a question.' She stepped closer and beckoned the others to do the same. They formed a secondary barrier – two of them blocking his exit over the front of the car and two of them keeping the door in place. He was well and truly trapped.

The window of the back door lowered. 'You!' he said. Ashley smiled and the window closed.

The woman pulled her balaclava off, revealing a severe scar that ran from just below her ear to the tip of her chin. She smiled. 'Terence Huddson.'

In every movie he'd ever seen it was a bad sign when a thug revealed their face – invariably it meant the victim would be killed. He braced his back against the wall, ready to fight.

'Come here,' she said.

He didn't move.

'It'll be a lot easier for me, and by implication a lot easier for you, if you do as I ask.'

He didn't move.

'Tedious.' She closed the door a little so she could move into his triangular metal and brick cage. She pushed him up against the wall with the heel of her left hand and held him there. She was tall and she was strong. She kissed the tip of his nose. He could smell the cherry flavouring of her lipstick. 'That's how you and her show affection, isn't it? Or would you like something a bit more intimate?'

He didn't move.

'You're a cool one, aren't you?'

He smiled. 'Takes a lot to scare me, scar face.'

She ran her finger along the scar. When she reached her chin she left it there as if she was thinking deeply. 'Me too,' she said. She moved her finger from her chin to his and pushed his head against the wall.

He kept smiling. 'Very theatrical,' he said and grinned. 'Care to tell me what a pretty girl like you is doing out and about so early in the day? I'd have thought you were a night person, in dimly lit bars.'

'Cocky too.' She clicked her fingers and the other three women each took out a knife. 'Now, Terry, let's reach an understanding, shall we?'

'I presume because that bitch is here this is about last night. I suppose I must have upset someone important who now wants me to understand my place. Am I right?'

The window lowered a little. 'No,' said Ashley.

'So what is it then?'

'Leave her. Walk away and let her rise to where she belongs.'

He laughed. 'Where she belongs! You people amaze me.'

'Leave her or else.'

'Or else what?'

'Show him.' The window closed.

The woman took out her own knife, slashed the sleeve of his jacket and then held its tip to his forehead, pressing enough to draw blood.

'Ooh, going to scratch me to death are you?'

She dragged it across his skin. Blood dripped from the cut, through his eyebrows and on to the pavement. She unzipped his jacket and cut the buttons off his shirt, one by one.

He blew her a kiss.

She ripped his shirt open and pressed the tip of the knife against his nipple.

'You're quite sexy, aren't you,' he said and blew her another kiss.

She traced a line from his nipple to his belly button with the knife and then quickly moved it out of the way and punched him hard in the stomach.

He doubled up. 'Better.' He coughed. 'Much better.'

'Leave her,' she said.

'No.' He looked up. 'And violence will never work. I grew up with it. You'll have to kill me and then she won't come with you, ever.'

She kicked him in the face. 'There's a lot of degrees to the violence I can dish out.'

He stood up. 'I know, but the trick is to remember it's always temporary. It'll end and I'll recover.'

She punched him again but he was ready for it and clenched his stomach in time.

'You don't recover from being cut. I could wreck that handsome face of yours. I could make it such a mess she wouldn't even recognise you.'

'You won't though because it won't get you what you want. She'll feel sorry for me and then she'll stay with me.'

'How well do you think she can stand up to physical violence?'

He laughed. 'This is a joke, right? You think I'm going to believe

293

you'll do anything to harm her? For some reason you want her but let's get this straight – I'm not going to let you have her. You can threaten me with anything you want, I won't betray her.'

Ashley got out of the car. 'Oh yes you will. Or at least that's what she'll think has happened.' She climbed over the car bonnet and sat cross-legged on its edge. 'Last chance, lover boy. Will you let her go of your own free will?'

He shook his head. 'Piss off, you inbred slut.'

'Temper temper.' She gave the woman a syringe. 'Do it.'

She pinned his head tight against the wall and injected his neck. 'What the—'

Ashley interrupted. 'It's a nano device that will transmit messages via your ruyi as and when we want. And it'll seem as if they've come from you. Untraceable too. Isn't it great?' She slid off the car bonnet. 'C'mon girls, let's leave Mr Huddson to contemplate the rest of his little life.'

FORTY-ONE

Max sat on the bench outside of Cambridge railway station and took out his polymer running shoes. He carefully wriggled each toe into its separate slot and pulled them up over his ankle. The tough but pliable polymer and the individualised toes gave him grip and lightness, as if he was running in bare feet coated in a plasticised rubber.

He drank an energy-boosting drink, slung his bag on his back and began his journey home. He focussed on the steady rhythm of his arms and legs as he weaved in and out of pedestrians and cycles. The pavement outside rows of houses turned into the long sweeping path around the BeWellCorp shopping complex. Hoards of affluent Cambridge yellows trudged from their cars across the vast parking areas to the bargains of the last day of the year. The corporations were doing everything they could to persuade these cautious consumers to spend. Some goods were being sold at cut-price but the vast majority of pre-Pay Day spending at this strata level was on credit. The jump from yellow to orange was so big that it was your position within yellow that defined you among your peers, not whether you were close to promotion, and this was an opportunity to appear more affluent in the eyes of your colleagues and neighbours.

The sun was warm on his face as he ran around the edge of the complex inhaling the fresh spring air. A car pulled up alongside and slowed down to match his pace. Irritated drivers tried to pass but there wasn't enough room without their engines cutting out. The noise of their protests grew and grew. A red flag appeared from the back corner of the stalking car and the noise stopped.

It pulled ahead of Max and stopped by the side of the road. The queue of cars passed and the flag retracted.

Max jogged on the spot until the last car had passed and then ran out into the middle of the road to join the back of the queue. As he drew alongside the stalking car it started to move again, keeping pace with him.

The window lowered. 'Can I offer you a lift?' said a man wearing a t-shirt with a faded RetailCorp logo being excreted from the back end of a bull.

'I'm fine thanks,' replied Max. He carried on running.

'You might be but the Fool on the Hill could do with a lift, couldn't he?'

'Who?'

'Maxamillion. Don't treat me as if I'm stupid.'

'Wouldn't dream of it... Who?'

'Maxy baby. Get on board while you can. It won't take much to tip him over the edge. Difficult thing to have on your conscience. Especially with all that empathy stuff racing around your insides.'

He slowed down a little. 'Who are you?'

'I know Dan. Or to put it a better way, Dan knows me and he knows what I want him to do. You did tell her you'd dropped the blackmail, didn't you?'

The car slowed and stopped. So did Max. 'You have my attention,' he said.

'Good. Get in.'

The door opened and Max slid into the seat next to the threatening man. 'Who are you?' he repeated.

'Lord Balfour, high-level recruiter.'

'And it was you that told Dan to tell me to stop blackmailing Amber Walgace?'

'Yes. We have plans for both of you that won't work if you're squabbling.'

'Me and Dan?'

'No. You and Ms Walgace.'

'Are you for real?'

'Take a look around you. What do you reckon? Real enough?'

'Vaguely impressive. Keep talking.'

'Dan has already made you the offer and it's thirty minutes before the deadline.'

'I know.'

'How do you fancy trying some of the perks of being orange before you decide?'

'Perks or bribes?'

'There's a difference?' Lord Balfour pressed his thumb against a panel and part of the floor opened to reveal a selection of tomatoes, including some that were dark green with deep purple stripes and some that were white with brown caps. 'I believe you have a predilection for illegal food?'

Max smiled. 'Not much of a bribe, or a threat.'

Lord Balfour smiled back. 'What about this? Does this count as a decent threat?' A small screen played the footage of Max in the illegal gambling bar.

'Better, but hardly the crime of the century.'

'How about blackmailing a high-ranking orange?'

Max laughed. 'Nice try, but I've never done that.'

Lord Balfour laughed mockingly. 'Oh yes you have. Or at least you will have once she's a high-ranking orange.' The screen showed footage of Max hacking into Amber's charta and sending the blackmail threats. 'There's plenty more – just in case you're thinking that's all we have.'

'She's going to be orange after Pay Day?'

'Yup. She's well on her way. And the authorities don't take kindly to threatening high-level citizens.'

'Citizens? Authorities? Are you seriously suggesting we have either of those?'

'Stay focussed, Max. Will you take the job at RetailCorp? Will you be our eyes and ears inside the corporations?'

'And if I don't? Is this all you have to throw at me?'

'Answer the question.'

'No. I won't take the job.'

'Okay, forget the threats. Let's concentrate on the bribes. Do you have any idea how exquisitely wonderful it is to be orange?'

'I can guess.'

'I wonder if you can. Imagine a world where you're so wealthy you don't have to work. Imagine a world where your wealth earns you more wealth. A world where you only have to tell the ship which direction to go in and other people do the rest. Can you imagine that?'

'And all the time you're in the shadows pulling my strings?'

'We're in the background giving you the information you need to make the right choices. Everybody wins. It's a privileged world that not many people get to glimpse let alone be a part of.'

'You can fall from grace though can't you?'

'Yup. But it doesn't happen that often.'

'It's not like being red though is it? I wouldn't be protected for life, would I?'

'No, not in the same way as red. But it's a very good place to be.'

Max looked out of the window at the passing countryside. The fields of his childhood stretched into the distance. He loved the natural beauty of the trees and the fields and out there was an alternative to the coercion of the corporation-dominated world he was being offered. He knew there had to be another way to help his dad. A way that wouldn't involve him betraying everything he believed in.

'Deadline approaching,' said Lord Balfour.

Max turned to face him. 'Thanks, but no thanks.'

Lord Balfour shrugged and pointed at the screen. 'Shame, take a look at this.'

His dad was being led across the front lawn of their house by his mum, like a prisoner that has lost all hope. His clothes were filthy and crumpled. Max felt a wave of anger. 'Bloody idiot, what's he done now?'

The image froze. 'Keep that thought in your head,' said Lord Balfour.

A feeling of emptiness welled up inside him. He was over-whelmed by a sense of failure and of an anger that was so deep he couldn't latch on to it. He sat back in his seat.

Lord Balfour touched his arm. 'That empathy trial…it was ours. You're now infected with all sorts of bugs and drugs and we can manipulate your empathy in whatever direction we choose. If you choose to throw your family to the dogs, imagine feeling the pain of Becka scavenging for food as a white. Imagine feeling her self-disgust at what she might do to stay alive. Imagine the hollowness inside your mum as she realises that she pushed your dad so hard he collapsed and took his whole family down with him. Is that what you want?'

Max screwed up his face with the pain of the images Lord Balfour had conjured up. 'Okay. Okay. You win. Let me out.'

As the car sped off his ruyi buzzed with a message from Dan to meet him in the local pub.

Dan was sitting in the corner with a half-drunk pint in his hand. Max bought an energy drink and joined him. 'Well?' he said in an exhausted voice.

'Excellent timing,' said Dan as the door opened and Martin and Jenny walked in.

Max looked at Dan, looked at Jenny, looked at Martin and then looked back at Dan. 'What's happening here?'

'I need to talk to you and your dad. About what just happened on the road out there. Get rid of your mum,' said Dan quietly so only Max could hear.

'Mum. Dad. What are you doing here in the middle of the day?'

'Your dad got a message from this…person…insisting they meet here immediately. I'm his chaperone.'

'What are you doing here?' asked Martin.

'Same message as you,' said Max. He took Jenny to one side. 'Mum, leave him with me. This won't take long to sort out, it's just a little misunderstanding from that festival at the weekend. I'll sort it easily. Okay?'

'Are you sure? He's so fragile. You're not exactly the best of pals are you?'

'We'll be fine. I'll look after him. Don't worry. Please let me do this. To prove I can.'

Jenny hesitated. She smiled at Martin. 'See you soon. Come straight back won't you.'

He nodded.

Max gave her a hug. 'I love you,' he whispered.

'I love you too,' she whispered back. 'See you soon,' she said to Martin as she waved goodbye.

Dan sat down. 'Now boys. I've got some good news.'

'Wait,' Max said to Dan. He held his hand up. 'Dad, there's a couple of things you need to know before Dan spills his beans.'

Martin nodded.

'I've been spying on you and I know you've been spying on me. I was trying to look out for you, trying to make sure you didn't get into any more trouble.'

Martin took a sip of his beer. 'I know. Same here. What happened to us, son?'

'Life?'

'Is that all?' said Martin.

Dan tapped the table with his pint. 'Very touching but I'm short on time and there's more. Martin – your Pay Day loan is cancelled, paid off. Oh, and there'll be no charge for the services of Sir Arthur. A gesture of goodwill to an old hacker, was how he put it.'

Martin was speechless but Max spoke on his behalf. 'Thank you and pass our thanks on to Sir Arthur. What about the troll?'

'Neutralised,' said Dan.

Max shook Dan's hand. 'Appreciated. Dad?'

'Appreciated,' said Martin.

'Dan, do you mind leaving us alone for a few minutes?'

'No problem. I'll be outside.' He picked up his pint and his ruyi and left the table.

'Dad. I've got something important to say. Will you listen to me? Properly?'

Martin nodded.

'I have to leave with Dan. I have to go, so you and Mum and Becka can get on with things. Do you understand?'

'You're never around anyway, are you.'

'This is serious. I might not see you again for a very long time but it's something I have to do. It'll mean that you guys can get on with your lives without all this. Promise me you'll look after them?'

Martin nodded.

'Say it.'

'I'll look after them. What's going on?'

'Nothing to worry about. I love you. Always have and always will. You're my dad and I'm proud of you. Please do the right thing for Mum and Becka. Please.'

'Okay. How will I know what the right thing is?'

'You'll know. You're a good man, that's your problem. But you can turn it into your strength.'

'Son…'

'Dad… Give me a hug. Please.'

Martin hugged Max tight.

As Max left the pub, both of them were crying.

FORTY-TWO

Groups of people were huddled along the side of the road clutching their ruyi. Occasionally, Amber would hear one of them exclaim with delight that they'd gained a few points or moan with exasperation that they'd lost some. The frenetic last day of the year was in full swing and she despised them for it. She despised their scrabbling around for a few points to make life seem a tiny bit more bearable. It was pathetic and demeaning. Couldn't they see the bigger picture? Couldn't they see that they were being played by the corporations? Couldn't they see that none of this would get them promotion, that it simply held them in their place with only small variations in their status?

She stopped outside her house and took a moment to soak it all up – the year of being married to Terence and the home she'd tried so hard to build. It'd been hard to drop a level to be with him and she wasn't sure he truly appreciated her sacrifice. He was a lovely, sweet man and their life here had been nice, but deep down she knew that she deserved better, either with him or without him. She sat on the doorstep and gazed across the street. She didn't belong here. She'd always felt disjointed from her peers, right from the first day at school, and now she had an opportunity to rise above it all but she wasn't sure where Terence fitted in. Maybe he did and maybe he didn't. It was a question that had to be answered before the end of the day.

She pressed the lock and the door clicked open. Terence was upstairs in the lounge. She took her walking boots off, crept up the stairs quietly and peeked through the crack between the door and the frame. He was lying on the sofa with a can of beer, his ruyi and the StrataLife game paused on the screen. With a soft step she entered the room, startling him.

'Amber! Babe! I didn't hear you come in.' He switched off the screen, put his ruyi and beer on the table and leapt up. 'Gissa hug, I missed you.'

'Looks like it,' she said.

'Babe, please don't start.'

'Sorry. What's that across your forehead? Is that from the wood?'

'Long story. Let me get you a drink.'

'I'm fine. We need to talk.'

'We do.'

They sat with the cushions propped up at either end of the sofa, facing each other. The sunlight was streaming in and fresh pink flowers oozed a sweet and deeply rich aroma. His beer smelled similar.

'How's the ruyi?' she asked.

'Aha, you noticed. I was getting us some last-minute points. It's busy busy busy on there today.'

She flinched. 'Your head?'

He took a drink. 'You're not going to like this but you have to know.'

'Go on...'

'I was threatened. By your friend Ashley. Her thugs did it.'

'Threatened? How? Why?'

'They told me to let you go. To let you become one of them.' He touched his forehead. 'This was a warning.'

'Really, Terence? Do you expect me to believe you?'

'That's not all. They injected me with a device so they can send you messages as if they're coming from me.'

'Get real. I'm not falling for this crap. What's got into you?'

'Amber, I'm telling the truth. They threatened me. They injected me. I don't want you to see them again.'

'Making stuff up to keep me trapped is pathetic. Even for you.'

'Even for me? You stupid bitch, they're all over you, turning you into some sort of plaything. Even if you don't stop for me, stop for yourself.'

'No. Why do you have to be so limited? Why do you have to control everything?'

'Okay. Okay. Let's take a breath. I'm not trying to control you. Look around – we have a lovely home, better than either of us would have thought possible. Let's not lose it, eh?'

'Lovely flowers, lovely sofa, lovely hubby – all waiting for me when I get home. Every day the same. Every day a little bit more cosy. Every day a little closer to death. C'mon, Terence, wake up.'

'Babe, calm down. Don't wreck things.'

She threw a cushion across the room and a vase smashed on the floor. 'I'll show you what wrecking is.' She stormed over to the screen and ripped it from the wall. 'StrataLife. Dead.' She threw his can of beer at their wedding photo. She picked up his ruyi, stormed to the window and dropped it on to the patio below – it smashed. 'You want to see me wreck things?' she screamed at him.

There was a knock at the door.

Amber ran down the stairs and yanked it open. 'Sam.'

'Hi. Your intercom system doesn't seem to be working.'

'You came all this way to tell me that?'

Sam hesitated. 'I came to ask you to stay in touch once you're promoted.'

'Piss off.' She slammed the door and ran back upstairs. There was another knock on the door but she ignored it.

'Who—'

She interrupted him. 'Soppy Sam. She's gone.'

He laughed. 'Her timing always left a lot to be desired. Babe, you can smash up the house as much as you want. It was wrecking us that I was talking about.'

'Smash us up? You think I can't do that?'

'We're strong. I love you.'

'Do you? Did you know I lost points for being unfaithful with an underage dropout?'

'What? What do you mean?'

'You heard. Unfaithful. Underage. Fling.'

'Who? When? Amber, talk to me.'

'You still want to cling on…to us?'

'Why do you have to hurt those of us that love you? What is

304

it with you? You hurt those who care about you and suck up to those who don't give a fuck about you. You are one massive self-destruct…thing.'

'Thing?'

'Thing.' He dropped to the floor and cried. 'I can't go on with this. Can you?'

'No.' She cried too.

He held her hand. 'I'm done. It's over. You win.'

She squeezed his hand. 'Thank you.'

'I want you to have those points back, the ones you gave me.'

'But you'll drop back down. What job would you do?'

'What job would I have done at yellow? I'm not like you, my job's not important. There's plenty of joinery work at blue – I'll be fine. What will you do?'

'Lord Balfour's offered me something. I'll find out a bit more about that and stay with Opo in the meantime.'

'And this place? Our home.'

'You can stay for a while, until you get yourself sorted.'

He sucked his lip. 'You had all this worked out didn't you?'

'A bit.'

She slung her bags in the back of the empty taxi and slid in beside them. Terence was standing on the doorstep with his hands in his pockets and the saddest expression she'd ever seen. It was the right thing to do but it had been hard for both of them. The hole he'd left behind in her stomach felt real. She waved once, faced front and didn't look back as they pulled away from the kerb.

The streets were busy with people going about their daily lives. Every so often she caught a glimpse of the five corporation flags as people prepared for the evening's celebrations. It was enshrined in law that the population must celebrate Pay Day as an acknowledge-ment of another year of stability and to welcome those new to their particular strata level; it was a good excuse for a party.

She pressed the intercom. 'Can you stop at the Bureaucracy on the way. I have to drop something off.'

'It's not on the schedule.'

'Charge it to Samantha Crawley, Head of the Disability Assessment Unit.'

She sat back and let the streets roll by, watching the minutes count down on her ruyi: four hundred and fifty; four hundred and forty-nine; four hundred and forty-eight… The soporific effect of the countdown was washing over her and the passing streets became blurred as she allowed herself some real tears for the first time in a long while. They were tears of relief, not regret.

The taxi arrived at an empty drop-off point. She tidied her face, combed her hair and straightened her clothes. 'Wait for me here,' she commanded.

She deposited her charta with the security check-in pod inside the foyer and on her way out she paused next to the mini-lake at the bottom of the waterfall. This was a stepping stone on her journey from violet to orange. She wanted to keep the reflection of the wooden panels and the tall atrium above it in her catalogue of memories to bring out on those bleak days when she lost sight of how much she'd achieved. She took a deep breath and turned on her heels, click-clacking to the front door and the waiting taxi.

'Thank you. Carry on with the original journey,' she said as she climbed back in.

This was the first time she'd visited Opo at his own home and she was impressed. The large house had bay windows on every floor with a balcony outside each one. There was a small, well-kept front garden with flower beds on one side and herbs on the other. A spotlight lit the dark-green front door and the light from inside caught some of the colour from the stained glass panels and projected it on to the doorstep.

She touched the intercom with her ruyi and waited.

The door squeaked open. Opo was dressed in black Lycra leggings and a grey woollen sweater. He was surprised to see her. 'Hun? What's occurring? Did we have a date?'

'I've left him.'

'Left him?'

'Terence. We've split up. Can I come in?'

He noticed her bags. 'Left him for how long?'

'For good. We're done.'

'Ah. You'd better come up then.'

She followed him along a bleak corridor lined with bins, up rickety stairs to the third floor and into a room with bare walls, a single bed and a small kitchen built into the corner. She put her bags down next to the only chair.

'I need a pee,' she said.

'Two doors back the way we came.'

'Opo. Why are you here?'

'Have your pee and I'll tell you. It's all a bit awkward really.'

The toilet was dark and damp and smelt of stale urine. Names and phone numbers had been scribbled all over the walls, offering all sorts of unsavoury services. She concentrated on peeing.

'Opo, it's gross,' she said as she walked back into the room.

'You get used to it.'

'I don't understand though. Is this a kind of experiment or a bet with someone?'

'It's where I live. You're the first person to visit me here. How did you get my address?'

'Balfy gave me it. He said I should come and stay with you if I left Terence. Can I wash my hands?'

'Of course. In the sink over there. It's not what you expected is it?'

'Not really, no. It'll be cosy with two of us.'

'You can't stay. It's not allowed.'

'But you're my friend.' She pointed at the bags. 'I'm homeless until the morning. One night?' She dried her hands on a towel and accidentally pulled a face of disgust.

He sat on the edge of his bed. 'Sit down,' he said, tapping the chair with his foot. 'The thing is…I'm not sure how to say this… the thing is…'

'Just spit it out. It's going to be one of those days, I can tell.'

'The thing is, Amber, you were a paid job.'

'A paid job?'

'Yeah. I befriend people for a living. And I'm good at it. I was asked to become your friend and take you to glamorous places.'

'Opo?'

'It's what I do.'

'And yet you live here.'

'I have some expensive habits that I can't really afford. Housing isn't one of them.'

'It was all false? You and me? A lie?'

'Honey, I'm sorry. You got what you wanted though, didn't you?'

His ruyi buzzed. 'She's outside.'

'Who?'

'Ashley. She's come to collect you. Good luck. Maybe we'll bump into each other at a party or something.'

Amber picked up her bags and left him sitting there.

FORTY-THREE

Jenny lay on her side watching Martin sleep. He looked peaceful but every now and again he'd twitch and shift his body slightly. The late afternoon sun was casting long shadows across the bedroom and the smell of baking bread was wafting up the stairs. The only sound was Martin breathing and the birds singing outside. It was a perfect moment.

She stroked his forehead and he stirred. 'Hello, you.'

'Hello,' she said and kissed his cheek.

'Did I dream that or did we—'

She interrupted him with a kiss on the lips.

'It's been a while since…in the afternoon…' He stretched and rubbed his back with the delight of someone waking from an afternoon nap.

She ran her fingers through the hair on his chest. 'It's a moment we must remember.'

'Agreed. It's quiet downstairs.'

'They're both out.'

'Jenny…'

'Yes?'

'I want to say goodbye to things – people and places. Will you come with me?'

She smiled at him, sadly. 'If that's what you want.'

'It is.'

'Okay. I need a shower first.'

'Me too.'

He lay in bed listening to her whistling above the rushing sound of the shower. It was strange that she should be so happy now. He checked his ruyi – three hundred and seventy-five minutes.

'It's all yours,' she said as she came back into the room wrapped in a thick white towel that covered her from the top of her chest to the top of her thighs.

'You still look good,' he said, tugging playfully at the edge of the towel.

'Still?'

'You know what I mean.' He tugged again.

'Don't spoil it, Martin,' she said and smacked his hand gently.

He smiled, jumped out of bed and picked up his clothes. 'See you downstairs.'

The hot water massaged his body and he savoured every last moment of the luxury of their home.

'See you outside,' called Jenny from downstairs.

He dried quickly and pulled on the first set of clothes he came to – a pair of battered jeans and an old sweater. Downstairs, he laced up his boots and put on an old leather jacket.

'What a sight,' said Jenny as he stepped out of the front door.

There was a faint trace of wood smoke in the air mixed with a hint of manure. He breathed in deeply. 'I'm gonna miss the smell of the countryside.'

Their shoulders touched as they stood looking at the house. She nudged him. 'It's beautiful, isn't it?'

'Yes it is. I've always loved the way it seems to be a face – the tall thatched roof its head and the windows tucked underneath those sticking out bits, like eyes with bushy eyebrows.'

'And the triangular bit that juts out over the door – that's like a nose.'

'And the bush growing around the door is the nose hair.'

They both chuckled.

He put his arm around her. 'I'm going to miss all this.'

'I know you are.'

'This way,' he said and clambered on to the grass bank at the side of the house. 'I've always loved it up here.'

At the top of the bank they were level with the upstairs windows where the view of their home was at its most dramatic. Smoke was curling out of the two chimneys.

'It'll be getting dark soon. Would you like to say goodbye to the pub before Becka gets home?'

'Yes please. Jenny…'

'Martin…'

'It's Max… He's gone away for a while. He asked me to tell you.'

'I know. He sent me a message. Sounds important. I'm sure we'll hear from him soon.'

'Are you okay about him not being here, today of all days? And missing his birthday?'

'It's weird. Everything I love is slipping away and yet I feel calm for the first time in ages. It all feels right somehow.'

He pulled her close. 'Thank you.'

'For?'

'You know.'

She broke free and kissed him on the cheek. 'Let's go see that damn pub of yours.'

The bridge creaked as they crossed from their safe haven into the village. The birdsong seemed to follow them down the street and the trees rustled as if they were saying goodbye. Almost every home had the warm glow of a recently lit fire radiating through their open curtains. Everything appeared calm and content.

Inside the pub, Fred sat alone in the corner with the last dregs of a pint.

'Can I? One for the road?' asked Martin. Jenny nodded. 'A pint of your finest ale please, landlord, and a gin and tonic for the wife.'

'Red wine,' said Jenny.

'Coming up. What about misery guts over there,' said the landlord, gesturing with his chin towards Fred.

'One for him too,' said Martin.

Jenny squeezed his shoulder. 'I'll bring them over for you. Go and see what's wrong with him.'

Martin pulled up a chair, sat down and rested his chin on his hands. 'What's up, Mr Fred?'

'Eh? Oh…nothing. Bad day, that's all.'

'Really? C'mon, you can tell me.'

'I had my end of year accounts for the music.'

'And?'

'Cost me more than I made.'

'Bummer. There's a pint on its way.'

Jenny arrived with the drinks. 'Hi, Fred, did he tell you his news?'

'What news?'

She took a sip of wine. 'Martin?'

Martin sighed. 'It's the last time I'll be in here. As a local anyway.'

'How's that?'

'Time to move on. Pastures new 'n all that.'

'Well that is a surprise. I thought you'd be part of the fixtures and fittings until the day you popped your clogs.'

'So did I, but it's not to be.' Martin raised his pint and Fred did the same. 'Cheers,' he said and chinked glasses.

'Cheers,' replied Fred and took a long, slow drink. 'Where are you off to then, my boy?'

'Now that would be telling…'

'That's why I asked.'

'My lips are sealed – we haven't told the kids yet.'

Jenny finished her wine in one big gulp. 'On that note we'd better get back.'

'One more?' asked Martin.

'Very kind of you,' said Fred.

Jenny coughed. 'Martin?'

'Sorry, Fred. Have to go. Look after yourself, won't you? I'll try to pop in when I can.'

Fred raised his glass. 'All the best.'

As they left the pub, Martin glanced over his shoulder. Fred was staring into the bottom of an almost empty glass again.

They held hands as they walked back towards the house. 'Thanks. I'm glad you were there,' he said.

'I love you,' she said.

The bridge creaked as they kissed and hugged. The brook was

trickling and the clouds were pink. Becka's music was a faint lullaby drifting across from their home.

'Was it worth it?' asked Jenny.

'I think so, don't you?'

'I'm not sure, but let's make sure we savour the good memories.'

'Agreed.'

'Agreed.'

Becka called from her window. 'Hey, where have you been? I had to take the bread out of the oven.' She noticed they were holding hands and had sad expressions. 'Is everything all right?' she shouted.

'We need to talk. In private,' said Jenny loudly.

Becka closed her window.

As they opened the front door they could hear her banging down the stairs. 'In the kitchen, darling,' called Jenny.

'Me too?' asked Martin.

'Seriously?'

He shrugged.

'Of course you too.'

He took off his boots and hung up his jacket. Becka was already sitting at the table with a glass of lemonade and a look of curiosity. 'What's going on? Mum? Dad?'

Jenny was busy making a pot of tea and Martin didn't know what to say. He tidied away the pots and pans and then stood next to Jenny, hoping she would take the lead.

'Dad, you're weirding me out,' said Becka.

'Becka!' said Jenny.

'Mum?'

'It's okay, but we need to explain something to you. And ask your opinion.'

'Okay? Is Max part of this?'

Jenny poured two cups of tea and slid one of them across to Martin, who was running his fingers along the table seemingly engrossed in the grain of the wood. 'I'll come on to Max, but there's some other stuff first.'

'Mum!'

'Okay. Max has gone away for a while but he'll be in touch as soon as he can, I'm sure. It's nothing to worry about.'

'Where's he gone?'

Jenny groaned. 'Becka, please let me speak. This is important. Max will be fine.'

Becka glanced at Martin who glanced back and then continued tracing the patterns on the table.

'Your dad and I have something to say. You know it's Pay Day tomorrow?'

'Two hundred and fifty-eight minutes,' he said without raising his head.

'Yes, thank you, Martin. Becka – Pay Day, do you know how important it is?'

'Duh…'

'Becka, please take this seriously. A lot of decisions get made for Pay Day and things change a lot. Quite a few years ago your dad got promotion to green and I was so proud of him. We bought this house and then you kids came along. It was lovely. It is lovely. But things change. It's been a struggle to keep it going. The corporations have demanded more and more to stay green and your dad's work has demanded more and more from him. It's all got a bit too much so we're changing things.'

'Are you splitting up?' asked Becka.

'Hear me out. We can't stay in this house, we simply can't afford it. There are two choices and we've talked them through, but we want to know how you feel about them.'

'What are they?'

'Martin, do you want to tell her?'

'No. You carry on.'

'Okay. One choice is to drop out and join the outliers. If we do that we'll never be able to get back on to a Strata. It's a one-way street. It would take the pressure off your dad though.'

Becka perked up. 'I like the sound of being an outlier. Would we live in the woods?'

'I doubt it. And there is one major hitch with that option.'

'What's that?'

'I don't think I could come with you. I've thought about it long and hard and I just can't see me surviving with no safety net. As hard as it is in the Strata, at least I know where I stand.'

Becka looked at her mum and then at her dad. 'So, you *are* splitting up?'

'If we choose that option then yes, and you'll have to decide who you want to live with.'

'What's the other choice?' said Becka anxiously.

'The other choice is to sell this house, move back to the city and become blue. Some of your dad's old friends have sorted out his debts, so we'd be okay.'

'And would you still split up?'

Martin stopped tracing his fingers across the table. 'No. If we go for blue then we think we can make a go of staying together. I'd get a junior management job in one of the corporations and your mum could go back to doing some admin work.'

'Would I have to move school?'

'Darling, I'm afraid that whatever happens you'll have to go to a different school,' said Jenny.

'I don't want you to split up.'

Martin moved next to Becka and put his arm around her. 'We don't want to split up either. Blue might be boring but I think we'll cope better. We can always try for green again once we've found our feet.'

'Martin! No we can't. This is permanent. We agreed.'

'Sorry, you're right.'

Jenny moved to the other side of Becka. 'What do you think?'

Becka kissed her mum's cheek and then her dad's. 'Let's stay together, even if it is a bit boring.'

They hugged her. 'Thank you,' they both said.

'You're welcome.'

FORTY-FOUR

Dan and Max had been sitting in the pub listening to one musician after another perform fifteen-minute slots on a small stage. Nothing much had been said except to comment on the varying degrees of competency each musician displayed and occasionally recounting the story of a night out that involved music and often an amount of debauchery.

'Not long now,' said Dan.

Max frowned. 'Until?'

'Until you're a grown-up.' Dan chuckled and play-punched Max on the arm.

'Hilarious. I need your help though.'

'Go on…'

'I want to become an outlier.'

'I know, but you promised Lord Balfour to work for a corporation.'

'You could make him change his mind, couldn't you?'

'Maybe. I want to show you some stuff before you decide. Becoming an outlier isn't a decision that's easy to reverse. You know that don't you?'

Max nodded. 'Show me what?'

Dan stood up and drank the last half of his pint in one gulp. 'Follow me.'

They walked along the river bank in silence, weaving in and out of the slow-moving tourists and dodging the fast-moving commuters coming towards them. They climbed the steps from the grounds of Southwark Cathedral to London Bridge and crossed to the east side. Dan leapt up on to the low wall and Max followed.

The bridge was filled with glum-looking people packed tightly on the pavement. The crowd, which was at least fifteen people across, jostled and bumped into one another, but didn't speak.

'Look,' said Dan. He pointed north across the bridge. 'What do you see?'

'A lot of grey people who've had their souls ripped out, trudging through life.'

Dan laughed. 'So wise for someone so young.'

Max climbed down. 'What's your fucking point, Dan?'

Dan sat on the wall. 'My fucking point, Max, is that most greens choose this.'

'Exactly, why do you think I want to be an outlier?'

Dan stared at him intently until Max looked away. 'I'm not sure. I'm not sure,' said Dan. He stood up, grabbed Max's arm and pulled. 'C'mon, this is too depressing.'

'Where are we going?'

'Just follow…it'll be worth it.'

They fell in step with the march of the commuters into the station. Dan touched Max's ruyi with his and then waved it near the platform barrier. Max did the same and followed Dan on to the platform just as a train was pulling in. Unlike the trains out of King's Cross, this had no specific carriages for different strata; they pushed their way on to the train and stood in silence as it trundled along the tracks. Max tried to see where they were going but his view was blocked by the arms and the backs of his fellow travellers. He shut down any desire to interact and turned inward to his thoughts so he could endure the journey. Occasionally he caught a glimpse of Dan smiling, nodding and even saying hello to those around him. Max was in awe.

He closed his eyes and replayed the past week in his head. He was in the middle of trying to formulate an argument that would convince Lord Balfour that he could be as useful as an outlier as he could inside a corporation when Dan tapped him on the shoulder and nodded towards the door. The train pulled into a station and they forced their way off.

'Where are we?' asked Max.

'Doesn't matter where we are, it's what I'm going to show you that matters. This way.'

Max followed him out of the station and along a country lane until they reached a locked iron gate in a tall hedge. Dan pressed a button and an eye-level slit in the gate opened with the scrape of metal on metal.

'It's me,' said Dan. The gate creaked open and he beckoned Max to follow.

Inside the gate was a large open space with a smattering of trees. Sheep, goats and cows were wandering around, grazing. On the far side was a group of tipis with smoke pouring out of their chimneys.

'Outliers?' asked Max.

'Yes. Let's say hello,' replied Dan as he walked through the animals, shooing them as he went.

As they approached one of the tipis, a thin scruffy man waved to Dan. 'Hi,' he called in a voice that gave the impression he was finding it hard to concentrate.

'Hi,' Dan called back. 'This is Max,' he said as soon as they were in speaking distance. 'A friend who's come to see how you live.'

'Creepy...' said the man, his voice fading towards the end of the word.

Dan lifted the canvas door to one side with one hand and held out the palm of his other hand. 'After you.'

Max stepped inside and Dan followed. The occupants looked up lazily and then one by one drifted back to staring at the fire. Nobody spoke.

'What's occurring then?' asked Dan.

Still nobody spoke.

'Too wasted?'

A couple of people nodded without looking up. They stood in silence for a few minutes until Dan beckoned Max to follow him outside.

As soon as they were out of hearing distance Max stopped. 'What's wrong with them?'

Dan smiled. 'They chose a different but equally brain-dead existence as those comatose commuters.'

'But they're outliers.'

'Yes. And they're very proud to have dropped out and to have rejected ruyi and charta, but all they do is sit around, take drugs and stare into space. I call them the dried-up dropouts. C'mon, let's head back.'

'Okay,' said Max quietly.

'I know a place we can get some sleep before the big day. Fancy it?'

Max nodded.

'Time to wake up,' shouted Dan through the bedroom door. Max checked the time on his ruyi. It was four o'clock in the morning and he'd managed to get six hours' sleep despite being in a spectacularly noisy hotel full of people celebrating the end of the Pay Year.

On the way they'd stopped at a bar close to the station. Dan had been in a quiet, reflective mood and hadn't really spoken. The conversations that Max could overhear were so mundane he had no urge to join in so they'd left the bar quite early and walked through the city to a hotel near Regent's Park. The streets had been full of loud celebrations, although every now and again he'd seen someone slumped in a doorway looking as if their world had collapsed in on them.

Dan was waiting in the hotel lobby. 'Let's walk,' he said as soon as Max joined him.

It was cold outside and there was a faint smell of smoke in the air which rapidly disappeared as the cold penetrated his nostrils. The neon signs in shop windows and the lights of the office blocks were uncharacteristically vivid against the dark sky. The park was closed to traffic, only allowing pedestrians through and the emptiness of the streets, the grand Regency buildings and the old lampposts gave the impression that they were walking on to a film set. No people, no traffic, darkness and quiet created a sinister atmosphere. It looked different under the glow of the city nightlight and Max felt as if he was seeing it all for the first time. He'd hardly noticed the fountains on previous visits, but now they sounded like rivers flowing over rocks. Mist hung around the base of the trees adding to the sense of mystery. A dog barked and a muffled voice called out. They both faltered slightly in their step.

'Look, now we're in the middle you can see the stars,' whispered Max, being careful not to break the eerie magic of the silence.

They walked on not speaking until they reached the zoo. Dan sniffed the air. 'Smells like fishy manure and chlorine,' he whispered. 'Amazing what we miss, rushing around all the time. I love being alone in the park at night. Don't you?'

'It's incredible,' said Max.

At the canal, Dan stopped halfway across the bridge. The streetlights bounced off the mottled frozen surface of the water and frost sparkled on the railings.

Max blew on his hands and rubbed them together. 'Why did we go to the outliers?'

'I wanted you to see the reality.'

'But you're not like that. It's not the only reality.'

'No. That's true, I'm not. The point I was making was that it doesn't really matter whether you stay in or opt out of the system, if you're apathetic and take the path of least resistance you'll end up sleepwalking through life. In a lot of ways outliers are no different to the Strata Straights, as you so eloquently named them.'

'Sure, but I don't want to put up with all that strata shit when I can live perfectly happy without it.'

'Or…you could change it from the inside.'

'Is that what Lord Balfour wants?'

Dan laughed from deep down in his throat. 'Hardly! His kind need this strata thing. No, this is my secret game. Care to join me?'

Max stared at the boats moored along the bank of the canal. He was surprised and intrigued by Dan's revelation. 'Can we walk for a bit more?'

'Of course, let's go and look at this wonderful city of ours from the top of Primrose Hill.'

They walked on in silence through the empty streets of large houses. A baby started screaming, a bedroom light came on and it stopped. Inside the park, two foxes strolled up to them, stared and then trotted away with their bushy tails held high.

'Shall we sit?' asked Dan as they reached the top of the hill. The panoramic view of London stretched out before them – the City of London, the Shard, NetCorp Tower and the London Eye. 'It's a beautiful city, isn't it?'

Max leant forward, resting his chin in his hands. 'It is.'

'I'm not going to rush you, Max. It's a big decision and you need to be sure.'

'Thanks.'

It was peaceful sitting there contemplating his future. If he did nothing he'd be given a green-level job, at least for the first year. The majority of his contemporaries had been waiting so long to become adults that they would grab the job and their sexual legitimacy with both hands and step on to the treadmill of work and parenthood eagerly. He knew he didn't want that, but he was torn between the romance of dropping out and the chance to change the world that Dan was offering. And he couldn't ignore Lord Balfour's threats.

'Can you neutralise this empathy stuff they've pumped into me?'

'Yes, I think we can.'

'Let's walk some more while I think. Is that okay?'

A single church bell rang out across the hill. 'Of course it is. Although it's six o'clock so we only have a few minutes before you need to decide.'

Max stood up and started to walk down the hill. Dan followed.

They reached the railway bridge that divided Primrose Hill from Camden Town. It was peppered with graffiti, signalling the shift from the higher to lower strata neighbourhood. A solitary tired-looking figure waddled along the street in front of them and the streetlight bounced off the layer of grime that covered the pavement. In the doorway of an office block a man was lying in a shoddy sleeping bag. Dan handed him a token of some sort.

'I'll do it,' said Max.

Dan's shoulders visibly relaxed and he put his arm around Max. 'I'll look after you,' he said and squeezed.

Max put his arm around Dan, squeezed and laughed with relief. 'Good, I'll hold you to that.'

Dan swiped his ruyi. 'I've told him we're on our way. Don't forget he knows nothing of our arrangement.'

'I'm unlikely to forget that, am I?'

'No. I'm sorry.'

Dan pointed to a dilapidated tower block. 'They're in here,' he said. 'He has the whole of the top floor.'

'Who'll be there?'

'Amber Walgace – she's the new Senior Executive of the Bureaucracy. She'll be your boss.'

'You're kidding, right?'

'No. Don't worry, it'll be fine. She won't rock the boat; Lord Balfour's got her exactly where he wants her.'

Max shrugged. 'Who else?'

'Some backroom guys that you don't know. Ashley, his right-hand woman, a tech specialist called Mildred and a data guru called Madeleine.'

The lift rocketed to the top floor. The door opened and they stepped into a large warehouse style room. Amber was sitting in front of them wearing a large floppy black felt hat, a deep-green felt coat with a large mohair collar that fringed the whole length of the coat, tight black ruched leggings and cherry-red and white brogues.

Lord Balfour was looking out of the window on the opposite side of the room. He turned to face them. 'Welcome. Max, I'm glad you saw sense in the end. I believe you know Amber, your new boss. This is Mildred and Madeleine.'

Amber smiled at Max. It was a cold smile. 'Welcome to my team,' she said.

'Thank you,' he replied, smiling back with as much warmth as he could manage.

'If you two don't play nice together…well let's not go there…

you have a new Pay Year to reveal to the masses. Shall we get on with it?'

Amber and Max nodded.

Dan gave Lord Balfour the thumbs-up and left the room.

Sam was sitting at her desk waiting for the new Senior Executive to arrive and announce this year's strategy for the Bureaucracy. Then she could induct her new team.

The office was buzzing with anticipation and every unit head was focussed on their charta, waiting for the arrival.

Outside, security had formed a guard of honour to welcome their new boss to the building. Two rows of neatly dressed men and women in dark brown uniforms stood facing each other, leaving enough room to walk between them from the drop-off point to the entrance. They stamped their feet to try and keep warm in the early morning chill – this was an unusually early start for everybody.

A klaxon blared from the doorway and they stood to attention. A brown limousine flanked by security personnel on foot carrying rainbow flags that fluttered in the slight breeze glided into view and eased its way along the gravel driveway that had been especially laid that morning.

Amber stepped out of the limousine and waved. She strutted through her guard of honour and in through the front door of the Bureaucracy.

ACKNOWLEDGEMENTS

A big thank you to everyone who helped me along the way, especially to Gail, Jane, Kim and Penn for their valuable insights and for being brave enough to tell me when something wasn't quite working. Also, a big thank you to the team at SilverWood and to Hilary Johnson for their professional support and advice. And a final slightly tongue in cheek thank you to my local supermarkets for prompting me to consider what a government run by corporations might be like!

ALSO BY STEPHEN ORAM

Quantum Confessions

"A veritable head trip; yet rooted in a believable and sometimes visceral near-future."

Grey is a high performing student with attitude. Aled is torn between his morals and his desires. They live in a world where those who believe in absolute truth are on a collision course with those who don't. Society is becoming dangerously polarised and despite a thread of history that binds Aled and Grey together they take opposite sides in the conflict; she is recruited by The Project and he is given custody of The Proof of Existence.

Against the backdrop of a failing society and experiments to find the link between quantum physics and a supreme being, the real question that unfolds is...

"Who chooses your reality?"

Find out more about the author at
www.stephenoram.net